ISLANDS OF THE CURSED SEAS
HAND OF THE REAPER

Hand of the Reaper
Print edition ISBN: 979-8-218-67288-1

Contents

The Lost Keys
Bounty Isle
Ramrod Island
Spitshine Spot
Buccaneers Isle
Fort McConnell
Spider Island
Swashbuckler Island
Tick Island
Blister Island
ISLANDS OF THE CURSED SEAS
N
W
E
S
Perdition Isle
Rogue Island
SkinnyCurvy Island
The Existential Deep
Guts Island
Wraithbone Island
Blood Island
Fort Levasseur
Rapscallion Island
Stab Island
Manatee Island
Pillager Island
Lonely Isle

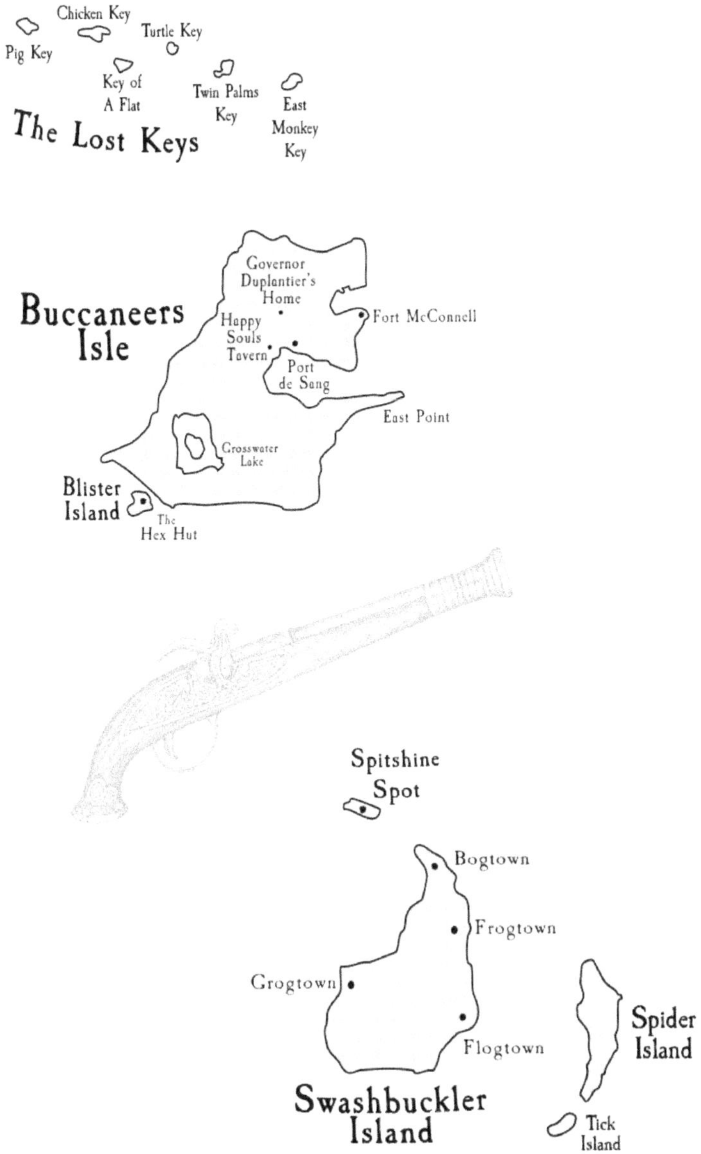

Chicken Key
Turtle Key
Pig Key
Key of
A Flat
Twin Palms
Key
East
Monkey
Key
The Lost Keys

Buccaneers
Isle
Governor
Duplantier's
Home
Fort McConnell
Happy
Souls
Tavern
Port
de Sang
East Point
Crosswater
Lake
Blister
Island
The
Hex Hut

Spitshine
Spot
Bogtown
Frogtown
Grogtown
Flogtown
Spider
Island
Swashbuckler
Island
Tick
Island

At the end of the seventeenth century, hidden deep in the Caribbean, there is a chain of small islands populated by the outcasts of society, men with no country, and seafarers...

"Magic is the means to an end. It is not the goal."
                                        – Golden Sea Grimoire

1

CONSCRIPTED

Despite living on a small island in the West Indies, Caleb had never been to sea. His entire life, he felt the sea calling out to him, but he had never even set foot on a ship. Unfortunately, he was never permitted to leave the island or even the plantation unless he was performing his very specific duties.

Since childhood, Caleb lived and worked as a slave in the home of the governor. Caleb knew no other life, but he still imagined that something out there called to him. It was not until he reached his eighteenth year that he would even consider answering the call. It was more than just the sea calling; it was also the whispers of a dark curse that would ultimately shape the next stage of his life.

But for now, Caleb was a prisoner in the home of François Duplantier, the current governor of Buccaneers Isle. Caleb had never known his father or mother; he was taken from them and sold as a child with no consideration for family ties. He had only vague recollections of a town on the other side of a long sea voyage in the hold of a dark, overcrowded ship.

On the island plantation, Caleb grew up in the service of the governor. Most importantly, it was up to Caleb to keep

Duplantier comfortable in the tropical climate. Many days, Caleb was tasked to simply follow the governor with a small fan to cool him off. Other days, Caleb would stand close by, providing shade from the hot sun using palm fronds attached to the end of a long pole.

Whenever the opportunity presented itself, Caleb attempted to educate himself in secret. The governor had a son named Jean who was a few years younger than Caleb; during Jean's lessons, Caleb would listen in, and eventually he taught himself how to read. He would take forgotten schoolbooks and look over them when nobody was watching. He cultivated an interest in sailing, economics, and exploration, but he kept the knowledge close to his chest.

All the education that Caleb had gleaned felt in vain, because he knew it was unlikely he would ever leave Buccaneers Isle or the home of the governor. And yet, whenever his duties would take him to Port de Sang on the coast, he would see the visiting ships coming to dock at the island, and his imagination would take over. He would remember everything he had seen pictures of or read about in books, and his mind would fill with possibilities of a free life out there.

One morning, Caleb was accompanying the governor outside to meet a carriage that had just entered the plantation. It was nearly midday, and the sun was already beating down, so Caleb did what he had done since he was a small boy: he carried with him a collapsible fan and a lengthy pole that had several large palm fronds at the end and followed the governor, shading him from the hot sun and fanning him when ordered.

Governor Duplantier, with Caleb just behind him, approached the carriage as a man exited.

"*Bienvenue!* Welcome to Buccaneers Isle, Mr. Lansky," Duplantier greeted in his thick French accent. "You're far from Cartagena, my friend. What brings you across the sea to our humble island?"

"I am here on business," Lansky answered. He was a British

man. Caleb had seen him around, but it had been some time. "If I may have a moment of your time, I wish to discuss some new matters that have come up."

"Is that so?" Duplantier challenged, lowering his voice. Despite his position as governor, the idea of international relations always seemed to weary him. He kept his hand out of affairs as much as he could afford to.

"You know how it is," Lansky said in a serious tone "The ever-deteriorating state between our mother nations have many of us concerned."

Duplantier waved his hand dismissively. "I want no involvement in my nation's silly conflicts! They are half a world away, and we are here. But let us not get ahead of ourselves. You have traveled far. Will you stay for a meal? Elliana is preparing meat pie and a fruit tart."

"Ah, that would be capital." Lansky dabbed at his sweaty forehead with a handkerchief as he was ridiculously overdressed for the tropical weather.

Duplantier ran his hands over various pockets, muttering to himself. "I have a few things I was to pick up in town today. Where is that blasted list? Ah!" He pulled out a small piece of parchment with writing on it. He quickly scribbled two more items onto it and handed it to Caleb.

"Run to the shop. Give this list to Monsieur Geoffrey and fetch these things right away."

Caleb took the piece of paper, folded it, and put it in his vest pocket. "Will this be on the account, sir?" he asked.

"Good point," Duplantier grumbled, searching his pockets for a coin purse. He emptied out several coins, counted them, and handed them to Caleb. "That should cover it for these items. You let him know that I will settle my account the next time I am in town. That should appease him. Now, go."

"Right away, sir."

Lansky raised an eyebrow. "You send him alone into town?"

Duplantier laughed. "Where can he get off to? He's a

grateful lad and knows better than to make trouble. You won't find a better master around than me, isn't that right, my boy?"

"Yes, sir," Caleb acknowledged, letting the insultingly dismissive attitude regarding his status wash over him as he had many times before. He secured the money given to him then bowed slightly once more to the two men and began his walk to town.

Caleb arrived at the main street of Port de Sang, and it was busier than usual, putting Lansky's earlier comments out of his mind. There was a large merchant ship – a three-mast ship – docked in the bay. *Could this be the vessel that had brought Lansky here from his home on the mainland?* As he wondered, Caleb found himself curiously drawn to the ship.

Almost in a trance, he stepped out onto the wooden planks of the dock, the salt sea water splashing under his shoes. Merchants loaded and unloaded crates of supplies, and sailors fastened and unfastened ropes. Though he had never personally experienced it, Caleb swore he could feel the deck of the ship beneath his feet, rising and falling at the whims of the sea; he could smell the wet wood of the helm and hear the whistles and calling of orders.

Another ship made its way into port. This one was significantly more imposing; it flew no colors, but it looked battle-hardened. It arrived without a fuss, and its crew also began to fasten lines to the dock.

"You a sailor?" Caleb heard a deep voice inquire. He looked down and realized he was out on the dock for the first time. The port town was back behind him, looking much duller and more uninteresting than it had ever looked. Standing in front of him was a large-framed man with a prickly short beard.

"Are you on the manifest?" asked the man, who was most likely the merchant ship's quartermaster.

"Manifest?" Caleb repeated back, stammering. Overwhelmed at the sight of all that was around him, he was at a loss for words. "Sorry," was all he managed to squeak out before running back into town in the direction of the general store.

The stout quartermaster shook his head and went back to his work, muttering something about "kids these days."

Caleb's eyes darted from the shop to the crowds of people moving about, then to the ships in the harbor, then back to the shop. He held the governor's list in a clenched fist as he went ahead into the shop, a general store with the words *"Golden Doubloon"* inscribed above the doorway.

A tall, lanky man wearing a bright outfit stood behind the counter.

"Good morning, son," he said, waving Caleb over. "You have more errands for the governor today?"

"Good morning, Mr. Geoffrey." Caleb held up the list of items he was sent to pick up. "I've got a list right here."

Geoffrey took the list from Caleb, noticing the distracted, vacant look on his face as he did so.

"What is the matter?" he asked. "Are you coming down with something?"

Caleb reached into his pocket and pulled out the coins Duplantier had given him. "No, sir. I'm fine," he said. "Monsieur Duplantier said this should cover the items."

Geoffrey took the coins and started to pack items into a bag – notably cheese, ground coffee, oats, and a box of tea leaves. Caleb guessed that the cheese and the tea in particular would be wanted for the guest, so he quickly gathered the items together and prepared to leave the shop.

"Lots of new folk coming to the island today," Geoffrey observed. "Best be careful on your way home."

"Yessir," Caleb said as he backed towards the door. "Busy day indeed."

Dodging the increasingly dense foot traffic in the town, Caleb hastily made his way up the street.

A group of rowdy men staggered from one of the docked ships towards the local tavern. The sight of pirates walking freely in town was not uncommon in Port de Sang. Governor Duplantier was, in many ways, a lenient man when it came to the laws of the sea. He did not turn away such men who would frequently come to resupply and be on their way. They usually brought commerce with them, and Duplantier did not care about what they had been up to while they were out to sea so long as they caused no trouble here.

Caleb picked up speed and walked quickly to the boundary of the plantation, where he could see Duplantier's foremen, Charles and Bert Walton, lounging there. They were no doubt taking a break from abusing the fieldhands.

It was common practice for those who worked in the governor's house to keep clear of the Walton brothers. Duplantier's fieldhands knew that if the Waltons were displeased for any reason, they would enforce punishment, no matter the source of the error. They were young and not particularly bright; if they were not good at a task, they would take it out on people who were. Caleb dreaded the day he might be moved under their care. He had spent his life close to the governor, and as bad as his life was, it was the best life he figured he could hope for in this world.

They sat up straight when they saw Caleb approach.

"What have we here?" Bert said, eyeing the items in Caleb's hands. To say that Bert was the ugly one would be to discredit the ugliness of Charles. There was a family resemblance between the two brothers that each might consider to be unfortunate.

"Looks like someone's been shopping in town," Charles said.

"The governor is expecting these items," Caleb said shortly, attempting to pass by without slowing down, but Charles would not have it. He stood firm beside his brother.

"Let's have a little inspection first."

Caleb had endured these "checkpoints" before. They were usually just a show of power from the young men, and apart from being degrading, they were mostly just wasting Caleb's time, so he acquiesced. He knew that if he refused, more time would be wasted, and it would take even longer for the governor to get his items, and that would ultimately be worse for him.

So, Caleb made a show as if he were frightened of them.

That way they could at least get some satisfaction and possibly get through with this demonstration of power faster. But truthfully, Caleb's thoughts lingered on the ships he had seen in the bay.

When they had finished harassing Caleb, Charles and Bert sent him on his way, but not without a swift whip of a riding crop across the back of Caleb's legs. He winced at the sharp sting and carried on as the two remained there, laughing with one another.

As he approached the house, Caleb did his best ignore the stinging in his legs and walk straight and tall. He found Governor Duplantier and Mr. Lansky sitting together at a table in the sun room, attended by Miss Elliana, who took the items from Caleb as he entered the home.

Like Caleb, Elliana had been a slave in Duplantier's house since childhood, which for her was many years ago. She had been Caleb's primary instructor, comforter, and caregiver as he had grown up in the house. Many in the house referred to her as "Mama Ellie" because of her maternal habits to the less fortunate in the home.

As expected, when Caleb had finished his delivery, Monsieur Duplantier requested the newly acquired tea be served to him and his guest as they began dishing up their food. Duplantier's wife and son Jean also sat at the table, but at a distance, so as not to distract from the business at hand.

Caleb went to his duties with practiced professionalism. He did not speak unless there was a question directed at him, and even then, he kept his answers brief and to the point. One of Mama Ellie's repeated lessons to him was *"Don't make trouble,"* and so he did not.

After the tea had been served, Caleb looked to the governor's family and their guest as they continued their discussion, paying Caleb no mind.

"The conflicts between his majesty King William and your King Louis and their interest in this area has led to a significant increase of activity in these waters," Lansky said. "You and I have been friends for many years, Frank, but we cannot ignore the tension between our nations forever. If you demonstrate your loyalty against these lawless men on the sea, that can be a step towards fostering good relations between us."

"These men have done me no harm," said the governor, focusing more on his food than on his guest's words. "And I am no military man. Surely, I cannot offer you significant means to fight them."

"We are not asking for ships or supplies," Lansky assured him. "We're merely asking for your vigilance. Condemn the pirates who have been roaming freely here. They have been attacking French and English ship alike. Even the Spanish have been accosted by them."

"Then go talk to the Spanish." Duplantier wiped sweat off his brow with a napkin then looked around for Caleb. When he spotted him putting away some of the dishes, he motioned him over. "Come, it's much too warm here. Get some air moving."

Caleb stopped what he was doing and fetched one of his small fans. Duplantier sighed in relief as Caleb began to gently fan him.

Lansky continued, showing only slight frustration at the interruption. "Allow the English to rebuild and refortify Fort McConnell here on your island. That alone would lead to a more secure sea and a demonstration of good faith that could lead to better relations between us."

"I understand your position," Duplantier acknowledged, "but hear mine: reinstating Fort McConnell with troops loyal to the English would be like I were declaring myself an enemy of France. I have no interest in this conflict. Besides, these pirates are good for business. The trade that they bring; if I were to frighten them away, my humble little haven here would suffer."

"The atrocities they commit while out to sea does not concern you?"

"Hearsay. What they may or may not do while on the sea matters not to me. They give me no trouble here."

"I should warn you, *Monsieur* Governor. His majesty King

William is enlisting the aid of privateers. He has been offering letters of marque to cooperative pirates who have experience fighting on the seas, encouraging them to fight for King and country in exchange for full pardons. He is using them to battle against the pirates in these waters. Are you familiar with Rafael Santana?"

"Santana?" Duplantier repeated the name, drumming his fingers on the table hesitantly. "The Italian pirate who sailed the *Devil's Thunder* and stalked the eastern shipping lanes?"

"That's the one. He has accepted a commission and has gone legitimate; he's bringing in bounties in the name of the King. It's worse out there than you know." Lansky leaned forward, attempting to add weight and sincerity to his words. "There is a rise in the use of dark arts in the Caribbean. We've recovered dangerous artifacts and tomes of unspeakable rituals. I've even been told of a Voodoo practitioner on the south side of your own island. He has a place there and is no doubt in alliance with these pirates."

Duplantier laughed. "The Hex Hut is just a tourist trap! Its proprietor is a businessman. Mr. Kingsley uses smoke and mirrors to lure in men whose superstitious minds are as open as their purses. Simply another lucrative business."

"Nevertheless," Lansky said, "If you continue to harbor these sorts of reprehensible men on your island, the Royal Navy will consider you complicit with their activities."

"Outrageous!" Duplantier stood from the table, raising his voice. "You say that I am to go against the pirate scourge, and if I don't, you mean to say that you will set them against me? *C'est incroyable!*"

"It is my duty to present this information to you and implore you to do the right thing."

Duplantier sat back in his chair and motioned for Caleb, who produced his fan and with a practiced hand began to fan the sweating governor. Duplantier set his cup on the table and sighed.

"Port de Sang is a free port," he said, definitively. "Whatever happens, it will remain a free port."

They continued with their meal, and the conversation turned to less serious matters including town gossip and complaints about the hot climate.

The rest of that day, Caleb's thoughts kept going to the ship he had seen pulling into the dock, and he wondered if it could have belonged to Santana himself, hunting down enemies of the King. One thought kept repeating in his head:

If a ship full of outlaw pirates can be commissioned for legitimate work, could there also be hope for someone like him?

The following morning, Duplantier went into town with Lansky as he returned to his ship. He would set sail to some of the other islands, no doubt in an attempt to convince others to ally with him against the pirates in the nearby waters. Caleb accompanied them, providing shade with several large palm fronds as they walked.

Duplantier and Lansky walked down the main street filled with sailors walking arm in arm, talking and laughing loudly with one another.

"You see all these men?" Duplantier asked. "These men are simply enjoying the hospitality of Port de Sang, as many others have done in the past. Now, if you wish to negotiate a trade for sugar or spices, we have plenty to offer."

"Nevertheless," Lansky said as they drew nearer to the dock, "I hope you will think hard about my offer. Each of us has our own way of contributing. Any of us stray, we will all pay."

Caleb could see that the other large ship was still there next to Lansky's ship.

"Why don't you seek out the captain of this vessel," Duplantier suggested, indicating the ship next to the one Lansky was preparing to board. "Maybe he will join you on your little errand, eh?"

Lansky observed the ship's stern and read aloud the ship's name. "The *Red Soul*?" he scoffed. "Mind yourself, dear Governor. These are dangerous men at your doorstep, and it is only a matter of time before they do something that you will regret."

He turned and stepped onto the deck of his own ship just as the crew were beginning to unfasten its ropes from the dock.

Caleb stood there, absentmindedly looking up at the ships, not noticing that Duplantier had stepped away until he heard him call out for him.

"Forgive me, sir," Caleb called out, clutching his shade-casting stick and hurrying after him. He positioned the large palm leaves so that they blocked the sun from the governor, and they walked together towards the general store.

"Wait here," Duplantier said just outside the store. "I'll settle up my account with Mr. Geoffrey."

Caleb stole a glance towards the docks. He could vaguely hear Geoffrey greet the governor as he entered the store, but Caleb's attention was on the ships: Lansky's ship was departing, and the other ship was being boarded. On its deck, men went about loading and securing barrels and crates for the voyage.

In a trance, Caleb found himself drawn back towards that ship. He could not say how long he had been standing there, but he soon found himself once again facing the ship's quartermaster, who stood there holding a pen and paper.

"You looking for something, lad?" the man said in a gruff voice.

"I'm a sailor," he heard himself blurt out, but what possessed him to say such a thing, he could not imagine.

He looked behind him at the general store where the governor was still inside, taking care of his bill.

"I see," the man said. "And who do I have the pleasure of addressing?"

"My name is Caleb," he said.

The man jotted down the name. "You're not on the manifest, but we are a bit short on deckhands. I am Callahan, quartermaster of the *Red Soul*. What makes you think you have what it takes to sail under Captain Benjamin Torch?" he asked.

The name of Benjamin Torch sounded familiar to Caleb, but he could not place where he had heard it, so he brushed it aside.

"I will do my part," he said. "What is the destination of the voyage?"

Callahan motioned for Caleb to come closer. He obliged, and the quartermaster lowered his voice. "We sail north," he said. "Our captain has sought out mystical passages in the north, and he is willing to share the bounty with his crew."

"Bounty?" Caleb repeated.

"Aye," said the quartermaster, "power and riches await us."

Caleb stood in silence, letting it all sink in. Perhaps it was too much for him to process at the moment, having never been offered anything so substantial before.

"Sounds great," he said, pushing aside any reasonable fear. "I've never had any power or riches myself, but I've always meant to get some. Is this a private venture, or is it backed by the crown?"

"Backed by the crown?" Callahan laughed, his voice rising. The other sailors who were gathered around laughed along. "You want to know who we sail for, do ye? We sail for ourselves. This expedition is backed by Benjamin Torch. It's a research expedition; ye might even call it a pilgrimage, but you can bet on it, there will be a profit. Captain Torch always makes sure to take care of his own in that regard."

"That sounds reasonable."

At this moment, Caleb still had never sailed and had much to learn; he wasn't sure he could identify a French flag, much less any of the metaphorical red flags that kept popping up.

"When do we sail?" he asked, glancing back towards the town. The governor would be reappearing any minute. This was an entertaining fantasy, but if he wished to avoid severe retribution, he really should be getting back to the shop.

"You're in luck, kid," Callahan said, interrupting his thoughts. "We're preparing to set sail presently."

Sure enough, men were already unfastening the ropes from the docks and preparing to bring up the gangplank.

From the direction of the town, raised voices called out. Duplantier was there, standing just outside the Golden Doubloon, looking for him.

Caleb stiffened.

"We must be shoving off," Callahan pressed. "What say you?"

Caleb said nothing and stepped onto the gangplank to the ship.

Callahan clasped his hands together. "Very well, then, young shipmate. Welcome aboard the *Red Soul.*"

There was a shout as Duplantier ran towards the dock. He had caught sight of Caleb on the ship, but it was too late: the gangplank was brought in behind him as the anchor was raised, and they soon began to move.

Seeing his enslaver standing alone on the dock, swearing in French while holding the palm fronds that had been left behind, Caleb felt a twinge of excitement mixed with fear as he hoped he had not just made a terrible mistake.

11

THE EDGE OF DEATH

The shape of Buccaneers Isle quickly shrank into the distance behind the *Red Soul* as it sailed into the sea. It was at this time that Caleb first saw the captain. The air was filled with nervous energy, and through his excitement, Caleb was unaware of the dark magic that even now surrounded the captain and his ship.

A hush went over the crew, and the men stood up straight as the captain stepped forward to the edge of the quarterdeck.

Captain Benjamin Torch was a tall man with a trim yet imposing frame. He wore a long frock coat and a simple tricorn hat on his head. His weather-worn face had sharp features resting behind a thick red beard, all of which gave him the appearance of a man older than he really was. His bright green eyes scanned the crew standing before him.

"Men," he greeted them with a commanding voice, "welcome aboard the *Red Soul.* I am grateful for your assistance on this most historic voyage. Many of you have sailed with me, but I am aware of new faces here with us today. Work hard, and you will be rewarded accordingly. Mr. Callahan shall assign your duties and see that your contribution here is of merit. We sail northwest past the keys to our destination."

Here, the captain lowered his voice, and Caleb felt a chill from the way he spoke his next words. "What lies there may well be the key to all our fates."

The men stood in silence as Captain Torch let these words sink in. He grinned and gave his crew a knowing wink. "And the key to treasure unfathomable!"

Those words the men could connect with. They laughed and cheered. Torch joined them in cheering.

"Carry on then, you black-hearted devils!"

Caleb and a half a dozen others were led below deck to be given their assignments. If the other crewmen guessed that he was a runaway, they did not seem to care; he needed passage, and they needed hands.

Most of Caleb's tasks for the governor had been focused on housework and domestic duties, so when Callahan introduced him to the master gunner, Caleb hoped that he could manage to pick it up without making a fool of himself.

"We'll see what we can make of you," the master gunner said. He was a tall, fair-skinned man by the name of Olaf Hanson. He wore a tattered red coat and spoke in a strange foreign accent. Caleb later learned Hanson was from a land called Sweden, far on the other side of the word. Hanson kept his blonde hair pulled back under a red cloth, and his long beard was neatly braided. "What sort of experience do you have?"

Caleb searched for the right words. He had never been this close to a cannon, and the governor of course kept no firearms in reach of the slaves in his home.

"Not much, I'm afraid," he said, a feeling of embarrassment washing over him. He began to doubt whether the skills he had in the house might be of any use here on a ship.

"No cause to fret," Hanson reassured him. "We'll start with the basics and work from there. We've got the cannons here, of course. The powder and the standard cannonballs are stored next to them. We also have got chain shot, powder flasks, and stinkpots, but we needn't worry about those for now."

"Is there a lot of call for all this?" Caleb asked, looking at all the crates of ammunition filling the area. "Does this ship see a lot of action?"

"It's seen its fair share, for sure," Hanson admitted, his manner giving away that he was not expecting this line of questioning. "Generally, when we take a ship, once that crew finds out who we are, they give up provisions without a struggle, and that's always preferable."

Slowly, the reality of his situation sank in.

"And who are we?"

"Have you not heard of the *Red Soul*?" Hanson whispered. "Captain Torch is a mighty feared buccaneer in these waters."

"Mercy!" Caleb exclaimed as he finally recalled where he had heard the name Benjamin Torch: he had heard the governor curse that name many times, saying that he gave pirates a bad name. In fact, many of the profanity-laced phrases Caleb knew were in association with the name of Torch.

What sort of captain might Torch be, he wondered, *if a man like Duplantier (whose relaxed stance on piracy was well known) would curse his name?*

"What have I gotten myself into?"

"What did you think we were? Merchant sailors?"

"I'm afraid I didn't get a good look at the ship," Caleb explained, and this was true: his attention had been set on getting aboard a ship – any ship. He had, of course, heard of the pirates who sailed to and from the port of his home island, but never had he imagined he would find himself counted amongst them.

"If it's all the same to you," he continued, shaking off the trepidation, "I'm willing to give it a go."

Hanson gave him a knowing look. "Not much to go back to, eh?" he said, guessing the nature of Caleb's departure. "You should count yourself lucky! If we had been a merchant vessel, you would no doubt be clapped in irons by now. You might count it a blessing you found your way here with us!"

Caleb swallowed hard, now realizing the great risk he had taken.

"It no longer matters," he said. "I won't be going back, and I won't be seeing him again." He did not have to say who he meant by "him;" Hanson understood.

"You never can tell," said Hanson, "but you're a part of this crew now, and as such, you'll have to learn what is expected of you here. Life at sea is different than on land: your legs will have to adjust, as will your stomach."

Over the next week, Hanson taught Caleb all he could about cannon maintenance and operations. They repeated the procedures until Hanson was satisfied that Caleb could readily assist, should the situation present itself.

When night came, Caleb was assigned a hammock below deck. A crew of fifty men in such close quarters was not a comfortable setup, even for a ship as large as this. The hammock was not as cozy as even his squalid living arrangements back at the governor's slave house, but here he was free, and that counted for a lot.

What Caleb had not learned was their destination. Throughout the course of the voyage, the captain remained isolated in his cabin. Occasionally, the crew could hear strange sounds coming from inside. It seemed as if he had locked himself in there to perform archaic rituals.

The *Red Soul* avoided the main shipping lanes as it sailed north, away from the more populated islands. When they did spy other ships, they did so with no fanfare: plunder of earthly goods was clearly not the purpose of this voyage.

It was quiet going for two weeks. When there was time for it, Caleb watched and studied the basic functions of the ship. After a few combat lessons, Hanson gave Caleb a small knife to keep for himself.

"It's not much," he said, "but it's best to keep something like this close to you at all times. You never know when you may need to use it."

It was the fifteenth day at sea, and Caleb watched the sunrise peek over the starboard side of the ship. The night helmsman and several night-shift deckhands were there, but they were all silent.

One point of discussion over the past few days was that these waters were frequented by Captain Reginald Hennesey, a large brute of a man who commanded a crew of particularly fearsome cutthroats. Torch had faced his ship in battle on more than a few occasions. They both preyed upon merchant ships, and while there was a general alliance amongst many of the pirates in the area, the two of them had often found themselves at odds with one another. There was a price on both of their heads, and each of them was willing to collect the bounty on the other.

More than this, the air was thick with conjecture as to the intended destination of their current voyage. Many believed it was gold, but there were those who had sailed with Torch the longest who insisted he had something more fantastic and spiritual in mind.

"Sailed with him to find the fountain of youth, I did," said an elderly man by the name of Bartholomew Knave. "As you might guess, we found no magic in those waters, but it did prompt the captain to start looking for other ways he might master life and death. He began to study occult practices. He researched death and life in multiple cultures. There's no real telling what he has found."

This was met with murmurs from the crew, but those words stayed with Caleb, and he mulled them over as he went up on the deck to ponder everything he had seen and heard over his time aboard the ship.

A fog hung low just above the calm waters. The captain stood on the quarterdeck just behind the helmsman, quietly surveying the sea.

"Southwest on the horizon, sir." The helmsman spoke in low tones, but even so, his voice carried in the still air. "Coming across to a possible intercept position."

"Aye," Torch acknowledged, looking through his spyglass. "I see her. Was she flying any colors when you spotted her?"

"I could not tell from this distance, Captain," he said, shaking his head. "Perhaps you can make it more plainly than I?"

"It is difficult," Torch admitted, lowering the spyglass. "Could be a merchant vessel. Could be a man of war. We must be at the ready to defend if necessary. Mr. Hennesey mustn't take us by surprise again – not when we are this close."

"Aye, sir."

"Keep an eye trained on her but maintain course straight and true to our destination."

The next hour proceeded slowly and without incident. The vessel in question eventually turned away and silently made its exit. Torch remained on the quarterdeck, watching the sea carefully. It was early in the afternoon, but the heavy fog continued to rise as they moved forward. This excited the captain, though he remained composed for appearances.

"What do you suppose all this means?" Caleb asked Hanson, standing at the bow of the ship, looking out into the fog. "This darkness is uncanny. Unnatural."

"That's just it," Hanson said as he lit one of the ship's lanterns. "I'd wager that what we're to find out here is dark and unnatural as well."

Then something caught Caleb's attention. He pointed, exclaiming, "Hullo. What's that?"

"More fog?" Hanson said.

"No," said Caleb a little louder. "In the fog. A green light."

From the stern of the ship, Captain Torch was attentive to the discussion and gestures and marched quickly forward to investigate.

"Aye, steady men," he cautioned as he reached the fo'c'sle of the ship. "What's that, lad?"

"In the fog, just resting on the water." Caleb pointed ahead. "It looks like a green light – like a light from a candle, but there's no candle. It's just a green flame resting above the water."

Torch peered through his spyglass and grinned devilishly. It was as Caleb had described.

"Maintain course and keep a sharp eye out for those lights, Mr. Davies," Torch said to the helmsman, pointing forward as he made his way back to his place at the quarterdeck. "If any of you see one, keep it not to yourself. Our path is set before us."

Then, to Callahan: "Run her easy. Let her drift."

"Aye, aye."

Callahan gave orders to the crew to drift the ship to its destination. "Haul in the head sheets and fore sheets. Easy, lads. Steady as she goes."

From the deck, Caleb and several of the other men pulled on the clewlines and buntlines, gathering up the main foresail and easing the ship's headway. The ship drifted forward in the nearly-still waters.

"Another off the port bow," one of the men called from the deck.

"Well-spotted, Mr. Delk."

The *Red Soul* drifted silently forward, following the lights. As they reached one, another appeared a hundred or so yards ahead of them. The sky quickly darkened, as if night were already approaching early. The dense fog enveloped them, so that nothing could be seen outside the ship, save for the sporadic green wisps of light sitting on the still waters. The silence became nearly unbearable, but no one dared to speak above a whisper.

Caleb prepared to light a lantern on the foremast, but Torch gave a halting gesture.

"Stay your hand, lad. The will-o-the-wisps be lighting our way."

"As you say, sir," Caleb said, closing up the lantern.

"In fact, douse all lights."

The men complied and extinguished all lanterns on the deck, but not without murmuring their own misgivings at this course of action.

"'Tis a bad omen," one of them muttered.

"I don't much care for these phantom lights," Davies said to Captain Torch while cautiously steering the ship. "The old tales say these lights lead a man to find his last rest, if you get me."

"Aye, for most men that be true," admitted Torch. "But we're seeking their source – there be the one who sends out the lights to trick sailors to come to him. And it be him whom we wish to see."

"Look! The compass." Davies drew the captain's attention to the chaotic motion of the needle on ship's compass.

"Blast the compass! Take heed of the lights!" Torch ordered in a raspy whisper. "Maintain current heading."

He looked down at his crew and summoned forward one of the older men – Mr. Knave.

"Knave, step up."

"Aye, Captain?"

"Ye know of the Grim Reaper?"

Old Knave nodded, hesitantly. "They say he resides in the land of the dead," Knave said. "And he can be summoned here to the living world."

"That is what they say," the captain said. "But he cannot be summoned by a man full of life. Ye must be close to death to seek an audience."

"Aye," Knave said. "That's how I hear it."

With a sharp thrust, Torch forcefully screwed a knife into the small of Knave's back. Knave's face contorted, and he gasped for air. Captain Torch looked evenly into Knave's eyes.

"I'll have to ask ye to do us a favor and knock at Death's Door for us while you're there. Your sacrifice will bring us the audience we desire."

Knave dropped to his knees, twitching in pain as life left him.

The lights over the sea ahead faded away into nothingness, and the ship moved silently forward into the darkness with no further guiding light.

Davies turned to address the captain but staggered backwards in surprise, because standing just behind Torch on the quarterdeck was a tall, pale man, still, solemn, and dressed in a black tattered cloak. Even more unsettling were the man's eyes, which were also completely black.

At the helmsman's reaction, Torch turned around to see the figure standing there. After an initial shock, he regained his composure. The men around him drew their cutlasses and stood trembling.

"Stand down," Torch said, holding one hand out in a calming gesture to his men and removing his hat with his other hand. "Weapons away."

The crew reluctantly obeyed.

The pale man moved closer to the captain, though nobody saw him take a step; it was as if he glided in the air.

"Captain Benjamin Torch," he addressed him in a cold voice and a low tone, yet in a voice loud enough for all to hear. "Art thou surprised that thy name be known to me? Thou hast yearned for an audience with the Reaper for many years."

"The Reaper?" Torch repeated, his voice dry, but his face showing no fear.

The pale man nodded.

"'Tis the title thou knowest me by," he said. "Thou seeketh immortality. Riches. Power. Thou art not the first to attempt this."

"We shall not fail, my lord," Torch said, taking a knee. "Command us, and we shall deliver what you request."

The Reaper backed away from Torch and ascended into the sky above the ship. A cold, circling wind surrounded them, and the Reaper spoke in a great booming tone. Contrasted with the preceding silence, his voice shook the floorboards of the ship and rattled its cannons.

"First, I must break free from this purgatorial existence," he said. "This can only be done with the full summoning ritual, which was lost many years ago. Find the words to be spoken. Once I am fully here, through me and my gifts to thee, thou shalt become the most powerful force upon these cursed seas. My power I pass to thee to be my Hand in the realm of mortal men."

At this, the Reaper extended his hands and revealed a great scythe from his cloak. From the sickle, a pale glow emitted. A cold, green light filled each member of the crew as they felt power being transferred to them from the Reaper.

"Every life taken by thee is a soul delivered unto me, and through their energy, power shall be given for the task to be completed. Perform the ritual, and thou shalt be rewarded."

He stretched his hand towards the fallen body of Knave. The same green light surged into his body, and he was lifted up, floating above the deck until life returned to him. But he appeared to be in an artificial state of life; the color was gone from his flesh, and his expression was lax. He landed on the deck in front of Captain Torch who watched as the pale green light faded from his reanimated crewman.

"Perform the summoning ritual by the first light of the new century," the Reaper continued, "else I shall have all thy souls as payment."

A murmur arose from the crew. The new century was now five years away, and the men feared what his words may mean, but the excitement at the promise of power and of riches quickly drove these thoughts from their minds.

"Return to me by that day, Benjamin Torch," the Reaper said as he drifted into the sky above them. "I will be waiting."

He raised both his hands, and as he turned away, he faded into a wisp of cloud. The men on the ship, speechless, looked off to the stern of the ship and watched silently as the fog lifted, and the light of day shone around them again.

III
THE REAPER'S CREW

Caleb stood at a loss, unable to wrap his head around what was happening. He could see what looked like a green cloud seeping into the pores of his skin. The lust for power and riches was in the eyes of his captain, and that same look was reflected in the faces of the rest of the crew as they spoke excitedly at the promise of the great reward.

Captain Torch braced himself against the railing of the quarterdeck and addressed his crew.

"A new century is upon us. Now is the time we prepare for the coming of the Reaper. I am to act as his Hand in the land of the living. We have all been chosen, and we shall be rewarded." He raised his sword above him in a dramatic gesture.

The crew cheered. Caleb hesitated, but not wanting to be the odd man out any more than he already was, he joined in the celebration.

"We have our task set before us. There is a ritual to be performed on the day of the return, and there will be items required. The ritual itself has been lost to time, but with his guidance, I believe it will be ours soon enough. We have five years to prepare for his return. Mr. Belfort, plot the course for

Spitshine Spot."

Martin Belfort, the ship's navigator, acknowledged the order and instructed the helmsman to adjust the ship's heading to south-southeast and stand by for further orders.

"Sou'-sou'east, it is," Davies repeated as he began to turn the wheel of the ship.

When the chattering died down, Caleb busied himself with securing lines at the foresail, going over this latest development in his mind. Less than a month ago, he had been a lowly slave at the mercy of the governor, and now he had been given some sort of otherworldly power by some spectral entity. He felt an uneasy chill running through him that had not faded even after the stranger had vanished.

Bartholomew Knave, whom the captain had sacrificed just moments ago, was now standing on the deck and going about his duties, but he was no longer the same man. His clouded eyes did not seem to focus. He moved on his own and showed some signs of life, but it was more like a crude imitation of life.

Caleb cautiously approached him.

"Mr. Knave, might I speak with you a moment?"

Knave mechanically turned his head. Caleb was unsettled with how inorganic and lifeless his movements were.

"Aye…?" Mr. Knave croaked, acknowledging he had been addressed but not pushing the conversation past that.

"Yes, well…" Caleb fumbled over his words. What does one ask a man who has just returned from the dead? He searched for the right thing to say, but he could not bring himself to directly address the matter. "What I mean to say," he stumbled, "is everything all right?"

"Aye…"

Caleb awaited an elaboration that never came.

"You're sure?" he pressed.

"Aye…"

Perhaps he ought to switch tactics. Caleb had not gotten to know Knave during the journey here, so he had no personal reference for conversation, but he went for it anyway.

"The skies south of us appear to be clear," Caleb noted, hoping to prompt further discussion. He remembered overhearing Mr. Knave speak favorably of his home in a region known as the Western Isles. Maybe if he were to bring that up, he could break through to him. "I'll wager you're looking forward to returning to the Western Isles. I've never been there. Can you tell me what it is like?"

"Western Isles…" Mr. Knave's voice trailed off. "They are to the west." He turned, facing away from Caleb as he spoke. "I'll be moving along now. Mind your post, sailor."

He shuffled back to his duties, leaving Caleb standing there in thought.

"Strange times are indeed upon us, boy," said a young deckhand standing nearby. He had witnessed the exchange as he was busy scrubbing the deck. "Mr. Knave appears to be a bit disoriented."

"I don't know whether he came back to us completely," Caleb said. "It is as if he had returned to the land of the living as a stranger and cannot quite remember what living is."

The young man gave Knave a sideways glance, then turned his gaze back to Caleb. "I suggest that we keep to our tasks and don't go minding these matters. Danger lies there. You'll be wanting to get that line there properly fastened."

"Of course," Caleb said, realizing he had been pulling absentmindedly on one of the lines without properly securing it.

The ship sailed for another two hours until a small commotion began brewing towards the bow of the ship. Four men standing at the fo'c'sle shared a spyglass amongst themselves and pointed to the distance whilst chattering excitedly. They quickly silenced each other and stood at attention when Captain Torch approached.

"Report."

"Henry spied it, he did," one of the young men said, pointing out in the distance. He offered the spyglass to the captain, but

Torch was already raising his own to his eye.

"Just three points off the starboard bow." The young man pointed ahead past the figurehead of their ship. "You see it? It's a merchant ship, sir, coming across the horizon; lightly armored, too, I'll warrant."

The captain put away his spyglass, satisfied with what he saw, and walked briskly aft towards the helm.

"Helmsman," he said, "adjust course to intercept. Mr. Bellamy, prepare the men to take the ship. Remember, we wish to disable. A sunken ship with sunken cargo does us no good. Who knows? Maybe they'll surrender to us without a fight!"

This was met with some chuckling and jeering. It was clear that most men here would prefer at least something of a fight.

Caleb was not one of those men.

"Hoist the black flag!"

Bellamy blew his whistle and gave the command for the men to go to their stations. A black flag shot up to the highest point of the main mast. The classic image of a white skull on the flag sat nested above the simplified image of two lit torches.

During the commotion, Caleb went towards the hatch along with a dozen other men and took his station at one of the larboard cannons below deck.

As Caleb gathered some small cannonballs from the storage barrels, he could feel the ship turn sharply as it approached the merchant vessel.

"Give it here, lad." A grizzled older man stood at the cannon. He held his hand out, reaching for the cannonballs Caleb clutched to his chest.

"Right. Sorry." Caleb loaded up the cannon and waited for the order to fire.

"Don't give me 'sorry,'" the man said. "Give me cannonballs!"

Caleb hastily returned to the storage barrels and prepared to reload the cannon. The order was soon given, and they fired one cannon after the other. Caleb remained assisting the burly ill-tempered gunner, who was called "Onion Jack," though why he was called that, Caleb was not told.

"That'll take 'em down, the fools!" Jack growled and laughed as he let loose his cannon on the ship. Now standing much closer to Jack as he spoke, the aroma emitting from his mouth helped Caleb guess how "Onion Jack" was given his nickname.

Even with the sound of the cannons, the men below could hear commotion on the deck as grappling hooks brought the two vessels together. Caleb unsheathed the knife Hanson had given him and looked towards the hatch, but nobody descended to his level.

Not long after the fighting began, the captain of the opposing ship gave the call to surrender.

When the noise above died down, Caleb stepped up onto the deck, where he saw a dozen defeated sailors surrounded by the crew of the *Red Soul*. It was obvious that most of the merchant sailors were not experienced fighters.

Captain Torch, standing on the deck of the merchant vessel, addressed its captain.

"I accept your surrender," Torch said. "I believe there is some information which I need that you can fill me in on, in trade for your lives." He looked around at the bodies lying on the deck. "We have no use for your main transport cargo, so you will be free to carry on with your voyage not completely inconvenienced. We do have our needs, so we will be taking whatever currency you have aboard as well as your ammunition stores, of course. As for the information, let us speak further, away from curious ears."

Torch addressed two young members of his crew who stood there with him. "Masters Boen and Boyle, take stock and mind what could be salvaged for our purposes, while I have a talk with this here captain."

They nodded and led several other men to the hatch of the ship leading below deck. Boen caught Caleb's eye and waved him over.

Torch meanwhile led the merchant captain to his cabin. What they spoke of there, neither crew knew.

The main hold of the ship was filled with crates of linens and silks to be transported to artisans and merchants on the main chain of islands. These items did not interest the crew of the *Red Soul.* What caught their attention was several casks of red wine and several stores of ammunition. After the crew of the *Red Soul* took all the weapons they could find to add to their own arsenal, Caleb grabbed crates of gunpowder and began moving them over to their ship while Boen and Boyle moved the wine and rum.

"Not much of a haul for a ship this size," Boyle muttered. "I don't see why we don't just strike the rest of them down and add this ship to our fleet."

"There's no sense in that," said Boen. "But the way I sees it, the haul ain't the purpose. It's whatever words the captains are sharing with one another. Information, Boyle, that's what the captain is after: he's looking for something he knows these merchant men know. And if these merchant men know it, rest assured Captain will soon know it. I'll wager we have an adjusted heading when we weigh anchor again – an adjusted heading and a few additional heads."

Caleb tended to the task. He didn't like to leave these sailors unarmed, but it was probably for the best they surrendered when they did, keeping their casualties to a minimum.

As he returned to the *Red Soul* with the new munitions, Caleb saw the two opposing captains emerge from the cabin onto the deck of the merchant ship. The merchant captain looked pale and disheveled.

Torch had a look of restrained excitement about him. He spoke some words to the merchant crew, but Caleb could not hear from his position on the pirate vessel. He could see nervous shuffling about as the crewman backed away. Torch stood above the bodies of their fallen shipmates and moved his arms theatrically.

A shockwave pulsed from where Torch was standing, rocking both ships. The sound of a soft, otherworldly hissing mixed with the creaking of bones filled the air as green smoke seeped from the deck's floorboards. Seven of the dead men lying on the deck dramatically rose to their feet and stood in a line facing their new captain. Their appendages twitched as their joints twisted and turned to support their bodies as they stood in a facsimile of life.

Without a word, Captain Torch turned and walked the gangplank back onto the deck of the *Red Soul.* The seven reanimated men followed closely after.

The surviving merchant crew made their ship ready to sail and departed with haste. Callahan divided up profits taken from the merchants and handed them out to the crew. Caleb stowed his share in a small pouch that he tied up and kept on him; it was more money than he had ever claimed for his own.

The next week at sea followed a similar course. It was mostly routine work, but the crew encountered two more ships which they subdued in the same manner. Caleb was given the chance to man a cannon himself this time. His first few shots sailed over the ship, but a few shots did land high on the hull. He also partook in the plunder of the ships; again, it was mainly foodstuffs and ammunition.

The number of new shipmates in the form of reanimated dead husks also grew. From one ship, the captain brought back nine slain men, and from the other, a dozen. As they drew closer to their destination, there were nearly as many undead as there were regular living crewmen. They behaved in the same as Mr. Knave: they comprehended orders and understood what people said to them, but they seemed to no longer have the mental capacity to act independently or creatively.

Captain Torch brought the husks with him when boarding the second and third ships to add to the theatrical nature of his attack. The skin of the captured undead men quickly lost color, and their eyes glazed over. To look at them, one might guess they were sickly. They certainly looked and felt (and smelled) *wrong.*

It was impossible to avoid them entirely while on deck, as crowded as the ship was getting, but Caleb did his best to keep his interactions with them to a minimum. To keep the living crew from being overly distracted and unsettled, the undead were mostly kept occupied with work.

The additional help freed the rest of the crew up for some downtime. But when the ship was not in combat, Caleb kept busy; he joined a number of the other men scrubbing the deck. Jack stood there, off duty, looking over the railing out to the sea.

Caleb waved to get his attention. "Good morning."

The gunner appeared to be munching on an apple for his breakfast. He nodded to Caleb. "Aye."

As Caleb drew closer, he could see that it was not an apple he was working on, but a red onion.

"They say onions are good for relieving joint pain," Jack remarked when he noticed the look on Caleb's face. "After ten years, I can't say my joints are much better yet, so it should be working any day now."

"I'll take your word for it," Caleb said as he scrubbed the deck with the other men. "This place that we are headed to – have you been there? What is it like?"

"I've been there. It's a rundown old Spanish fort on a small spit of land just north of Swashbuckler Island. Captain Torch claimed it years ago and set up base there. We'll divert southwest by Buccaneers Isle for some more supplies, but we should turn northeast from there and arrive at Spitshine by the end of the day tomorrow."

"I see."

Jack noticed the unease in Caleb's voice. "You have somewhere else to be, lad?"

"I am just anxious to know what will happen to us now."

Caleb eyed some of the undead crewmen mechanically working the sails. He let that thought linger in the air as Jack returned to his breakfast onion.

Hanson, who was also there scrubbing the deck, followed Caleb's gaze and closed in, keeping his voice low. "It is unfortunate what happened to poor old Knave," he said, "but you and I, we have nothing to fear. Keep to your work, and all will be well. The Reaper has promised us riches and power, so long as we do the tasks given us."

His tone gave him away; he had doubts and was trying to convince himself of what he was saying.

"Before anything can be done, the ritual itself must be found. If the ritual cannot be completed, I imagine our fate will be worse than the poor lost wretches who have joined us on this ship, leaving their souls behind."

"That's not comforting," Caleb thought aloud.

"No, I suppose it's not."

"Are you saying there is no hope for any of us, then?"

Hanson was silent for an uncomfortably extended moment. "I would never say that," he finally assured him.

"What about this ritual? If it is lost, what is there to be done?"

Hanson stopped his scrubbing.

"Did you notice how our captain has been speaking with the captains of the other ships in private? He's been gathering information. When we get to the fort at Spitshine Spot, I'll wager the *Red Soul* will be given a new heading."

Caleb returned to his task in silence. What bothered him most about the current voyage was not even the soulless men who were becoming more and more deathlike in appearance and manner as they sailed on, but the fact Caleb was beginning to feel used to their presence.

The final day of the voyage was uneventful, giving Caleb more time with his thoughts until he ultimately became convinced that nothing good could come of him staying here with the increasingly macabre crew.

The sun went down, and a large island came into view. Few

of the regular crew were on deck, but they were engaged in some sort of dice game with one another, focused on the stories they were telling. The rest of the crew standing around were the increasingly cursed looking undead men, but they paid no heed to anything besides their work.

After gathering his courage, Caleb looked at the crew then slipped himself through the railing and dropped into the sea.

Caleb sank a bit longer than he had intended and felt his heart race as he furiously kicked his feet and grasped with his hands against the current pushing him down.

He finally breached the surface of the water and took a deep breath, nearly choking on the seawater that splashed into his open mouth. He rubbed his eyes and squinted, watching the ship sail off into the night.

Ahead of him, Caleb saw the large island. Jutting out from it was a small swampy bit of land with a raised thatched building built into some trees, illuminated by the warm glow of welcoming torchlight. As the *Red Soul* continued to circle the island, Caleb swam towards the light.

"A curse that binds itself to the soul twists the mind and fills it with dark thoughts and desires. The stench of Death is ever-present, and its gaze is never relenting."

– Golden Sea Grimoire

IV

THE VOODOO MAN

"There is a dark cloud coming. It is a cloud of change. Dark, evil spirits want to lay claim to this land and its peoples."

Aiden Kingsley spoke these words in a thick Haitian accent, his eyes closed in concentration, and his natty dreadlocks falling dramatically over his face. He sat behind a small booth in a thatched hut, surrounded by the warm glow of lanterns. Another man sat in the corner of the hut, banging softly on a tanbou drum and occasionally vocalizing, adding to the atmosphere.

"The forces of darkness may be on their way at this very moment," Kingsley continued, dramatically, "but fear not, seekers of truth! We can be made safe."

"What ought I do?" squeaked a shaky voice just in front of him.

Kingsley opened his eyes. Across from him stood a man wearing a colorful shirt. A sly grin made its way to Kingsley's face.

The hook was set. Now to reel him in.

He pulled out several ornate dice and tossed them into a small shaker cup and rolled them out on the counter in front of

36

him.

"Yes, very interesting. Allow me to consult my tome to see what the spirits suggest."

He pulled out a large tome from under the booth and landed it open with a thud, quickly thumbing through the pages until he found the appropriate passage.

"This seems to be right on your path. We provide sacred items here, offering protection by the loa Dan Petro who shall look after you and see that no harm comes to your land. Aisle 2B. Everything is labeled."

He gestured to a nearby section in the shop, for that is what this place was. Specifically, this was "Mr. Voodoo's Hex Hut," with Kingsley himself being the eponymous Mr. Voodoo.

"It is fortuitous you arrived here today," he said, "for we are running a sale on Dan Petro related items this week."

He was, in fact, not running a sale, but the list prices were always bumped up, and a discount was an enticing incentive that could encourage sales. If it translated into a purchase, then Kingsley saw nothing wrong with that.

"A thousand thanks upon you," the man said, bowing low as he scurried over to the aisle which was tackily labeled "Isle 2B."

Got him.

Kingsley gave a big, toothy grin.

"Mr. Voodoo is here to help."

The Hex Hut was located on tiny Blister Island, just off the southern coast of Buccaneers Isle. It was, for the most part, a tourist trap souvenir shop. Aiden Kingsley had taken over the place from his parents and planned to leave it to his niece Corine when he moved on to do something more fitting to his education in the spiritual arts. For now, he did his best to lend an air of mystery and authenticity to the place while also selling cheaply made voodoo dolls at inflated prices.

The wind picked up outside, blowing the bamboo wind chimes, and an unexpectedly cool morning breeze came through as the door swung open. A dark figure stood silhouetted in the doorway.

The shopkeeper shook off the chill that quickly subsided and cautiously greeted the man.

"Welcome to Blister Island's Hex Hut, young stranger," he said. "Glad you blew in here today. I'm Aiden Kingsley. Let me know if there's anything I can help you with. A charm to keep you from harm, a hex to put on your ex." His usual sales pitch greeting that he had prided himself on in the past now sounded rather trite as he spoke it in this situation.

Another customer in the hut, a middle-aged well-to-do looking tourist wearing a vest with palm trees crudely drawn on it, spoke up. "How about this weather, eh? If you don't like it, just wait a few moments, am I right? Only in the Caribbean, yeah?" The lack of response indicated that in fact, he may not be right, so he went back to looking at some kitschy shrunken head trinkets that, as he would put it, "the wife would just love."

The man in the doorway moved steadily forward into the shop.

"My name is Caleb," he said, stepping into the light. "I would like to know if you can help me."

"You looking for something specific, friend?" Kingsley asked.

"You call yourself the Voodoo man?"

"Mr. Voodoo," Kingsley corrected. "That's me." He watched a small puddle of water form at Caleb's feet. "Can I offer you a towel?"

Caleb's eyes moved down to see the water pooling up underneath him.

"Sorry about that," he said. "I don't mean to mess up your shop. I wanted to ask you some advice. I have heard of your place, and I understand that you have some knowledge of the spirit world."

"That's right," Kingsley said with a measured tone. "I will certainly try to give you what assistance I am able. What ails you, friend?"

"What do you know of curses?" Caleb asked quietly, stepping forward.

Kingsley searched Caleb's face for any hint of deception.

"You're not messing with me, are you, brother?"

With a cursory glance of the room, Caleb took stock of who all were present. His focus turned back to Kingsley, who looked increasingly concerned and more than a little skeptical.

"Come speak with me in the back," he finally said. Then, louder, he called out, "Corine, watch the shop while I'm speaking with this fellow."

A dramatic, exasperated sigh could be heard across the way as a teenage girl stepped around a corner, her nose buried in a book. Without taking her eyes off her book, she planted herself behind the counter.

"Thanks, doll," Kingsley said. "I know it's a chore; I'll be right back." He picked up a few books to take with them to the back room. "My niece," he explained. "Everything's an inconvenience for her. Sometimes, I think this new generation of youngsters is spoiled rotten."

Kingsley led Caleb through several doors until they came to a small room that looked more like a living area than a shop and sat down. Caleb took a deep breath and collected his thoughts.

"My name is Caleb," he said again. "I was recently a crewman on the *Red Soul,* under Captain Benjamin Torch."

He proceeded to tell Kingsley what had happened to him since his departure from the island a month ago, the strange meeting with the cloaked figure, and the cursed crew under Captain Torch's command. Kingsley listened attentively, without interruption.

"That's quite a story," he said after a prolonged silence as he processed what he had heard.

"So, what now?"

Kingsley lit a long pipe and took several long draws from it before speaking again.

"Let's take a step back and go over what we know. Assuming

you're being straight with me and not just yanking my rudder chain, if nothing else, I can further my own personal research in these matters. You say the cloaked man cursed the entire crew of the ship you were on, yourself included?"

"That's right."

Kingsley moved to his bookshelf and began running his fingers over the spines of several books. "Baron Semedi is the loa of death and fertility. He greets your soul after you've been buried and leads you to the underworld. Did your 'Reaper' wear a top hat and smoke a cigar by any chance?"

"I'm afraid not," Caleb said. "He was a pale, solemn figure."

"I see." Kingsley considered this information a moment. "It sounds like your man is more of a classical stoic entity, more akin to the imagery that rose to popularity during the Black Death in the Old World several hundred years ago. Who knows? Maybe we can call upon Baron Semedi to aid us, if it comes to it."

"Really? Caleb said, impressed. "You have experience in that?"

Kingsley laughed. "Of course not. I'll level with you: I do know some of the basics, yet while I may be 'Mr. Voodoo' in the shop, that's mainly for tourists. They like the big show. It sells trinkets and pays the rent; visitors eat it up. But if all you say is true, this sounds like one high-level curse by a top-tier perpetrator. I mainly deal with small hexes and charms."

"But you do have training, do you not?" Caleb asked. "You have been educated in these things?"

"I've been studying Voodoo for years, as well as many ancient languages, local and remote. I have never encountered anything quite like this." Kingsley searched his memory back to his days learning occult history before taking over the Hex Hut.

"A curse affecting a group of individuals is an interesting matter. Can one even break the curse for yourself independently of the rest of the crew? I don't know. Of course, there is also the question of what will happen should the contract be fulfilled, and this Reaper gets what he is after. Would the curse break? Maybe it would, but I think you will find that the entities who make these kinds of deals are not famed for being trustworthy. I would have to check other sources, as I'm not sure the books I have here would cover everything. Quite honestly, this is all above my skill to advise."

"Is there no one who can help?" Caleb asked. "Where did you learn the things that you know?"

"There were several teachers," Kingsley recalled. "I'm not sure where they all are now, but there was this Boston woman, Cynthia Cove; her area of expertise was 'Curses Throughout History.' She has a place on Swashbuckler Island just to the east. If you can get on a ship that is going that way, she may be able to provide answers."

Caleb shifted nervously in his seat. He had not been forthcoming about his reason for leaving the island in the first place.

"I don't exactly have the means for traveling," he said. His meaning was not difficult for Kingsley to guess.

"There could be a way for us to go there that would not involve us getting swept up by another pirate crew," Kingsley said.

Caleb felt a hint of hope. "You would accompany me?"

"I'm not completely sure you are not trying to hoodwink me," Kingsley said, "but you capture my interest. Meet me at the Happy Souls tavern in Port de Sang this afternoon. I have some business matters to take care of here, but once I have them settled, we can put together a plan for setting out."

And with that, Caleb made his way out of the Hex Hut. A small craft ferried him from Blister Island to the nearby mainland of Buccaneers Isle, and he made his way northward towards the all-too-familiar town of Port de Sang.

Much of the walk to the town was spent considering his new situation. He certainly felt different than he had felt weeks before the trip. His old home island was now seen through fresh eyes, but could that just be an effect of going to sea for the first time? He *had* seen the strange man on the ship, had he not? *Was* it all somehow in his head?

Absentmindedly, Caleb held in his hands the knife that Olaf Hanson had given him on the *Red Soul.* It brought back the memory of being out to sea.

Caleb did not know how long he had spent looking at his knife, but he snapped out of his memories when he heard voiced up ahead.

He hid behind some nearby underbrush and waited. Sitting in the dirt, hiding amongst a patch of rhododendrons, he closed his eyes and caught his breath.

When he was calm enough, Caleb opened his eyes and saw ahead of him Jean Duplantier, the governor's son, an adolescent man several years Caleb's junior. His speech was soft, and Caleb could not easily make out the words. Eventually, Jean walked away, and the voices and sounds of their movement faded into the distance.

Caleb stepped out of the undergrowth and turned to face the small port town. As he did, he found himself staring into the faces of the two men he least wished to see: Charles and Bert Walton, the foremen and taskmasters of Governor Duplantier's plantation.

Blast it.

"Do my eyes cheat me?" Bert said to his brother as they both looked down at Caleb's surprised face.

"If it isn't the house slave Caleb," Charles quipped with a devilish grin. "Where have you been? Your master has been so worried!"

Running was not an option at this time. Behind him was the difficult terrain of the underbrush and standing between him and any other way out were two men who would readily take him back as a prize for the man who claimed Caleb as his property. The punishment he would face on the plantation at their hands was not something Caleb cared to imagine.

All this flashed through his mind in a single instant. What

did not flash through his mind was what he actually did. He whipped his knife up in front of him, holding it at arm's length. The brothers had not expected this and after the initial surprise found the threat amusing.

"What are you going to do with that, boy?" Bert mocked. "Cut some shallots?"

Charles squawked an annoying, stuttering laugh.

But Caleb was not laughing. His body surged with adrenaline, and he was ready to do what he had to. Charles Walton held up a machete in response to Caleb's threatening gesture.

"Don't make me –" Caleb began, but he was interrupted by Charles, whose smile wrenched itself into an angry scowl.

"Don't make you what?" he growled. "I can make you do whatever I well please. You belong to the governor, which means…" He pulled back his machete, preparing to swing, "… you're mine, boy."

Quick as a flash, Caleb flung his knife forward. It cut through the air and struck Charles directly in the center of his chest. The force of the blow threw him backwards, his eyes wide and his mouth gasping.

Stunned, Bert cried out, "Charlie!" and started fumbling for his own knife.

Lying on his back, Charles still held the machete out above him, pointing it forward at Caleb. Caleb wrenched it out of his hand just in time to use it to parry an incoming blow from Bert.

Caleb rolled away out of reach, now wielding the machete. He spun around and swung. The blade struck Bert, and he fell to the ground next to his brother.

What happened next was the real surprise for Caleb. At first, he thought it must be a hallucination from the shock, or maybe it was a trick of the light? But it couldn't be that; he saw it clear as day, for it was still day. A dull green glow escaped from the bodies of the two men and then shot into him. It was as if energy from their dying souls had entered him.

Caleb rifled through the pockets of both Bert and Charlie. It was a horribly morbid affair, he thought to himself, but the deed was done, and he may as well take any advantage he could. There were a few Spanish doubloons and several gold rings between the two of them. He also made sure to retrieve his knife as well as a few other small knives strapped to Bert's hip.

A premature discovery of the bodies could make leaving more difficult, so Caleb dragged the bodies deeper into the underbrush and away from view. He stood over the two of them, trying to comprehend what he had just experienced. On examining his hand, there was no odd glow nor any discoloration showing anymore; had he just imagined it all?

With a concentrated effort, Caleb extended his hand towards the two bodies. The ground rumbled beneath his feet. A green swirl of energy seeped from his outstretched hand. The bodies twitched, and their arms began to reach forward. With a gasp of shock, Caleb withdrew his hand, and the effects immediately ceased. The bodies fell limp, and the green glow faded away.

"That's peculiar," he said under his breath, his eyes wide.

It was nearly midday; crowds began to form in Port de Sang. Several ships were docked, including a noteworthy three-mast galleon. The name written clearly on its hull was "*Devil's Thunder.*" There was no sign of the *Red Soul*; if it had docked here on its way to Torch's stronghold, it had already passed through.

Staying under the cover of the dense foliage and ducking behind fences to stay out of sight, Caleb slipped into the town undetected and approached the rear entrance of the Happy Souls Tavern.

Inside, a group of men gathered around a ragged sailor playing slow music on a squeezebox. The men drank and talked with each other, but in an uncharacteristically reserved manner. Overall, the tavern was calm and empty.

A few heads turned as Caleb stepped cautiously into the room and to the bar, but the men slowly went back to their business as he ordered a grog. He paid for it with one of the coins that he had picked up from the Waltons.

"Ain't I seen you somewhere before?" the man at the bar asked, carefully looking over Caleb as he handed him a tankard. It was a horrible looking drink; the liquid was greenish brown, and it had a slice of an overripe lemon floating in it.

"I don't think so," Caleb said, racking his brain for a possible quick way out of an explanation. All he could come up with was, "I never been anywhere before."

The demeanor of the bartender changed, and he chuckled grimly as he thought about the response. "Boy, if that don't sum it all up. You know, I ain't never even been so far as East Point. Me mother gave birth to me in this tavern, and Lord knows I'll most likely die here. Never been anywhere myself, neither."

Caleb gave a hesitant but polite smile as he took a sip from his drink. He could taste the citrus as well as coconut and a generous portion of sweetened rum only slightly watered down. It was not as bad as it looked, but the unexpectedly high alcohol content made him shudder. He set the drink down, deciding to pace himself.

Caleb's thoughts drifted to the galleon he had seen docked in the port.

"Anything to speak of happening in town?" he asked. "Any visitors?"

The man waved of his hand. "People come and go – some more than others, and myself not as often as any of 'em. Captain Santana and his crew of the *Devil's Thunder* just made port today." He spat on the floor. "I reckon you know of him?"

Caleb nodded. "What brings him here?"

"This is Buccaneers Isle!" The barkeep said. "He has a right to come here as much as anyone, though I'll wager you won't find many 'round here very happy to see him. As long as he don't drive all my customers away, he can do what he likes."

Caleb took his tankard, stepped away from the counter, and found an unoccupied round table in the corner. He claimed it for himself and waited for Kingsley.

When Kingsley arrived, Caleb was nearly finished with his drink. He wondered if they would be able to make it off the island before anyone found the bodies of the Walton brothers.

"What's the news?" Caleb asked as Kingsley took a seat. "Can we leave this island now?"

"These things take a little time," Kingsley cautioned. "Is something the matter?"

Obviously, Kingsley could see that there was indeed something the matter. Caleb was a cursed man, but something had changed in his attitude since they had spoken earlier that day. He was much more anxious. Maybe it was because they were back in town.

"The sooner the better," Caleb said, not giving himself away.

Kingsley nodded. "The *Devil's Thunder* is docked here in the bay. I happen to be family friends with the ship's physician, Dr. Rockwell. With a good word, I think we should be able to join the crew."

"That's great," Caleb said, distracted.

"Is there something I should know?" Kingsley asked. "Did something happen?"

Caleb's eyes darted around. "It's nothing," he assured him. "What about Captain Santana? Is he on the dock?"

"I saw several men out there. It looked like they were unloading some things. I didn't get a good look." He studied Caleb's worried face. There was something he was not telling him. "Are you sure nothing else happened?"

"Two men from the governor's home," Caleb blurted out.

"They saw me on the way here."

"I see," Kingsley said, not understanding his full meaning. Caleb had been evasive concerning his former life on the island, but Kingsley was no fool. What he had not been told, he was able to piece together: Caleb had run away. The men from the governor's home were men who could identify him. "If they make it back to the governor, that could make things complicated."

Caleb shook his head, not wanting to say the words. He didn't have to.

"Oh."

"I've seen them deal out terrible punishment to men in the field. I had to act. I had to defend myself. But that is not the worst of it. There was something that happened to the bodies." He felt foolish as he attempted to recount the details, especially to a stranger. But he was in too deep, so he pushed through.

"There was a wave of something that hit me. It was like it went through me. Some sort of ethereal visage that arose from the bodies and came into me."

"Ethereal visage," Kingsley repeated slowly.

"You know, like this energy that came from their spirits, but I could see it."

"This is old magic," Kingsley said, his mind going back to his years of study. "There is much we do not know. As you say, the sooner we leave, the better. I reckon we find this Captain Santana and see whether we can be on our way."

V

DEVIL'S THUNDER

Kingsley and Caleb left the Happy Souls Tavern, keeping a watchful eye on everyone.

"If you're going to walk around here," Kingsley said, "you're going to need to look less like you and more like a sailor. What's that you're wearing?"

"This is what I had on me when I left the governor's house," Caleb said, looking down at his ragged trousers and simple shirt. "I don't have much of a selection to choose from."

"Well, you do now," Kingsley said. He looked at Caleb's face next. "Not sure if there's much of a way to change up your face, but we can hide it a bit. Maybe we can cover up an eye as well." He looked around and spotted the General Store. "Let's pick up a few things."

"You'll have to go in without me," said Caleb. "I've run errands there many times, and I'm afraid the owner Mr. Geoffrey knows me by now. I cannot have him see me."

"Yes, that would be a problem," Kingsley agreed. "Tell you what. You stay tucked away here." He indicated a corner at the end of a dark alley. "Keep out of sight, out of view, and I'll be in and back with a few things."

Seeing no alternative, Caleb handed over the coins he had taken from the Walton brothers as well as the money he had made aboard the *Red Soul,* trusting Kingsley to make the purchases for him. Kingsley nodded and went into the store, and Caleb had nothing to do but wait.

Tucked away from prying eyes, Caleb shuffled under cover of the shadows to the edge of the general store and looked towards the street.

Men and women went about their day, some of whom Caleb recognized, but most were strangers. He took mental notes on how different classes of people held themselves: how they stood, how they walked, and how they spoke. Caleb had observed a lot of well-to-do travelers who had come to visit the governor, so he felt certain he could affect something of a similar confident air if he put his mind to it. He practiced walking a few steps in the manners he observed.

The *Devil's Thunder* sat anchored at the far dock; people stood around it as others loaded it up for a voyage. Whether or not they were going to sail to Swashbuckler Island, boarding this ship was his best way to get off Buccaneers Isle. He tried to guess which of the men near the dock was Captain Santana.

The door to the General Store opened, and Kingsley stepped out, wearing a lightweight long coat over his other clothes and carrying a small bundle. Caleb slipped back into the alley as Kingsley met him there.

"That's amazing!" Caleb said, taking the bundle. He rifled through the clothes and began to put together his new outfit.

Kingsley took his extra coat off and handed it to Caleb. "See how this works."

"That's fine," Caleb said, excited about his new look. He hastily put the coat on and began to adjust it. "Oh, this is very fine."

"It's the cheapest coat they had," Kingsley admitted, "but it should start you off well." He wrapped a strip of material over Caleb's head as if he were dressing a head wound. "That should help a bit."

"What is that?"

"It would be good to bandage up part of your face," Kingsley said as he covered one of Caleb's eyes and part of his cheek. To finish, he tied off the ends atop Caleb's head. "As much as we can hide, the better."

"I suppose," Caleb said, a little less enthusiastic about this part of his costume.

"Top this off with a hat, and *voilà!*" He brought out a ratty tricorn hat and set it on top of Caleb's head.

Caleb caressed the hat. It was a simple poor man's hat and not in great condition, but to him, it was the best hat he had ever hoped for.

"Very good, my friend," Kingsley said, stepping back to admire his work. "You are a spectacle."

They began to walk in the direction of the *Devil's Thunder.*

Several paces from the dock, Caleb's eyes widened in surprise at seeing Jean Duplantier standing there in front of him. Caleb's body briefly tensed up, but he fought to contain himself and made a courteous bow as he passed by.

"Good day, sir," Caleb said, his heart pounding, but doing his best to not give himself away. He affected a slight upper-class accent and a confident manner to help complete his character.

"*Bonjour,*" Jean replied, tipping his hat, clearly not making the connection. He did turn to give Kingsley and Caleb a second glance, but that was more because of the high-class mannerisms coming from someone who looked like a common deckhand. With a shake of his head, he continued walking on his way.

"Maybe choose a character that fits the costume," Kingsley suggested when Jean had left hearing distance.

The two of them laughed at the absurdity of it all.

"Any suggestions?" Caleb asked.

"You could be my cousin Caleb Kingsley from Ramrod Island."

"Is he wealthy?"

"No, he's fictional," Kingsley said. "The point is to create a character you can embody."

"If he's fictional," Caleb challenged, "why can't he be wealthy?"

"Because you will be him, and you are not wealthy."

"That's fair."

They approached the ship where three men stood poring over inventory and documents.

"Do you see your doctor friend?" Caleb asked.

"No, but maybe we can speak directly to the man in charge."

As they drew closer, they approached one of the men standing by the ship who was most likely the captain; there was some gray in his short black beard, and he had a stern but respectable look about him. He wore a brown tricorn hat that was in much better condition than the one Caleb wore; he also wore a red coat that came down to his ankles. He was not a short man, but the man standing next to him almost made it seem like he was by comparison.

The tall man appeared to be an indigenous person, an Indian, as some of the settlers called them, but he was dressed in seaman's clothes matching the rest of the crew.

The third in this odd trio was a younger man with a boyish face and dirty blonde hair pulled back in a tight ponytail behind his head. He was speaking to the captain but stopped as Kingsley and Caleb approached.

"Something we can do for the two of you?" the young man asked.

"Forgive us," Kingsley said, bowing low. Caleb followed his lead. "My cousin and I are seeking passage to the port of Swashbuckler Island to the east of here."

"This is not a passenger ship," the man said, turning away from them. "I'm afraid you must search elsewhere."

"We have, sir," Kingsley pleaded, "but as I am sure you are aware, this island is full of pirates, and many of the ships coming in and going out are filled with their kind, and we, upstanding men as we are, do not wish to associate with them. It is part of the reason we wish to sail away from here." He did not have a hard time stressing this, as much of it was actually very true, and Kingsley counted on these men knowing this.

"I trained as a ship's gunner," Caleb offered, "and we would both be willing to lend a hand should the occasion arise."

"I'm sorry," the young man started, "but —"

He was cut off by a gesture from the captain.

"Belay that, Mr. Johansen," the captain said, stepping forward to speak with the two inquiring young men. "You say you have some experience as a ship's gunner, young one? What was the ship's name? And answer me this: why wish you to sail on the *Thunder* rather than return to it?"

Kingsley started to speak, most likely a hastily constructed lie of a story, which Caleb was certain the captain would be able to see through. Caleb laid a reassuring arm on Kingsley's shoulder.

"The truth is," said Caleb, "I was taken aboard a ship of pirates, and they pressed me into service, but I managed to cut ties with them, but not before they gave me my training on the guns. Now, I would sail against them if I could, to bring them to justice. I've no love for pirates."

"Is that so?" said the captain. He stood there a moment in silent contemplation. "Then it seems we've a common purpose. I trust your eye won't cause too much trouble?" He gestured to the bandage on Caleb's brow.

Caleb raised the bandage a little, revealing his eye.

"Oh, no sir," he said. "It is mostly healed up. It's just a little sensitive."

"And your friend, here: what training has he?"

"No formal sea training, I confess," Kingsley said. "But I can lend a strong hand where needed, and I am also quite good in the kitchen. If Dr. Rockwell is still aboard your ship, he can vouch for my character."

The captain spoke the matter over with Johansen. "We could use some extra hands for a while. And with Mr. Brenner leaving us, we could use a new cook."

"At your discretion, Captain."

"Swashbuckler Island, you say?" said the captain. "We are not headed there directly, but it shall be in our path in a few months' time. You would be willing to work for us on the ship until we arrive there?"

Seeing no greater alternative, Caleb and Kingsley gratefully accepted the offer.

"In that case, welcome aboard the *Devil's Thunder*. I am Captain Rafael Santana. This is my sailing master and navigator, Mr. Johansen. And lastly, our quartermaster, Mr. Atsadi. He will see to it that you fulfill your duties aboard the ship. Atsadi, take their names down and add them to the roster."

The tall man nodded and took down the names of Aiden Kingsley and Caleb. With a little hesitation, Caleb gave his name as "Caleb Kingsley."

The sky was a clear blue when they set out, and the weather was pleasantly warm. Caleb stored his new coat and shirt below as he went to work in the sun on the deck of the ship. He repurposed the rag covering his eye as a sweat-rag tied around his forehead. Caleb was in decent physical shape, but standing shirtless amongst seasoned sailors, his small frame looked scrawny. He worked hard, nonetheless. Much of the work involved pulling ropes against the force of the wind and the waves. With this consistent routine, he would no doubt catch up to the physical condition of the other men before long.

Many of the crew were not unlike those who served on the *Red Soul*. A variety of nationalities were represented, and many of them were rough looking fellows. It was soon learned that the captain had himself been a pirate in his youth, after having come from Italy to the New World, but he had received letters of marque from King William of Orange in England during the recent deposition of King James. Though Santana was Italian of origin, his skill was known, and his loyalty had been purchased by the English. As a privateer, he helped the English fight against its enemies the French in the Caribbean. Also, he and his crew, many of whom were former pirates themselves, now hunted pirates.

While Caleb stayed on deck, Aiden Kingsley was sent to work in the ship's galley. Because he was new to the ship, he officially worked under one of the men there – a man by the name of Melville Bilgewater. Mr. Bilgewater was not much of a cook at all, but he was loyal to the captain. He was primarily there to see to it that nothing harmful went into the food. Several live chickens were kept in the hold, so they were the meat that would make up most of the non-seafood-based meals. The ship was stocked with vegetables and spices, allowing him to experiment with recipes, usually with Mr. Bilgewater looking over his shoulder, mentally taking notes. It did not take long for Kingsley to impress him and the captain with his cooking.

Caleb put to use all he had learned while on the *Red Soul,* and he soon found himself learning more, first in the area of tying proper knots. He was glad for the sea air again and felt a glimmer of hope, but the mystery of the full extent of his current condition gnawed at him.

"Turn hard to starboard, Mr. Bogall!" came the voice of Johansen. Caleb snapped back to attention from his musings.

Atsadi started calling out orders to the rest of the crew. "Set the mainsail, and brace the bowlines to leeward!"

Jake Docks, one of the sailors working nearby, motioned for Caleb to assist at the sheets. He did so and stood ready, waiting for the next order and hoping he would be able to understand enough what he was supposed to do.

"Keep the sheets tight, Mr. Kingsley," Docks said to Caleb.

Caleb leaned back, putting all his weight into pulling the line attached to the sails. His foot began to slip. He caught himself and regained his footing without giving the line slack, but he received a nasty gash on his arm as he slid against the railing.

"Bring it around," Atsadi called. "Keep going. Keep going. Get 'em tight!" The wind blew hard into the ship's full sheets, and with a sharp movement at the ship's tiller, Bogall used the momentum from the wind to launch the *Devil's Thunder* out to sea with an impressive jolt of speed.

"Now, steady the bowline and get the tack aboard. Let go and haul! Keep her true, lads."

With that, it felt like things were beginning to calm down. Caleb's heart raced with adrenaline; all the sailing aboard Torch's ship had been more understated, whereas here, it was almost as if Santana wanted to draw attention as they left Buccaneers Isle.

Other ships coming to Port de Sang gave a wide berth to the *Devil's Thunder* as she made her way out to sea. Captain Santana stood tall and secure behind the tiller as they made their swift exit from port. Perhaps he wanted a show of strength to dissuade any pirate vessels from challenging them. Whatever the case, they were in the open ocean, and the crew fell into a more relaxed routine.

When everything had become calm, Atsadi sent Caleb to visit Dr. Albert Rockwell, the ship's surgeon.

As Caleb entered the cabin, Dr. Rockwell stood to greet him. Rockwell was a middle-aged man, clean cut and more civilized in appearance compared to the rest of the crew, even the captain.

"Well, well, what have we here?" he said, taking a look at the bloody arm. "Only just out of port and already an injury? This is hardly a good omen." He took a closer look at the wound, which was a rather unsightly gash running halfway down Caleb's arm. "Isn't this a beauty?"

"You think so?" Caleb asked. There's no denying that he was in pain, but there was a part of him that was still exhilarated from the experience, and he felt some excitement about his first scar.

"Don't get too excited now," the doctor said. He wet a rag and began to dab the wound. "They tell me you're Caleb Kingsley, but I don't believe we've met. I thought I knew all the Kingsleys."

"I'm Aiden's cousin," said Caleb. "From Ramrod Island."

"And taken by pirates, I hear?" the doctor said, letting the issue of the Kingsley family slide. If the young man did not wish to explain himself now, that was up to him. He trusted Aiden, and he would trust him in this for now. If it were worth coming to light, the truth would come out eventually.

"You have had quite a time already," he continued. "We must make sure there are no stray fragments remaining in this wound." He examined it closer.

Caleb fidgeted. "Have you any scars?" he asked.

Rockwell raised an eyebrow at this. "On my leg. I'll show you sometime. Got hooked on a line while dealing with a terribly massive shark near The Deep."

"The Deep?"

"Aye." Rockwell stepped aside and rifled through his bag. He produced a small bottle and a wooden block. "You'll be wanting some of this for the pain."

Caleb took a swig from the bottle. It was straight whiskey that didn't go down smooth, but he was still grateful for something to dull his senses.

"And bite down on this. This will sting a little."

Caleb set the block of wood in his mouth. Rockwell began stitching up Caleb's arm. Caleb bit down hard and endured the ordeal as Rockwell explained what he knew of the Deep.

"Southeast of here, there is a stretch of open ocean that sailors call 'The Existential Deep.' It is a place of inclement weather and sea monsters, some say; a place where all sorts of horrors dwell. I don't put much stock in such stories; I figure that it's men misremembering things due to fear and then exaggerating for the sake of a good story. I was on a ship sailing around it once, when we were set upon by a shark twice the size of any other shark I had ever seen. Faith, it was a giant of a shark, but a giant shark is still a shark, if you get me; there was nothing otherworldly of it. I imagine that's what many of these stories really are. I avoided the shark's jaws, but as my luck would be, my leg got caught in a fishing line. Who could have predicted that one?"

He shook his head as he finished stitching Caleb up and

took a sip of the whiskey himself.

"Now, this will take a while to heal," he said. "Be sure to keep it bandaged tight. We can check on it tomorrow and change the bandage. Try to keep it as dry as possible."

Caleb retrieved his shirt from his belongings and put it on as he went out on the deck, wondering just how he would keep his bandage from getting wet here on the sea. He joined several crewmen he had spent the day shadowing who now stood idly on the ship's fo'c'sle.

"So, Caleb," said a man by the name of Stephen Kennedy, "I hear you're off to Swashbuckler Island. What's happening over there these days?"

"I couldn't say," said Caleb. "Have you been there? What's it like?"

"Like any other island, I'd guess," Kennedy said. "It has been years since I have made port there. As for me, I'll take the sea."

"It's really peaceful out here, isn't it?"

"She's peaceful now," said Kennedy, "but she can really bring up a storm. You always want to be on her good side, and even then, she can blindside you."

"Aye, that be true," said Jake Docks. "You haven't spent much time at sea, have you, boy?" It was more of a statement than a question. "That's fine. You'll get a feel for it, though you'll be a bit more mindful of the railing when you're attending to the sheets I'll warrant." He indicated Caleb's bandaged arm. "Don't want to go losing a limb now." He let out a wheezing laugh, revealing a mouth that was missing a few front teeth.

"It's nothing," Caleb said, though it was beginning to throb. He was grateful for the shot of whiskey that had already started kicking into his senses.

At this time, one of the younger sailors rang the ship's bell.

"That'll be dinner for us," Kennedy said, hopping to his feet. "Let's hope your cousin's cooking is better than Old Bilgewater's."

He led the way down the hatch where the dinner was distributed. Another group of deckhands stepped onto the deck to relieve the current shift as Caleb, Docks, and Kennedy went below.

For the first time since they started their new assignments, Caleb and Kingsley saw one another. Kingsley had taken to his task well. He brought out a pot of stew from the galley, and with the assistance of old Melville Bilgewater, he served the crew. The stew was thin but made good use of the chicken and vegetables. After the day's work, Caleb thought it smelled heavenly. When all hands had received bowls of stew, Kingsley fixed one for himself, joined the others and sat down.

Docks did not bother waiting for the others; he started eating right away and was nearly half finished by the time Kingsley sat with them. Caleb waited for his "cousin" before he began eating.

"This looks wonderful," Caleb said. "It seems you're fitting in here well, 'cousin.' If I'm not careful, I may lose you to Captain Santana."

"It is quite a setup. We're well-provisioned, and there's no customers to deal with."

"Don't forget we will be departing when we reach our destination."

Kingsley waved a hand dismissively. "Of course, of course. I only mean to say the experience here is most rewarding."

Caleb held his spoon up to his mouth, revealing the bandage to Kingsley for the first time.

"Looks like you're taking this work a bit seriously."

"Just a scratch," Caleb insisted. "I'll be fine."

"Aye," said Docks through a mouthful of stew. "He got cut good, but he kept a steady foot all the same. This here stew is not bad. Better than Old Bilgewater's boot leather stew at any rate!" He laughed as if he had said something particularly clever. When nobody else joined him in the laugh, he went back to eating quietly and muttered something about 'kids these days' not appreciating a 'finely-crafted joke.'

They ate their meal and shared stories with one another.

Like many of the crewmen, Docks and Kennedy were reformed criminals. Docks had been caught picking locks and helping himself to treasure, while Kennedy had a more violent history on the sea, though he did not share the details at this time.

As they finished their meal, the sun disappeared below the horizon. The night crew was on deck, and now was the chance for Caleb to get some rest. He sat up a few minutes in the corner in the crew quarters away from the others. A lantern above him cast a soft orange light.

Against the recommendation of Dr. Rockwell, Caleb unwrapped the bandage on his arm and looked at it; it was an unpleasant sight.

A tingling sensation crawled up his spine. It was different from the pain of his wound. He could swear that he could feel a dark energy within himself. He did his best to suppress it, and it faded.

He looked up and around. Everything appeared normal from here. Nobody else had stirred. But the memory of that dark feeling gnawed at him. He closed his eyes and focused. The strange sensation returned. Charles and Bert Walton's faces flashed briefly in his mind.

As he opened his eyes, his right hand had a dull, green glow. It reminded him of what he saw on the Walton brothers' bodies just after he had killed them. Slowly, he moved his glowing right hand over to his wounded left arm and touched it on the scar.

A wave of energy so powerful it took his breath away flowed from Caleb's right hand into his left arm. Like a ghostly appendage, it ran over the wound, caressed it, picked at it, and closed it up. All that remained was a barely visible scar. The ghostly hand faded away, and it was as if it had never been there.

Caleb sat for a moment, baffled and in shock. For appearances, he re-wrapped his arm in the bandage.

"Well, that's new," he said quietly.

"Oi!" came a voice from a nearby bunk. "You going to put out that light or what?"

VI

FALSE FLAG

The second day aboard the *Devil's Thunder* started off poorly for Caleb when Atsadi called out for him to tie a scaffold knot, and instead, Caleb tied the only knot he knew, which was a simple overhand knot. He was surprised to find out just how many knots there were and afterwards spent much of his free time learning from Stephen Kennedy the names of the knots and how to tie them.

Life on this ship was not terribly different than it had been on the pirate ship. In many ways, the crew was a similar mix of people. Most were strong young men, hardened by a life at sea. Some were older, more experienced sailors, and a good number of them, like Kennedy and Docks, had been experienced pirates before they had been given letters of marque to hunt down their former compatriots on behalf of King William of England.

While practicing knot-tying with Kennedy, Caleb asked him how he found working under Santana compared to his former life as a pirate.

"I suppose it's not that different," Kennedy said after some consideration. "It's certainly got to be better 'an crewing a ship in the King's Navy."

"How's that?"

"Oh, you know; there, you've got uniforms, stricter discipline, that sort of thing."

"Have you ever been in the King's Navy?" Caleb asked.

"Perish the thought!" Kennedy exclaimed. "Now, I'll warrant maybe there's not as much freedom here on this ship compared to when when Docks and me sailed under Old Captain Jim Pompey, but here's much more respectable. The pay is fair, and we still gets to help take down ships."

"Who's Old Jim Pompey?"

"Eh? What's that? Who's Jim Pompey?" Kennedy repeated. "Well, he weren't no privateer, that's the truth. He was a shrewd old salt who marauded along the southern shipping lanes, ransacking, taking guns and slaves from vessels in the shipping lanes from Pighead Island and back up and around to Ramrod Island. Hauled in some good booty on those ships, we did, before he got himself captured and hanged for his trouble out on the eastern islands. He got the rope, and Docks and me got a chance at going straight with letters of marque, courtesy of Rafael Santana."

"He stole slaves?" Caleb asked. "What did he do to them?"

Docks stepped in. He had been off to the side, listening in on the conversation. "With the slaves?" he said. "Some of 'em he'd use himself, working the tasks free folk wouldn't. Sure now, you wouldn't want to be a slave under him, true as true. The rest of 'em he'd sell off to slave traders for cheap just to be rid of the lot. Couldn't say which would be worse."

"And what of you? Who'd you sail under?" Kennedy asked. "I heard you had been press-ganged onto the crew of a pirate ship."

"Oh," said Caleb, not wishing to recall details of his time on the *Red Soul*. He kept himself occupied by undoing a practice knot and tying it from memory. "I don't recall much."

"Od's bodkins!" exclaimed Kennedy. "What *do* you remember? Who was the captain?"

"It was Benjamin Torch of the *Red Soul*," Caleb finally said.

"You don't say!" said Kennedy, his eyes widened. "Cap'n Torch, himself? Is that a fact?"

"You know him?"

"There's not many a sailor in these parts who don't know of Captain Benjamin Torch. Old Pompey never directly ran into him, but he told us tales. Word is, Torch was into mysticism. What manner of a man was he?"

"I don't know how I would put it to you," said Caleb, wishing that were truer than it was. He recalled the cold hard look in Torch's bright eyes. He had seen enough of him to be able to form a reasonable understanding of his character. Torch kept a level head whenever he had been on deck giving orders, but it was always as if there was a fire under him preparing to light a fuse that would set him off in a murderous rage. Caleb had never seen that rage, but he always felt it was there under the surface.

"Truthfully, I saw very little of him," he said. "I stayed at the guns, mostly."

"Very well," Kennedy said, his disappointment clear. "Let me see what you have learned. Show me a bowline knot."

Caleb undid the knot he had been practicing and looped the end of it around into a sturdy bowline.

"That's keen," Kennedy said. "A little more practice and you'll be golden." He looked closely at the knot, and his eyes strayed down to the bandage on Caleb's arm, darkened by his dried blood. "And how's the arm? You ought to get the doc to take a look and change out those bandages."

"It's fine," Caleb said, and that was true. He had kept it wrapped for appearances, but he knew that even the scar under the bandage had faded.

At Kennedy's insistence, Caleb returned to the doctor. Doing this would allow him to avoid further discussion about Torch and his time aboard the *Red Soul*, and for that, Caleb was grateful. However, he was worried what sort of reaction the discovery of his unnaturally fast healing would elicit in the doctor.

Dr. Rockwell was busy writing something at his desk when Caleb came to see him. Whether it was a journal, medicinal, or something more recreational, Caleb could not say. Rockwell put away the papers as soon as Caleb entered.

"Young Master Kingsley," he greeted. "Come for some fresh bandages?"

Caleb nodded but hesitated to move forward, but an excuse for stepping away did not come to him, so he remained motionless.

"Come now," said the doctor, affecting a reassuring smile. "Up anchor and step forward. There's nothing to be afraid of. Has your arm been giving you any trouble?"

Caleb shook his head. "Not at all. It's mending quite well. Must be the sea air."

Rockwell shook his head and laughed politely. "I'm not sure it works that way, but let's have a look. Some men are known to heal quicker than others."

But as he unwrapped the bandage, Rockwell's smile faded. He moved a light so he could get a better look at the scar, for that's all that remained: a faded scar covered in some dried blood. Caleb searched his mind for a reasonable cover, but there was no story that immediately came to him. He hoped that when the time came, he could bluff his way through a conversation without fully giving away his condition.

The doctor tempered his shock and began washing Caleb's arm with a damp cloth.

"By my blood I've never seen a wound heal that fast," he remarked, running his fingers over Caleb's skin.

"Lucky me, I guess," Caleb said. "I guess I heal quicker than others. I've always been this way."

Rockwell looked into Caleb eyes just long enough for Caleb to feel uncomfortable. "Healing this quickly is beyond anything I've seen. It's unusual. Are you certain you did nothing to it after we wrapped it?"

Caleb broke Rockwell's gaze and shrugged it off. "No. I mean, maybe it wasn't as bad as all that to begin with."

Rockwell's skeptical expression was enough to say that this was not a sufficient explanation. The doctor had cleaned the wound himself and saw with his own eyes the unsightly gash on the arm, yet all that remained was a scar that looked as if it were from a long-healed wound.

"I reckon you've seen stranger things than this while at sea," Caleb said, gathering his things and preparing to leave the doctor. "Maybe the ocean has blessed me with its healing."

"Perhaps the sea offers healing to a new sailor." But Rockwell's voice betrayed him: he surely did not believe that this was the case. "Perhaps," he repeated, but Caleb knew from his earlier interaction with the doctor that he did not put stock in such tales. Rockwell was a practical man. Only a practical explanation would truly satisfy him, and that was something Caleb did not have, even with the help of the truth.

His own deceptions were stacking up against him. Rockwell undoubtedly knew Caleb was not a member of the Kingsley family. It was clear he knew he was hiding something regarding his arm, and it was a fair assumption he could guess he was running away from something on the island. But how much of it could he put together?

"You seem to be fully recovered," the doctor said at last. "I would however like to continue to observe it. You will alert me if there are any changes?"

Caleb nodded and left the doctor who returned to his desk and sat there, stroking his beard in contemplation.

The *Devil's Thunder* sailed into the open ocean. The lack of action over the next several days stood in stark contrast to the flashy exit from Buccaneers Isle. Kennedy continued to instruct Caleb the different knots he needed to learn. If his time on the *Red Soul* introduced him to the workings of a ship's guns, his time on the *Devil's Thunder* taught him how to sail.

Much of Caleb's time over the next several days was spent with Kennedy and Docks, who taught Caleb about sailing. A crewman by the name of Harrison spent time with Caleb, instructing him how to fight.

A week passed.

One early morning, as he returned to the deck at the end of one of his rests, Caleb found himself in the middle of a great commotion. Men scrambled about. Atsadi shouted orders.

"Hands to braces!" the quartermaster called.

Caleb stepped faster and ran into Kingsley who was helping to turn the sails to catch the wind.

"Aiden, what's happening?" Caleb asked.

"Not sure," said Kingsley. "Mr. Atsadi called us all out here."

"Step lively. All hands to general quarters," the orders continued.

Captain Santana stood on the quarterdeck with Johansen, looking forward across the length of the ship towards the left – the port side of the ship. He had a stern and focused look about him. Caleb followed his gaze. There, ahead of them, was a brigantine.

"Can you make it out?" Kingsley asked, also looking forward to the other ship. Caleb shook his head.

"They fly the Spanish merchant flag," came Santana's voice from behind them, speaking to the helmsman.

"Hoist the Red Ensign, Mr. Grant," Johansen called to one of the men. A young man nodded and began to raise a British merchant flag at the main mast.

"If she truly be a Spanish merchant," said Santana to Bogall, "she'll like as not let us go on our way. If she be something else entire, well, best we give them a surprise. Keep her steady and ease helm to larboard."

Bogall nodded at this and slowly adjusted the ship's heading to drift closer to the vessel in question.

"Men," Captain Santana addressed the crew in a louder voice, "it is our duty as privateers in the employ of the Royal Navy to help stamp out pirate threats in these waters. If that be a proper merchant vessel before us, we'll let her carry on her way with our blessing, but if she be a wolf in disguise, we'll disable her and bring in prisoners for a proper criminal trial. Gunners, be ready at the cannons. Everyone else, swords at the ready, but do not show your hand until the order is given."

"To your cannon, Mr. Kingsley," came Atsadi's voice.

Caleb nodded and stepped towards one of the front starboard cannons.

"What about me?" Aiden Kingsley asked, his voice shaking. "I'm no fighter."

"You are today," Atsadi said.

Harrison handed him a cutlass. "Stay back and remember, much of the battle is in the mind. If you can cut down your foe at a distance with fear or shame, the battle is half won."

Kingsley held onto the cutlass and stepped backwards to the security of the main mast.

Atsadi addressed the crew.

"That goes for the lot of you," he said. "Cut 'em down to size. Give 'em the fear of God, then the fight will be ours. But steady as you go until the attack is sounded. Make like you are simple merchant sailors until we are upon them."

"What's the sense in that?" Caleb quietly asked Docks, who was with him on the fo'c'sle cannon.

"Don't you see?" said Docks, "we run up on them, and they on us, thinking we're an easy-prey merchant ship, then when we're in range, they'll fly their true colors and let loose upon us, thinking they've caught us by surprise, but we will be prepared to let loose upon them. It's what we in this business call a 'false flag.'"

"But what if they are just merchants?" The approaching ship's colors could now be plainly seen by the crew, and their flag identified them as such.

"If that's what they are," said Docks, "they will not challenge us, and we will not parry them. But 'tis better to prepare."

"Stow the chatter," Atsadi said, and the men fell silent.

"Ready the cannons and hold fast," Johansen ordered. "And take heed: we aim to disable, not to sink."

"Caleb," said Docks in a low voice so as not to distract from Johansen's orders, "get this here cannon loaded, and get yourself ready to reload as needed."

"Aye, as you say."

Caleb retrieved a cannonball from the nearby ammunition barrel and loaded it into the cannon's muzzle. When it was set, he returned to the barrel and picked out a second.

Movement on the deck settled as the *Devil's Thunder* drew closer to the other ship. Despite their proximity, Caleb could not see its crew. It was as if they were hiding.

As they silently approached, Caleb saw it: the captain of the other ship, standing on the quarterdeck. He was a younger man than Santana, clean shaven and dressed in finery that seemed to Caleb too fine for a merchant captain.

The young captain said something to his helmsman, too low for anyone on the *Devil's Thunder* to hear.

Caleb looked back towards Santana for a sign. He, too, was studying the other captain closely. He held a steady hand up to Bogall, bidding him to wait but be ready to turn at a moment's notice.

"Keep your legs on you, sonny," Docks warned. "Secure your stance." Caleb spread out his legs and braced himself as the other ship turned violently to port.

"Show 'em our true colors, lads!" came the cry from the opposing ship. In the next moment, its merchant flag was replaced with a black flag; on it was an image of an hourglass in one corner and a knife in the opposite corner; in the center of the flag was a white blunderbuss gun.

Cheering and jeering came from the enemy ship as heads of the crew popped up from behind cannons. Then, with the help of a speaking trumpet, the captain of the vessel addressed the *Devil's Thunder*.

"Approaching merchant ship! Stand down and prepare to be boarded by Captain Blunderbuss Bailey! Receive us or be taken by force. Relinquish your goods, and no harm will come to ye."

Unflinching, Santana signaled for Grant to strike down the false merchant flag. "Hoist the 'Bolt!" he ordered. The merchant flag was promptly taken down and replaced with a flag which common pirates in these waters knew and feared: it was a red flag with the British Union Jack in the corner; in the main setting of the flag was a single white cutlass. It was a flag that alerted ships that not only was this ship operating as a privateer under the authority of England, but more specifically, this was the *Devil's Thunder*, a ship experienced in taking down pirate ships in the Caribbean.

The flag was raised, and Captain Santana called back through his own speaking trumpet as the ships had begun circling much closer to one another.

"Attention, approaching miscreants. This is Captain Rafael Santana of the *Devil's Thunder*. In the name of his majesty King William the Third of Britain and Ireland, I bid you lay down your arms and surrender."

But the young upstart captain would have none of this. Rage poured out of him as he shouted back at Santana.

"Double-faced Sea Sponge!" He cried out. "Stand to't, me bullies!" He gave a downward motion with his extended arm. "Fire all!"

With a deafening *boom*, cannons fired, violently hitting the railing of the deck of the *Devil's Thunder*.

Johansen called, "*Return fire!*" At least, that's what everyone assumed he called out; his voice was drowned out by the sound of the men already carrying out this order.

The cannons rang out. Caleb nearly lost his footing due to the ringing in his ears. Wood splintered from the deck around him. He reloaded the cannon, and Docks fired again.

On orders from Johansen, Bogall steered the *Devil's Thunder* into a more powerful position, and its cannons fired broadside on the enemy ship, whose name could now be seen displayed prominently on its stern: the *Vengeful Goose*.

"Hands to the halyards," Atsadi called out, readying the

crew for close combat. "Haul away!"

Kingsley stepped up to join the men, pulling on the lines to help catch wind in the sheets.

"Let's see if we can't hit their mainmast, Mr. Kingsley," Docks said to Caleb. "Bring me a chain shot and look sharp: we'll be upon them in no time."

Caleb nodded and fetched the chain shot, which was two small cannonballs attached to each other by a strong bit of chain. He loaded it into the cannon and stood back. The *Devil's Thunder* cut through the water at a great speed, a speed that seemed amplified thanks to the proximity of the *Goose.*

"She's coming 'round," called Atsadi. "Make ready. Musketeers, stand by. Boarding axes and swords, step lively!"

The cannons boomed, and the chain shot spun through the air, tearing through the rigging of the opposing ship.

The crew cheered.

"She's bleeding out!" called Harrison, aiming a musket.

"Out hooks! Prepare to board!" called Atsadi.

On Santana's command, the crew of the *Devil's Thunder* took in the sails to reduce speed.

Kennedy took a grapple on the end of a long rope and swung it to the lines of the other ship. It held fast. Half a dozen other men did the same. All the gunners who had been at the cannons helped to pull the two ships close together. Then, after a volley of fire from the muskets, the boarding crew of the *Devil's Thunder*, armed with axes and cutlasses, leapt to the other ship and engaged the enemy in combat.

"Having the heart of a traitor can make a spell difficult to perform unless it is one of the required components for the spell."

– Golden Sea Grimoire

VII

THE *THUNDER'S* PRIZE

A flurry of motion and sounds overwhelmed Caleb as he stepped onto the enemy ship with a cutlass handed to him by Mr. Kennedy moments ago. Kennedy was the first of the crew on the opposing ship, and he threw down the attacking pirates in quick fashion, ramming them with his body and striking with his elbows, all whilst shouting epithets like a madman.

Docks boarded the ship alongside Caleb. They stood back-to-back with cutlasses drawn, fending off the rather disorganized crew of pirates.

With only a trivial amount of sword training, Caleb relied a lot on luck and confusion on part of the others at this point. What he lacked in skill and experience he made up for in opportunity and circumstance. The opposing crew had not counted on facing such resistance from their mark, so they were off balance and ill-prepared.

The pirate captain fired his blunderbuss from the quarter-deck into the attacking privateers, not hitting anyone, but adding to the already considerable chaos.

A sunburned man came shouting at Caleb, swinging his cutlass wildly. With a circular motion, Caleb met steel with steel

70

and spun the weapon out of the man's grasp.

The disarmed man fell to his knees, pleading with his hands for Caleb not to end him. The fear in the man's eyes affected Caleb, and he hesitated, not finding it in himself to strike down an already defeated man. Caleb gestured with his hand that he accepted the surrender.

"Lay yourself down, and our captain may show you mercy when your ship is taken," Caleb said to the man.

The man bowed his head and recoiled briefly. He balled his hand into a fist and punched Caleb in the gut, nearly knocking the breath out of him. He then spat on the flooring of the deck and scurried away from the mêlée, chattering to himself. Before Caleb could react, the pirate was lost in the crowd.

Kennedy, who had witnessed the encounter, let out a full belly laugh. "That'll teach ya!" he said while trading blows with another man.

The discarded sword was picked up by one of the fleeing man's mates who charged Caleb with both that cutlass and the sword he had already been holding. Bracing for the impact, Caleb slipped aside. Fortunately for him, the man, big as he was, was also rather slow due to his left leg being a peg leg, and his moves were easily predicted.

"Have at thee, you son of a sea cook!" the large man called out while thrusting the cutlass in his right hand.

"You're mistaken," Caleb retorted while parrying the blade. "My parents were not sea cooks."

The man was at a loss for words with that comeback, and he fumbled first over his words, then with his sword.

"Be that so, I'll cut ye down just the same!" he said. He was distracted just enough for Caleb to land a cut on his hand. The large man dropped the cutlass then refocused his energy to the weapon in his other hand.

The man fumbled a bit while swinging his secondary weapon, giving Caleb just enough time to find an opening.

Caleb met the man's cutlass with his own, pushed it out of

the way, then swung low and hit him straight in the chest. Caleb pulled his cutlass back to himself, and the man slumped forward.

A hot burst of dark energy shot into him from the fallen body.

Behind Caleb, Jake Docks fought off a wave of attackers closing in. in the chaos of the action, one of the pirates' blows landed and took away Docks' left hand clean off. He had been using that hand to steady himself on the ship's halyard lines, and as he lost the hand, he cried out in pain and fell down to the deck.

As he lay there, Docks found a sash on one of the fallen men and fashioned it into a tourniquet, tying it around the stump at the end of his arm. Then, dizzy from the shock of it all, he stumbled to his feet and gathered himself. Holding up his sword in rage, he went after anyone who came close to him.

A team of a half score men from the *Vengeful Goose* who had either turned against their own crew or had never been loyal to this crew in the first place, now fought alongside the men of the *Devil's Thunder*.

The leader of the turncoats stood out from the rest of the men, primarily because it was in fact not a man, but a young woman, her golden blonde hair pulled back and tied behind her head. It looked as if her right eye had been replaced with an onyx black glass eye.

The young woman raised her cutlass and with a yell led the men behind her in a skirmish against the crew of the *Goose*.

It did not take long for the crew of the *Devil's Thunder* to overpower the pirates. Captain Santana boarded the vessel and made his way to Captain Bailey, whose guns' ammunition were spent.

Each captain pulled out a rapier, and the two began to duel with one another on the poop deck. The pirate captain ducked and weaved dramatically, while Santana stood straight with the look and manner of an experienced fencer.

"Treacherous mock-man," the pirate said between parries. "I know you – a pirate like me, you once were."

"A pirate, yes," Santana retorted. "Like you? Perish the thought." He advanced upon the pirate until he had him cornered on the deck. "But there is a chance to turn your life into a more noble pursuit as I have done, if you but make the call to surrender."

He pinned Captain Bailey back against the railing, and their swords locked. The younger captain gritted his teeth and sneered angrily back at Santana.

"You miserable misbegotten monkey!" he said, pushing back and breaking out of the locked position, driving the fight back onto more even ground. "I'd scuttle this ship with all of us aboard before I'd let you take it."

But as he said this, Santana struck his hand with the point of his rapier. The captain reflexively dropped his sword onto the deck with a childish cry of "Ow!" and in an instant, Santana moved in and placed the tip of his rapier to the man's cheek and moved in closer so that their faces were nearly nose-to-nose.

"Surrender your ship," Santana said to the captain, "Or I'll remove your ears and wear them on a necklace."

He conceded and gave the signal for his men to surrender.

Santana smiled and took a step back as the men began laying down their arms.

"Smart choice, lad," Santana said, sheathing his rapier. "Now then, Captain Blunderbuss Bailey. Your ship…"

The *'Vengeful Goose*," he said, hanging his head.

"…The *Vengeful Goose*," Santana continued, "the *Goose* is surrendered. It seems that your wings have been clipped. Now, we shall take aboard your men and you along with them will await trial for your crimes on the sea. Perhaps, we can see if your talents can be of some avail to us, for we are always looking for more men to help fight against the scourge in these waters. Looking about, it seems as if some have already taken this choice to heart."

Bailey scoffed. "How different are we, Captain? Here, we plunder the corrupt wealthy by our own discretion and for our own accounts. Yet you, you 'privateers,' you rob and harass the poor in the name of a king halfway across the world."

"That's a filthy lie, that is!" said one of the men from the *Goose* who had fought to aid Santana during the fight. "Stole us as slaves, he did, press-ganged us into his crew, and made us work for him for no pay."

"We have to cut costs somewhere," Bailey shrugged.

"Whatever the case," said Santana, "that's not for us to decide here an' now. We'll be taking you to Swashbuckler Island where you will be held until you can appear on trial for your actions. This is the mark of a civilized society."

When the matter was settled, Caleb helped Jake Docks back to the *Devil's Thunder* where Dr. Rockwell dressed his wounds.

Captain Santana approached Docks with a bag of coins.

"For your sacrifice in the heat of battle," Santana said, setting the bag of coins on the table beside Docks. "As per the articles: five hundred pieces of eight for the loss of your left hand while performing your duties to your ship and crew."

"Thank ye, sir." Docks managed to strain a smile of gratitude. "It seems for my part, I be a lucky man."

"Are there any further injuries?" Rockwell asked the captain. "How many more need to be tended to?"

"Nothing immediate. They can see themselves in if they feel the need, but you should be permitted to focus on Jacob here."

"And the captured crew?"

"Most are cooling their heels in the brig. I'll have an escort bring to you anyone who needs immediate attention."

"That's fine," said Rockwell. "Any new additions to the crew?"

"We've had one shy of a dozen swear upon the articles of the *Thunder*," the captain said.

"A good size."

"Aye, many had been captives of the ship, but a few were part of the crew, fearing the hangman's noose, I'll wager. Captain Bailey's first mate Mr. Thomas Fullery was quick to come over to this side; he said he'd swear to the articles and speak concerning his former captain at the upcoming trial. Captain Bailey was not too pleased to hear that, as you can well imagine. If Bailey could fire cannon shot out of his eyes, Fullery would be blown off the deck."

The captain laughed at his own analogy.

It was true: the young captain of the *Goose* seemed entirely out of his depth in this encounter, and he could imagine the look upon his face at the betrayal of his right-hand man after everything else that had gone wrong for him that day.

"And as for you, Mr. Kingsley," Santana said, clasping a hand on Caleb's shoulder, "you showed true initiative out there today. Your swordplay may be a bit rough, but your heart was shown, and I'm grateful to have seen the charge you made. Took down two of the men yourself, did you?"

"Three, Captain," Caleb said, hardly reacting to the gratitude shown him.

"Three," Santana repeated, impressed. "You're proving yourself to be a rather good resource. You'll get your share of the plunder as well as a share of the reward once we make port. You'll be under no obligation to continue with us, but should you wish to remain, you would certainly be welcome to stay aboard."

"Thank you, Captain."

The captain reiterated his thanks and returned topside.

Caleb remained behind to assist the doctor. Rockwell was glad for the help and the company; it gave him a chance to have Caleb close by.

"Maybe your unprecedented healing translates into medical practice as well," Rockwell said as a way to not-so-subtly remind Caleb he suspected something was amiss. Caleb forced a half smile, but that comment would hardly be enough for him to give away the secret to his condition. They carried on, speaking mainly in trivialities or about the task at hand as other injured men filed in for treatment.

It was late in the evening by the time Caleb left the doctor and found Kingsley in the galley. He was sitting in the corner, his head resting in his hands, when he found him.

"Hey there, 'cousin,'" Caleb said, shaking him gently by the shoulder. Kingsley stood with a start and embraced Caleb.

"Caleb, my friend! I thought for certain you were going to die when I saw you over there."

"It was madness." The battle still weighed heavily on Caleb's mind. "God save me, I don't know how I can deal with it. These men, we're basically doing what they are doing – attacking ships, taking prisoners and stealing. And I had to take three of their lives; how does one reconcile it all?"

"They take from the innocent," Kingsley reasoned.

"And what if they were pressed into this life thanks to an unjust society?" Caleb asked. "The 'innocent' they take from are the same who legally took me from my parents as a youth. Who is innocent, and who is just?"

Kingsley looked at him in silence. He had always had his own freedom, and he had known Caleb only a short time now, so he felt he could not reasonably address such a topic.

"For now," he considered, carefully choosing his words as he spoke, "we can take solace in the fact we set free some of those prisoners held on the ship against their will."

Caleb nodded. "How are you holding up?"

"I'm fine." But he sounded tired. "Few men made it over to where I was on the ship. I didn't have much to do, I'm afraid."

"Let's hope we don't have much more of this before we get to see our contact."

"Any word on that front?" Kingsley asked.

"We're in luck," Caleb said, sounding more hopeful at this change of topic. "They're taking us to Swashbuckler Island as we speak, to turn these pirates in and collect the bounty on them."

"That is indeed good news.".

"I just hope we can make it there without further incident. Do you really think this person you know there can be of any help?"

"If anyone can be."

Caleb's thoughts strayed to the rest of Torch's crew. "I wonder where the *Red Soul* is now," he wondered aloud. "Maybe they're setting on their own quest for answers."

"Or maybe they're fully invested in their current mission," Kingsley cautioned. "Don't doubt that leaving them was a right decision on your part. Joining them in the first place was a foolish thing to do."

"I suppose you're right. I wonder what I would do should we meet them out here on the sea."

"Hang it all!" exclaimed Kingsley. "Don't tempt the fates with such words!"

Caleb opened his hand and stared at his palm, looking for any visible sign of what was plaguing him. He closed his fist and opened it again. It was ever so faint, but surrounding his hand, thin green wisps of energy dimly glowed in the dark and curled around his hand.

Kingsley noticed this and moved uncomfortably close to look at it.

"Is that it?" he asked softly.

Caleb nodded. "You see it too, then?"

"By all that is great and good, I have never seen a thing like that. Are you all right?"

Caleb did not respond. Physically, he felt in peak condition apart from a little bit of soreness brought on from the work on the ship, but this wore heavily on his mind. It was all compounded by the unsettling words from the captured captain of the *Goose* that had prompted him to question the morality of what they were doing. He still did not understand the scope of everything, and that is what concerned him the most.

The crew of the *Devil's Thunder* began repair work on the *Vengeful Goose*. Some of the *Thunder*'s crew were carpenters, and they were sent over to make the captured ship seaworthy again so that they could take it in with them.

As they settled in, it was discovered that there were seven here who had been taken captive and press-ganged onto the pirates' crew. They, along with four of Bailey's formerly loyal men, pledged themselves to the articles set forth by Captain Santana and officially joined the crew of the *Devil's Thunder*.

The young woman who had taken it upon herself to lead the attack from within the *Goose* was called Susan Hawkins; it was determined that she had been taken from another ship and forced to sail with the pirates. She pretended to be loyal to Bailey until the opportunity arose to betray him.

When the *Thunder* had begun firing upon the *Goose*, Hawkins set free the captives in the hold of the ship and led them in the fight against the crew of the *Goose*.

The particulars of what she had been forced to do in service of Bailey no one said, but the way the men gave her quarter indicated strongly that she had perhaps played her part as Bailey's crew well. However, the men's attitude towards her softened when they saw the way the captive Captain Bailey now regarded her. In the end, she was also instrumental in getting the first mate, Mr. Fullery, to agree to the articles and join the crew of the *Devil's Thunder* as well.

Johansen returned to the *Devil's Thunder* and informed Santana that the *Goose* was now ready to sail.

"Well done, Benedict," Santana said. "I trust you can take her into port?"

"It would be my pleasure." Johansen saluted the captain.

"Get to it then. Let me know whom you need to bring with you to handle her, and we'll have it done."

Johansen selected a small crew for the task and boarded the *Goose* and worked the rest of the day making her ready to sail.

Santana gave the orders to bring up the anchor and put the sheets to the wind, and they, too, were promptly on their way to Swashbuckler Island.

Caleb manned the lines back on the poop deck near where Santana stood. When the main work was done and they were on course, Captain Santana approached Caleb.

"You've done good work," he said. "You showed initiative in battle. But something else troubles you?"

"It's nothing." This would not be enough to dissuade the captain from further prodding, so Caleb elaborated. "I can't help but think on what Captain Bailey said."

"Go on."

"The differences between his line and ours. Sailing the seas, seeking out ships, and bringing them down. I realize there is an official capacity to what we do, but – forgive me if I speak out of turn – is that all that makes us different?"

"Aye," said Santana, looking thoughtfully out to the horizon. "You're not wrong, lad. You've a good head on your shoulders. These are good questions, and I'm not certain the answer is always what I want it to be. It be true, the similarities are plain as day on the surface. I'll lay it out that the true differences lie in our intentions and the manner in which we carry ourselves.

"Forget for a moment the letters of marque; forget the King, just for now. What do we have? For one, we have our articles we sail by. I like to think of the ship's articles as something that enforces our honor and holds us accountable, captain and crew. A ship is only as strong as its articles. You can use it to measure the heart of the ship. The pirates – they pillage and plunder; what's in their articles? A fair share for those aboard? Aye, that's a good thing, but who are they taking it from? That should be taken into consideration.

"If you sail a ship with no statement – with no articles, then you take from anyone solely for your own benefit at the expense of others. I like to think we help to restore a balance on treacherous waters, that we take up arms in defense of the powerless."

"But how can we know that?"

"That's the true question, isn't it?" Santana said. "Our intentions may sometimes be tested. If we focus on actions we know to be in the right, that is the best way to steer our attitude to the proper course. Choose a path with a fundamental focus on justice. If you sail with that as your guiding star, it may not always be the easy path, but ultimately I believe it is the most rewarding, if not in this life, then in the next."

That gave Caleb a little comfort, but his mind was still not entirely at ease. He went over these words in his mind as they sailed to the western port of Swashbuckler Island, a place called Grogtown.

The port was not terribly unlike Port de Sang on Buccaneers Isle, but it was considerably smaller and less busy. the *Devil's Thunder* docked, followed closely by the *Vengeful Goose.* Captain Santana, with the assistance of Benedict Johansen and a dozen of the crew, escorted Captain Bailey and his loyal crewmates to the courthouse, where he was then taken to a cell to await trial.

When Bailey and his crew had been processed, a representative of the English Navy was selected to oversee the transfer and trial of Captain Blunderbuss Bailey and the transfer of him for a proper hearing. For now, Bailey was safely in their custody, thus completing Santana's part. The English representative saw to it that Santana and his crew were paid for Bailey's delivery and provided him with information on several other potential targets.

When Santana gave Caleb his proper share and released him from his service, he extended his offer once more.

"Your journey lies beyond us," he said. "But remember, should you ever require a haven or a crew that will stand by you, the *Devil's Thunder* will welcome you back."

"The authors of the *Golden Sea Grimoire* cannot be held responsible for any of the actions caused by vengeful spirits resurrected by the reading of passages in this tome."

– Golden Sea Grimoire

VIII

THE GRAVEDIGGER OF SWASHBUCKLER ISLAND

Caleb and Kingsley left the company of Captain Santana together and walked further inland, following a path out of Grogtown.

"How far away is this Cynthia Cove person?" Caleb asked. "Do you really think she'll see us?"

"She'll see us, for certain," Kingsley said. "She's a businessperson, like me. She's over in Frogtown, about a half hour's walk from here, on the eastern side of the island."

"What sort of business is she in?"

"Last I heard, she is the groundskeeper at the Frogtown cemetery."

Caleb stopped and turned to face Kingsley. "Run that by me again; how is a cemetery groundskeeper supposed to offer us any help?"

"How's someone who spends her days surrounded by the spirits of the dead supposed to help us out in some wild curse perpetrated by some fellow passing himself off as the Grim Reaper?" Kingsley challenged. "I don't know. It's all I got."

Caleb shook his head and carried on, up the road.

Half a mile from the town, they came to a graveyard with a

81

simple sign that labeled it the Frogtown Cemetery.

"This is the place."

It was still early afternoon, but the cloud cover was so heavy that the skies darkened, and it felt like it was already late evening. A small shack was nestled into the perimeter of the cemetery near one of the crypts; from a window there came the faint warm glow of a lantern, lighting up the inside of the crude building. Kingsley and Caleb cautiously approached.

"Hullo!" Kingsley called as he rapped on the heavy wooden door. "Madame Cove, are you in? It's Aiden Kingsley here with a friend. May we speak?"

There was the sound of shuffling about and what seemed to be a chair being knocked over, followed by a loud crash and a string of unintelligible shouted expletives. Outside the door, Kingsley's eyes shifted as he stood there awkwardly, not knowing whether he should acknowledge the commotion.

The noise from inside settled down, the door opened partially, and a woman's face appeared in the crack. Caleb couldn't imagine a person who would more fit the look of a cemetery groundskeeper than this woman. Her pallid face looked as if it were carved from stone with her sharp features. Her long black hair was pulled back from her face and braided behind her.

"Aiden Kingsley," she said with a low, even voice. "It's been some time. Come in."

She opened the door wider and allowed the two men to enter.

"Thank you." Kingsley gave a polite bow as he entered. "It's nice to see you again. I hope you have been keeping well."

"Indeed." Cynthia turned her attention to Caleb. "And who is this?"

"I'm Caleb," he introduced himself.

"A pleasure, of course," she said, gently taking his hand. Her eyes flashed for a moment as if she sensed something, but she did not address it. "I am the groundskeeper; I look after the dead here. I spend much of my time studying the properties of life and death when not attending to my duties."

Caleb and Kingsley took a seat on a small wooden bench in the back of the room. A table took up much of the center of the room, and it appeared to have been the source of the crash they had heard moments ago, as there was a shattered ceramic container swept underneath it.

"I hope we weren't interrupting anything important," Caleb said, his eyes scanning the hastily swept mess on the floor.

"Pay it no mind," Cynthia said, pulling up a chair for herself and taking a seat. "Just a little project I was working on; it was going nowhere. I apologize I have nothing to offer you. I don't tend to have many living visitors. What brings the two of you to my door? Not that it isn't a pleasure to see you, Aiden."

"If it's not too much of an imposition," Kingsley began carefully, easing his way to the subject, "my friend and I have some questions concerning – well, concerning death, and we hope that your knowledge on the subject might shine a light on a few things."

Caleb recounted his time aboard the *Red Soul* with the captain and their encounter with the specter referred to as the Reaper. Cynthia sat still, but as Caleb spoke of the otherworldly being, it was clear that the groundskeeper was intrigued.

"You saw him yourself?" she asked in a hushed tone. "And you heard his voice?"

"As clearly as I see and hear you now," Caleb said, fighting back a shudder as he recalled the feeling. He described to her the ghostly energy that seeped into him following the deaths of the Walton brothers, and he also showed her his arm that had been healed by the same energy.

Cynthia's eyes widened. "By taking their lives, you have acted as a delivery system for the Reaper; he does with the souls what he wills and gives you the power to do what he allows."

"But if he is Death," Caleb thought aloud, "like '*The* Death,' doesn't he already have access to souls that have passed on? Why would he need someone to do this work for him?"

"Precisely," said Cynthia. "We don't know exactly whom or what we are dealing with. This man could merely be an interloper from the other side trying to break free, and the only way he can access the power to do so is with servants such as your former captain. You and the rest of your unfortunate crew have access to great power, but that power is an illusion. Ultimately, this 'Reaper' maintains control over you all. And there will be those seeking to exploit you, if they can find ways of harnessing and controlling this power."

"Are there ways of controlling it?" Caleb asked.

Cynthia closed her eyes and ran her hand over the scar on Caleb's arm, muttering some words in some foreign tongue. She opened her eyes and looked at the arm; for a moment it gave off a green glow that promptly faded away.

"I sense you have already begun to control it," Cynthia said. "If, by this, you healed your wounds, the Reaper's power is now alive within you."

Caleb stood and looked out the window; he saw graves, crypts, and tombs of the dead. His heart raced as he began to feel them. It was not the souls of the dead he could feel, for they had passed on, and the souls were gone from their bodies, but he could sense the empty vessels all laying out there, waiting to be commanded. His mind focused on this, and the floor shook beneath his feet.

"Stop it!" Caleb cried out. "I can feel them!"

Cynthia stopped uncomfortably close behind Caleb and grabbed his shoulders with her thin, cold hands. She spoke into his ear as they both looked out on the cemetery. A flicker of excitement lit up her hazel eyes.

"It is the call of the Reaper," she said. "His power within you is calling out to be used. Concentrate! What is it calling for you to do? Drain the life of the living? Awaken the bodies of the dead?"

Energy pulsed in Caleb's arm. Something from within him longed to direct this energy; some power at his command was straining to deal with life and death, but something even deeper cautioned that if he did, he would lose himself to it.

"I just want to be at peace," Caleb groaned, and his eyes closed. "I want them to stay at rest."

The rumbling subsided, and Caleb's elevated heart rate slowed back to normal. He opened his eyes and looked at Cynthia, who raised an eyebrow in response and gave him a chilling look.

Stepping back, Cynthia addressed Kingsley, who had watched the ordeal in fascinated fear from his seat.

"What are your thoughts, Aiden?" she asked.

Kingsley rubbed his head with his hands. "This is beyond me," he said. "There's no guidebook for this."

"Perhaps there is," Cynthia said slowly. "There is a tome, a *Grimoire* that is said to have been lost somewhere in the islands here in the Caribbean. I see in your face that you are skeptical. You yourself have heard of the *Golden Sea Grimoire,* yet you suppose it to be just a story. They say that if the book is read by someone who is capable, it can bend the fabric of reality to its holder's will. Its authors are forgotten, and the men who studied it years ago grew fearful of its potential, and they even tried to destroy it so that the knowledge of its power might be forever lost.

"But such power is not so easy to destroy. It has been hidden, locked away from all prying eyes. Obtaining this book may be dangerous, but it could well have the answers you seek. It could explain what has happened to you, Caleb; it could teach you how to control it, and it could contain the rituals that may help fight against the forces of darkness that you face."

"How do you know of this?" Kingsley asked. "And how can we trust that seeking out this myth is worth the danger?"

"For generations, my family has studied the forces that link life and death," Cynthia said. "The ability to commune with these forces has been passed down through my bloodline, and a lifetime of study and dedication to understanding it has granted me a special insight.

"My grandfather obsessed over the history of the *Golden*

Sea Grimoire. He tracked it down to these islands; that is the reason our family moved here. We traveled this far and have come this close. I have taken up my family's quest and have narrowed the search down even further, where I believe it is guarded by a host of men who do not comprehend the scope of its power. Our destinies have brought us together: your need and my search have aligned, but to what purpose, we have yet to discover."

Caleb idly messed with the change in his coin bag. What he had here would hardly be enough to sustain them for another voyage. It was unlikely that Santana and the *Devil's Thunder* would undertake the quest.

"We need to get this book," he said.

"Fine idea," said Kingsley, "but without a ship or a heading, what options do we have?"

"What if we had a ship of our own?"

"We don't have the funds to purchase a ship," said Kingsley, "even if we were to combine our resources."

"Suppose we got together some of those men from the *Thunder*," Caleb suggested. "Some of the poor fellows we picked up off the *Vengeful Goose* might join us."

"However you acquire a ship," said Cynthia, "I hope you will call on me. I have been researching the *Grimoire* for so long, I care to see this through to its conclusion. When you are ready, send for me, and I will accompany you on your journey."

IX

FURY OF THE *RED SOUL*

Kingsley and Caleb spent the night in a room at the Frogtown Inn. During the night, Caleb's mind kept turning to his former home. The other people he had left in their enslaved state had endured much worse conditions than he had, and they were still trapped there while he was out here. Captain Santana had seemed respectable and trustworthy, but how far his kindness would extend was hard to guess. Santana did not know Caleb's full story, even if he had likely pieced some of it together.

As Caleb lay on the bed in the inn, he could hear a mild commotion in the tavern below, as sailors carried on, laughing, drinking, and singing. The sounds were too muffled for him to understand the words, but he closed his eyes and focused on the singing until he eventually drifted off.

His sleep was uninterrupted, and he awakened early in the morning. He went down into the tavern to find Kingsley already there, sitting at a table with Rockwell, the doctor from the *Devil's Thunder*. They both looked incredibly serious. Caleb started to back away, but it was too late: they had seen him and waved him over. He sat, and they endured a moment of uncomfortable silence as they waited for Dr. Rockwell to finally speak.

87

"I like to think of myself as an honest man," he said. Caleb looked to Kingsley for a sign. He looked uneasy but gave nothing away.

"No, your friend has remained faithful," the doctor continued, correctly interpreting Caleb's glance, "but I don't especially care for being left in the dark, particularly when I have been roped into some kind of plot without my consent. I don't suppose you would mind telling me what this is all about, now that we are all here?"

He stared intensely at Kingsley. Both he and Caleb knew what he was referring to, but Kingsley was willing to keep up the bluff as long as he could.

"What all of what is about?" Kingsley innocently asked.

Rockwell's patience was clearly thinning. He pointed his finger right into Kingsley's face. "Don't give me that, Aiden. Not here, and not now. I've known your family for many years. I know your relations on Ramrod Island and I know of no 'Cousin Caleb.' I did not contradict you in the presence of my captain. Do you know how serious this is? I lied to my captain, vouching for a boy I have never met, know nothing about, and know is not whom he claims to be. I vouched for him to a captain whom I'm certain knows just as well as I that he is not who he claims to be. *I lied to the captain for you.* I believe I am entitled to an answer."

The guilt that Caleb felt for putting both Aiden and this doctor into this situation weighed upon him more and more.

"If I may," Caleb began.

Rockwell held out a halting hand. "I wasn't asking you."

Kingsley drew in a deep breath. "This young man is in trouble," he said. "We needed to leave the island."

"Needed to leave the island," Rockwell spat. He turned to Caleb, who met his unflinching gaze. "Why did you need to leave the island?"

It is likely that Caleb had never before stood so firmly when questioned this intensely. He was now ready to own up to what he had done. Aiden had stood by him, and it was now Caleb's turn to stand by his friend. The room fell uncomfortably silent. The other few patrons in the tavern were talking amongst themselves in low murmurs, but Rockwell's words, quiet as they were, sounded as if they could be carried atop that noise.

"Are you a runaway slave?" Rockwell finally asked.

Kingsley stirred in his seat, but Caleb motioned him to stand down.

"I am a sailor," Caleb said confidently. "And I am a ship's gunner."

"Are you a runaway slave?" Rockwell asked again, only slightly louder. Nobody at any of the other tables reacted, so it must have been quiet enough, but to Caleb, it sounded as if he was shouting.

Caleb was still and silent for several long seconds. Months ago, he might have cowered before this man's questioning, but the adrenaline coursing through him made him bolder. He had feared what would happen should the truth get out, but now that it had, fear turned into frustration that then turned into indignation. This doctor who had been cordial to him on the ship, patching him up, and sharing tales of the sea, had now turned against him. His language now dripped with prejudice and condescension as he referred to Caleb as a "boy" and as the property of another man.

"I was enslaved," Caleb confessed. "But no more."

Rockwell kept his voice low but was visibly maintaining his composure.

"It was my worst fear, then. You pulled us both along with you after all the work I've done to go straight. Are you not aware that it is now my duty to inform the authorities on both of you? Otherwise, you've placed a noose around my neck as well."

"Come now, doctor," Kingsley said, attempting to diffuse the situation, "he's been through a lot."

"I don't doubt that. Unfortunately, the law will not take that into account. You are criminals, the two of you. And you have made me into an accomplice."

"I know that you have no reason to trust me now," Caleb said, "but you must know that I sailed with Captain Benjamin Torch. He and his crew are holed up in the fort at Spitshine Spot not far from here, and he's becoming more dangerous."

"And the two of you are going to bring him down?" Rockwell challenged. "We're well aware of Captain Torch. If we encounter him, the *Devil's Thunder* will subdue him, and we'll take him in. I'm sorry, but we'll have to do it without your help."

As Rockwell spoke, Caleb's hand slowly caressed the hilt of his sword. If he was going to have to fight for himself, he was going to be ready. After what he had done to the Walton brothers, there was no going back to the plantation.

"You don't understand," Kingsley implored. He searched for the words he could use to help explain the situation, but he was interrupted by the booming of cannon fire.

Outside, there was a great commotion. Rockwell went to the front door to take a look. Caleb and Aiden also peered outside.

Several buildings were ablaze. Townspeople ran about; some were armed and preparing to engage the enemy, while others were fleeing or seeking shelter. Out of the fires stepped several pirates whom Caleb recognized: Onion Jack, Boen, and a few others whose names he never caught. As they stepped through the town wreckage, fire caught on their clothes; they paid it no mind and let it burn as they cut down people without remorse.

Through the fire stepped Captain Benjamin Torch, the light of the surrounding fire and the rising sun reflecting off his red hair and beard, giving the appearance that he himself was on fire.

"That's him," Caleb said, looking out from behind Rockwell.

A dozen shapes nearly unrecognizable as members of the human race followed behind Captain Torch; the flesh had been burned off or had fallen off so that all that remained under the clothes were living, animated skeletons. Some of them set fire to buildings as they passed by, but Torch and his immediate entourage seemed focused on a specific destination.

Caleb drew his sword. Rockwell followed suit and stood

blocking the door.

"I cannot allow you to leave," Rockwell said.

"My fight is not with you, Doctor," Caleb said, squaring off against him, "but I cannot afford to let the captain find me here."

"Then come with me quietly," Rockwell insisted, "and I will see to it you are given the chance of a fair trial."

Caleb smirked at this. He was unsure if Rockwell actually believed there would be a fair trial or if he just said that in an effort to calm him down. Either way, Caleb was a runaway and had killed, so even a fair trial was not proper assurance now.

Another blast of cannons sounded in the distance, hitting the building next to them. Five of the skeleton pirates crashed into the tavern and spotted Caleb and the others.

Rockwell's attention shifted from Caleb. He held out his sword in defense as the figures approached.

The remainder of men in the tavern cleared out quickly, leaving Kingsley, Caleb, and Rockwell to deal with the threat. Caleb did not wait to see if any of the cursed pirates would recognize him but instead lunged forward after them with his sword. They dodged and parried, but one thrust from Caleb hit its mark in an exposed rib cage; unfortunately, there was no longer anything vital in there to hit.

"Oh, for goodness' sake," he said, remembering what they were up against. "Any ideas?"

"Cut them down!" Rockwell said, engaging two of the others.

With no better plan coming, Caleb attempted this. The skeletons were a little slower and more stiff than proper living opponents, so he was able to push forward rather quickly.

The sound of bones creaking alerted Caleb to another skeletal pirate behind him, preparing to strike. Caleb crouched to avoid the blow, the rusty steel just missing him as he braced against the wall. Caleb planted his feet on the floorboards and lunged forward, letting go of his sword as he flew through the air and grappling one of the skeleton men.

The two rolled on the floor; Caleb wrapped his arms under the skeleton man's arms until he got a firm grasp on its head. Using his legs to clench the body, Caleb wrenched off the skull.

The body went limp, but the skull continued to threaten and bite at Caleb while crying out, "Unhand me!"

Another skeleton stood off to the side and saw this happen. He ran towards Caleb as best as his bone legs could manage and engaged him in combat.

"Destroy the skulls!" Kingsley called out while fending off an attacker.

Unarmed and backed into a corner, Rockwell desperately searched for a weapon to use to defend himself, but he was trapped, and everyone else in the room was otherwise engaged. He reflexively held up his hands in defense from the oncoming attacker.

With a crash, the door to the tavern opened, nearly thrown off its hinges, and standing there were Stephen Kennedy and Jake Docks. Behind them stood two other crewmen. Caleb recognized them as Harrison and Daniels, both from the *Devil's Thunder*. Susan Hawkins, the young woman with the glass eye who had recently joined them from the *Vengeful Goose* was there as well. Rockwell and the skeleton man advancing upon him turned in unison to see the new arrivals.

The strange scene in front of him made Kennedy's jaw drop. He raised his flintlock pistol and fired, hitting the skeleton in the side of its skull, causing it to spin in place.

Rockwell sprung forward and tackled the skeleton, throwing it to the floor. When he was certain it was down for good, he struggled back to his feet with the help of Docks.

The room seemed to be taken care of for now.

"What are you doing here?" Rockwell asked Kennedy, wincing as he tended to his wounded side.

"Have you seen it out there?" Kennedy responded.

Caleb watched through a window as Captain Torch continued to march through the burning town.

"He's headed to the cemetery."

"The cemetery?" Kennedy repeated, joining Caleb at the window. "You said he's been seeking information. If he gets to the graveyard, he could see Miss Cove and find out about the *Grimoire.*"

"We have to get there first," Caleb said, putting his sword away.

Rockwell raised his sword, still clutching his wounded side with his free hand. "Not so fast. Nothing has changed."

"Doctor," said Caleb, "this is not the time."

Nevertheless, Rockwell lunged at Caleb with his sword. "I cannot allow you to leave," he said.

Caleb whipped his sword out and parried the strike.

Kingsley moved forward with his sword drawn as well and positioned himself between them.

"Look what is happening!" he said. "This town is falling down around us. None of us are safe here."

Holding a flintlock pistol by the barrel, Kennedy approached the doctor from behind. He swung and knocked Rockwell in the back of his head with the butt end of the gun, sending him to the floor.

"That works," said Kingsley.

"What's this *'Grimoire'* you mentioned?"

Caleb left the building with the others close behind. Kingsley briefly filled Kennedy and the others in on the situation as they approached the cemetery, which was not far from the town.

The sun was still low in the sky, and an early morning mist hung over the graveyard. Strange figures walked forward past the graves, carrying lit torches.

"There they are." Jake Docks pointed at the lights.

"Looks like he's headed for Cynthia Cove's shack," Kingsley said. "I don't know if we can do anything from here. We cannot stop him, and we certainly cannot head him off and beat him there."

"He's only got a few men with him," said Caleb. "If we take

them off guard, we might have a chance. The men back in the tavern did not put up too much of a fight."

"You sailed with him," said Hawkins. "If you think we have a chance, I say let's go for it."

"Right," Caleb said, though now that it came to it, he was feeling a lot less confident. "Mr. Docks. You, Kingsley and I will move in from the left side."

Kennedy nodded and gestured to Hawkins and the other two men.

"Daniels, Harrison, Miss Hawkins, and I will flank from the right side," he said.

They moved through the foggy graveyard and drew near to Captain Torch and the half-dozen walking corpses accompanying him.

But before they could spring their attack, Captain Torch turned around as if he could sense them approaching, his eye fixed on the crypt that Caleb was hiding behind.

"Who goes there?" Torch asked in a low voice. There was no response. He stretched his arm out in front of him and spoke some strange words under his breath.

Caleb felt a hot piercing sensation in his shoulder. He winced and tried to resist, but the pain was too great. Though he struggled against the movement, he found himself walking forward into the open air, towards the captain.

"What are you doing?" Kingsley hissed, but it was soon apparent that Caleb was not in control of his own movements.

Kennedy watched from the other side of the graveyard. From there, he could see that Torch's attention was focused on Caleb, and he seemed to be controlling him in some way through some sort of magical means.

"Torch has a hold of him somehow," Kennedy said. "If we could break his concentration, Caleb may be free to move again."

That was all he needed to say. At her feet, Hawkins found a cracked headstone. She picked up a piece of it and launched it at Captain Torch's head. It hit, and Torch's eyes flashed as he turned his attention to Hawkins. Caleb immediately was in control again.

Without waiting for any further orders, all the others ran forward with swords drawn. Caleb, meanwhile, ducked behind one of the crypts to catch his breath. *Of course I can't directly attack the captain,* he thought to himself.

Torch gave his new attackers a quick sizing up, then bent down on one knee and grabbed a fistful of grass beneath him with both hands.

The earth shook.

A headstone next to Kennedy toppled over as the dirt in front of it was broken. Two bony hands shot out and grabbed at the ground. Pushing itself up and through the earth was the reanimated corpse of an old sailor.

The same thing happened throughout the yard. A pulsing energy went through the dirt, resurrecting dozens of corpses, all reinforced by Torch's magic, doing his bidding.

One of the undead shot up directly in front of Docks and began ferociously grasping at him and bit his foot. Docks cried out and drew his flintlock pistol, shooting it in the head. Docks fell on his back, clutching his wounded foot.

Hawkins moved through the graveyard battlefield at top speed to reach Captain Torch, but the opposition facing her was too great, keeping her at bay as Torch turned away and went towards Cove's shack. Hawkins cut through several of the reanimated dead without suffering more than a few insignificant cuts from them.

Kingsley had the lease experience in combat of all of them, so he stayed farther back, throwing rocks at the attackers.

Nearby, a small swarm surrounded Harrison and Daniels. Using brute force, Daniels managed to break free and tuck and roll to relative safety, but Harrison was not so fortunate. The attackers were unarmed, so they resorted to clawing and biting at the men. Two bit Harrison in the neck, and they continued until he stopped struggling and fell limp.

It was clear they would soon be completely overwhelmed if they continued moving forward, and Torch was nowhere to be seen.

"It's too late," Kennedy cried out. "Fall back towards the town."

"We have to keep pressing forward," Caleb called back as he cut through several more of the attacking creatures.

"We can make it through," Hawkins said, but she lost her footing, and one of the undead men knocked her on her back.

Caleb ran to her and slid on the ground, pulling Hawkins out of the way just as the undead man's hands came down. She looked up at Caleb who helped her up. She nodded her thanks and finished dispatching the attacker.

The two of them were now closest to Cove's shack, so they sprinted for it together. They burst through the doors, swords ready, but the building was empty: there was no sign of Captain Torch or Cynthia Cove.

"Blast it!" Caleb exclaimed through gritted teeth.

Hawkins looked at the walls for another exit. There was another door in the back, but peering out, there was still no evidence of Torch. She went back out the entrance, where she could see Kennedy and Daniels out there, finishing up the dwindling numbers of the attacking undead. Kingsley held Docks up, keeping weight off the injured leg.

"His foot is in a bad way," Kingsley said. "I don't suppose any of you know any surgeons?"

Of course, the first who came to everyone's mind was Rockwell.

"I mean any *other* surgeons," he quickly corrected himself, suspecting their thoughts.

The wooden door of a crypt near the shack slowly creaked open. Cynthia Cove's Face appeared and cautiously scanned the scene. When she saw Caleb and Kingsley, she stepped out.

"Cynthia!" Caleb called out in relief.

"I saw your captain approaching, and I decided to make

myself scarce," she said. "It looks like he's headed back towards his ship."

"What did he want?" Kennedy asked.

"I can only guess," said Cynthia, "but look at this mess. It will be a nightmare cleaning all this up."

X
LAUNCH OF THE
VENGEFUL GOOSE

As Kennedy wrapped up Docks' foot, he regarded the body of Harrison, who lay in the middle of the cemetery.

"Is there nothing that can be done for him?" he asked.

"I don't think that's how it works," answered Caleb. "I don't know that it would truly be him that returns."

"Can you at least try something?" Kingsley pleaded.

Caleb closed his eyes and nodded, though he did not like where this could go. He outstretched his hand and focused his thoughts.

Kingsley looked on, but nothing was happening. There was no glow and no movement.

"Well?"

Caleb opened his eyes and shook his head. "I feel none of it."

"Could be you're tapped out of energy," Cynthia said.

Kennedy and Daniels managed to get Docks wrapped up and stood him up. They stood on either side of him and helped him to walk.

"We need to get him into town," said Kennedy.

The others agreed. Cynthia said she knew of someone who might be able to help them. They stepped outside and looked around; the graveyard was still, and there was no sight of Torch or his men.

Cynthia led them back into town to the house of a doctor by the name of Peter Gold. Though it was midday, there did not seem to be much activity; the people must have hidden away due to the commotion in town. A housemaid answered the door. When it was brought to their attention that it was a medical emergency, Dr. Gold appeared and took Docks into a small operating room at the front of the house.

Gold unwrapped the bandages and looked at the foot.

"This is a mess, isn't it," he said, shaking his head. "I'm afraid the rest of the foot will have to come off. I've a nice assortment of pegs or even some newly designed false feet if you desire to take a look. I see you already have a hand replacement. Have I worked on you before?"

Docks shook his head.

"That was the handiwork of our ship's doctor," Kennedy explained.

"Ship's doctor, you say?" Dr. Gold repeated as he began to gather his tools to work. "What ship do you sail on?"

"We sailed under Captain Santana on the *Devil's Thunder,*" said Caleb, "but no longer."

"It's a fine ship, I've heard. Good man, Santana. I've never met their surgeon. Now, if you'll excuse me, I'll get started."

Kennedy and Daniels left the doctor to his work and returned to the waiting room where Caleb filled them all in on the situation.

"We're have to get out to sea," he said after briefly summing up their situation. "We cannot afford to rejoin with Captain Santana."

"Aye," said Kennedy. "The only course of action is acquiring a ship for yourself. You know, there's a lovely ship in port that's not doing anybody any good at the moment."

"You mean the *Vengeful Goose*?" Hawkins said.

Kennedy nodded. "That's the one. We should be able to

crew her."

"It's going up for auction," Caleb said, "but I don't know that even with all our resources we could afford to purchase it."

"I don't mean to suggest we purchase it," Kennedy said.

Caleb was sure he did not like where this was going. "No. No, we cannot do that."

"You're already a wanted man," said Kennedy. "You cannot stay here, and we must make our own way. We needn't become like Torch. We'll just be our own freelance buccaneers, not under the thumb of a distant monarch. We'll set our own course and take the jobs we choose."

It was not the optimal plan, but there was seemingly no other way. From the moment he had decided to run away from his life of slavery at the governor's plantation, it seemed this path had been set.

"Very well," he said, giving in, "but we need a captain, and I've no head for that sort of thing."

"I would be happy to fill the role," Kennedy volunteered. "I have been at sea for many years, and I believe I can find it in myself to take on the task."

"All right." Caleb looked out the window; he could see the *Red Soul* just beginning to leave the bay.

"I think that if we're going to do anything, the sooner the better," he said. "While the men of the town are focused on giving chase to the *Red Soul,* maybe we can slip out on the *Goose,* preferably under cover of night."

Kennedy went to check on Docks and the doctor. He had given Docks a bottle of whiskey for the pain and was wrapping up the leg where it had been amputated just under the knee.

"Can he be moved?" Kennedy asked.

"I wouldn't recommend it."

"We can't afford to come back here," Daniels said. "If we're going to leave, we need to leave quickly."

"You are departing on a new voyage?" Dr. Gold asked.

"Yes," Kennedy said, hesitantly. "As a matter of fact, we are."

"Do you have a ship's surgeon signed on?"

"Not as yet."

Gold shook his head. "Well, you can hardly go to sea without a surgeon. Imagine if something like what happened to unlucky Jake here happened while you were out at sea? How would you manage?"

"What would you suggest?" Kennedy asked, hoping to lure the doctor into volunteering himself.

"What sort of voyage are you undertaking, if I may ask?"

Caleb spoke up. "We're searching for some lost artifacts of…" he searched for the word to properly, yet vaguely, describe the *Grimoire*, "…religious significance."

The doctor stroked his short, prickly beard. "A treasure hunt, you say?" His eyes lit up. "And what might the value of these artifacts be?"

"Historical and sentimental, primarily," said Caleb, "but I'm sure we could come to an arrangement that would be beneficial to us all, if you would hear us out."

That enticed the doctor further. "I would certainly be interested in what there might be to gain," he said. "I've been meaning to get out to sea for a while anyway, shake the sands of this island off my boots and see other lands."

"We cannot assume the *Goose* will be fully stocked with all the necessary supplies," said Kingsley. "Either way, we'll likely need to come back or make port somewhere else to supply up."

"There is the armory by the docks," suggested Kennedy. "If we stock up the ship with enough munitions from the armory, we can get whatever else we need."

"Aye," said Caleb. "I don't like it, but necessity drives us."

"There is a smaller port on the south side of the island," Gold said. "I can gather a few things of my own and have Mr. Docks ready to travel and meet you there by sunrise tomorrow. We'll have some additional supplies to carry with us."

"That sounds reasonable to me," Caleb said. He stood and dusted himself off. "Lead the way, Captain."

"Captain?" Kennedy scoffed at the premature use of the title, though something in him already did like the feeling of being called that. "Don't let's be getting ahead of ourselves. I haven't a ship yet. I don't even have a proper hat."

"We'll get you both shortly," Caleb said, patting him on the shoulder.

They left Docks with Dr. Gold as the rest of them went quickly across the island back towards the west coast of Swashbuckler Island to Grogtown, where the *Vengeful Goose* remained docked. It was early evening by the time they arrived at a small armory by the docks. They were pleased to see that it was currently open, as other men were hastily coming in and out to arm the various ships.

Daniels pointed to the ship, which had several men already walking onboard with crates.

"How do you like that?" he said. "They're already getting our work done for us!"

"They must be loading up to give chase to Captain Torch," Kennedy guessed.

"Chase Captain Torch?" Caleb repeated. "That's a fool's errand!"

"Right," said Kennedy. "Let's grab some ammunition and see if we can't save one of their ships from such a fate."

Caleb picked up a box of cannonballs and chain shot. Kingsley followed suit; if they were to defend themselves, they would need as much ammunition as they could take, he figured. Daniels and Cove took several pistols, while Kennedy and Hawkins took no additional armaments, but held their swords at the ready.

Other men at the storehouse paid them no mind as they took what they needed and left.

Kennedy motioned for the boarding party to halt as they assessed the situation.

"Can you see who is on board, Miss Hawkins?" he asked. "Anyone you recognize?"

Hawkins took a small spyglass out and put it up to her eye for a moment and scanned the ship before handing it over to Kennedy.

"The man on deck," she said, "that's Mr. Fullery. He was the first mate when I was aboard."

"Aye, it seems he's moved up to captain now. Anybody else?"

"Just crew loading in supplies." Hawkins took her spyglass back and put it away. "Nobody I recognize. If we move in quickly, we may be able to take it. I'll subdue Fullery. He could be persuaded to help us. A half dozen pairs of hands is not a lot; we could use more men when we can get them."

"Agreed," said Kennedy. "As this last party leaves the ship, we'll make our move. Caleb: you, Daniels, and Mr. Kingsley, board the ship from the water on the starboard side. Cynthia, Susan, and I shall board from the dock. We'll have to depart as quickly as we can."

Caleb nodded. "We'll get to the capstan and weigh anchor as soon as we board."

"Aye, but watch your back," Kennedy said. "Now, let's move."

Hawkins and Cynthia picked up the ammunition crates and walked the dock with Kennedy. Caleb, Daniels, and Kingsley went into the water. Another larger ship was also getting resupplied and prepped to make chase. *That could be a problem*, Caleb thought, but he continued moving.

When they reached the ship, they scaled the rope ladders on the side and stood ready by the railing, waiting for Kennedy to make his move.

Kennedy confidently walked directly onto the deck of the ship and approached its current captain. Fullery turned around at the sound of the footsteps and was shocked to see Kennedy's drawn sword at the ready, just in front of his face.

"What is the meaning of this?" he exclaimed indignantly. "My good man, are you havin' a laugh?"

Hawkins set down the ammunition crates and aimed her flintlock pistol at one of the lingering shipmates. When he saw the pistol trained at him, he dropped the crate he was carrying and backed away towards the side of the ship.

Caleb hopped onto the deck as well and went straight for the capstan, with Kingsley and Daniels close behind.

"I'm terribly sorry, Mr. Fullery," said Kennedy, edging his sword closer to the man's chest, "but we're commandeering this ship."

Caleb and Daniels pushed hard at the capstan, raising the anchor. Kingsley and Cynthia unfastened ropes that tied the ship to the dock and began setting the sails for a quick departure.

"You want to join the voyage or stay behind?" Hawkins asked the sailor she had at gunpoint. His eyes darted from the dock, then to the sails, then back to Hawkins, who was smiling a devilish grin at him.

The sailor reached for his own flintlock pistol on his belt, gambling on his captor not seeing it.

She, however, did see it. Hawkins trained her pistol at the man's hand and fired. The shot did not connect, but it served its purpose: the man dropped his pistol onto the deck of the ship.

"All right then," Hawkins said. "Off you go."

She advanced towards him. The cowering man fumbled over the side of the ship and fell onto the dock, stumbling as he ran back towards town.

At the sound of the shot, Kennedy turned but kept his sword on Fullery.

"What about you, then?" he asked. "Do we send you back to town as well, or will you be joining us?"

"You haven't told me what this is all about," Fullery said.

"That ship that came here," Kennedy said, "you cannot hope to catch it."

"And you can?" Fullery asked, unimpressed.

"Not yet," Kennedy admitted, "but we have a plan in place, and we need this ship in order to put that plan into motion."

"What sort of a plan?"

Kennedy lowered his sword and raised an eyebrow.

"So, you are interested?"

The would-be captain straightened his posture and attempted to put on a brave face. "This is all highly irregular, and I protest your methods. But I admit, I do not like the prospect of a direct attack on this enemy. I saw the crew, and they are highly unconventional."

"Most unconventional." Kennedy relaxed his threatening position over Fullery. "I hope you will not give us any trouble, or we'll have to clap you in irons and stow you below."

"You'll have no trouble from me." He glanced at Hawkins and Cynthia. "Though I don't know what trouble you're asking for, bringing these here women aboard."

Cynthia took the comment in stride, but Hawkins responded with a series of rude gestures.

"You sailed with her," Kennedy reminded him.

"And look where I am now!" Fullery grumbled. "Ship's captured – twice, mind you – and the old captain is set for a trial, likely to end in swinging the hempen jig."

"Yes," said Kennedy, "but you're fit to be a fine sailor aboard this vessel once again." He stepped up to the quarterdeck and took position behind Hawkins, who had taken the helm.

"Miss Hawkins, take us out and around the east of the island."

"Aye."

Hawkins maneuvered the ship as it departed the docks of Swashbuckler Island. There was a commotion back at the dock as some sailors noticed the unscheduled departure of the *Goose*. Hawkins held aloft her hat and gave the men a farewell wave.

Men ran about the other ship, tossing around crates of supplies and fumbling with the ropes as they finished departure procedures.

"Caleb, ready your cannon," Kennedy instructed. "Fire a warning shot across the bow of their ship if they give chase. Take care not to needlessly damage them. If they do pursue the *Red Soul*, they'll have plenty of time to get damaged enough."

"Aye, aye," said Caleb as he loaded one of the cannons.

As predicted, the ship did begin to pursue, but the *Vengeful Goose* had a head start and a favorable wind.

Kennedy signaled, and Caleb fired. The shot landed much closer than he had intended, tearing off the tip of the bowsprit of the approaching ship.

"Sorry about that!" Caleb called back to his captain. "That was my fault!"

"Don't give it a second thought," said Kennedy. "Douse the lights. Maybe she'll lose her bearing on us as she recovers."

Cynthia and Daniels went about the deck, blowing out the lanterns around the ship, helping to vanish the ship from view.

"That'll do it." Kennedy was pleased, for he could see the other ship had turned away from its pursuit, no doubt in no small part due to the grazing hit it had just received. It was headed more directly for the direction the *Red Soul* had taken, which was inclined northwest, and the *Goose* was traveling east along the coast of the island.

Kennedy pulled out a chart that mapped the area. He called Caleb over so that he could help him navigate.

"That's Spitshine Spot," he said, indicating a small island north of Swashbuckler. "That's where Captain Torch makes port."

"Then it's fortuitous we're headed in the opposite direction," said Kennedy. "We'll meet the doctor in the morning on the south side of the island, but for now we'll have to make ourselves scarce. There is Spider Island to the east. We'll circle around and stay on the far side of it until we are ready to move for the rendezvous point."

"Yes," said Caleb. "That's the smart path."

Kennedy called out the course adjustments to Hawkins,

who turned the ship south.

"We'll be returning to the southern side of the island in the morning," Caleb said to Fullery. "We'll let you disembark then."

"If it's all the same," Fullery said, resigned to his fate, "it seems I am destined to serve this ship one way or another. I would see to it that when all is done, this ship is not sunk."

"So be it," said Kennedy. "Welcome back aboard, then, Mr. Fullery."

"Remember to keep your cursed dolls separated from your uncursed dolls."

– Golden Sea Grimoire

XI

SHIP'S ARTICLES

Night came and passed. The crew took shifts between watching, steering the ship, and sleeping. The ship was a newer model and boasted a wheel to steer rather than the common tiller that most of the ships employed. Hawkins was familiar with the workings of the ship from her time aboard, so she took the helm. They took in the sails and traveled at a controlled pace as they circled the uninhabited Spider Island, east of Swashbuckler Island.

As dawn approached, Kennedy ordered full sail, and they traversed quickly to the southern side of Swashbuckler. There was a small town significantly less busy than the northern towns, and at this time no ships larger than the *Goose* were docked. Even so, Hawkins gave the shore a large berth and steered them past that area. Dense foliage covered the southern beach. As the sun began to rise, Kingsley looked to the shore and spotted a small boat. He called out and pointed.

"Longboat on the shore," he announced.

"Take her easy," Kennedy said to Caleb and Daniels, who were working the lines." Take in the sheets but look vigilant. Can you see our men, Mr. Kingsley?"

"I see two men in the thicket off the shore," said Kingsley. "Yes, I can make them out now. It is Dr. Gold and our man Jake. He's got a fresh peg on his leg."

"That is good. Signal them with the lantern and prepare to come to full stop."

Kingsley took a lantern and moved his hand in front of it then away several times. That was good enough: the two men launched their boat into the water and began to row to the ship.

The order was given, and Daniels dropped the anchor. He and Caleb stood by, ready to raise it again once the longboat was secured.

It took several minutes for the boat to make it to the *Goose*. Cynthia stood watch in the crow's nest, scanning the horizon for any other ships. So far, it seemed that they were in the clear.

As the longboat approached the ship, Fullery and Kingsley tossed down some lines to Gold and Docks. They secured the boat and came aboard.

"Welcome aboard the *Vengeful Goose*," Kennedy said.

Docks tipped his hat. "Thank ye, Captain. Glad to be here."

"Now, up anchor, and set sail."

Caleb and Daniels began turning the capstan. "Unlucky Jake," as the crew took to calling him after his second amputation, sat on the rigging and helped direct the sails to the wind.

Hawkins kept her position at the helm. "What's our heading?" she asked.

"Take us southwest," said the captain. "Steer clear of the islands for now. We may encounter merchant ships that might add to our supplies."

"Begging the captain's pardon," said Fullery, "but I would suggest we write up ship's articles if we're going to undertake such a venture. It would be good to know what shares we can expect as well as know what is expected of us whilst on ship."

Kennedy was slightly taken off guard by this request, but he relented. "A fine suggestion," he said. "And good initiative shown here by you. Would you assist me in the cabin as we write these up? Mr. Caleb, would you care to be present as well, as you are hosting this voyage?"

Caleb nodded. "Thank you, sir."

"When these articles have been written, they shall be shared amongst the crew, and if there be any amending, that will be taken into consideration as well. We'll then sign them and be on our way."

With that, Kennedy, Caleb, and Fullery went into the cabin and began to go over the provisions they felt would be fair to the crew.

Whatever money they received, a percentage of it would first be put into provisions and ship repair. After that was taken out, the captain and each crewman would receive their shares. If anyone were injured while on the ship or while serving in the interest of the ship while on land, various insurance payouts would also be given.

Caleb suggested that there be provisions for the treatment of the crew and the treatment of any captured person. He did not wish to be like the slave traders who would treat any sort of men as less than human. Captain Kennedy was hesitant on this article; he argued that any enemy they encounter would be subject to their mercy, but he was outvoted by Fullery and Caleb, so he stood down.

Several other provisions were made concerning the activities they would participate in and what the overall purpose of the ship was. The main mission of the *Vengeful Goose* was to seek ways of combating Captain Torch and the crew of the *Red Soul*. The secondary mission was outfitting the ship for defense, and that included preying on other ships. Caleb made the point that the ships they target should only be pirate ships, leaving the merchant ships alone, but he was outvoted here; limiting their targets in this way would be riskier and would ultimately give less of a reward. But in the interest of satisfying Caleb's wishes, they arrived at the consensus that they would focus primarily on pirate ships.

"We're not exactly outfitted properly," Kennedy said. "We haven't even proper flags on board; we only seem to have flags from the King's navy. That can be fine if we wish to present ourselves in this manner, but I would suggest we find a port to stock up on flags as well as other goods."

"That is reasonable," said Fullery. "There is an island nearby that would be perfect. It has plenty of resources, shops, and everything we might need."

"How are our coffers?" Kennedy asked.

"We do have some coins," said Fullery, leading him to the place where the money was kept. "We planned to set out mainly to attack Torch, so we will need to make more money soon, but we should have enough to get some of the necessities."

"Very well," said the captain. "Where is this place that you suggest?"

Fullery pointed to a place on the map that was labeled "Bounty Isle."

"It's a trading outpost. Not much else there, but it boasts a fine market; some of the locals refer to it as the 'Shopping Isle.' It should have all we need."

"I see." Kennedy studied the map. "I have never been to this region; I have only stayed to the west of here, so if you are familiar enough with the place, I would be grateful if you could take the lead as we adjust course."

"Thank you, sir."

Kennedy finished writing down the details of the articles, gathered them up, and returned to the deck with Kennedy, Fullery, and Caleb. He called for the attention of the crew as he began to read aloud. There were some murmurs when it came up that they might be attacking merchant ships, even though that was not a priority.

When Kennedy got to the part about the compensation for lost limbs, Unlucky Jake spoke up.

"Is that a retroactive policy?" he asked. The others laughed at this, but he was quite serious.

"We'll see what we can do," Kennedy said.

When he finished detailing all that was written, there was some discussion on some points, but not much was amended save for clarifying language.

The crew swore their allegiance to the newly-established articles, and with a renewed sense of purpose, they set sail. Fullery made the calculations for getting the ship to Bounty Isle and relayed the information to Hawkins.

The *Vengeful Goose* took a winding roundabout passage, passing behind Spider Island then turning northwest, avoiding any ships from Swashbuckler Island who may still be searching for them. They circled around and passed Spitshine Spot and continued west past Ramrod Island until they reached the dock on Bounty Isle.

Captain Kennedy went ashore with Caleb, Hawkins, and Kingsley. The rest of the crew remained on the ship, awaiting orders and ready to set sail if there was any sort of emergency.

The town seemed unsuspecting as they arrived. It was about midday, and everybody there was ready for business. Caleb had seen shopkeepers on Buccaneers Isle who were pushy and eager at times, but it was nothing compared to this.

There were all sorts of shops and stands in the marketplace; there were grocers, flag shops, ship accessory shops, ammunition shops, and anything else a young sailor could imagine.

Captain Kennedy, joined by Caleb, made his first stop at the flag shop, where there were all sorts of flags, organized by kind. There were merchant flags, flags of various nations, and there was an assortment of skull and crossbones flags. There was even a section that advertised custom flag designs.

"What can you tell me about these?" he asked the salesman.

"Ah, you need some flags for your ship?" the salesman said. "What sort of vessel are you running? Merchant? Fisherman? ...Privateer?"

"For a privateer," said Kennedy, carefully choosing his words, "what sort of flag would you suggest?"

"Ah, I get you," the salesman said with a wink. Many pirates of the day considered themselves privateers and would call themselves that rather than use the word "pirate," and this flag salesman knew that.

"There are all kinds of flags you'll be wanting in order to either let people know what sort of person you are or to let people *think* they know what sort of person you are, if you get me. You raise a merchant flag, let the enemy come upon you, then *huzzah!*" He made a performative gesture that nearly knocked Kennedy back a step. "You've bamboozled them. You fly your true colors and set upon them while they are unaware and unprepared. For something like that, you'll be wanting different nation flags: the popular ones like England, France, and Spain. They can also help you not get undue attention from otherwise unfriendly eyes if you are able to match their flag before they spot you."

"What about these?" Kennedy asked, looking at a pile of black and red flags with various assortments of skulls and skeletons drawn on them.

"The obligatory Jolly Rogers," the salesman said. "There is of course, the classics. They let people know your intent and can put a pang of fear into them. It's certainly a tried-and-true flag, but don't sleep on the variations. We've got dancing skeletons, which are always fun and add just a bit of whimsy. Then there are the ones with the hourglass, which is a cheeky way to let your target know that their time is running out. Then there are these babies." He held up a bright red flag with an hourglass and a cutlass. You put up a flag with a red background, and that tells anyone you encounter that no matter what, you intend on spilling blood: there will be no quarter given. If they run, they will die. If they surrender, they will die."

"Oh, my," said Caleb. "That does seem a bit excessive."

"Some privateers are excessive people!" the salesman said with a shrug. "You fly a flag like that, and anyone you meet on the sea will be fussing about so fast to get away that they'll no doubt make a mistake, making them easier to catch. Trouble with that is, if you end up letting people go after flying a red flag, word would get around, and the meaning of it diminishes. So, for the sake of the rest of us, if you fly a red flag, please follow through and kill everyone, won't you? Either way, when on the sea, I'd watch out for anyone else flying a red flag, if I were you."

"Noted," said Kennedy.

Kennedy picked up a few national flags, a merchant ship flag, and a standard black and white skull and crossbones flag. "You do custom flags as well, I see?" he asked.

The salesman smiled and began telling Kennedy the different custom flag options.

While Caleb and Captain Kennedy were busy with the flags, Hawkins admired the swords at the blacksmith. One caught her attention: a three-bladed device the blacksmith claimed was a "swordbreaker," designed to catch one's opponent's blade and snap it from the hilt. Always ready to try out a new weapon, she picked up the swordbreaker and made her way past the other vendors until she reached a stand selling various eye patches.

"Good afternoon, madame," the patch salesman greeted her when he saw her approaching. He was a short, wiry older man who wore an eye patch over one eye.

"Anything here catch your eye?" He then laughed as if he had said something clever. In truth, it was likely this was his main greeting for anybody coming to his shop, yet he seemed so proud of that joke and found it completely amusing, as if he had not said it countless times a day. "You may call me Patches."

"What do you have here?" Hawkins asked.

"Patches!" He then went straight into business mode. "Take a look at this here," he said, picking up one of the plain black eye patches. "This is the latest thing. It's a revolutionary new design that has practical applications that you would not believe."

"Oh, really?" Hawkins asked. "What exactly does this 'contraption' do?"

"You see…" He stopped himself. "Pardon the expression." He giggled at his own choice of words and corrected himself,

"You will *notice* that this is an eye patch, yes? But of course, it is. I reckon you are familiar with eye patches?"

Hawkins stared back, expressionless. Her dark glass eye reflected the afternoon sun.

"Maybe you are, maybe you are not," he said, shrugging. "But this here eye patch is what I like to refer to as a 'night-vision patch.'"

"What is that?"

"It's really quite a revolutionary new concept." Patches spread out his hands in a dramatic storytelling fashion. "Imagine you're on the deck of your ship, a great galleon out on the sea. It is a sunny day, the sun is shining on your face, but then, *wham!*" He clapped his hands, giving Hawkins a bit of a jump. "Your ship is attacked! Cannons fire, and a crew of cutthroat pirates raid your ship."

"Sounds terrifying," Hawkins said evenly, playing along.

"Oh, it is frightful," he continued, not breaking stride. "Your precious cargo is stored in the hold below, and of course, that is what these vicious men are after. You want to defend your cargo, do you not? Of course, you do! So, you follow below to engage them in combat. But you've been in the sun, and your eye is not accustomed to the dark."

"That is true," she said.

Patches leaned forward, so uncomfortably close to Hawkins' face that she could smell his breath. She caught herself imagining him eating garlic chicken earlier that day.

"What if I told you it didn't have to be this way?" he said. "Take one of these limited-edition night-vision patches, and you wear it over your eye while you're out in the sun. it allows that covered eye to get used to the dark, so that when you go below deck, you switch the eye patch over to your other eye, and by an amazing scientific breakthrough, your eye is used to it being dark, and you can now see perfectly down below! You can therefore take down your heartless attackers with no issue, and your cargo is safe!"

He smiled, satisfied at the tale he had just told.

"So, what do you say?"

Hawkins held the eye patch in her hand. It was a rather nice-looking eye patch.

"I do have a glass eye," she said aloud to herself.

Patches waved a dismissive hand. "You can use the patch to cover that as well," he said. "Though the night-vision is not guaranteed to work on that eye." He considered this statement for a moment. "But if it does, please report back to me immediately; that would be an amazing breakthrough!"

Hawkins raised the eyebrow over her good eye.

"But if you do wish to use it as advertised," Patches continued, "you will want to put the patch over your good eye while you are on deck. He reached over and helped Hawkins put the patch on. "Then, when it is time to go below, take it off, and you will be able to see better than anyone else down there."

Kingsley, who had been watching this whole time, stepped in close to Hawkins and whispered into her ear.

"It's a scam, Susan," he said. "The whole 'eye patch to see in the dark' thing? It's a story that was invented by salesmen to sell eye patches to guys who have two good eyes. Trust me. I have a gift shop of my own. I know how these people operate. If you want to get a patch for your eye, get it because you have lost an eye."

Patches noticed Kingsley's interruption.

"You're not going to listen to him, are you?" he asked. "Who is this for – him or you? If you want a nice patch, why would you let someone tell you that you cannot have one? In fact, I'll offer you a special deal. Buy this one, and I'll throw in the next two for half price."

"I only have two eyes," Hawkins said.

"These would be for your friends," Patches said. "It's a matching set. People will see you and know that you are all together."

Hawkins glanced at Kingsley, who was shaking his head.

"Don't do it."

She sighed and pulled out her coin purse.

"I'll take three."

"Excellent decision," Patches said, putting the patches into a pouch for her.

"I will not be wearing one of those," Kingsley said.

Hawkins took the patches, and she and Kingsley left to meet up with Captain Kennedy and Caleb, who were both finishing up gathering their new flags from the flag vendor.

"That should do us for now," said Kennedy. "Now, if we just get some food supplies, I think we should be set. Mr. Kingsley?"

"Yes, sir?"

"You were a fine enough cook on the *Devil's Thunder*. Would you be willing to take on the task again for us?"

"I would be happy to do so," Kingsley said, "until you find someone better."

"I'll leave it to you, then, to figure out what we need." Kennedy handed Kingsley some coins. "Here is the money allocated to our food. Go find us some hardtack, fruit, maybe some chickens, and whatever else you think our crew would eat, then meet us back at the ship."

"Aye, aye, Captain." Kingsley went with Caleb and Hawkins to purchase the necessary items as Kennedy returned to the *Goose*.

"By the way," Hawkins said to Caleb, "I have this special eye patch I think you might appreciate." She explained all she had been told about being able to see in the dark.

"Very well," Caleb said. "I'll hang onto it."

As the three entered the food section of the market, Kingsley first went to the livestock section. They purchased a few chickens, which were kept in crates. They also picked up some hardtack, spices, and a barrel of apples. Hawkins suggested they keep some fishing supplies stocked on the ship as well.

They finished gathering their food items and headed back to the dock, where the *Vengeful Goose* was waiting for them. Before they could reach the clearing, however, they would have to make their way down a path through the woods.

"What's that, there?" Kingsley said, pointing at what appeared to be another ship pulling into the bay.

"I don't know," said Caleb. "Let's pick up the pace."

He flung the barrel he was carrying onto his back, secured it with a strap, and started running faster to the dock. Kingsley and Hawkins also sped up. The chickens in the crates complained loudly as they bounced about. When they reached the dock, they all recognized that the new ship in the bay was, in fact, the *Devil's Thunder.* It was already turning into an intercept course against the *Goose.*

The *Goose's* sails were already being put to the wind, and Daniels and Fullery were pushing the capstan, bringing up the anchor.

Kingsley and Hawkins took a running start and jumped onto the ship. As they landed and rolled, their crates hit the deck, causing the chickens inside to squawk and flap their wings, irritated at the commotion.

The *Vengeful Goose* had just finished raising anchor as Caleb, trailing behind the others, made it to the dock.

Dr. Gold stepped onto the quarterdeck with a length of rope in hand. He called out to Caleb and tossed an end of the line to him and tied the other end to the ship's railing. Caleb caught it, and as the *Goose* began to sail away, he swung onto it, the barrel of food items still attached securely to his back, and he hit the back hull of the ship.

Kingsley joined the doctor on the quarterdeck. As he and Dr. Gold began to pull, Caleb climbed the rope, sore and dizzy from the impact. When Caleb made it to the top, Kingsley grabbed the barrel and pulled it with Caleb attached to it the rest of the way on board. They lay on the deck for a moment, catching their breath.

"All hands to general quarters!" Captain Kennedy called out.

Kingsley unhooked the barrel from Caleb's back and took it

to the hold below. He returned with two muskets; one he tossed to Caleb, and the other he kept for himself.

"What is the situation?" Caleb asked.

"It's our old friend, Santana," Kennedy said. "I was hoping we would not run into him for a while. Stand ready at the guns, but do not fire. Our goal for now is to flee, not fight."

Daniels and Hawkins worked on the sheets, desperately trying to catch the wind as quickly as they could.

"We have a favorable wind," Daniels said. "Let's hope that's enough to outrun these fools."

Unlucky Jake was at the helm, turning the wheel hard for a sharp turn away from the island.

A call was heard from the approaching ship; it was Captain Santana, his voice carrying over through a speaking trumpet.

"Crew of the *Vengeful Goose*," he called out. "You have unlawfully seized this vessel. Drop your anchor and surrender the ship. Come peacefully and turn yourselves in for a fair trial. Otherwise, we will be forced to take action."

"Full speed out of here," Captain Kennedy cried. Gunners, load chain shot and aim for their mast. Cripple them, if we can."

"Aye, aye," Caleb and Kingsley said in unison as they prepared two cannons on the starboard side of the ship.

A warning shot from the *Devil's Thunder* whizzed past Caleb's head. The wind from the shot knocked him off his feet. Caleb sat there, dazed from the blow.

As he stumbled to his feet, Caleb loaded the chain shot into his cannon. He shifted the cannon over, carefully aiming towards the *Thunder*'s main mast. He fired the cannon and dove for cover.

The shot was off by several feet. It tore harmlessly through the main sail.

"Pity," he said to himself.

"Fire again!" Captain Kennedy called out.

Kingsley fired a chain shot from his cannon. It whistled through the air and struck a beam. It was not quite the same damage that hitting the mast would have caused, but it was something. From their station on the *Goose*, they could see and hear the *Thunder*'s crew running about to deal with the damage.

Unfortunately, this aggression also prompted the *Thunder* to begin firing as well. It had more guns and more experienced hands, but the *Goose* had a good start and favorable winds. Most of the shots missed the *Goose* completely, but two managed to strike the hull.

Cynthia Cove dove away as splinters shot out from the impacts. Some stray bits of wood grazed her arm. Clutching her wound, she ran to the relative shelter of the cabin. Dr. Gold followed her there, so that he might see if there was anything he could do right away, even while they were still under attack. He was able to remove the splinters and treat her arm, but the two of them remained in the cabin until the encounter was over.

The *Goose* caught a strong wind in its sails, and Docks steered it so that it picked up speed as it sailed away from Bounty Isle. The *Devil's Thunder* lingered behind them, not able to match their speed thanks to the damage she had sustained.

"Keep full speed ahead!" Kennedy called. "Mr. Docks, adjust course south. Take us along the edge of the Deep."

"The Existential Deep?" Docks clarified, his voice uneasy.

"That's right," Kennedy confirmed. "No need to take us through it; just take us around it."

"Aye, aye," Docks said quietly as he turned the wheel. "Lord, have mercy."

Caleb ran to the stern of the ship and looked behind them; the *Devil's Thunder* had given up chase. They were too fast, or perhaps they knew what was out there in the Deep and wanted nothing to do with it.

XII
THE ROGUE SHIP

The *Goose* passed closer to the area labeled on the map "The Existential Deep." Caleb received no clear answer from anyone about what they could expect to find out there, but there was a universal reaction of trepidation whenever it was mentioned. The waters of the vast sea in the direction of the Deep looked darker and rougher in the distance, though Caleb wondered if that could just be the influence from what others had said about it. Whatever the case, he knew he would be grateful when they were clear of this particular stretch of ocean.

There was finally a bit of downtime, and the sailing on the edge of the Deep was smooth, so Caleb used this time to practice his skills with a sword. He took turns sparring with and learning from Susan Hawkins and Thomas Fullery, both of whom were skilled with the blade. Caleb seemed to be improving; he kept up with not only the movement of the sword, but with the footwork needed to move around the swaying deck.

The others sat on the quarterdeck and watched, placing wagers. Because Caleb's skill level was not yet matched with the others, nobody bet on him winning; instead, they bet on any good moves he might make or how long it might take for him to yield.

After yielding from a particularly exhausting round, Caleb took an apple from a barrel on the deck and went to the rails to look out at the dark clouds forming in the distance.

His mind went to Dr. Rockwell, who said that all the tales of monsters were made up, and nothing significant was out there, that map makers like to draw images of strange monsters to fill in the blanks of uncharted waters, but Caleb wasn't convinced. He had overheard Docks telling tales about creatures out on the sea: monsters with tentacles that can pull a ship below, and others with claws the size of palm trees.

"I think it's because he doesn't understand what is truly out there," Kingsley said to Caleb when he asked his opinion about this. "There could be something terrible out there, sure, but I also believe that there are a lot of great things there as well. To seek out the great things in this world is worth the possibility of encountering some of the terrible things, if you ask me."

As Caleb looked out towards the Deep, he saw something disturb the surface of the water. *Probably just a fish,* he thought. He stared as the *Goose* sailed closer towards the spot.

A pang of dread shot into Caleb, when, in the darkness of the sea ahead, he saw a large shape reflecting the sunlight in the water. It was far ahead of them still, but the size was massive, much larger than their ship. For a brief moment, Caleb swore he saw a glowing red eye.

Then it was gone.

I needn't let my imagination take over, he said to himself. *If I'm not careful, I'll go mad!*

His mind still on these things, Caleb's sight drifted forward as his gaze followed the flight of a seagull until something else caught his attention.

Taking his personal spyglass up to his eye, Caleb stood on the fo'c'sle of the ship and looked ahead. Docks noticed his eagerness and shuffled up to him.

"What is it, Caleb?" he asked quietly after moment of silence.

Caleb lowered the spyglass.

"There's something up there," he said. "One point off the starboard bow, crossing the horizon."

"That's past the Deep," Docks said. "There are shipping lanes crossing between Rocky Isle and Pighead Island. Could be anything from a merchant vessel to a pirate ship."

"Aye," said Caleb, handing the spyglass over. "See what you can make of it. I see movement, but my eyes are not yet as trained as yours."

Docks took the spyglass up to his eye.

"It is indeed a ship," he said. "A medium sized brigantine. Call the captain. Let's see what his mind is on it."

Captain Kennedy was already making his way forward, noticing the commotion at the bow of the ship.

"What is it? What have you spotted?" he asked, taking out his own spyglass.

"A ship," Caleb said, pointing forward. "Could be friend, could be foe."

"This could be our lucky day," the captain said, his excitement growing as he looked forward. "I see they are flying a merchant flag."

"Could it be a trick?" Caleb asked, knowing full well that some pirate ships lie in wait while disguised as merchant vessels.

"It's always possible," Kennedy said, "and we must be ready should this be the case. We'll be coming up on them rather quickly. We've still not many hands, so let's see if we can't scare them into a quick surrender. Hoist the Jolly Roger, and let's give them a sight that will make them shudder!"

The crew cheered. It was to be their first fight, and though their numbers were small, the ship in question was not much larger in size than their own, and they had the confidence they could handle themselves, provided they were intimidating enough.

Unlucky Jake Docks made his way to the main mast and began running up the black flag.

"Full sails; full speed ahead! Run these men down!" Kennedy called out.

Hawkins took the helm and steered the *Goose* on an intercept course with the ship ahead of them. The wind was in their sails, and they were at top speed. Daniels and Gold stood by the sheets, ready to take them in when they got close. Caleb and Kingsley stood at the cannons, waiting for them to close the distance.

As they drew closer, it was clear the ship was preparing to retreat. It made a sharp turn and was going back in the direction from where it had come. Men could be seen on its deck, scrambling about.

Kennedy gave the order to fire a warning shot.

Kingsley aimed his cannon across the bow of the ship and fired. The shot rang out and nearly clipped the bowsprit of the merchant ship.

Captain Kennedy took out a speaking trumpet and addressed the ship.

"Attention, Merchant Vessel," he called out. "This is Captain Stephen Kennedy of the *Vengeful Goose*. We advise you to anchor yourself, surrender peaceably, and no harm will come to you. Resist, and you will be fired upon, and your men will die. We leave it to you."

There was some further commotion on the deck of the other ship, until finally, they raised the white flag of truce. The ship stopped still in the water; its anchor had been dropped.

Hawkins steered the *Goose* to boarding distance next to the merchant ship. Fullery and Daniels tossed grappling hooks that caught on the ship's rigging and then took a long gangplank and dropped it across the side of the ship, connecting the two. Kennedy, joined by Caleb, Fullery, and Daniels, walked the gangplank to the other ship.

The captain of the ship stood firm on the deck, with fear in his eyes, but a defiant look forced upon his face. Kennedy approached him.

"You are the captain here?" he assumed.

"I am," he said. He was a middle-aged man who spoke with a shaky voice in a strange variant of a Scottish accent. "I am Captain Robert Van Morrison. We are a simple merchant vessel, and we wish to offer you no trouble, sir."

"Well, then, Captain Robert Van Morrison, the merchant," Kennedy said with a cocky grin, "I am grateful for your cooperation. Two dozen of my men are ready at the guns to blow you out of the water if you decide to cause trouble. You see that unfortunate fellow with the peg leg up on the rigging?" He gestured to Docks, who sat high above them on one of the beams of the *Vengeful Goose.*

"I see him."

"If I signal him or if he himself sees something happening here that he does not like, he will give the order to unleash hellfire onto your ship. But as I said, we have no wish to harm any of you."

He stepped uncomfortably close to the merchant captain.

"Tell me, what is it you are delivering?"

The captain wiped sweat from his brow and nodded, attempting to regain his composure.

"We are transporting spices and tea, Captain," he said. "If you follow me below, I can show you."

Van Morrison led Captain Kennedy and the others into the hold below. "I will tell my employer of the misfortune that came upon us," he said. "Though I fought bravely, I was eventually forced to surrender."

"Of course," said Kennedy, clapping the merchant on his back.

They stepped below, where they saw a number of men, primarily African and Asian men, but a few white European men as well, chained up.

"What is this, then?" Kennedy asked the captain, motioning to the men. "Are you involved in the slave trade as well?"

"What?" Van Morrison asked, sweating profusely. "No, no, this is my personal crew. You see, there is much to move in my business: barrels, crates, and so on. You couldn't expect me to lift all that myself, at my age."

Kennedy laughed loudly. "No, my dear fellow. And what's this back here? I would hazard a guess these are the rum barrels?"

Van Morrison swallowed nervously, disappointed at the implication. "Yes," he said. "It keeps our spirits up, so to speak. A bit o' grog after a day's good work."

"Tell you what, Mr. Captain Van Morrison," Kennedy said, "I'll be taking these rum barrels, and I'll leave you half your cargo."

The captain seemed a little disappointed upon hearing he would be losing the rum barrels, but he was gratified he would not be losing the entirety of his stock.

"Very well," Van Morrison said. "You'll be taking these over yourself?"

Kennedy laughed again. "You hear that, boys? Me, at my age, lifting all these barrels? Nay, you see, you make good sense, my good man. We'll be needing some assistance taking these aboard."

Van Morrison's eyes widened as he took the captain's meaning.

"You wouldn't," he lamented. "You wouldn't deprive a man such as myself of my help – my livelihood?"

Kennedy's smile faded and his carefree nature turned to anger. He unsheathed his sword and closed the distance between him and Van Morrison, his expression mad in a way Caleb had never before seen. Van Morrison cowered in fear.

"I suggest you do not interfere with what I have come here for," Kennedy said as he moved closer. "Your very lives are ours to do with as we wish. Pray that I do not decide to take you along with me as a slave, for the lashes I give to my slaves aboard my ship would make you wail just to witness."

The poor merchant captain fell to his knees, hyperventilating in fear. His eyes were closed, but his hands were fidgeting, searching for his keys and anything else he might find that would appease the captain standing above him.

Kennedy relaxed his aggressive demeanor and took a step back. "We will be needing these men to assist us. Hand us the keys now, good sir."

Caleb took the keys from Van Morrison and began unchaining the poor men. Fullery instructed them to take the rum barrels, a crate of apples, and half of the crates of tea and spices.

When Captain Kennedy began leading the slaves onto the deck, the members of the merchant crew began to murmur amongst themselves in indignation. A few well-placed threats from Kennedy and Fullery quietened them down quickly, though.

Kennedy led the men back to the *Goose*; Caleb and Fullery promptly removed the gangplank behind the last of them. As the former slaves stepped onto the deck, they were surprised at the small numbers aboard.

As they sailed away, and the merchant ship faded off into the distance, the crew of the *Goose* laughed and cheered at the successful trick they had pulled, more than doubling their numbers with the thirteen new men who had joined them, not to mention the new supplies, all obtained without bloodshed.

The *Vengeful Goose* sailed west along the trade routes. They did not encounter any more vessels, so they kept themselves busy training their new crew with seamanship drills and fighting exercises. Mr. Fullery took on the role of quartermaster and made sure that everything ran smoothly with the new men.

Now stocked with more food and spices, Kingsley experimented more in the galley; it was not fine dining, but the food was at least more flavorful than it had been. A few of the new men were experienced fishermen, and they were able to help bring in fish for Kingsley to prepare.

Though they seemed to have a good start and were doing well for themselves, Caleb still had a growing concern about the *Red Soul*. Eventually, they would have to face Captain Torch and his crew, and they were still not equipped to deal with such a threat. Apart from seeking the *Grimoire*, Caleb did not know how they could be.

With the recent success against the merchant ship, Captain Kennedy became confident and in good spirits. If they were able to take that ship with such a minuscule crew, what might they be able to accomplish with twice the men?

He frequently sat in his quarters poring over maps of trade routes. Captain Van Morrison had offered no resistance when he was taken, but Kennedy knew that others would. Having sailed under Captain Santana, Kennedy had seen pirate ships attack merchant vessels that put up a great fight. Then, of course, there were ships like the *Devil's Thunder* out there hunting them. If they were to have any hope in facing them, they would need the weapons and experience.

Two months after taking on the new crew, the *Vengeful Goose* sailed on an open stretch of the sea. They had circled back and were not far from where they had come upon the merchant ship.

"Keep a sharp eye," an older man by the name of Jackson said to Caleb as they moved quietly on the water. Caleb looked ahead at the vast sea. It was open water, but he knew that this was the same place they had been before: the Existential Deep.

"I seen eyes watching from the depths looking up at you, waiting to tear you down to the bottom of the sea," Jackson continued.

"You ain't seen nothin' but what the grog showed you," one of the other men said. He was a young African man, a little older than Caleb, by the name of Aaron Cobb.

"Don't be disrespecting the sea," Jackson warned. "We do not know the sea, and we cannot know the sea."

He went back to swabbing the deck, shaking his head and humming to himself in an effort to calm his nerves.

"Don't mind him," said Cobb to Caleb. "He's been serving Captain Van Morrison longer than any of us, and I think he has lost a bit of sense. And from what I hear, some of the crimes he committed that got him sentenced to a life of slavery… let's just say, he wasn't all there in the head even before he started serving on the ships."

Caleb contorted his face. "Is that supposed to comfort me?"

Cobb laughed. "No. No comfort. Just know that he's a madman without sense. That makes it all better, does it not?"

"I suppose it does," Caleb lied. "What about you?"

Cobb shook his head. "I may have gone mad, but who's to say? I just long to find a way to go back home."

"Where is that?"

"I've been gone so long, I don't know if I would even recognize it, but it was back in the Old World. I have some memories of the village. They took me away from there when I was a child and had me work for some family up in Jamestown. Two winters ago, they sold me and brought me down here to the islands where they've had me work on a sugar plantation and on ships. What about you?"

"I've always lived on these islands. I don't know of any home."

"Shame, that," Cobb said, solemnly. He looked out at the dark sea ahead of them. "The sea isn't so bad. You treat it well and hope it treats you well back. But some days, it can be wild with no reason, but it treats all men the same; it don't play favorites. I like that. I've seen plenty of monsters and devils, but most of them owned big houses or sailed big boats."

There was truth in what Cobb said, but Caleb couldn't shake the memory of what he thought he had seen out there in the sea.

His thoughts were interrupted by the sound of Docks shouting from the crow's nest.

"Ship ahoy!" he called out. "Dead ahead."

Captain Kennedy stepped out of his cabin and forward to the fo'c'sle, where Fullery stood with a spyglass.

"It's a medium size ship," he said. "Looks like it is built for combat."

"King's navy?" Kennedy asked, taking the spyglass.

"Unlikely," Fullery said. "Could be privateer. Could be pirates."

Kennedy considered his options for a moment and walked back with Fullery to the quarterdeck.

"Maintain course, Miss Hawkins," he said. "We'll see what these devils may have in store for us. Prepare the men for combat. Stand by for orders."

"Aye, aye," Fullery said. Then, stepping down onto the main deck, he gathered the men. "All men to general quarters. Stand by the cannons. Prepare boarding cables and stand by to strike to disable."

Caleb moved across the deck to the larboard side cannon. Mr. Cobb stood by him, ready to assist.

As they drew closer to the ship, they could hear a shot ring out, as forward-facing cannons from the other ship shot across them.

"Hard to starboard!" Kennedy commanded.

Fullery repeated the order. "Hard to starboard! Prepare larboard cannons and fire a broadside volley on my order!"

Hawkins spun the wheel, and the *Goose* cut through the sea, taking a sharp turn to the right.

The other ship closed in rapidly. As it came more clearly into view, Caleb looked up and saw the flag: a black flag with a red skeleton holding a knife that dripped blood.

"Fire broadside!" Fullery called out.

The shout brought Caleb back to the present. He aimed high and fired the cannon. The shot landed at the railing of the ship, sending the men on board flying for cover.

Cobb, standing next to him, handed Caleb another cannonball. He loaded it and quickly fired again. It skimmed past the main mast. The *Goose* was also taking some damage. As the ships drew in close to one another, Hawkins turned the wheel so that they began circling tightly. Grapples were thrown from the other ship, and men began to swing across, boarding the *Goose*.

Caleb continued firing, but one of the men from the other ship came up behind him and swung a cutlass, nearly taking Caleb's head off; thanks to a warning cry from Cobb, he ducked out of the way of the swing just in time. The attacker lost his balance and tumbled onto the deck, giving Caleb just enough time to recover and draw his own sword.

The man got to his feet. He was an ugly young man, sunburned and scarred. His dark hair was tied up in a rag, and his eyes were wild. He wasted no time; as soon as he was on his feet, he sprung forward again. Caleb parried the strike with his sword and lunged forward, piercing the man's shoulder. This did not stop him; he continued swinging wildly, shouting what may have been insults in some foreign language or just gibberish as he swung wildly at Caleb.

At the last wild swing, Caleb stepped out of the way, causing the wild man to stumble again. The man turned around and lunged for Caleb, but Caleb struck him in the chest. As he did, he felt the now-familiar wave of dark energy go into him.

More men swung onto the ship and began attacking. They all had the same wild energy. Most of them wore all black clothes with black grease smeared around their eyes.

A tall man wearing a long coat made of shiny black material stepped onto the deck as well. A multitude of silver chains hung around his neck. He had long black hair that fell straight and dramatically over his eyes. He seemed rather young and spoke with an affected voice, as if he was attempting to sound older than he was.

"You have been defeated by the *Death-Blade*," he said, even though the battle was obviously far from over and the victor was undecided. In what he no doubt assumed was a dramatic gesture, he raised both his arms above his head. "I am Captain Night-Heart the Bloodletter. Your day of reckoning is at hand. The dark forces that – "

He stopped short as Susan Hawkins moved in towards him and lobbed off his right hand with a forceful swing of her cutlass. The young captain screamed in pain.

In an insulted, complaining tone that was likely his more natural voice, he cried out, *"I was talking!"* He tucked his arm under his coat and started walking back towards his ship, whimpering.

The other pirates who had boarded the *Goose* continued their fight, swinging wildly and yelling as they did so. Normally, while engaging in combat, Caleb appreciated some dialogue to get a feel for his enemy and to catch them off guard, but all these people seemed to do was yell unintelligibly as they attacked; they acted more like wild animals than people.

Caleb, Cobb, and several other shipmates pursued the captain as he returned to his ship. They struck down several people as they did so, but despite their superior skill, they were still outmatched and soon surrounded.

Seeing the fallen bodies around him, Caleb tapped into the Reaper's energy and resurrected the fallen enemy pirates. The captain's eyes widened in fear.

"Get us out of here!" he called to his men. "Run away! Help!"

As several of the undead men fought under Caleb's thrall, the other men frantically set sail.

The ship began to move. Caleb looked around; a complete victory seemed unlikely, but with the help of the men under his thrall, maybe they could get out of here with some sort of net gain. He tapped Cobb on the shoulder.

"Follow me," he said. "Let's see if we can't get something out of this."

Caleb led the four of his crewmates below deck while his zombie pirates covered them. There were all sorts of crates stacked below in the hold. They stopped and looked at them in awe.

"Od's bodkins," one of Caleb's mates said under his breath as they beheld the treasures before them.

"Get what you can," Caleb said, "and throw them overboard.

We can fish them out of the sea once they've gone."

They each grabbed a chest and hurried back up to the deck. The captain was seated there, clutching his arm with his good hand, muttering to himself as he watched his men fight the resurrected bodies of his fallen crew. When he saw the five men from the *Goose* emerge from the hold, each with a chest of plunder, he cried out again.

"Don't let them get away! Kill them!"

But it was too late. His men were too focused on fighting back the undead to concern themselves with Caleb and the other living men. The *Death-Blade* had begun sailing away from the still stationary *Vengeful Goose*. Caleb and the others jumped into the water with their treasures. Captain Night-Heart leaned over the railing and shouted at them.

"You will never escape!" he cried as they escaped. "The Bloodletter will have his vengeance and will find you. Darkness will take hold of your sorry lives, and the black curtain of death will fall on the stage of your existence!"

He sat back on the deck of his ship in defeat as the crew finished dealing with the zombified forms of his men.

Caleb and the others treaded water alongside five crates of goods taken from the *Death-Blade* and waited for the *Goose* to pick them up.

The *Goose*'s longboat was lowered, and one of the formerly enslaved men rowed it out to them and fished them and their treasure out of the water.

When they returned to the *Goose*, they set the chests on the deck in front of the crew. Captain Kennedy looked at it all in amazement.

"You say they had more on board?" he asked.

"Aye," said Caleb. "Much more in their hold."

They opened the chests. Three were filled with coins. The other two had silver plates and goblets in them.

"Well done, men!" Kennedy said, beaming with excitement. "Your quick action turned the tide of this encounter. Those pirates had us outmatched, but you managed to spin this into a victory. Mr. Fullery, an extra ration of grog for each of these men, and for Miss Hawkins for her efforts against their captain. And an extra share of this plunder for each of them as well."

They clapped Caleb on the back. He felt good about the outcome, yet he began to feel an ache in his chest after the experience of raising the dead men on the other ship.

"Common side effects of this curse may include dry throat, nausea, and shared dreams and visions of others who are afflicted by the same curse."

– Golden Sea Grimoire

XIII

VISIONS

The *Goose* set sail again with few casualties reported from the previous fight. Old Man Jackson and two others were killed in the attack, and Mr. Jim Daniels was critically wounded with a shot to the stomach. Dr. Gold did what he could to stabilize his condition, but the damage was too great. Gold called for Caleb to see if he could work any wonders on him.

Calling upon the dark energy he had gathered during the fight, Caleb was able to seal the wound, but Daniels still appeared pale, and the color of the skin around the wound was rotten. Caleb admitted he didn't know if what he was doing might make him worse in the long run. After all, the men he had seen raised had never been the same as before.

Looking at his own hands, Caleb felt that some of the color of his skin was beginning to fade ever so slightly. He excused himself, saying that he was not feeling well and needed to go lie down.

It was early evening, and the rest of the crew celebrated their recent victory on deck while Caleb took to his hammock below. He closed his eyes, and after tossing and turning for several minutes went into a deep sleep.

As he slept, in his dreams, Caleb found himself standing on a rock in the middle of the ocean. Waves crashed around him. There was no land to be seen. There was no other person or vessel around; he was completely alone.

The rock he stood on began to shake. Caleb looked into the water: there were two glowing orbs. They rose slowly until they emerged from the water, forming two red eyes in a large, featureless face that regarded him with familiarity.

"Caleb," it spoke in a booming voice.

The features of the face became visible as flames surrounded it like flowing hair: it was the face of Captain Benjamin Torch. "Caleb, you have abandoned your post. You have forsaken your destiny."

He tried to respond, but his throat was constricted. The enormous form of Captain Torch's face was surrounded by darkness. The stars in the sky were snuffed out, and the image of the captain burned away, leaving a flaming skull in its place.

"The Reaper must be summoned, Caleb."

A large flaming sword emerged from the sea. The looming figure of Captain Torch raised it over his head and swung it down, straight into Caleb.

He awoke with a start. Panting and sweating, he looked around him. It took a moment for his eyes to adjust and for him to get his bearings, but he soon recognized the cramped quarters below deck in the *Vengeful Goose*. There was movement not far away from him. It was the slim figure of Cynthia Cove, staring at him.

"Bad dreams?"

"Yes," said Caleb. "What is it – what are you doing here?"

Cynthia walked gracefully across the room, almost eerily, considering the ebb and flow of the ship. "Same as you," she said, "I needed rest. What did you see?"

"It was nothing," he said, dismissively. This obviously wasn't going to be enough to satisfy Cynthia; she continued to stare at him, expressionless, but expectant.

"It was Captain Torch," he continued. "There's something more I need to be doing while we're out here."

"What more could you be doing?"

"Anything," he said. "Going after other ships is one thing, but the *Red Soul* is still out there. There's no telling what it's up to. We could go after it, learn about it, anything."

Cynthia came over to Caleb's hammock and sat on a stool next to him. She took Caleb's hands in her own.

"You're so cold," she said. "What happened in the dream? What did Torch say?"

"I don't know if he can sense me out here," he said, pulling his hands away, "but it was like he was trying to call me back. Like he was preparing for something big. I should speak with the captain."

He stood up, gathered his coat, and headed for the deck.

It was a starry night, and several lanterns were lit on the deck of the ship. A few men played cards, wagering their newly acquired treasures. One of the new young men that had joined the ship was playing a peaceful tune on a violin.

Hawkins stood at the helm; she had an eye patch over her good eye, so she was, in actuality, steering the ship blind. One of the other crewmen, a man by the name of Roland, sat next to her, occasionally speaking to her, helping her adjust course. Aiden Kingsley stood behind them, looking out to sea, unaware of Caleb and Cynthia on the deck below.

Captain Kennedy was not on the deck. Caleb went to the door of the captain's cabin just below the quarterdeck, where he saw light from a lantern shine through the cracks on the door. He knocked firmly, and the captain's voice came forth.

"Yes, what is it?"

Caleb opened the door; Kennedy was at his desk, going over several maps that had trade routes drawn out on them in different colors. Upon seeing Caleb, he stood to welcome him.

"Ah, Mr. Caleb." He stopped himself. "Caleb… do you have a last name?" he asked in a way that suggested he had not considered this until now.

"It's always just been Caleb, sir."

"You're a free man, you know," Kennedy said. "And free to give yourself a name that can help command respect and help set you apart from the many other Calebs that are no doubt roaming about."

"I will consider that," Caleb said, and he promised himself that he would, but for now, what people called him was not exactly on the forefront of his mind.

Kennedy stopped as if he were lost in thought. "But excuse my rambling. You wish to speak with me? Any particular matter?"

Cynthia stood just behind Caleb in the doorway. Kennedy saw her and addressed her as well.

"Miss Cove," he said. "Come in, both of you."

Caleb and Cynthia stepped into the cabin and shut the door behind them.

"Have a seat," Kennedy said, standing and gesturing to two of the chairs in the cabin. He went to a cabinet at the side of the room and took out a bottle of wine. "How about this?" he said, holding it up. "A holdover from the previous captain. Let me get some glasses for you."

"I'm fine," Caleb said, dismissing the drink with a wave of his hand.

The captain poured two small drinks for himself and Cynthia and took a seat.

"Tell me," he said, "what is this about?"

"I'd like you to consider our next destination," Caleb said, eyeing the map. "You see, we've set ourselves out here with a purpose."

"And we're well on our way to that purpose," Kennedy boasted. "Forgive me. You were saying?"

"It's all well and good that we take on ships like that unfortunate pirate ship we encountered yesterday, but the reason I am out here has to do with Captain Torch and the *Red Soul*. He came to me in a dream. I fear his power is growing."

"In a dream, you say?" It was apparent that Kennedy was unimpressed. Still, Caleb recounted what happened in the dream.

"It seems to me that it is your own fears and concerns getting the best of you," the captain said. "We have a good thing going here. I'm sure you know of the whole situation with our King back in the old country, conscripting vessels, offering letters of marque to hunt down other ships and all. It is what the good Captain Santana was engaged in, and I considered that maybe it could be our destiny as well, but I believe we can be completely self-sustaining without even having to consider working as the King's bounty hunters or whatever you want to call them — privateers, if you like. The hauls we have taken just from the last two ships are more than enough for us to operate on our own for the next several months. We can truly be free out here."

"That's good," said Caleb. "That should free us up to do what I propose."

"About that," Kennedy interrupted. "No, you see, in order to maintain this level of profit, we have to keep striking. You've seen Mr. Daniels? Poor soul is likely to succumb to his injuries. I fear he will not survive the night due to his wound. And we have already lost others. I suggest we take on ships that are not as dangerous to our crew. There are plenty of other ships out there ready for the taking — other merchant ships. We need to focus on those. There's no sense taking such big risks, even with such rewards. We'll work our way to that."

"Let me get this straight," said Caleb. "You are saying that we should only target innocent merchant ships and leave everyone else alone?"

"Was anybody harmed when we took our first merchant ship?" Kennedy asked. Caleb shifted uncomfortably in his seat. "I ask you again: was anybody harmed? No one. None of our men. None of their men. They went on their way and reported to their employers that they were attacked, and they were probably even compensated. Everybody came out ahead."

"But what happens when ships constantly report attacks like

these?" Caleb challenged. "They are already recruiting privateers to hunt ships like us. They will just keep escalating this. More men will take these letters of marque and work for the crown and fight people like us."

Kennedy nodded and sat in silence for a moment. "That may be," he finally said, "and when the time comes, maybe we will join them. In the meantime, my orders are that we go after the merchant ships. We will be returning to Bounty Isle for more supplies in the morning. If you wish to depart, you may do so."

"I helped you get this ship," Caleb said, standing up. "We got this ship for the purpose of mounting a defense against Captain Torch. I will not leave it."

Kennedy stood as well, setting down his drink. "If you interfere with the missions this ship is set to accomplish, you will have no place here," he said firmly. "I don't wish for you to leave; you have been useful under my command, but you are replaceable. If there is nothing further, I ask that you leave me to my work."

He escorted Caleb and Cynthia to the door, and before they could completely process everything that had happened, they found themselves standing out on the deck of the ship with the rest of the crew who were going about the evening unaware of the argument.

"Come," Cynthia said, taking Caleb's arm, leading him up the steps of the quarterdeck. "Sit with me up here."

Kingsley sat on the quarterdeck as well, quietly eating apples and looking out at the sea behind them. He turned as he heard Caleb and Cynthia approach.

Susan Hawkins, still blinded by the eye patch over her good eye, greeted the two of them as she heard them step onto the quarterdeck.

"It's a beautiful night," she guessed. "What's the matter?"

Caleb looked around, unsure what prompted this question. She obviously couldn't see either of them, but apart from Kingsley and Mr. Roland, there was nobody else present she could be addressing.

"Come now," she said, "I can sense tension and unease. There's something going on. I'd like to know."

"It's nothing," Caleb said. "I'm worn out from the fight."

"I did want to say congratulations on a foolhardy but ultimately successful attack," Hawkins said.

"Foolhardy?" Caleb repeated.

Hawkins laughed. "Following a wild captain back onto his ship? You were truly outnumbered and surrounded by a bunch of people who had spent their lives dying their hair and applying black makeup, trying to be tortured individuals."

"I guess when you're actually somewhat tortured with a curse, a little manufactured drama isn't that frightening."

"Just don't start dressing like them, or I'll have to take some sort of drastic action against you."

"No need to worry about that," Caleb assured her. "But then, you could always just keep that eye patch on, and you wouldn't have to see it. How's that working out for you, anyway?"

Hawkins raised her head and leaned back while holding onto the wheel with both hands. "I can tell that my other senses are truly heightened. You should try this."

Caleb caught Roland's eye, who gave him a dubious look. He subtly shook his head, discounting Hawkins' claims.

She must have assumed this was happening, because she followed up with, "And don't listen to Mr. Roland. I tell you, if something were to happen here and now, you would all just need to look to me."

Hawkins continued steering the ship, listening to the sounds of the ocean and the occasional directional guidance from Roland.

"Caleb," said Kingsley, quietly "something is the matter. Even 'Black-Eye Susan' can sense it. What is it?"

"None of this is how I imagined it would be," Caleb lamented, exhaustion evident in his voice. "Captain Kennedy wishes to increase attacks against merchant vessels. He says he wants to decrease the risk to us, but I get the feeling there's more to it than that. The way he reacted to our recent hauls, he wants more of the same. I fear he may be willing to step over a line that I don't wish to cross. And it's not only that; the very reason that we are out here: we need to focus our fight on Captain Torch, not on innocent merchants."

"But we don't know if we can even do that yet," Kingsley said. "In the meantime, we can only really survive however we can."

"What about the *Grimoire*?"

Kingsley shook his head. "We still don't know enough about that or even how to acquire it."

"So, we find that out."

"And how would we do that? We don't exactly have any leads."

"Somebody must know," said Caleb. "When I was in employ of the governor, he spoke with a man called Lansky who claimed that there were mysterious items that the Navy had taken into their possession. It could be that the *Golden Sea Grimoire* is locked away in some outpost."

Cynthia and Kingsley both sat up straight upon hearing this.

"What's that?" Kingsley asked. "You never mentioned this before."

"It was something I had just overheard," he said. "And he was rather vague, but it's a start."

"That's it then," said Kingsley, getting excited. "Mention that to the captain. Maybe we could adjust the course to seek him out. We find this man, maybe we could find the book?"

"No," said Cynthia. "The fewer people who know about this, the better." She glanced at Roland, who was giving them the side eye. "Obviously, everyone up here knows now, but I suggest we keep to a minimum the number of others we let in."

"I agree," said Caleb. "But there's still the matter that we don't know where this man Lansky is now."

"What about the governor?" Kingsley suggested. "Might

he know?"

"That's a possibility," Caleb said, "but we'd have to return to Buccaneers Isle to find out."

"We may be able to manage that," said Kingsley. "We're not far from there anyway with our next stop tomorrow. I've been intending to find time to check on the shop, and there are some things I'd like to pick up from there. I'll put in a request."

"I could help put together a small landing party," Susan said. "I think there are enough men here whom we can trust to accompany us."

"Very well," said Caleb. "But not a word above what is necessary.

They went about their duties. It was early morning when Caleb's rest was interrupted by Kingsley.

"It's Daniels," he said. "He's asking for you."

During the night, James Daniels' condition deteriorated, and he was now near death's door. Caleb went to where the doctor was tending to him, and they were given privacy to speak alone.

"We have not known each other for long," Daniels said to Caleb, "but I believe that you have some honor. Keep the ship on the right course, and the men as well."

"I will do my best," said Caleb, not sure why Daniels had felt the need to say this to him in particular. "Ultimately, it's not up to me. I'm not the captain. The course of the ship is up to Mr. Kennedy."

Daniels coughed and winced at the constant pain in his side as he shook his head.

"I've known Stephen for many years," he said. "He has many fine qualities but given the choice between an easy path and a moral one, he will take the easy one. He needs a moral rudder, so to speak. You must help him find the right path, and if you can't…"

He was cut off by another coughing fit. Hearing it, Dr. Gold returned with some whiskey for him. He took a few sips of it then lay back.

"Watch over the men," he continued. "You have a good crew here. I don't know what sort of voodoo you have, but don't waste it trying to bring me back. It's not…" Daniels looked as if he wanted to say more, but he ultimately gave up after another coughing fit. Caleb stepped back, giving him room, as Daniels put his efforts into his labored breathing.

About an hour later, he gave in to his injuries and passed away.

Caleb quietly returned to his bunk to finish the night's sleep, what little of it there was left.

"In order to master your power, first master yourself."

– Golden Sea Grimoire

XIV

A VISIT TO THE GOVERNOR

The *Vengeful Goose* arrived at Bounty Isle early in the morning. Aiden Kingsley spoke with the captain about returning to Buccaneers Isle in order to allow Kingsley to pick up some items at the Hex Hut, including a rather large book of recipes he had gathered over the years. It took some convincing, but anything that would improve the quality of life on the ship while out to sea was a great incentive, and ultimately, Kennedy conceded.

The market on Bounty Isle was not as crowded as it had been the first time they had been there. Captain Kennedy claimed for himself a proper coat and an impressive wide-brimmed hat, so that he may more fully embody the part of a great captain. Some of the rest of the crew also used their new wages to purchase new clothes, though most of the money was spent at the tavern, where drinks were sold at an inflated price. Unlucky Jake Docks spent his earnings on a stylish new hook that matched his peg leg.

The man in the flag shop was pleased to see Captain Kennedy return, and he proudly presented a custom flag that had been ordered for the ship.

"What is it?" Caleb asked, holding it up to get a better look at it. It was a black flag with a white silhouette of a bird and a knife hovering over a horizontal bone. "A swan?"

Kennedy scoffed and took the flag from him, looking at it. "A swan indeed! It's a goose, of course! A vengeful goose."

Caleb gave the flag a closer look. "Ah, yes. I see it now."

"They have it in red as well," he said, also picking up that flag from the flag shop owner. Caleb shot the captain a concerned look, though not purposefully. The captain noticed and did what he could to alleviate his concerns. "For emergencies, you understand. Something to put fear into the ships we encounter."

There was not much else to get at the market but some food to replenish the stores on board the ship. They were loaded up and on their way before noon, and they soon found themselves approaching the familiar docks of Port de Sang, back on Buccaneers Isle.

Caleb stepped cautiously onto the street, concerned that the familiar sights would make it difficult to return, but as he caught his reflection in the water, he realized that he now looked like a completely different man from the youth who had escaped the island many months ago. For one thing, a short beard had begun to grow on his youthful face. Another difference was the clothes: he wore a ruffled white shirt, nice burgundy breeches, a fine waistcoat, and a black leather tricorn hat. He now looked the best he had ever looked.

It had been more than a year of living at sea, and Caleb had also started putting muscle on his formerly thin frame. But most of all, he had begun to conduct himself in a completely different manner. He had always kept a put-together appearance when he worked at the governor's home, but he now presented himself with an air of newfound self-respect.

On the street, he passed by Mr. Geoffrey, the owner of the Golden Doubloon. He tipped his hat and received a cordial response, but there was no recognition in the eyes of the shop-keeper. Caleb stayed his course, walking to the border of the town with Aiden Kingsley and Susan Hawkins by his side.

"Are you sure you wish to do this without me?" Kingsley asked as they passed the final shop of the town.

"I'm certain," Caleb said. "You take care of what you need to at the shop. The governor and I are just going to talk. I think I can handle myself here. Miss Hawkins, if you are willing, you can keep an eye on our exit."

Hawkins nodded.

Kingsley bade him good luck and walked away towards the south side of the island towards the Hex Hut.

Caleb looked warily at the road ahead that led to the governor's home. Hawkins noticed his hesitancy.

"I can take the lead on this if you wish," she offered.

"No," said Caleb. "This is something I need to do."

Steeling his nerves, he walked forward to the governor's home. There was the familiar open road that led to the front of the house. He knew that he should avoid going this way, for that entrance was for people who wished to be announced and welcomed. Instead, Caleb led Hawkins down a nearly indiscernible pathway that weaved through a wooded area, towards the back gardens.

From there, Caleb could see several carriages parked at the front of the house.

"Looks like some sort of house party."

"Just our luck," Hawkins said, disappointed.

Caleb, however, smiled at this. "Yes," he said. "Just our luck, indeed."

They went around to the back of the house and came to a patio. Caleb looked into one of the windows. There were about a dozen finely-dressed men there; it looked like they were involved in some form of business. Governor Duplantier himself was there as well as his son Jean, who was speaking with a very familiar face: Captain Rafael Santana.

"Some luck, wouldn't you say?" Caleb repeated quietly, pointing Santana out to Hawkins. "It's the good Captain Santana himself! They must be discussing the means of our extermination."

"I don't recall seeing the *Thunder* in the bay," Hawkins remarked as she looked over the guests in the house.

"Do you suppose he's here on the island while it's out under the command of someone else?" Caleb asked.

"Unlikely," said Hawkins. "My guess is that it's docked elsewhere."

Caleb watched as the party went on and the governor made his rounds. He kept his eye out for Mr. Lansky, but he was nowhere to be seen. He was likely off elsewhere, gathering more privateers. Part of Caleb wished that he could be one of those privateers, but it was not to be. On the governor's word, he would be put in irons and sentenced to a disgraceful execution and set as an example for other would-be runaways and pirates.

His thoughts were interrupted as he looked into the kitchen window and saw two figures moving. One of them was a young black man he did not recognize – possibly, it was his replacement – the other he recognized as Mama Ellie.

"Here's as good a chance as I'm likely to have," he said. "Keep watch out here; I'll be returning this way."

The young man in the kitchen gathered refreshments and eventually left to serve the guests, while Ellie remained in the kitchen, washing up used glasses.

Caleb rapped quietly next to the window. Ellie stopped what she was doing for a moment to listen, but unable to figure from where the sound was coming, she shook her head and went back to work, mumbling to herself. Caleb knocked a little firmer at the window. Ellie froze and looked up. Caleb had moved from the view of the window, so she still saw nothing.

This time, Ellie cautiously approached the double doors at the side of the kitchen. As she opened them and stepped out looking for the source of the sound, she could see nothing. But just beside her, at the wall of the house, stood Caleb, silent and still. When Ellie turned and saw him, it took a moment to register that he was a living person. As it did register, she nearly gave out a cry, but Caleb grabbed her and held his hand over her mouth, silencing her.

"Please, keep quiet," he said, seeing her concern as he stared into her eyes. When she relaxed, likely out of fear for her own safety, he took his hand away and stepped back.

"Miss Ellie," he said, removing his hat. "It is Caleb."

She looked him up and down. "You sound like him, but you sure don't look like young Caleb to me. You've got a good five years on him at least, probably more."

"I guess I have changed more than a little this past year," he said. "But nevertheless, it is I."

Ellie stepped closer and looked deep into his dark brown eyes.

"Why, I can hardly believe it," she gasped, recognition registering in her face. Then concern mixed with a hint of anger – an anger from her that Caleb had never been on the receiving end of.

"What in blazes are you doing here?" she said, striking him in the chest with her fist. "Don't you know that when Master François sees you, you will be taken and hanged? Possibly worse? You've betrayed trust, and those of us left behind have been the ones who have paid. Where there used to be trust and free roaming on the grounds, there are now curfews and punishments when they're broken. I have half a mind to call the master here and turn you in myself!"

"That is close to the reason I am here," said Caleb. He was incredibly disheartened at this reception, but he kept his voice low. "I wish to speak with his excellency the governor."

"You are truly mad," said Ellie, backing away towards the door.

"No," Caleb said, reaching out to stop Ellie. "Do not bring him back here. And do not tell him of my arrival. Instead, have him come to his study. Make up a reason but have him go there alone. I promise no harm will come to him or to you, if that is your concern."

Ellie stepped back into the kitchen, but kept her eyes fixed on Caleb.

"Please," Caleb implored. "I will make it up to you, somehow."

"There is no way to make it up to us, *troublemaker*," Ellie said. The name and the resentment behind it stung. Ellie had never spoken this way to him. "No way but to be captured and punished yourself. I'll have him come to his study, but if you are having me bring him there to kill him, know this: there are many men here who would come down upon you. I will tell them who it was, and my heart would feel no guilt of it."

"I understand," said Caleb, his heart breaking as he felt a a tremendous amount of sorrow for the remaining enslaved people left here under Duplantier's roof, resigned to their fate and insisting on calling their enslaver "master."

Ellie stepped away into the main room. Through the window, Caleb could see her headed straight for the governor. He hurried over several rooms from the outside of the house. When he came to the window of the governor's study, Caleb pushed open one of the windows and stepped in, closing it most of the way behind him.

A number of papers and maps were littered about the desk. Caleb was tempted to go through them, but there was no time. Instead, he concealed himself on the far side of the door; he held his knife ready as he awaited the presence of the governor. He only hoped that Miss Ellie would do as he had requested of her, but from the reception she gave him, he knew it was likely that she would speak to some of the other men who may in turn be setting a trap for them.

Even worse, Caleb thought if she did alert any of the others to his presence, Captain Santana may pull himself away from the party to launch a search of the town. If he were to see the *Vengeful Goose* docked there at Port de Sang, then they would need to make a hurried getaway.

His thoughts quickly returned to the present as the door

slowly opened. The large figure of Governor Duplantier stepped into the room cautiously. Caleb had positioned himself to where he could stand behind him as he stepped in. The governor was about to open his mouth to call out for his visitor to show himself, but Caleb had his knife out and stuck it at the small of his back: firm enough to be felt, but not forcibly enough to break the skin.

"If you wish to live, I strongly suggest that you remain quiet," Caleb said in a low voice.

Duplantier began to instinctively sputter out of surprise and fear. Whatever Ellie had said to get him in here, it wasn't enough to make him suspect a hostile visitor.

"Keep that noise down," Caleb said. He quietly but firmly used his foot to close the door to the room. He locked it and maneuvered the governor to the desk in the center of the room.

"I have a few simple, but very important matters to discuss with you," he said. "You may now turn and behold your guest."

Duplantier turned and for the first time was given a full clear view of his adversary who bowed theatrically before him. He squinted at first, trying to make out why the face seemed vaguely familiar. Confusion turned to shock and disbelief when he made out the face of Caleb. Shock quickly turned to annoyance and then to smug satisfaction.

"My boy," he said slowly, "how you've grown. We've been considering how we might find where you had gotten off to, and here you come back to me of your own free will? Did you get lost? We thought maybe something happened to you, but it seems you've been doing quite well for yourself. I offer my congratulations, *mon ami*. You have made it back, and I welcome you back into my home."

"Your home seems to be as easy to enter as it was to leave," Caleb said. It would be a lie to say that he was feeling no satisfaction in this encounter. "But I won't be here for long. I just need you to answer some questions for me."

Duplantier's smile faded and his expression became stern.

"You will not speak to me like that in my house," he said,

raising his voice.

Caleb raised his knife up to Duplantier's throat. Duplantier promptly stopped talking and moving altogether.

"I'd rather us not get too excited," Caleb said softly and with a wry smile. "You will remember that I was not the only one who went missing all these months ago."

Duplantier froze and eyed the knife. He looked into Caleb's unflinching eyes. Caleb could see in his face that he was working out his meaning. A spark of realization hit him.

"Bert and Charles Walton," he said when he had put it together. "Their bodies were discovered some time after you had gone from us!"

"That, they were," Caleb said. "I wish I could say I had more remorse for them, but they, as you know, were wicked, cruel men."

"And was I ever wicked or cruel to you, my boy?" Duplantier challenged, now pleading for his life in the best way he could: by negotiation.

"Wicked or cruel?" Caleb repeated, considering. "You never beat me. You provided food and shelter."

"Yes," said Duplantier, feeling more relieved. "I never harmed you, and you always had food to eat."

"You bought me, I was torn away from my family, never to see them again, because men knew that someone like you would pay for me, and pay for me you did. You set me to work as a *child*. You yourself did no wicked or cruel things to me, but were it not for you and men like you purchasing other men, women and children, I would have lived my life with my family. The notion of responsibility is an interesting point that could be debated, but that is not why I am here."

After a moment of careful consideration, realizing how much of a disadvantage he was at both physically and argumentatively, Duplantier relented.

"Very well," he said. "What do you wish to know?"

"You remember your friend, Mr. Lansky?" Caleb asked.

"Of course, I do," Duplantier said. "The man wanted to

have my assistance in taking down the pirates who visited my shores. I was initially hesitant, but you – you have joined those pirates, have you not? It seems you have given me a reason to accept his offer."

"Is he here?"

"Here, at this party?" Duplantier asked. "I am afraid he does not spend much time here with us. Either he is returned to his home in Cartagena, or he's out recruiting more men like me to help take down pirates such as yourself."

Caleb removed the knife from Duplantier's throat, giving a quick cut to the side of his neck, just enough to draw a little blood. The governor closed his eyes and made a concerted effort not to do anything that might provoke Caleb any further.

"The day I left," Caleb said, "Mr. Lansky spoke of artifacts recovered by the Navy, items held at their outposts. I want you to tell me what you know of these items and outposts."

"I have no idea what you're talking about or where they could possibly be. He did not say specifically,"

"I know that is not true," Caleb said.

"You were there when we discussed this," Duplantier said. "Therefore, if he said where it was, you would have heard."

"Many things that were discussed that day that I was not present for. And I was not a sailor at the time."

"It won't do you any good now," said the governor. "This island is no longer friendly to your kind. Fort McConnell is reoccupied and has been supplied. I will alert those men, and they will spring into action. Your ship will not make it out of the bay."

"Be that the case, there's no harm in telling me on which island I might find what I seek. Otherwise, you're of no use to me, and you can die here and now." Caleb returned the knife to the governor's throat.

"There is a fort," Duplantier stammered. "Fort Levasseur. Wraithbone Island. On my honor, that is all I know!"

"It is a shame that your honor means so little to me," Caleb said, putting his knife away. "But I thank you for your hospitality.

You have good help here. Treat them well. You have my mercy today."

He gave a final bow then stepped back out the same window he had entered. The governor was already on his way back to his guests, no doubt to have men sent after him.

Outside the house, when Caleb landed on the grass, he was met by Susan Hawkins.

"There are several men that side of the house," she said, indicating the way they had entered.

"More will be coming shortly," Caleb said. "We'd better return to the *Goose*. The governor did not seem happy to see me."

"Did you get what we came for?"

"Fort Levasseur," he said. "On Wraithbone Island."

"Well done." Hawkins walked Caleb to the garden. "This way is clear."

"Most of the help will be busy with the party, I would imagine."

They followed a perimeter wall that circled the home until they came to the property border.

"Now, to see if we can get the *Goose* to go the direction of the island," Caleb said. "I fear that will be the next task."

They arrived at the ship to see the captain waiting impatiently for them. They were both hurried onto the ship for a hasty departure.

As the *Goose* set sail, Kingsley was down below, arranging the new provisions they had brought aboard. Kennedy summoned Caleb and Hawkins to speak with him in his cabin.

He stood there looking out the windows back at the island, which was quickly shrinking into the distance behind them.

"Take us past East Point and circle around south," he said to Roland, who was at the helm.

"What is the matter?" Caleb asked, his concern growing.

"I am sure you know," said the captain, "that our status is that of wanted men. I am sure you also know that when we set foot on an island that it is of utmost importance that we stick to planned schedules and company."

"Yes, of course."

"You were to assist Mr. Kingsley with his errand at the south side, and you were to return with him. As he returned, you were not present. He had no satisfactory explanation why you lagged behind. There was the great possibility you had been seen and taken. We were prepared to set sail, leaving you behind. We received word that the governor has reoccupied Fort McConnell here; this island is no longer the safe haven it once was. I hope whatever it was you found to occupy your time with was worth it. Do you care to share what the two of you were up to?"

Hawkins, who had been silent until now, spoke up. "There was some reconnaissance we needed to do. We had to follow up on a fresh lead to a trove of treasure."

Kennedy raised an eyebrow. "A trove of treasure, you say?"

"Aye," said Hawkins. "A treasure that is said to be guarded at the fort on Wraithbone Island."

Kennedy scoffed at this. "Wraithbone Island?" he repeated. "I'm sure they have treasure at Fort Levasseur, but whatever is there will remain there as far as I am concerned. Aye, I appreciate the eagerness to find work, but there is plenty bounty out on the open sea that will call to us regularly and at a fraction of the risk. We'll not be setting foot on that island. As for the two of you…"

He looked over the two of them as he contemplated a punishment. "Twenty-four hours in the brig."

"According to the articles – " Caleb began, but Kennedy cut him off.

"Hang he articles!" he retorted, turning back sharply to come face-to-face with Caleb. "You have both shown insubordination and put us all in danger. There must be consequences."

"I was unaware you felt this way of the articles when you signed them yourself," Caleb said.

"There are some very fine principles in there, my boy," said Kennedy, "but like all charters, it is open for interpretation and revision. We shall revisit them, and they shall steer this ship and its crew. In order to do that, we'll start with respect to leadership. How can a ship function if there is no clear command and its men go about the islands doing whatever they wish while putting the ship in danger? No! Forty-eight hours."

Kennedy opened the cabin door and stepped out onto the deck, where the crew were working the sails.

"Armando. Absalom. Please escort these two to the brig, where they will be kept for the next two days."

"Aye, captain," said the men. They grabbed Hawkins and Caleb and led them away.

Captain Kennedy stepped up onto the quarterdeck and leaned forward at the railing beside the helm to address the crew.

"Miss Susan Hawkins and Mr. Caleb have committed an act of defiant insubordination against this ship and its crew. For their punishment, they will be spending the next two days and nights in the brig. Please carry on with your duties and remember, what any of us do is a reflection on the rest of the ship." He motioned for the two crewmen to carry out his order.

Caleb gave Hawkins a sideways glance. She was clearly holding herself back. *Now is not the time to challenge,* she seemed to be thinking. *But soon, the time will come.*

XV

TORCHED & SCUTTLED

For the rest of the day, Susan Hawkins and Caleb sat in the brig of the *Vengeful Goose*. It was not a particularly large enclosure, but it was comfortable enough, so long as it was just the two of them in there.

"If the captain keeps going down this path," Hawkins said, "someone is going to have to deal with him."

Caleb nodded. "That's crossed my mind. I'd like to give him the benefit of the doubt. We'll have to see how it goes from here."

Kingsley entered the room and approached the brig.

"This isn't good," he said, looking at the two prisoners locked up in front of him. "You mind telling me what's going on?"

"We have a location," said Caleb. "The fort on Wraithbone Island."

"So, it is true," Kingsley said softly. "The *Grimoire* is here in these islands?"

Caleb nodded. "That's the best lead we have. According to a man the governor knows, there's all sorts of artifacts there, and it's as likely a place as any for this book to be. But it's not going to do us any good if the captain is not willing to entertain the idea

157

of going there. What's the situation on deck? Have you heard if we have a heading?"

"We're headed southeast," said Kingsley. "I believe Wraith-bone Island is in that general direction, but it seems the good captain is keen on focusing on the merchant ships in the area. He's had some pretty strong words to say, hyping up the men."

"Do they seem to be with him?" asked Hawkins. "I've been part of a revolt before, on this very ship no less, so I can help rally the men if it comes to that."

"There is a general agreement that we can get more by attacking delivery ships and merchants than we can targeting other battle-ready ships," said Kingsley. "I think he is also considering that we may want to ally with other ships to share in plunder."

"I don't know how good of an idea that is," said Hawkins. "Alliances of this sort can be fragile at best."

"And the captain?" Caleb asked. "Is he treating the crew well? He hasn't come down on any of the men apart from us, has he?"

"He seems to be in good spirits."

"That's promising," said Caleb. "Now, you best get back to the galley. You ought not to be seen with us too much; it might be construed as collaborating and scheming."

Kingsley considered that a moment. "Isn't that technically what this is?"

"Of course!" said Caleb. "And we can't have him making that connection."

Kingsley nodded. "You guys hang tight, then, you got it?"

The rest of the day was uneventful for Caleb and Hawkins. They spoke little to one another as time passed. Kingsley later returned to them at mealtime with some stew for them, which they ate in silence.

As the sun set, Hawkins put her eye patch over her good eye and slept soundly. Caleb stayed awake longer, sitting against the bars of the brig in contemplation. He thought of Miss Ellie and what she had said to him back at the house. *Maybe she was right. Maybe everything he had done made things worse for everyone.*

He eventually fell asleep with these things on his mind. He slept uninterrupted through the night and without any further visions from Captain Torch.

The next day in the cell dragged on. Caleb and Hawkins did not speak much to one another, and they had no visitors apart from when Kingsley came by for a small serving of lunch. They sat in silence. Caleb's thoughts continued to go back to the home he had left behind.

It was an undignified slave's life, he thought, *but had he been wrong for leaving it?*

The sun finally went down again, and he fell asleep, contemplating his situation once again.

When he woke the next morning, Caleb saw that Hawkins was already sitting up in quiet contemplation with her eye patch covering her glass eye. The sun was just beginning to rise, and some of the early morning light began to hit them through the grating above.

The hatch opened, and Captain Kennedy approached slowly and seriously. He was followed by two men: Absalom and Cobb. Caleb stood up quickly; Hawkins followed suit.

"I would like to start off by saying that I think you two are fine crewmen," the captain said. "I think you both have the potential to be great assets, and I'd like to see what you can do. Can I count on you today, as we set our sights on fresh prizes? Can I count on you for following orders from now on?"

He spoke in manner and words that were softer in tone, but it also gave the appearance that he was attempting to curry favor, as both of them were liked by most of the rest of the crew. Nonetheless, both Hawkins and Caleb knew that it would be foolish not to go along with him at this time.

"Aye, Captain," they said in unison.

"Open the cell door," he said to Cobb.

Captain Kennedy led them back up to the deck of the ship

as the morning sun was just peeking over the horizon ahead of them and to the left.

"Where are we heading, if I may ask?" Caleb said, looking out ahead for land. There was none currently in sight.

"There's a trading route in the Eastern Islands," Kennedy said, "running from Swashbuckler Island in the north, down past Rogue Island, all the way down and around to Manatee Island. There are several stops for ships; we can intercept them before they arrive at their destination, and we can take whatever supplies they have aboard. If we take them after they are at their destination, we can take their earnings. Either way, it's a good chance we'll see some profit for ourselves."

"Do you think ships along this potentially perilous route might not be armed for defense?" Caleb asked. "They might put up a fight."

Kennedy looked off ahead of them, shielding his eyes from the sunrise.

"Aye," he said. "They'll be armed, but we've got the more skilled boarding party and more skilled gunners, isn't that right?"

Caleb gave an uncomfortable half smile.

"Now, Miss Hawkins," Kennedy said, "would you kindly give Mr. Denis a rest and take the helm?"

Hawkins nodded. "Aye, Captain."

Jacques Denis, who was currently at the wheel, stepped down as Hawkins took over.

Mr. Fullery gave detailed sailing directions to Hawkins, and the *Vengeful Goose* sailed silently for another hour as the sun continued to rise. They flew a neutral English merchant flag in cause another ship sighted them first. In the distance ahead of them, Cobb caught sight of a spit of land.

"That would be the southernmost tip of Rogue Island," said Fullery. "Adjust course south. Keep the land on the larboard side."

Hawkins nodded. She had once again put the eye patch over her good eye and let Mr. Roland assist her in the finer movements.

"Are you sure it is quite necessary to blind yourself while

steering?" Roland asked her as she turned the wheel.

"Quite necessary," she said. "I get a feel for the sea this way. Of all the senses I need right now, sight is hardly one of them. I'll save that for when I am needed in combat."

"I'm not sure I entirely agree with that."

"I understand what you mean. However, I must train this way. If I can fight completely blind, I will have a true advantage over my opponents in the dark."

"If that's what you think," said Roland, conceding defeat, "then go for it."

The *Vengeful Goose* continued past Rogue Island until finally Jake Docks spotted from his perch a ship coming directly towards them from the south.

"Ship spotted!" he called out. "It's a big one. Three masts. Possible complement of cannons."

"Is it a man of war?" Kennedy called up. "A Navy ship?"

"I don't believe so, sir," Docks yelled back down. "It appears to be a merchant ship, but strong and well defensible."

Kennedy looked through his spyglass. Sure enough, it flew the British merchant flag, but it was heavily armed.

"It's larger than us, sir," Fullery cautioned.

"Aye, that it is," said Kennedy with a gleam in his eye. "Large and no doubt full of precious cargo they be wanting to keep safe. If we put the fear of God in them, these dogs will no doubt surrender right off."

"And if they don't?"

"We'll have to make a statement," Kennedy said.

Fullery studied the captain's face. It was clear that he was set in this course of action. "Hoist the black flag, then?"

There was a glint in Kennedy's eye. "Aye. Hold, until we are up on her, then raise the black flag. Ready the men. We'll show 'em what we are made of."

"All hands to general quarters!" Fullery called out. "Load the guns and prepare boarding parties. The enemy is well-armed, so we will be showing no mercy until their surrender. Mr. Docks, prepare to run up the black flag."

The men cheered. There was a new energy in the air as the *Goose* sailed on its intercept course against the unidentified vessel.

They closed in on the ship. Docks raised the black flag, and the *Goose* let loose the cannons. Caleb loaded his cannon with chain shot and aimed high for the main mast. The chain shot grazed the side of the mast, doing minimal damage.

In response, the merchant ship adjusted its course and began to fire volleys back. Several shots tore into the *Goose's* hull. Men worked on the necessary repairs to keep the ship from taking in too much water.

One shot from the merchant ship whizzed past Caleb, throwing him off his feet. Fullery soon gave the order for a party to board the other ship.

Mr. Roland took the wheel as Hawkins drew her cutlass and blindly felt her way to the side of the ship with the boarding party.

A cannonball hit the *Goose's* main mast with a loud *crack*, exploding splinters across the deck.

Caleb, along with half a dozen men led by Cobb, cast out grappling hooks to the other vessel. Amongst a flurry of cannon fire and small arms fire, they boarded the larger ship.

Hawkins moved her eye patch over to her bad eye and leapt to the deck of the merchant ship just behind Caleb, She went to the hatch, dodging strikes from the men. Below, a dozen men operating cannons were firing at the *Goose*. Light shone in through the cannon portholes in the walls and through the hatch above them. Hawkins convinced herself that she could see especially well now with her freshly-uncovered eye and would later insist that it was thanks to the eye patch she had been wearing. She advanced on the men, taking their focus away from the cannons.

On the deck, Caleb and the others engaged the enemy, who seemed enthusiastic fighters for merchants. The captain seemed to present an air of authority as he stood on the quarterdeck at the rear of the ship, giving orders to the men.

Jeffreys, one of the members of the *Goose's* boarding party, drew his sword and moved in against the captain. Caleb attempted to join him to offer support, but one of the other men landed a shot from a flintlock pistol in Caleb's shoulder. He doubled over, clutching his wound. The stinging pain shot through him as he struggled back to his feet.

Another cannonball from the *Goose* crashed into the ship, just missing Caleb and nearly knocking him back off his feet. Jeffreys had engaged the captain in sword combat while both ships continued to fire upon each other.

Two merchant sailors closed in on Caleb; one of them was the one who had shot him. Reapplying his focus, Caleb fought back.

"Surrender your ship," Jeffreys said to the captain as he advanced on him. "Are your lives worth your cargo?"

The captain stood his ground. "We will not be preyed upon. Your ship is the more damaged. We will do what we can to eliminate your kind."

Jeffreys called down to the others. "He's not surrendering."

Caleb struck down the two men attacking him. He outstretched his hand and commanded them to stand back up. It took all the focus and energy he had to do so, and as he looked at his own outstretched hands, the skin began to wither away. All over his body, his skin felt dry and cracked, even with the spray of the ocean consistently hitting him. He was surrounded by a pale green mist that fell around him as the two dead men stood up. He cried out in a mix of pain and determination.

The men defending the ship saw what was happening and immediately began murmuring, speaking of curses and dark magic. Most of them dropped their swords and surrendered them to the men they were fighting.

The captain, however, refused to back down. He barred his teeth and pushed his attack forward onto Jeffreys.

"So, dark magic," he said. "You are not the ship full of

dark souls that has been stalking these waters. What are you, an imitation?"

"Your men have surrendered," said Jeffreys, parrying the captain's blows as he spoke. "Stand down and our necromancer might spare you."

But the captain was not deterred. He struck Jeffreys in the shoulder and caused him to drop his sword and fall back. The captain pulled his sword out of Jeffreys' shoulder and stabbed him again.

Cobb witnessed Jeffreys drop to the deck and cried out, thrusting a knife into the captain's back.

One of the other sailors, possibly the first mate, gave the order to surrender.

"Please, take what you wish and leave us," he pleaded with outstretched hands.

At this time, Hawkins returned to the deck from below, leading several surrendered survivors onto the deck, their hands on their heads. They dropped to their knees in submission.

Captain Kennedy stepped onto the deck of the merchant ship and looked over the fallen men, the cannons, and the fallen captain.

"Tell me," he said, addressing the man who surrendered, "what sort of a ship are you that you are this heavily armed and that you fight this hard to not lose your cargo?"

"We were commissioned to fight back," he said.

"So, you are not merchants? You are just a trap to lure ships like ours in?"

"That man," he said, pointing at the captain lying on the deck, "was a Naval officer. Many of us have training, but we are all non-commissioned sailors. We were all told to expect encounters with pirate ships while we ventured north. If we could take them down, we would be given a bonus."

Kennedy paced the deck. "So, this is what it has come to. Tell me, what is in your hold?"

The man swallowed nervously. "Guns and ammunition. We

are headed to Buccaneers Isle to resupply the fort."

"Not exactly the usual job for a ship like this, is it?" Kennedy asked.

"The Navy has its hands full dealing with the growing pirate presence as well as the threat of a dark force sailing a phantom ship. I didn't put much stock into the stories, but now, I fear those tales are true."

"Aye," said Kennedy. "I've seen the ship you speak of and its crew. That is why I'm afraid we are going to have to take what you have in your hold in order to defend ourselves. The sea is getting more and more treacherous, and we'll have to do what we can for our own survival."

He turned to speak to Cobb. "Well done here, Mr. Cobb." He saw the body of Jeffreys on the deck below. "Pity, that. I trust he fought well. Take what armaments we can move over onto the *Goose* as well as any repair materials so we can get her back into proper shape."

Cobb saluted. "It is done, sir." He took Hawkins, Caleb, Absalom, and Armando Martín below deck to pack up whatever they could take back with them.

Kennedy stayed on deck, watching over the crew along with several of his own men. He managed to recruit a dozen of the merchants to assist with the transportation of the goods and had them swear by the *Goose*'s articles. Even with the help of these men, it took over an hour to get everything squared away. The *Goose*'s mast and hull were adequately patched up by the time the majority of the crates of ammunition were on board. Kennedy was the last to return to his ship.

"I am sorry that the rest of you will not be joining us," he said to the crew as he departed. He held up his hand to stop Absalom and Cobb, who were carrying the last crates of gunpowder across the deck. "Set that down there, Mr. Absalom," he said.

Absalom looked at him quizzically. "Sir?"

"I think we have enough gunpowder, don't you?"

Unsure of what the captain meant by that, Absalom shrugged and set down his crates of gunpowder. Cobb did the same, and the two of them returned to the *Goose*, empty-handed.

The men of both crews looked at Kennedy, expectantly. He casually walked into the captain's cabin and returned to the deck with a lit lantern.

"It is a shame it had to be this way," he said, standing at the railing of the ship. He tossed the lantern into one of the open crates of powder and returned to the *Goose*, cutting the lines connecting the two ships when he was safely over.

The crates went up in a flash of flame and spread quickly across the deck. The remaining crew scrambled about for buckets of water to douse the fire, but it spread too quickly. The men attempting to put the fire out could not get close enough to it because of the heat, so they abandoned it and instead went for the longboats. As many as could fit into the two boats did so and began paddling away in the desperate hope they could come to land.

The *Vengeful Goose* pulled up anchor and began to move again. Caleb watched the burning ship behind them as they sailed away.

Several of the men who came over from the merchant ship began to integrate into the crew of the *Goose*. While he was impressed by their verbal commitment, Captain Kennedy declared that they should have an integration period; they had set sail in opposition to them, after all. They first spent several days in the cramped brig. Then, when they had passed several tests and had spent some time with the captain, they were gradually permitted jobs on the ship.

Caleb continued about his work in silence but kept a watchful eye on everything. After another week at sea, he finally managed to gather Cynthia, Hawkins, and Kingsley together to speak with them below deck.

"I feel like it's important that we have a discussion," he said quietly. The others nodded, listening intently. "It's come to my attention that we have lost our way on this voyage. We're filling our pockets, but we are doing nothing to combat the threat that is out there."

"Yes, the captain seems to have set the mission aside in favor of more immediate monetary goals," Cynthia added.

"He's taken advantage of his new position," Caleb continued. "We are now setting our sights for merchant ships, burning them, and causing destruction, all in violation of the articles we drew up when we set out."

"But is there anything that can be done about it?" Kingsley asked. "We could speak to him."

"I will confront him about it, to be sure," Caleb said, "but I am afraid that it may soon be time to forcibly remove him."

"Are you suggesting what I think you are suggesting?" Hawkins said quietly, not daring to utter the word aloud.

Caleb nodded. He lowered his voice. Even whispering it was a dangerous prospect on any ship, but he knew it must be said. "If we can get the support of the crew, I believe we have no other choice."

He took a deep breath then said the forbidden word:

"Mutiny."

XVI

MUTINY ON THE *GOOSE*

The clandestine meeting disbanded, and the four of them went back to work. Each who was present during the meeting tried to gauge who else on the crew might be sympathetic to their efforts. Mr. Fullery seemed to be getting close to the captain; he could be a potential issue.

During his short time on the ship, Cobb had confided in Caleb on occasion, so Caleb decided it was time to give him a chance to be in on the plan.

It was an overcast and foggy morning when Caleb approached Cobb on the deck of the ship as he was finishing his night watch. Carter Roland was at the wheel. Peter and Davy, two of the new crewmates that had joined them from the previous ship, were there, their attention focused on catching the wind in the ship's sails.

While the others were focused on their duties and most of the rest of the crew were still asleep down below, Caleb took Cobb aside and spoke quietly with him about his concerns about Captain Kennedy's command.

"I have no quarrel with the rest of the crew," Caleb explained, "but the current trajectory of the ship is contradictory to why we took the ship in the first place."

"I see," Cobb finally said, slowly. "Unfortunately for you, aside from a few of the fellows in the brig, many of the men like the direction things are going; I believe most are likely to side with the captain."

"And what about you?"

Cobb shrugged. "Things don't seem that bad to me now. If the situation begins to deteriorate, maybe I would feel different, but I have my freedom, the ship is running, we're getting a profit, and it's all good for me. You and me against the rest of the ship does not sound like good odds."

Caleb was clearly disappointed at this, but he felt it was best he did not reveal any of his other collaborators just yet.

"Don't worry," Cobb said, seeing Caleb's reaction. "You are a decent sort; I won't sell you out, but I also cannot be sneaking around for you."

"Understood."

Defeated, Caleb looked out across the bowsprit of the ship. The sun began to peek over the horizon to their right, off the starboard side, meaning that their course was northbound. Caleb had been studying the charts when he got the chance, and he knew that Wraithbone Island was on one of the southern islands.

"Any ideas where we are headed now?" he asked Cobb.

"We're circling back around the east side of Swashbuckler Island. Captain was keen on taking the fort on the northeast side of Buccaneers Isle that is being resupplied. I think he means to approach it from the north, catching them by surprise."

"He means to take Fort McConnell?" Caleb asked in shock. "Does he really think this ship is cut out for that?"

"He hasn't elaborated on the strategy, but I imagine when we get closer, we will all be filled in on it."

"I see."

Cobb saw the concern on Caleb's face. "You don't think we are up to it?"

"It's not just that," Caleb said. "Sailing us this way takes us close to Spitshine Spot, where Captain Torch and his allies are. Fort McConnell may be the least of our problems."

The morning passed into midday and the *Vengeful Goose* continued north on the west side of Buccaneers Isle as Cobb had said. Caleb and Kingsley went about their work next to one another in silence, keeping their eyes on the crew and their reactions to the captain.

Standing on the quarterdeck behind Roland at the wheel, Captain Kennedy watched over his crew. He also was mostly silent, save for the occasional word with Fullery about the navigation of the ship. He caught Caleb stealing a glance at him once. Caleb quickly turned away, returning to his task, but the captain kept his eye fixed upon him.

Caleb spent what time he could spare near the brig, getting to know the men who were there. At this time, there were four prisoners locked up; the rest of the men had integrated into the crew, but these men here were taking more time. All four of them, as well as several of the others who were walking freely on the deck, had been assigned to Fort McConnell on Buccaneers Isle. Two of the men seemed particularly morose about being here and unwilling to pledge themselves to the ship. Without explicitly stating his intentions to them, Caleb felt certain they would be with him should it come to it.

After mealtime, Caleb relaxed on deck with Kingsley again.

"Where are we?" Caleb asked, looking out to the starboard side of the ship. "From what I understand, we should be close to the island by now. It should be out there."

Kingsley shook his head. "I couldn't say. Captain had us adjust course north a while back."

"That doesn't make any sense," Caleb muttered, his concern growing. "There's nothing but a string of small keys up here, if my memory of the map serves me right. What has he been up to?"

"He's been silent all day," Kingsley said.

Caleb lowered his voice. "Have you spoken with anyone?"

Kingsley matched Caleb's volume. "Martín and Denis are with us. Absalom and Abraham may be trouble. What about you?"

"Dom and Percival are on our side for sure," Caleb said, "so long as we can get them out of the brig in sufficient time. I could not get a read on John or Paul, but I think that they would follow once things begin to happen, again, assuming we get them out of the brig in time."

"And the women?" Kingsley looked around. Susan Hawkins and Cynthia Cove were not currently on the upper deck. "What are they up to?"

"Once they get the word, they should be good to go. Cynthia is waiting below. I will go get the keys to the brig and set the other men free. That will give us more manpower to get this thing done."

Kingsley began to forcibly control his breath as the anticipation welled up. "So, this is really happening? Now?"

"Be calm," Caleb cautioned. "We cannot reveal our intentions until it is time to act. As soon as we have the men from the brig, we'll come to the deck, and I'll confront the captain."

"It is very risky."

"But necessary," said Caleb. "Be ready to fight when I return topside."

Caleb crept towards the hatch, looking behind to see Kingsley waiting nervously near the mainsail ropes.

As he slipped silently below deck, Caleb gave Susan Hawkins a subtle gesture with his hand. She understood the signal, nodded, and stepped onto the deck.

To unlock the door to the brig, Caleb first needed the keys. Fortunately, they were kept not too far away. He found them with little trouble and approached the cell door with them. On the far side of the ship, Caleb could see Cynthia standing in wait, back towards the galley.

The eager men inside began chattering upon seeing Caleb approach with the keys. Tempering their excitement was no small task.

As Caleb began to put the key in the lock, a hand reached out and grabbed his wrist. Caleb gasped and looked up: it was Thomas Fullery, who looked decidedly not amused.

"I think you're a bit turned around, Caleb," he said flatly. "The captain will be wanting to speak with you on deck."

Caleb stammered, looking for the right words, but none came. What was Fullery doing down here anyway?

As if to answer that question, Aaron Cobb stood from out of the shadows just behind Fullery. He had a blank expression on his face. It could be guilt, or it could be disappointment that Caleb was, in fact, planning to go through with his plan. Either way, he had alerted Fullery to this attempted jailbreak.

"Back away!" Caleb said, slapping away Fullery's hand and drawing his sword, but Fullery stepped out of the way of Caleb's blade and drew his own sword.

"Not the best idea, lad," Fullery warned him, running his sword across Caleb's blade.

Compelled to take action, however futile, Caleb hit Fullery's blade away and sprung forward, thrusting his sword threateningly towards Fullery who quickly recovered and countered the attack.

"Let's talk this over with the captain," Fullery insisted.

Caleb swung again, but this time Fullery stepped out of the way and hit Caleb in the back with the hilt of his sword, knocking him off balance.

"Bind his hands."

Cobb led Caleb onto the deck of the ship. Susan Hawkins was there, too, her hands bound with a short rope in the same manner as Caleb; something must have given her away. Aiden Kingsley watched on, undiscovered and ready to spring into action. Caleb caught his eye and gave a very subdued shake of his head, and he relaxed, watching expectantly to see what would come of this.

The other men on deck began to murmur at the sight of the captured Hawkins and Caleb being marched towards the captain.

Captain Kennedy stepped forward and looked down upon them.

"Caleb," he said in a disappointed voice, "what have you been up to now?"

"I caught him attempting to free prisoners and conspiring to mount a mutiny, Captain," Fullery said. "Cobb here says that Caleb tried to recruit *him* for this endeavor as well."

"Is that the truth, Mr. Cobb?" Kennedy asked.

"Aye, Captain," said Cobb quietly. He cleared his throat and repeated his words a little – but not much – louder. "Aye, Captain."

"We found a co-conspirator attempting to coerce others into action." Fullery said, indicating Hawkins.

"Who else was party to this?" the captain asked.

"We were acting alone," Caleb said loudly. "We sought help from others, but when we could find none, I turned to recruit the prisoners in the brig."

Kennedy stepped forward to speak face-to-face with Caleb. "You two and the men in the brig?" he asked, not believing what he was hearing. "What would you possibly hope to achieve, with such a meager force?"

"I wish to challenge you," Caleb said defiantly. Kennedy did not find this amusing.

"You wish to challenge me?" Kennedy repeated. "On what grounds?"

"You have not kept to the articles we agreed to sail under," Caleb accused. "You have set us against innocent ships and have avoided the task we clearly laid out."

"And you have committed mutiny," Kennedy countered. He stepped back and made performative gestures as he carried on. "You have attempted to overthrow your captain and only now submit your grievances after you were caught. You would have put the ship and its crew at great risk had you managed to free dangerous prisoners who were not ready to be freed. You should know that we have our reasons for what we are doing. The last ship we encountered were full of men and weapons that were going to be used against us. Do you think they would have been kind to us if we had sailed on by?

"Nay, Caleb, we are not avoiding the task we set out to perform. We are simply going about it in a way that you do not fully comprehend. I am sorry that you have decided to take these drastic measures, because you are a fighter. You may not be the most skilled fighter, but you have knowledge as to what's out there. I would have liked for you and Miss Hawkins to be involved in our fight against the fort, but I see now that it was not meant to be. Do you maintain that the two of you were acting alone? If there were others who were involved, we might be able to make things easier for you."

Caleb stood his ground. Hawkins stood in defiant silence beside Caleb.

"It was just us, Captain."

Kennedy turned away. "Very well. Mr. Fullery, return Caleb's pistol to him, if you please."

"Sir?"

"The punishment for mutiny," said Kennedy. "We have several small islands out here. I think they'll make a good home for these conspirators. But we don't wish to leave them empty-handed. Remove all but two shots and return it to him. He can then make use of it however he wishes."

Kingsley stepped forward. "No, you cannot do this!" he cried.

Kennedy raised an eyebrow at this outburst. "You know, there are a great many other small pieces of land. I'm sure each of them could use someone if you feel so strongly about this."

Absalom and Martín held Kingsley back as he struggled forward.

"Caleb's connection to Captain Torch will be invaluable to us," Kingsley reminded the captain.

"It's fine, Aiden," Caleb said. "You keep up the fight against Torch in my stead."

Kingsley wrestled himself free of the hands holding them, but stood still, watching the proceedings.

Fullery took Caleb's flintlock pistol and tucked it into Caleb's belt. His hands were bound behind him, so he could not reach for it.

"Toss them over." Kennedy gave the order and walked back towards his cabin. He stopped to speak with Roland. "When it is done, resume course for Fort McConnell."

"For deserted island survival tips, see our companion book, the *Golden Sea Survival Guide.*"

– Golden Sea Grimoire

XVII

CALEB OF THE KEYS

Caleb hit the cool water and went under. The current swirled around him, and he kicked furiously to upright himself. Eventually, he hit the bottom, planted his feet firmly on the sea floor, and pushed himself upward.

As he breached the surface, Caleb took a gasping breath and spat the saltwater and sand from his mouth. When the water cleared away from his eyes, he scanned the horizon, keeping himself afloat by continuously kicking.

Ahead, he saw a small island: one of the keys. Hawkins had already reached the shore. Caleb spun himself around and looked in the opposite direction and saw the ship sailing off into the distance. He obviously could not swim to catch up with it, so he turned back and kicked until he was in shallow enough water to stand.

When he came to the beach, Caleb searched for a rock large enough that he could lean back against and use to help free his hands.

"That did not go as planned," he said.

Hawkins said nothing as they worked on each other's ropes. It took longer than he predicted, but with a little help, Caleb eventually tore himself free.

"We may be here a while," said Hawkins, casting her ropes onto the sand. "Who knows for how long? So, how about we find some food?"

There was vegetation on the small island and there were even some feral chickens running around. If they caught them and could start a fire, they could sustain them for a while, Caleb thought. Exploring the entirety of the island only took several minutes; there was a thick underbrush and two tall palm trees on one side and a sandy beach on the other side. Caleb spent some time gathering coconuts he found strewn about on the ground.

On one side of the beach, Hawkins discovered several wooden planks. She gathered them together and put them next to the pile of coconuts near the bushes. Together, they took the rope that had bound their wrists and used them to tie several palm fronds to use as shade.

The day passed slowly into evening. Neither had eaten anything since they had left the ship, so as the sun went down, they conserved their energy and went to sleep, covered by several palm fronds.

The next morning when Caleb awakened, Hawkins was busy foraging for food. She had managed to gather a few unripe bananas and some guavas.

"It's not much," she said, handing over a bruised guava, "but I thought we could have some breakfast.

Caleb took a bite of the fruit. "We should get our bearings, find out what resources we can have here." It wasn't the best meal either had ever eaten, but it was better than nothing.

They would need to gather some wood for a fire (not to mention, find a way to start one), food, and eventually a means to leave this island. He clasped his hands together and looked down at them. His hands looked a lot worse; it was as if life was leaving them. A part of him felt like he was weakening, but he knew he could not rest – not when there was work to be done.

There was another small island in the near distance similar

to the one they were on. Caleb swam towards it and was able to reach it with no problem. It was, however, even smaller than the Twin Palms Key, as they came to refer to the first isle. There were no trees here, only sand and rocks. There was a skeleton of a giant turtle lying on the beach, but nothing living.

One more island seemed close enough for swimming, so Caleb pressed on. While it was still a small island, it was larger than the previous two put together. It also seemed to have an abundant chicken population.

By the time he made it to Chicken Key, it was late afternoon. This last swim wore him out, so he sat on the beach to catch his breath. Hawkins explored one of the adjacent keys in the distance.

Caleb closed his eyes and let the sun beat down on his face as he drifted out of consciousness. As he slept, he dreamed once again of Captain Ben Torch. This time, it was just the two of them standing on one of these small islands.

"Young master Caleb. Marooned in the keys. Where is your ship?"

Caleb did not respond. He stood there, frozen in place, fear overtaking him.

"You have abandoned your new crew just as you have abandoned me," Torch said. "Or could it be that they have abandoned you?" He laughed and stepped closer to Caleb. With each step, Torch's face changed. His skin was now like a clay mask, and each step he took worked at shaking it loose, revealing fire behind it.

When Torch reached Caleb, his human face had completely fallen away. All that was there standing before him was a skeleton in the captain's uniform, wreathed in flame. Caleb instinctively held out his hands in front of him in a defensive gesture, only to see the skin on his own hands burn away, leaving behind nothing but fingers of exposed bone.

"Return to the *Red Soul*, Caleb," Torch commanded. "Return and complete the ritual with us. The time is near."

Caleb forced himself to turn away. He was no longer on

land. He seemed to be on the ocean, though the water was only up to his ankles. He looked down into the water he was standing in and saw his reflection staring back up at him was also a skull with the skin burned away.

With a gasp for breath, Caleb opened his eyes and shot awake. He was back on the beach of the Chicken Key, and a quick self-examination revealed he was back to his usual self.

"Thank goodness for that," he said aloud. It was now late afternoon, and he was starting to feel parched, having only had a little coconut milk and no fresh water all day.

He removed his shoes and waded barefoot in the water as he circled the perimeter of the island. The sea stretched out in front of him into an endless expanse. If there were any other islands out there, they would not be within swimming distance. Running his hands through the sand on the beach, he came up with some rocks and seashells.

When he had completed a cursory perimeter sweep of the island, he put his shoes back on and started for the interior, which consisted of a few thickets and a dozen palm trees.

The first thing he noticed as he left the beach was another plank of wood. He picked it up and looked it over. Possibly, it was from a supply crate of some kind.

"That would be a turn of luck," he said, "if there's some supplies out here for us." He discarded the plank on the sand. He saw no further sign of civilization.

The image from his dream kept spilling into his mind.

Maybe it was not just a dream, he thought. *Maybe it was some kind of a vision?*

He closed his eyes and concentrated, but there was nothing to concentrate on, so nothing happened. He opened his eyes and sighed, exasperated. It was a calm, sunny day. If it weren't for his current situation, it would be very peaceful. He latched onto that thought and closed his eyes again, focusing on the rhythmic sound of the waves on the shore.

There was something like an indistinct voice behind the

sound of the waves. *Was it Captain Torch's voice?* No, it was different from that, but it was a familiar voice. Then it struck him. It was the sound he had heard when this affair began: he was hearing the sound of the being that cursed him and the rest of the crew, but he could not make out the words.

Focusing on the sound of the voice, Caleb steadied his breathing. A wave of heat shot through him, and he opened his eyes; his left hand was on fire! He yelped from surprise. But he soon realized that while he did indeed feel the heat from it, it caused him no pain. He lowered his hand to the pile of sticks and allowed the fire to catch. As he pulled his hand back out, it was no longer on fire, but the skin was burning away.

"One problem at a time," he muttered to himself, and he wrapped his hand with some loose cloth that he had in his jacket.

The growing fire drew Hawkins' attention; she swam to the small island and found Caleb cooking a caught chicken over the fire.

"Looks like you've got some survival skills after all," she said, impressed. "I heard a strange shout from over here as well. Is everything all right?"

"I didn't hear anything," Caleb said. Ashamed of the outcry he had made, he played it off as if it had not happened and instead focused on preparing their food. He had spent a lot of time in the kitchen, but none of that time was spent actually cooking, and this chicken hardly compared to Ellie's dinners. Nevertheless, they both welcomed the food graciously.

"I wanted to thank you," he said. "Standing next to me against Kennedy. It means a lot."

"It is a shame I could not help more," Hawkins said, still eating.

"No," he said, shaking his head. "It was foolish of me to try. There was nothing to be gained."

"Nonsense," Hawkins said firmly, setting down the bones of her finished meal. "You have a code and a plan that you have bound yourself to. I would support it where I can, as would your friend."

Caleb's thoughts returned to Kingsley. "Poor Aiden," he said. "Now he is trapped aboard that ship, surrounded by faithless pirates, and it's all my doing."

"You cannot blame yourself for the wrongs that others have done," said Hawkins, but that was little comfort.

"I have always held out hope," Caleb continued, "even for the men who have wronged me the most, but what has this trust gotten me in the end? Cobb should have been our ally, but he ultimately sold us out. Sometimes I wonder if I should not have trusted anyone. I thought that life away from the plantation would make things clearer, but it seems to me that morality is even more muddled out here than it was there."

"Putting your faith in the wrong people is not your failure; it is theirs," said Hawkins. "But maybe there's something we can learn from it, moving forward."

When he had eaten his fill, Caleb cracked open another coconut and got what he could out of it. He was beginning to pine for a nice refreshing mug of grog.

That night, as they let the fire die down, Caleb went to sleep with troubling dreams, but they were more feelings and images this time. He sensed fire and the dark figure drawing closer to him. He tossed and turned in the sand, muttering to himself in his sleep until morning when he awakened.

The new day promised more of the same. Hawkins attempted to erect some sort of structure out of sticks and stones, but she was no architect, nor did she know what building materials they would need.

Caleb tried his hand at fishing, using a sharpened stick. While his methods left something to be desired, he managed to spear one fish of impressive size.

He set several hours aside to meditate and practice controlling the dark energy that had been given to him. While he still could not decipher the voice, he felt he was beginning to at least get a better handle at what he was able to do, though every expenditure seemed to take something from him physically, sometimes in the form of a scar and sometimes in the form of dead or burnt looking skin.

The skies began to darken, so Hawkins brought together large palm fronds and vines to fashion a large bowl to collect rainwater. She also set out opened coconut halves in the sand to catch as much water as they could.

As the rain came down, Caleb lay on his back on the beach, bare chested, letting the rain hit him and collect into his various containers set about him. Hawkins, meanwhile, sat under her crude shelter, respectfully giving Caleb some space.

It was not a long shower, but it was refreshing enough, and they were able to store some of it for the next few days. Of course, not knowing how long it would be before the next rain, they each drank a minimal amount from storage over the following few days.

A week passed.

Hawkins and Caleb spoke little, but they began to feel more bonded to one another as survivors, forced to rely on each other for their well-being. Caleb improved his fishing skills, but they still ate little as the days went by. Much of his time was spent in meditation and mastering his connection to the dark energy within him. Hawkins maintained her distance, spending most of her time reinforcing their shelter, as her concern for him grew.

On the fifteenth day of being marooned on the islands, Caleb was wading in the water looking for some fresh seafood when he caught a glimpse of something in the distance.

It was a ship.

Of course, it could be any ship. It could be the *Vengeful Goose*, patrolling these waters after having dealt with Fort McConnell. It could be the *Red Soul*, looking for more ships to prey on. It could even be a navy ship or privateer ship that would take him back to Buccaneers Isle for a hanging. Whatever the case, he figured they would still have a better chance with them than alone out here.

"Susan!" he called out, but she had already noticed it herself. "Give 'em a signal they can't miss!"

Caleb went with Hawkins back to where their small fire was burning and piled more cut pieces of brush onto it, causing it to blaze more intensely and cast dark smoke up into the sky. Caleb stood in front of it, jumping and hollering out to the ship.

To his relief, the ship turned in the water to make its way closer to them. A longboat dropped from the side of the ship, and two men rowed ashore to meet him.

Caleb's expression dropped when he recognized the ship. It was the *Death-Blade*, no doubt still filled with a bunch of rowdy, brooding, and violent pirates. But something was drastically different as he got a closer look at the men in the approaching longboat.

"A pinch of rosemary added to concoctions that deal with removed limbs can help improve blood circulation."

– Golden Sea Grimoire

XVIII

THE RETURN OF NIGHT-HEART

Caleb and Hawkins stood side by side, awaiting the long-boat's arrival at the small island. Two men stepped out of the boat, brandishing their swords. Their skin had been completely burned away; all that remained of them were skeletons, with their torn clothing hanging off their exposed bones.

"Come aboard," one of them said with a raspy voice. "The captain wishes to have a word with you."

"Captain…" Caleb prodded.

The two skeleton men turned their skulls to look at one another a moment, then they looked back at Caleb and Hawkins.

"Yes," the second skeleton man answered. "The dark lord of the sea, Night-Heart the Bloodletter, requests your presence onboard the *Death-Blade*."

Caleb winced at the audacity of the names. It had not gotten any easier to hear.

"Very well, then," Caleb said, stepping aboard the small boat, followed closely by Susan Hawkins. "This should be good."

The skeleton men turned the boat around and rowed back out to sea with their two living guests. They all stepped aboard the ship. It was indeed the same ship Caleb had been on with the hold full of treasure. Above the door to the captain's cabin was an ostentatious plaque with the name of the ship, *Death-Blade,* written in dripping black and red paint.

"How gaudy," Hawkins muttered to herself upon seeing the tacky lettering.

The captain stepped down from the quarterdeck of the ship to greet Caleb. It was the same captain who called himself "Night-Heart" (though Caleb wondered if that was in fact his Christian name), but the skin had withered away from his face, leaving not much more than a skull behind a short black beard.

"We meet again," he said to Caleb, specifically. "Your captain, Benjamin Torch, said we might find you here. Now, we will take you to be reunited with him. He has missed you."

"You're looking more…" Caleb trailed off, searching for the proper words to describe him and the crew. "You're looking much more extreme than the last time we met."

Night-Heart threw his head back and cackled. The effect would have been frightening if it weren't so cliché.

"That's right!" the captain bellowed. "Torch found our ship and killed us all, but then he gave us the gift of resurrection. You have something in you, I sense, but you fear to let it out. Maybe when you and your captain are reunited, you can have your full experience heightened as ours is."

Another man who had been standing silently behind Night-Heart stepped forward. It took Caleb a moment to recognize the master gunner who Caleb had sailed with on the *Red Soul.*

"Mr. Hanson?" he said.

Hanson looked solemn. He still had all his features intact; he just looked pale and had a slight green tint to his skin. "Caleb! I feared we would never meet again."

"What are you doing here?" Caleb asked.

"Captain Torch presented me with the responsibility of overseeing this ship after he converted its crew," Hanson explained. "You can see that they still have their free will; we have just resurrected them and tasked them to patrol the waters.

I think they actually prefer themselves this way."

Night-Heart stepped forward, ignoring Hanson's comments.

"If you please, Mr. Hanson, take these scoundrels to the brig." He gave a gesture with his bony arm, and Hanson took Caleb and Hawkins below.

They walked past the crew, all of whom were skeletal forms of the men who, in life, had sailed this ship. Caleb recognized some of them from their earlier encounter, and by their reaction to him, they seemed to recognize them as well.

"Is this what you have all been up to?" Caleb asked. "Forming undead armies?"

"It's more complicated than that," Hanson said, shutting the two prisoners in the small cell. "And what have you been doing all this time? Playing pirate? It seems to me that you have been just going on with your life as if none of this had happened. This concerns all of us, you know. We have only a year before the new century is here: the deadline the Dark One gave us. The captain is close to gathering all he needs for the ritual to bring him back to the world of the living. What do you think he will do to you when he finds that you have taken no part in his return?"

"I would take no pride in helping him return," Caleb said, but a part of him did feel a pang of guilt; he felt that maybe there was more that he could have done to help fight back, but his inexperience landed him on an island where he had become powerless to do anything.

"Surely, you don't think it can be prevented?" Hanson asked in such a cautious way that made Caleb wonder if there was perhaps some hope for him.

"I think it is up to us to try and find something," he said, hoping to lead Hanson to reveal his true feelings on the matter.

Hanson shuffled about uncomfortably and nervously scratched at his beard. "There is one thing," he said slowly, lowering his voice, "but I cannot help you with this. There is no reason to believe it could actually work."

"What is it?" Caleb insisted.

"One thing I am sure you are aware of that we need to complete the summoning ritual is the proper incantation. We believe it can be found in something called the *Golden Sea Grimoire.*"

Hawkins and Caleb attempted to not react when they heard the name, but Hanson noticed something in their eyes that gave them away.

"So, that is something you have heard of?" Hanson said flatly. "I don't know if I should be encouraged or disappointed that this means it is likely really out there. You see, Captain Torch has been searching for clues to its whereabouts. He has seemed rather anxious about it."

"What are you suggesting?" Hawkins asked. "We find this book and destroy it so that he cannot perform the ritual?"

"No, nothing like that," Hanson said. "Technically, yes, that would prevent it from happening, but as a punishment, the Dark One whom we have been serving will take the rest of our lives and our souls as recompense. He still exerts power over us, even if we are here and he is still trapped in the Lands of the Dead."

"It would be a sacrifice," Caleb admitted, "but it would be our lives in exchange for the rest of humanity."

"I don't believe so," said Hanson. "You see, he would punish us, but he would find someone else, some other way to have done what he wants to be done. He would still be out there."

"Is there any way this 'Dark One' can be defeated, then?" Hawkins asked.

Hanson leaned in closer and lowered his voice to a near whisper. "I don't believe he can be killed directly, but there are other rituals in the *Grimoire.*" He trailed off.

After all the betrayal he had witnessed just since he had left Buccaneers Isle for the first time, Caleb wondered if Hanson could be trusted. He had put his trust in others who had betrayed him; could he be any different?

"I have said too much."

"If I told you that I thought we could stop Captain Torch,"

Caleb said, "would you join us?"

Hanson chuckled at this. "'We'? Who do you mean? The two of you?"

That's a good point, Caleb thought.

"If I could join another crew," Caleb said, "I think maybe something could be done."

"With respect, I think that's part of your problem," Hawkins said.

"How's that?"

"You've been hopping around the islands, joining crew after crew. First you joined Captain Torch, then Captain Santana, then Captain Kennedy. You had to sail under their flags and under their command. Maybe it's time that you took the lead?"

Caleb scoffed. "With the luck I've had, you really think anyone would sail under me?"

Hanson did not respond to the question. He instead reached into his coat pocket and pulled out a flask. "You're no doubt thirsty. Take some of this. I squeeze a bit of lime in it to help fight the scurvy."

He tossed the flask to Caleb and left. Hanson disappeared to the upper deck, and Caleb took a long drink from the flask. He shuddered at the high alcohol content but felt strangely refreshed, if a little light-headed.

"You know," Hawkins said as they settled in their cell, "For what it's worth, I would sail under you."

Caleb raised an eyebrow. "Yeah?"

"Yeah." Hawkins couldn't help but smile. "You've got promise," she said as she took his hand in hers and gave it a reassuring squeeze. "I know there are others out there who would sail under you, too. And not just because of that thing you can do with dead bodies."

The last comment elicited a surprising laugh from Caleb – something he had not expected but welcomed, nonetheless. All the stress that had been building up in him from the events of the past few weeks felt like they were coming to the forefront of Caleb's mind, and having someone by his side alleviated that pressure in a way he could not explain.

"Thank you." The words didn't feel adequate to express his gratitude. He was surprised to find tears welling up in his eyes, for he was not used to being shown such kindness and loyalty, much less from a woman like Susan.

A commotion on the deck interrupted their thoughts as the captain spoke with Hanson, but the voices were muffled through the floorboards, and the conversation was unclear.

Caleb and Hawkins sat together in silence. One crewman came by in the evening to give them an apple apiece, but that was the only food provided that day. They began to miss the island, where they could at least have some fish and chicken, though they had to work hard for it.

That night, Caleb slept on the floor of the brig. Hawkins sat with her back to the bars, her eye patch over her good eye.

They awakened to the sound of men running about on the deck above. The hatch opened, and two skeleton men came running down, chattering as they fussed over a crate of cannonballs that they hurriedly took with them to the deck.

"What's going on up there?" Hawkins asked, moving her patch over to her bad eye, but they ran off back to the deck without giving them so much as a glance.

"Don't mind us," Caleb said to the empty room. "We'll just wait here!"

Loud shouting could be heard from above. It seemed they had come upon another ship; that would account for the cannonballs, obviously. *But what sort?* Caleb wondered. *Could it be one that would fight back?*

With a *crash!* a cannonball tore through the hull of the ship not far from the brig.

It was definitely a ship that would fight back.

Caleb and Hawkins continued to call out for help, not wanting to be locked away helplessly as the ship sank. One of the skeletal crewmen came down to fix the new hole. He hammered away at a board, crudely covering it and ignoring the prisoners' pleas for assistance.

Going back to his practiced meditation, Caleb closed his eyes and focused, reaching out his hand towards the skeleton man. He turned around, and his skull, though lacking eyes, looked back at him. He shook his head as if fighting against an external influence that he did not wish to heed. Hawkins watched, perplexed, but intrigued.

Caleb lowered his hand in defeat, and the skeleton scurried back on deck after grabbing a musket.

"I guess I still have some practice to do with that," he said.

"What was that?" Hawkins asked.

"I might be able to influence them on a subconscious level," he said, "but Torch's thrall is strong."

He took out the flask that Hanson had given him the day before and looked at it.

"Maybe there was something about this that could be used to open the door," he suggested. Hawkins looked dubious, but Caleb continued to openly theorize. "I've heard about strange objects used as keys." At least, he thought he had heard that. Nevertheless, he was convinced that there was some sort of clue on the flask itself that would be his way out of here.

"See if there is any writing on it," Hawkins suggested, getting into the spirit of the plan.

"Nothing," he said. "Maybe a hidden lever? No. It doesn't open."

Another *crash*, and the boat rocked, causing Caleb to lose his footing and fall onto the floor. The hatch opened, and Olaf Hanson came running down. He immediately went for a key ring that was hanging just out of reach of the cell door and opened it for Caleb.

"I would have figured it out if I had more time," Caleb said.

"What are you talking about?"

"This flask," he said. "It was a clue, right?"

"That was a drink," Hanson said, reaching his hand out for

it. "And I'll be having it back now."

Caleb reluctantly gave the flask back to him.

"What's going on up there?" Hawkins asked.

"It's Torch's old rival, Reginald Hennesey," Hanson said. "He's not a kind man, but he has no love for Torch. If you could convince him that you are sailing against Torch, he might be merciful to you."

"Sounds like a long shot," Caleb said, unconvinced.

"You have a better idea?" Hawkins asked.

Hanson handed Caleb his sword, knife, and his pistol.

"I suppose not."

Hanson led Caleb and Hawkins into the sunlight on the deck of the *Death-Blade*, where a boarding party had already begun engaging the skeleton crew in combat.

Hawkins grabbed a sword and started cutting down the crew of the *Death-Blade* as well. She cut down one of the men by surprise, taking his skull clean off. His body continued fumbling about, frantically, waving his sword.

Caleb dodged the flailing body and caught the skull.

"Unhand me, traitorous fiend!" the skull cried out. "Your death will be most painful and ironic as well!"

Caleb reared back and lobbed the skull into the air, over the side of the ship, and into the water.

The directionless headless body dropped its sword and ran, arms outstretched into the water after the skull.

Hanson found Captain Night-Heart standing near the helm of the ship atop the quarterdeck and made his way to him. Night-Heart drew his sword as Hanson leapt towards him.

"Treachery!" the captain called out in surprise as he countered Hanson's blows. "I'm going to tell Captain Torch!"

"You will be unable to do such a thing," Hanson said, "for I intend to strike you down here, today."

"You?" the skeleton captain laughed. "You dare to challenge me? I will destroy you and then I will tell the captain of your treachery! What do you think of that, you sorry excuse for an undead pirate?"

Hanson smirked in spite of the situation. "I think I can take on a childish fool of a captain such as yourself," he said.

"Childish!" Night-Heart exclaimed. "Childish? What talk is this! I am leaps and bounds more mature than you, you witless lout!"

The two of them continued fiercely dueling while jabbering away at one another. Caleb and Hawkins continued the fight below, aiding Captain Hennesey's crew.

When Hennesey's men saw them, they did not question them as they fought alongside them. As the battle seemed to be turning in their favor, Hanson advanced upon Night-Heart.

"A fool you were, and a fool you remain," Hanson said. "Know now that you are beaten, Captain, else a fool you shall die."

Night-Heart growled back in frustration, "Captain Torch will not be lenient. You are dead men, all!"

Hanson thrust his sword forward, and the blade lodged itself in Night-Heart's chest.

"May the sharks find you swiftly," he said, landing a blow with his free fist into Night-Heart's skull.

Night-Heart lost his balance and stumbled backwards to the railing. He fell over the side of the ship and repeated his final threat as he plunged into the sea:

"*Dead men, all!*"

The remainder of the skeleton men were quickly dispatched by Hennesey's crew with the help of Caleb.

A large-framed middle-aged man wearing an impressive coat and a large hat stepped aboard from the other ship. He carried himself like a gentleman, and Caleb correctly guessed this was Captain Reginald Hennesey. He had a stern expression on his rugged countenance.

"Well done, men," he said with a gravelly voice. "You, there." He pointed at Hanson. "I do not know you, but you have assisted in dispatching this rather disagreeable fellow. I am Reginald Hennesey, Buccaneer of the Eastern Seas, Captain of the *Nordlys*.

Who might you be?"

Hanson gave a courteous brief bow as he introduced himself. "My name is Olaf Hanson, Captain. I was sailing under the orders of Captain Benjamin Torch and assisting the captain on his voyage."

Hennesey raised an eyebrow at this. "You turned on your captain? Not a particularly honorable thing to do."

Hanson got down on his knee and bowed his head. "I am at your mercy, Captain."

"That won't be necessary," said Hennesey. "You may be of use. I might wish to send a message to your captain – your former captain, I should say – if you would be willing to deliver it. And this young man?"

"Caleb, sir," Caleb said, following Hanson's example and getting down on one knee, though he did so rather awkwardly in comparison.

"Caleb?" Hennesey repeated. "And who is this Caleb? Caleb Who?"

"We picked him up on the Keys," Hanson said. "He and his companion were set adrift, and we were to bring him to Captain Torch for questioning."

"And what would the Reaper's Hand want with you?" Hennesey asked.

"I was there with him," Caleb said, "the day he met with the Reaper. I was on his crew, and I shared in his curse. If I may be so bold, I have a plan to defeat him, both of them. If we sail together as allies, you could assist me."

"Oh? Let's hear it."

XVIX

BUCCANEER OF
THE EASTERN ISLES

Captain Hennesey had his men return to his ship, an impressively large galleon called the *Nordlys*. His crew secured as much treasure and supplies as they could as water began leaking into the *Death-Blade* from the holes caused by cannon fire. The *Death-Blade* once again hauled a significant storage of treasure in its hold. The damage to its hull was so extensive that when all provisions were gathered, Hennesey set several fires at key points around the ship and let it sink.

"This was a well-fought victory," Hennesey declared to his men. "Shares will be divided from this plunder, with a bonus amount going to Mr. Olaf Hanson, who managed to defeat the captain – what was his name?"

"That 'ere was Night-Heart the Bloodletter," Hanson said.

"Neptune's teeth!" Hennesey exclaimed, contorting his face. "That's rubbish." Then, louder to the crew, he continued, "Mr. Olaf Hanson, who managed to defeat Captain …Night-Heart in combat. We thank you for your assistance. Now, we will head back east to familiar waters and recuperate after such a successful venture."

The men went about their duties adjusting course and

setting sail for their destination. Caleb and Hawkins followed alongside the captain as he made his way down the steps toward the door to his cabin.

"If I may have a word?" Caleb said. "I think you will want to hear our plan."

"You do have a plan, then?" The captain opened the door and entered his cabin, motioning for Caleb to join, along with Hanson and Hawkins. It was a very impressive cabin, built and accessorized for someone with good taste in decor and models of all sorts of sea vessels.

"I am listening," he continued. "What exactly is it that you propose?"

"You know of Captain Torch's situation, then?"

"Does it have anything to do with the ship full of living skeletons that we just dispatched moments ago?"

"It does," Caleb said, "in part." He went on to explain the extent of the deal that Torch made with the Reaper and the power over death that he seemed to have been given as a result of it.

"And you have this power as well, the two of you?" Hennesey asked.

"A portion of it," Caleb said, "but we were meant to act under him as an extension of his power, not as his equal."

"So, that makes you vulnerable to him and susceptible to his influence?"

"Possibly," Caleb stammered. "I don't know to what end, though. I've managed to evade him for some time."

"The thing of it is," Hanson cut in, "there is a ritual that he needs to perform, and the details of it is hidden away in the fortress on Wraithbone Island. If he can perform the ritual, it is likely he will bring a new wave of terror that will dwarf what he has done up until now."

"Very well," said the captain. "We just make sure he does not obtain that book. Are you suggesting that we destroy it?"

"Something along those lines," Caleb said. "If we can beat

them to it and make sure he is never able to perform the ritual, then that would at least stop it from getting any worse. I am, however, hoping that there is something in there that could weaken Captain Torch and stop him once and for all."

"It's an ambitious plan, I'll give you that," Hennesey said. "But there are so many things that could go wrong. You realize that your plan hinges on not only obtaining this book, but that you must also have an experienced practitioner in magic to perform whatever rituals you may find inside?"

"I think it could be done," Caleb said confidently, despite the inner doubts gnawing at him. "We have a voodoo specialist on our side."

"I have to admire your grit, boy," Hennesey said, "and I have no love for Ben Torch, but it seems you are in over your head. You don't have a crew. You don't even have a ship. Didn't I hear you were just picked up off one of those keys out there?"

"That's true."

"And correct me if I'm wrong," he continued, "but I had heard Governor Duplantier of Buccaneers Isle has issued a reward for an escaped slave by the name of Caleb. By his description, it follows that you would be him. He seems quite interested in having you return."

Back around to this again.

Caleb felt lightheaded. "And I trust you would be interested in collecting on that reward?" he asked.

Hennesey paced. "Sailing into Port de Sang is hardly as simple as it was years ago," he said. "Merely docking without the proper paperwork could get authorities on us so fast that such a thing may not be worth it. Besides, there's the issue of the newly-fortified Fort McConnell. Word is, the latest pirate vessel it sank was one called the *Vengeful Goose.*"

Caleb and Hawkins perked up at the name of that ship. Hennesey noticed the look of recognition in their eyes. "You are familiar with that ship?" he asked.

"We know its crew," Caleb said. "Any word of survivors?"

"The captain and a few others escaped capture," Hennesey said. "No word on their whereabouts. Some went down with the ship, but there were a few who were captured and are now awaiting trial and hanging. What of you, then? Will you be staying on with us? You seem to be able to handle yourself, so if it's agreeable to you, you would be welcome to stay."

"If it's all the same to you, when we arrive at our destination, I believe it will be best for me to strike out on my own. I need to see my mission through."

Hennesey shrugged. "Have it your way."

The *Nordlys* sailed two days more until it reached Rogue Island, one of the easternmost islands in the region. Beyond that, it was open ocean for days. The ship anchored at a small peninsula on the south side of the island, away from the main port where the bulk of visiting ships were docked.

Caleb stepped onto the sandy beach with Hawkins and Hanson and looked around. There was a ring of black rocks surrounding a circle of burned ground in the grass not too far off.

"This here's Black Spot Point," Hanson said. "I've never been here personally, but it's been talked about by the crew of the *Red Soul* as being near the place Hennesey and his men hide out."

Captain Hennesey joined them on the beach. "I'm sure you understand I cannot risk taking you to the heart of my encampment for security purposes. It is only for current members of the *Nordlys* crew."

"Of course," Hanson said.

"Now, as promised," Hennesey said, assisted by three men, each holding a wooden crate, "in these crates are your equal shares for the defeat of Captain Knife-Wound or whatever his name was. I apologize for the bulk, but we made good here. I will be going into the market, if you wish to accompany me. It is a hike up the western beaches up to the town, but that is as it must be. There is a tavern called The Twisted Hull that I recommend. Its owners are trustworthy people."

"Thank you," said Caleb. "We'd be glad of the company."

The captain attended to a few matters at the ship, and when he was finished, they walked north along the beach together. The pleasant manners that Hennesey had exhibited to them surprised and intrigued Caleb. Of course, having been a shipmate on his rival's ship gave a remarkably different picture of the man. Men from the *Red Soul* spoke of the violent manner that he would tear through ships, gunning down everyone in sight, and it could very well be that that was how he acted on his raids, and it was likely he would behave that way if he were to board the *Red Soul,* but it was hard to picture unbridled rage coming from this middle-aged man with the slick hair and pencil mustache, however worn his face may be.

"I hate to see what has happened on your home of Buccaneers Isle," he said to Caleb. "We have spent many a shore leave there. It is a fine port, and it is disheartening to see McConnell fortified once more. Many years ago, when he and I were much younger, I knew François, the governor. He was not a governor then. He had no grand interest in international or even local affairs. I'm not sure what happened to him. Maybe he lost his way.

"But I'm sure he would say the same about me: outlaw, man on the run, pirate. Maybe I lost my way, too. Who knows? What is our way anyway? I don't put much stock in destiny. I think lots of times we just improvise and go with what comes our way."

Caleb absorbed this but did not respond. Destiny never really occurred to him, but he did know that living his life with no control was entirely unfulfilling. Maybe that's all he wanted: a little control. And as possibly the ultimate test of his control, he would now be seeking a command of his own.

They arrived at a small town, and Hennesey bade them farewell as he went off in the direction of some small shops. The shopkeepers greeted him with pleasant familiarity.

"They seem to like him here," Hawkins noted.

"Yes," said Caleb quietly. "They do." He quietly recalled the bonds he thought he shared with Mama Ellie back home, Dr.

Rockwell on the *Devil's Thunder*, and even Stephen Kennedy and Aaron Cobb before it had all gone wrong.

"It's probably best if we get away from here as quickly as we can," he said.

"Very well, then." Hanson looked ahead and saw a small dock that appeared to have several vessels listed for sale. He pointed it out to Caleb who took the lead and stepped up in search for someone to speak with.

"The prices seem rather inflated," Hawkins noted.

"This one here is a good size," Caleb said, standing in front of a two-mast brigantine ship. It was just a little larger than the *Vengeful Goose* and much newer looking.

"You have a good eye for ships, my boy," said a voice from behind them. Caleb and Hanson spun around to see a stocky middle-aged man standing there with his hands on his hips, ready to do business.

He extended his hand. Hanson took it and received a vigorous shaking from it.

"Call me Oak," the man said. "We've got the finest ships in the Caribbean."

"Is that so?" Hawkins challenged. "Where are they?"

Oak laughed a loud, raspy laugh. "Why, you're lookin' at them!" He raised his large, tattooed arms and gestured at the ships. He nudged Hanson in his side. "Looking for a first new ship for your son, here?" He eyed Caleb.

Hanson and Caleb gave each other puzzled looks, for Hanson's pale Scandinavian complexion and blonde hair stood in stark contrast to Caleb's dark brown skin.

"Something like that," Hanson said carefully.

Oak laughed loudly again and continued on with his pitch.

"Fresh out of assembly and constructed with authentic Caribbean rubber trees, giving the whole thing a nice bounce to it. Come! Come stand on the deck and tell me what you think."

The three men and Hawkins stepped onto the deck of the ship. The waves gently rocked it from bow to stern.

"Careful now, friends," he said. "Now, come with me to the front of the ship. We call this section of the ship the *forecastle*, or *fo'c'sle* for short. Isn't that neat? It may be a 'four castle,' but I'll only charge ye for one!" He went into a hysterical fit of laughter all to himself.

When he had regained composure, he instructed them to stand side-by-side at the bow of the ship.

"How's the traction on your shoes, there?" he asked, looking down. "Oh, you'll be fine. Feel the waves as it rocks the boat down. Now, feel it as it comes up, and *jump!*"

As the ship rocked up, they jumped up into the air together and were able to get significant height. They landed solidly back on the deck.

"That spring you felt gives you a taste of the quality material that goes into a ship like this. It's got options, too: reclining captain's chair with attached tankard holders is my favorite, and they can be installed in under a day with a minimal markup!"

"I think that just the basic model will be fine," Caleb said.

"Suit yourself," Oak said, "but if you change your mind, you can always come back here and add them later. It does have the essentials: a nice row of cannons on either side of the deck, a new top-o'-the-line wheel for steering (the tiller is so *passé!*), and a generous hold for your personal affects or for anything you may pick up along the way – what you do after you sail away from this place is your business, but I will of course welcome you back if you ever decide to go with any of those add-ons or upgrades. That is, after all, my business."

Caleb took Hanson and Hawkins aside. "I don't think I could afford any of these ships, basic model or not."

"What if we pool our resources?" Hawkins offered. "Use my share of the bounty. You can pay me back later. The important thing is that we get to Wraithbone Island."

"You have mine as well," Hanson offered.

Oak waited eagerly for them to return to the sales talk.

"Well, then," he said. "Have we come to a settlement? And

what is the young skipper's name?"

"Caleb."

"Captain Caleb…" Oak waited for him to finish the name. "You got to have a surname for this whole captain thing to sound right. It gives a sense of respect. It's a title. Don't be shy."

"Something from your recent experience, perhaps?" Hanson suggested. "You proved yourself resourceful on the island where we found you. Caleb of the Keys."

Caleb considered this for a moment. Whenever he hears the name, he would be reminded of the failed mutiny he took part in. But perhaps that could also inspire him to be better than his previous captain. He accepted the name with a sense of humility.

"Keys," Caleb said to the ship salesman. "Caleb Keys."

"Shall I put that on the bill of sale, then?" Oak asked. "Now, I want you to be certain about this. I have a strict 'No Refunds' policy, and I think we should be clear on everything up front."

Caleb nodded. "Yes. Captain Caleb Keys." The name still felt strange in his mouth.

"Splendid," Oak said, getting a fountain pen and preparing some paperwork. "I know someone who does christenings if you wish to make that official. Local. Affordable. Just let me know."

Oak led them into a small building where they finished the official paperwork on the ship.

"Now," he said, "you realize that while this ship is perfectly capable to be manned by three, it is recommended you have a much larger crew to operate it to its full potential."

Caleb nodded. "I understand. We'll be picking up a full crew shortly."

"That's good to hear," Oak said, putting away his pen. "Congratulations on your new purchase, Captain Caleb Keys."

"Thank you," Caleb said, standing up and looking at his new ship parked at the docks.

"One more thing," Oak said. "It is considered bad luck to sail a ship that does not have a name."

Caleb smiled as one name came to mind.

XX

TROUBLEMAKER

Captain Caleb Keys and his small crew prepared the ship for departure from Rogue Island. A temporary plaque on the stern of the ship displayed the name *"Troublemaker."* The three of them picked up essential items for the sea while in town: food, ammunition, and a few flags, Hennesey was kind enough to lend them three sets of clothes that could help them pass for merchants.

"You know," Hawkins said as she took the helm, "it's great that we are sailing into port disguised as merchants, with merchant flags and merchant clothes, but do you think it might raise some eyebrows that our "merchant ship" is called *'Troublemaker'*?"

Caleb considered for a moment then brushed the matter aside. "I believe we're focusing on the wrong thing. When we get to port, we need to find out where everyone is and then devise a way to break them out."

The wind was picking up. Hanson braced himself on the deck as he pulled the lines controlling the direction of the sails.

"And how do you suggest we do that?" he asked.

"First of all," Caleb said, "I think that for appearances you ought to present yourself as the captain. I'll be your manservant."

"Your first outing as captain, and you want people to think I'm your lord?"

"Trust me," Caleb said, "I'd prefer it if I were going under a better circumstance, but I have experience in this. They won't look twice at me if they think I'm just your property."

"OK," said Hanson. "Then what?"

"Then we find our people."

Hanson nodded. He meant *"How do we find them and how do we liberate them?"* But of course, Caleb knew that and was still formulating that plan. Rather than pressure him about it, Hanson decided to let him make the plan in silence.

Because of the strong winds, the *Troublemaker* made good time as it sailed southwest from Bounty Isle toward Buccaneers Isle.

They did not, however, sail to the docks at Port de Sang. Hawkins instead steered the ship along the south coast of the island until they came to the small bit of land where Kingsley's Hex Hut was. They dropped anchor just offshore. Caleb and Hawkins rowed their longboat to the hut while Hanson stayed onboard the ship.

The Hex Hut was not busy at all. They approached the door but heard no activity inside. Caleb carefully pushed the door open and entered. There was a lone girl sitting behind the counter with her eyes closed and mouth hanging open.

"Excuse me?" Caleb said, clearing his throat.

The girl stirred, then opened her eyes. She nearly fell out of her seat when she saw Caleb and Susan Hawkins standing in the shop in front of her.

"Oh, pardon me!" she said, stumbling to her feet. "Welcome to the Hex Hut, Home of Magical Items and Souvenirs. Hey, don't I know you?"

"You're Aiden's niece, Corine, aren't you?" Caleb answered.

She stepped closer to Caleb and examined him uncomfortably close. Her eyes widened as she recalled.

"You!" she said, pointing her finger in his face. "You're that strange guy that Uncle Aiden ran off with!"

"I have a feeling we should have tried our luck asking the governor for help," Hawkins said to Caleb.

"What do you want?" Corine asked.

"Are you here alone?"

She nodded.

"My name is Caleb Keys," Caleb said, speaking slowly and in as calming a manner as he could manage. "I am pleased to meet you. This is my friend, Susan Hawkins. We got separated from your uncle, and we came back here to help him."

"Yeah, well, he got locked up and is set to be hanged for piracy up at the cemetery no thanks to you!"

"Then it is true," Caleb said softly. "Where is he being held?"

"The jailhouse in town," Corine said. "Where else would he be? Where have you been, by the way? Why didn't they arrest you as well?"

"I had a disagreement with the captain of the ship," he said, knowing there was nothing he could say or do to make up for what was now happening to his friends. "I went my own way, but I'm back now, and I want to help."

"Good luck with that," Corine scoffed. "The hanging is tomorrow morning."

Caleb and Hawkins left the hut and made their way northward on foot. They walked in silence, keeping a quick pace as they passed through the center of the island.

When they approached the main town at sunset, they ducked to the right side of the main road to avoid passing by the governor's plantation. They cut through some underbrush and arrived at the backside of the Happy Souls Tavern, near the water.

"Can you see any ships in the harbor?" Hawkins asked.

"A few," said Caleb. "Nothing significant, but we should still be wary. Anybody out and about on the coast?"

Hawkins shook her head. "The coast is clear. You know how to get to the jailhouse?"

"It's just across the way, next to the Golden Doubloon General Store."

They casually walked across the street hoping not to draw suspicion to themselves in case there was anybody else out and about.

There was a notice board next to the jailhouse entrance; a section of it was dedicated for bounties on various criminals, runaway enslaved men, and pirates. In the center, there was a handbill with an illustration of Caleb that included a personal notice from Governor Duplantier condemning him and promising a cash reward.

"Looks like you've already begun to make a name for yourself," Hawkins said.

Caleb removed the handbill from the board and rolled it up.

"To remind me of home," he said, tucking it away in a pouch.

They circled around the side of the general store around the back to the jailhouse. There were windows to the sheriff's office and a view of the cell block, but there was no close access to it.

"What do you see?" Hawkins asked, keeping watch around the side of the building.

"I can see Martín, Fullery, Simon, and Absalom," he said. "I see others, but I cannot make out their faces. Hold on; there's Aiden." He came away from the window and stood with his back to the wall of the building.

"What do you plan to do here?" Hawkins asked.

"There's not much we can do from out here. They're locked up and guarded pretty good."

"So why did we come here?"

Caleb stood silent for a moment.

"Captain?"

He snapped back to the present. "Sorry. I just had an idea. We should return to the ship and get a good night's sleep."

Hawkins didn't follow. "You're just giving up, then? I suppose this was rather hopeless."

Caleb couldn't help but smile as he dwelled on his idea. "Hopeless?" he repeated. "No, good Ms. Hawkins. I think we've got just the thing, you and I."

Back at the *Troublemaker*, Olaf Hanson waited for Caleb and Hawkins to return and fill him in on the details. When they did, Caleb had Hanson tell him everything he had experienced while being with Captain Torch – the abilities he had seen, how they manifested, and where the power came from. As Caleb had guessed, the energy he had been able to harness was something that derived from life, usually drawn out from an external force, like the killing of another person. The energy was then housed in the person who took the life and then used to heal or even to manipulate the dead.

Captain Torch had taken soul energy from the crew of the *Death-Blade*, essentially killing them all, but he was able to resurrect them by giving a portion of that energy back to them so they were able to sail on their own with a sense of preserved identity, though they were still under the thrall of Torch.

Caleb listened intently and shared his own experiences, particularly of what he learned and felt while on the Keys.

"This energy," he said, "do you think it can come from any sources other than other people?"

"I couldn't say for sure," Hanson admitted, considering. He had not seen Torch or any members of the *Red Soul* crew generate that energy in any other way. "But I have observed that some of the crew, the captain included, can draw upon energy from their own selves. It comes at a cost. As you may have seen, some of the crew have a more extreme deathly pallor than others. The more energy you draw from yourself to do these deeds, the more humanity you lose. If you go on using these powers, you will lose yourself to it and become like Night-Heart and his crew: the living dead."

This made sense to Caleb, given the toll on his body he had noticed.

"It may be too late for us," he said, as the reality of it all sank in. "Whatever happens, we may end up losing ourselves to it, but even if that's the price, I believe we need to do whatever we can."

"What's on your mind?" Hanson asked. "What exactly is your plan?"

Caleb and his crew of two rested well that night on the ship and were up bright and early at sunrise. When they arrived back in town, Port de Sang was already bustling, in stark contrast to the empty town the night before. In the streets, there were not as many pirates as Caleb had been used to seeing, having lived on this island his whole life, but many of the people who were there did not all look well-off, either. Some middle-to-high-class folk walked about town. Also present were an assortment of commissioned sailors, many of whom no doubt were stationed at the newly restored Fort McConnell. There was also an increased population of poor fishermen, beggars and similar men. Some of them could be heard murmuring about a hanging that was to occur later this very morning. Some mentioned it with excitement, while others spoke with disappointment and fear.

Another ship had docked that morning, and people unloaded crates and barrels onto the pier. Caleb did his best to conceal his face. He pulled out the spare eye patch that Susan had given him many days ago and strapped it over one eye. Hanson walked ahead, placing himself between the view of Caleb and anyone they guessed might recognize him.

Hanson occasionally said things like "Come on, keep up," to him to put on a show of a master-servant relationship, to which Caleb walked on silently, with his head down. They reached the northern edge of the town where a short path led to a small cemetery.

"I just wish we had been able to dock the ship closer," Caleb lamented, looking behind him at the hills beyond the town.

"It can't be helped," said Hawkins. "I believe we can make this work."

A small group of onlookers gathered around the graveyard. A new set of gallows had been erected there and could be seen from the town.

"Do you think the governor will be here?" Caleb asked.

"It is highly likely," Hanson said. "Are you prepared to do this?"

Caleb nodded. "You?"

"Ready, Captain."

The title seemed to boost Caleb's confidence. "I think if we try, we can get a real rise out of this town."

They took inconspicuous positions on either side of the viewing area in front of the gallows. Hawkins stood next to Caleb and kept her hand at the hilt of her cutlass.

Several armed men stepped forward with the bound prisoners. Aiden Kingsley was in the front, and his presence was causing a little bit of a stir due to him being a recognized shopkeeper on the island. Some people were genuinely distraught that he was there as a convicted pirate.

Behind Aiden walked Martín, Fullery, Simon, and Absalom, all bound with rope. Unlucky Jake was there, too, his good arm now in a sling. He also now wore a patch over one eye. Dr. Gold was also present. Behind him were five other men, whom Caleb recognized as the former merchant sailors Paul, Dom, Percival, John, and George.

Caleb signaled to Hanson with a subtle nod. Both of them got down on one knee and placed their palms on the grass underneath them. A few of the bystanders gave them inquisitive looks before dismissing it as some sort of gesture of solidarity or mourning. That wasn't what they were here to see, so they refocused their attention back to the platform where Governor Duplantier now stood, accompanied by a young boy, holding a large palm frond to shade the governor from the hot sun as he addressed the crowd.

Seeing a young child taking his old position gave Caleb a flash of righteous anger. Another child was forced into a life of involuntary servitude to undeserving man.

"As your governor," Duplantier began as the crowd quietened down, "it is my unfortunate business today to present you with a dozen persons tried and convicted of piracy. Their ship lost in the futile attack against Fort McConnell, which still stands in defiance of their illegal and violent acts, these are the pirates who were caught. Few surrendered and took the high road, accepting our employ, and they have pledged themselves to help hunt down the others of their crew who have slipped away beyond our grasp. Those rascals will be caught and tried as well, and they shall meet a similar fate. And now – "

He hesitated as a murmur began to grow from the crowd. The prisoners standing on the gallows awaiting the noose also looked around in confusion. The trees in the area began to quickly whither. The grass beneath their feet wilted. The color from all the foliage around them that had been alive and vibrant was now gray and dead.

The earth beneath them shook. Murmuring from the crowd progressed into gasps and screams as a bony hand erupted from the dirt in front of them. The door of one of the distant crypts swung open and dead men began to slowly step forward.

Duplantier looked on in shock. "Voodoo witchcraft!" he said, pointing at Kingsley.

Kingsley's eyes darted back and forth. "I must protest!" he said. "I deal in tourism, but I think things are going to be a little different after today!"

The governor, speechless, backed away and ran back into town towards his home. The men who had brought the prisoners out here began forming a protective circle, training their rifles at the advancing undead.

"Fire!" one of them shouted.

Shots rang out. One of the undead was struck in both

shoulders but continued to advance. Three more completed unearthing themselves from the ground and started shuffling forward, arms outstretched.

The guards reloaded their weapons.

Caleb stood, taking his hands off the ground. His head spun, as if he had rapidly stood to his feet while severely dehydrated. The skin around his face looked disheveled and dry. He shook off the discomfort, took out his knife, and ran toward the bound prisoners. Hawkins drew her cutlass and stood threateningly behind him, ready to defend if any attackers came at them, but all were focused on the unholy dead advancing upon the scene.

"My brother!" Kingsley cried out when he saw who it was who had come to his rescue.. "I knew it was you."

Caleb finished cutting his ropes and gave him a knife as well. With Hanson's help, Kingsley and Caleb quickly cut the ropes from the other prisoners' hands.

"New friend?" Fullery asked, indicating Olaf Hanson.

"Another former member of Torch's crew," said Caleb.

"Good first impression."

"So, are you with us?" Caleb asked, loosing the bonds on Fullery's wrists. There was little time to argue.

"Aye, Captain."

Then with a shout, Fullery ran passed by several of the undead and tackled one of the guards. They rolled in the grass, and Fullery took the gun from the guard's hands and struck him once with the butt of it. He then dropped it and took a saber from the man's sheath and wielded it against the other men standing around him.

"I trust you have a ship to pick us up?"

"Something like that," Caleb said. "We must make a run for it."

Jake stepped off the platform, planting his foot and his peg leg on the ground. "You're having a laugh, right?" He sighed and loosened up what remained of his limbs.

Caleb led his crew through the cemetery into the jungle,

away from the town. The sound of the guards clashing with the undead men faded into the distance.

"Where are you taking us?" Percival asked, checking behind them for any followers. "There is no harbor here."

"We have to avoid the main roads," Caleb said. "It is safer this way. We'll make our way south past Grosswater Lake towards Blister Island."

"I have to see Corine," Kingsley said. "She needs to know I am safe."

"That's up to you," Caleb said, "but we are pressed for time."

"I'll run ahead," he offered. "I can be there before the rest of you."

Caleb nodded. "Very well, then. Mr. Hanson, you're my quartermaster; you run along with him and ready the ship for us. We'll be wanting to set out of here as fast as we can move."

Hanson and Kingsley ran on ahead; Caleb led the rest of the crew at a steady pace across the island. Fullery supported Jake's bad arm around his neck, helping him move faster. They matched pace with Caleb as they hobbled towards the west coast of the island.

"I must say, Master Caleb," Fullery said between breaths, "your appearance is most unexpected and equally appreciated."

"Then I trust there will be no problem between us?" Caleb said. "You stood by your captain against me. Can I count on you to stand by me when the going gets tough again?"

Fullery nodded. "Kennedy led us into a foolish assault against the fort then left us to be overwhelmed. As we began to dig in, Mr. Roland was the first to go down, still at the helm of the ship as our landing party pressed forward on land. We were surrounded and did not even notice when Captain had abandoned us. I ordered the surrender, I thought, to save our lives."

"Why didn't you take the governor's offer and fight for them?" Caleb asked. He looked over at the four former merchant sailors who were walking with them. "Surely, especially with your history, they would have welcomed you."

"We attempted to!" Percival lamented. "We told him we would pledge ourselves to sail under his flag and under his authority."

"They didn't even listen when we insisted that we were prisoners," Dom said in disgust. "It seems they wanted to make a statement with us more than they wanted allies."

"Indeed," said Fullery. "They marched us up there anyway with the wild story that we were the stubborn ones who refused to join them. Despite his claims, nobody was offered letters of marque."

"What about the Cynthia?" Caleb asked. "What happened to her?"

"I was on the ship when it was going down," Dr. Gold said. "I saw Miss Cove make it to a longboat. Where she went to or whether she made it away safely, I'm not sure, but she was not taken prisoner with the rest of us."

"And Cobb?"

Fullery shook his head. "Shot down during the ground assault."

"Heavy loss," Caleb said, and he meant it. Despite his betrayal, he felt sorry for Cobb and understood the predicament he had been put in.

They came to the west coastline of the island and followed it south. Dom pulled out a spyglass, put it to his eye, and looked out to the sea.

"I see a shape on the horizon," he said. "There's a ship out there. It couldn't be yours, could it?"

Caleb took the spyglass and looked out. "I think we're in trouble," he said. "As much as we can, pick up the pace."

The ship was, in fact, the *Devil's Thunder*, and it was on a course south towards where the *Troublemaker* was waiting, unmanned.

"Having the proper components for a ritual is important, but the most important is the voice and how it is used."

– *Golden Sea Grimoire*

XXI

PARLAY

The crew sped along the western shore down to the crossing to Blister Island. The *Troublemaker* was there, waiting for them, with Hanson already on board. Kingsley was on the shore, loading supplies into the longboat when Caleb and the others came running up to him.

"We have to get the ship under way immediately, Mr. Kingsley," he said as he and the others began to crowd into the boat.

"Hold up," Kingsley said. "You cannot all fit in here. And there's the supplies to be considered."

"Take half of us, then," Caleb said. "The *Devil's Thunder* will be closing in on us momentarily."

Caleb took Hawkins, Jake, Dom, Martín, and Percival into the longboat with Kingsley, and they rowed as quickly as they could to the *Troublemaker*. When they arrived, Hanson welcomed them aboard. They unloaded the boat and sent it back with Kingsley to pick up Fullery, Absalom, Simon, Paul, John, and Dr. Gold.

"What is the status, Mr. Hanson?" Caleb asked. "Are we ready to set sail?"

"Aye, Captain," said Hanson. He sensed the urgency in the men as well as in the captain. "What news?"

"The *Devil's Thunder* is on its way and will be here momentarily," he said. "I do not think we are ready for a conflict. We should be prepared to flee if need be. I will attempt negotiation, but we cannot be delayed any further. Understood?"

"Right," said Hanson.

Caleb addressed the present crew. "All right, men," he said, looking about. "And Miss Hawkins," he added, "be ready to weigh anchor as soon as the reset of the crew is aboard. Mr. Martín, I understand you are a ship's pilot, is that correct?"

"*Sí, Capitán,*" said Martín.

"If it's agreeable to you, then," Caleb continued, "I will have you take the helm. Mr. Docks, go aloft and keep a lookout for us. Mr. Fullery, Dominic, Percival, be ready at the capstan and pull up anchor as soon as the others are aboard. We'll be ready for them."

"Aye, Captain!" the men called back together.

"And for you, Miss Hawkins," Caleb said, turning to face Hawkins, "would you do me the honor of being my navigator and first mate?"

"Aye, Captain," she said with a salute.

The longboat returned shortly, and the rest of the crew made it aboard. As soon as the longboat was secured, the men began to raise the anchor. John and Absalom, the largest of the men who came aboard the second boat, assisted bringing up the anchor.

"Good job, men," Caleb said. "I would like to take a brief moment to welcome you all aboard the *Troublemaker*. I, Captain Caleb Keys, am honored to have you all. Some of us have had some differences in the past, but I believe that we can all work together for a common purpose. We have an important goal on this ship, but I will also make sure it will be profitable for us all."

The men cheered at this.

"Now, Captain Santana of the *Devil's Thunder* is approaching us. I believe him to be an honorable man, so I am pleading with you to not fire unless I give the word. I have hope that, should we engage with him peacefully, we may be able to come to terms. Understood?"

There was a mixed reaction to this.

"He is here to take us back to the gallows!" John called out. "I will not stand by and surrender after just walking free!"

Caleb scanned the faces of the crew. He could see that he had to offer them hope. "If that is his intent," he said, "then we will blow him out of the water!"

This was met with cheering.

"But I ask you to put your trust in me to speak with him first."

"The *Devil's Thunder* is approaching!" Docks hollered down from the crow's nest.

"Raise a flag of Truce, Mr. Docks," Caleb called back.

"Aye, Captain," Docks said, rummaging through the flag box for the white flag.

"I hope you know what you're doing," Hanson said quietly to Caleb.

"Me too."

Caleb kept his composure in front of the men, but his face gave away a small hint of uncertainty. He stepped forward onto the fo'c'sle and drummed his fingers impatiently on the railing.

The *Devil's Thunder* approached at such an angle to avoid a broadside, but whether they were being cautious or preparing to turn for a surprise barrage of cannon fire, it was impossible say. Through his spyglass, Caleb recognized Benedict Johansen standing on the deck and looking back at him through a spyglass of his own.

"Your word, Captain," Hanson said, standing by.

Caleb figured there should be someone familiar accompanying him, but also someone imposing to help give him credibility. Kingsley was familiar and nonthreatening, but of the crew, Dom was the largest. If he had both of them by his side, he guessed that would be a good look.

"Have Aiden and Dominic prepare to come with me to the other ship."

Hanson nodded. "Aye, Captain."

"Bring them here and fetch the speaking trumpet," Caleb added.

"Mr. Dominic and Mr. Kingsley," Hanson called, "step forward."

Dom released the line he was pulling and handed it off to Percival, who took over his duties for him. Kingsley brushed himself off and joined Dom. Hanson led them to the captain at the bow of the ship.

"Mr. Dom," Caleb said, "I understand you have some experience in negotiations?"

"Limited, sir," he said. "They had me on the speaking trumpet on the merchant ships partly due to my natural loud voice."

"That will do, then," said Caleb, taking the trumpet from Hanson and handing it to him. "I'll guide you in what to say. Now, hail them and request speaking arrangements, if you please."

"Aye, Captain." He took the trumpet in hand and put it to his lips as the ship entered vocal range.

"Attention, approaching vessel," he called out in a voice so loud and commanding Caleb nearly stumbled backwards. While he was physically imposing, Dom had been relatively soft-spoken.

He was no longer.

"Attention, approaching vessel," he repeated. "We offer a flag of truce. The benevolent Captain Keys wishes to come aboard to speak with your good captain."

"Come again?" Johansen called back. "Captain Who?"

"Captain Caleb Keys of the *Troublemaker*," he said. "He wishes to peacefully negotiate an alliance. We will make no trouble," he added.

"'We'll make no trouble'?" Caleb repeated under his breath. Dom shrugged.

Johansen stood there a moment, speaking with a rather animated crewman.

"Stand by, sailor," he finally called back.

The crewman ran back across the deck of the *Thunder* to the stern, where Captain Rafael Santana stood alert behind Mr. Bogall at the tiller. The man said something to Santana then rushed back to the Johansen at the fo'c'sle, delivering a message.

"Our captain, the honorable Rafael Santana will permit your captain and one companion aboard, unarmed, for discussion."

Dom looked to Caleb for confirmation.

Caleb nodded.

"That is acceptable," Dom called out.

"Bring your ship alongside ours," Johansen said.

They went through procedures to bring the two ships alongside one another. Men from the *Devil's Thunder* tossed grappling hooks to connect them and brought out a gangplank for Caleb to cross over.

Caleb stepped across it with Kingsley close behind him. Dom stood on the *Troublemaker* and watched.

As they stood there on the plank, Santana's pace quickened as he greeted them.

"By the sea," he exclaimed, his countenance lifting. "Is that young Caleb? It cannot be." He took his hand and shook it. "You look terrible. I hardly recognized you."

"It is good to see you," Caleb said, genuinely relieved to be standing in front of his old captain, "but I must emphasize that we are boarding your ship in an act of faith. When our business is finished here, we wish to return to our ship unharmed. If we do not return, my men have orders to sink this ship with us in it."

Kingsley remained silent but turned his head slightly to look back at their ship. As far as he knew, no such order had been given.

"You have my word," said Santana. "On my honor, no harm shall come to you or your crew, and you shall be returned safely to your ship."

Caleb nodded his gratitude and stepped the rest of the way onto the deck of the ship.

"What is this 'Captain Keys'" business?" he asked. "Just how many names do you have?"

"No more, I hope," said Caleb. He gestured to Kingsley. "You remember Mr. Kingsley?"

Santana took his hand. "A pleasure to see you again," he said. He ushered them to the doors under the ship's quarterdeck. "Join me in my cabin, if you don't mind. We can speak freely there."

They went into the room where they each took a seat.

"I must admit," Santana began, "I have mixed emotions seeing you here, now. You are well aware that I am tasked with the capture of pirate ships in these waters. While you were a fine crewman under my command, you are, in fact, a wanted man on multiple accounts. Your old friend Dr. Rockwell had some choice words to say of the two of you after your rather foolish departure from Swashbuckler Island."

"But you will honor your agreement and let me return to my ship?" Caleb asked.

"I will not go back on my word."

"Not that I object to it, but why may I ask, did you agree to those terms?"

"You made a rather bold gambit, and I respect that. The question is, why would you take such a risk to speak with me? It is only fair to hear your side."

Caleb recounted his tale to Captain Santana, filling in all the gaps in his story.

"Captain Benjamin Torch is terrorizing the islands with his navy he has been assembling. But it is just the beginning. He has been growing in power these past few years, but there is something that he is after that could make all of this that he has been doing seem like nothing. He has made a deal with a dark entity that resides in the Land of the Dead. This Reaper gave him power, making Torch his Hand, acting in his stead in the Land of the Living. But this thing that Torch is seeking may be the key to stopping them once and for all."

"And what, may I ask, is that thing?"

Caleb hesitated. "I cannot tell you," he said, "for our own safety. But it is something that we are close to obtaining. When we do so, we will launch an attack against the *Red Soul,* and we will want any assistance we can get."

Santana poured a cup full of wine and took a sip of it.

"So, you are here to ask me to let your ship go so you can then ask me to later fight beside you?"

"Yes," said Caleb, confidently, "to fight against the ship that threatens us all. And whatever my personal past is, this ship that is out there has never engaged in piracy. I wish to make it clear that I do not align myself with Stephen Rockwell or approve of his actions when he led the assault on Buccaneers Isle shortly after betraying and abandoning me. Our path is one that is focused on justice, not greed."

"Perhaps," Santana conceded, "but your spokesman who called to us looks very much like one of the men who was scheduled to hang this very morning for an assault upon Fort McConnell. Are the men on your ship innocent, or are they running from the law the same as you? I am sorry, Caleb. Good intentions aside, you are playing with fire."

"That's all I can afford to play with," said Caleb. "What else would you suggest I do? Given the choice between a life as an enslaved man and that of an outlaw, I may as well see what I am capable of doing out here. The man you heard at the speaking trumpet was a merchant sailor set to hang because he was on a pirate ship, even though he was there as the pirates' prisoner. Like me, he was betrayed by Governor Duplantier and never given the chance to pursue a free life. Meanwhile, Captain Torch is out there threatening all of us, free men and slaves, privateers and pirates.

"Give us a fortnight. You bring your ship to confront the *Red Soul* on my signal, when we have obtained what we need. I will personally surrender myself and my ship to whatever punishment is due."

Kingsley sat up at this. "Captain…"

Caleb quietly held up his hand to keep him quiet. Kingsley reluctantly stopped speaking as Santana considered the proposal.

"My commitment is to justice in all its forms," Caleb finished.

"I will take it to my superiors," he eventually said. "We will be prepared to set sail from Buccaneers Isle in fourteen days' time. If you still wish to set sail together, approach Port de Sang with the white flag of truce flying, and we will speak again. But no tricks, or we will be forced to take you in."

Caleb stood and shook Captain Santana's hand.

"Thank you, Captain."

"A mind focused on the task at hand can work wonders, but if it is left unchecked, it can lead to obsession."

– Golden Sea Grimoire

XXII

ROGUE ISLAND RENDEZVOUS

The crew cheered when Captain Caleb Keys and Aiden Kingsley returned to the *Troublemaker* safely.

"I have to hand it to you," Fullery said, taking Caleb's hand, "I had my doubts, but it seems you have a golden tongue."

"What happened over there?" Hanson asked. "What sort of alliance did you rope us into?"

"This ship is not a criminal ship," Caleb said. "He has no claim on it. They know they are being threatened with total destruction by Torch and his men, and they need ships like ours as allies. We set a time and place that our ships will meet to sail against the *Red Soul* in allied combat."

The crew murmured contentedly about this. Caleb stepped into his cabin. Kingsley followed and closed the door behind him.

"What about the rest?" Kingsley asked. "That bit about promising to surrender to him when this is all done. How do you think those privateers will react when we do not surrender to them?"

Caleb stood silent.

"When we *do not surrender*, Caleb," Kingsley repeated. "If we surrender ourselves to them, we'll be sent to the gallows

221

again, and there will be no one coming to help us this time."

"This is of course assuming that we make it successfully to the other side of the confrontation with Torch," Caleb said. "If we stop him, then whatever happens to us afterwards won't matter."

"You can say that for yourself," Kingsley retorted, "but do not presume that for the rest of us."

Caleb remained even-tempered. Resigned to the situation, he looked exhausted. "Are you going to tell the rest of the crew?"

"No, I'll keep silent," Kingsley assured him. "Under protest, I'll keep your secret, but only because we need them."

"We're going to need a little more help," said Caleb as he laid out a map of the nearby islands on the table. "Can you send Miss Hawkins in here?"

Kingsley fought the urge to resist Caleb's request but said nothing. He stormed out of the cabin and onto the deck. Caleb took a seat and sat there in silence a moment, studying the map.

They sailed around the south side of Buccaneers Isle and adjusted course eastward. They could make it to Rogue Island, where maybe they could meet up with Hennesey before striking out to Wraithbone Island. To get there, however, they once again would be passing the dangerous waters of the Existential Deep.

Caleb had sworn he had seen something himself when they were out that direction before, *but had he? Had it just been the influence of tales mixed with the influence of his actual current situation?* He looked at his hand. The skin was drying up and beginning to peel off. Like the skeleton pirates of the *Death-Blade,* his life was beginning to fade away.

When all of this was over, would he even be alive to face judgment and execution? he wondered.

His thoughts were interrupted by his cabin door opening. Susan Hawkins entered, looking concerned. Caleb hastily put a glove over his hand, but that did not hide the discoloration that had begun to spread on his face.

"What was it you wanted, Captain?" Hawkins asked.

It was intended as a sign of respect, but hearing his friend call him "Captain" instead of his name gave Caleb a cold and distant feeling. He brushed it aside and got to the point.

"I could use some of your navigational advice," he said. "I've been going over the charts; the fort lies on the north side of Wraithbone. If we strike from the north, we might be able to get in, get what we need, and leave if we are fast enough.

"The fort is set up to defend against ships arriving from that sea," said Hawkins. "We would be going against a fully stocked array of cannons. It would be safer to land and approach on foot from the south."

"If we could dock, have a landing party, then have the rest of the crew move the ship for a quick pickup while some of the men sabotage the fort's defenses, that could be something."

"That would be risky," said Hawkins, looking over Caleb's shoulder at the map. "The waters are treacherous, and we don't have much manpower at our disposal. It's just this ship, and the crew is small and inexperienced in that sort of maneuvering."

"You're right," Caleb said. "We need Captain Hennesey's help."

"Rogue Island, then?"

Caleb nodded. "Yes. Thank you, Susan. If you will do me the favor of making the course adjustments, I'll remain here for a moment and organize my thoughts."

"Consider it done."

Hawkins left Caleb alone in his cabin.

As the day went on, the *Troublemaker* passed the north side of the Existential Deep. Caleb stepped onto the deck and spent some time silently looking out across the starboard railing on the fo'c'sle, the vast, dark water, and the constant dark clouds that hung over it.

Once or twice, he saw something break the surface of the water. *It was likely just a large fish jumping,* he said to himself. Whatever the case, he felt uneasy as he scanned the waters. It was as if that part of the sea had been cursed with darkness. Could the Reaper be using this part of the sea as a gateway already? But nothing so significant was out there: it was just the open ocean.

To calm the crew's nerves as they sailed past the Deep, Simon played a peaceful tune on his violin. Absalom sang softly along to the music, his voice unexpectedly sweet.

Hawkins approached Caleb and stood beside him. He acknowledged her, and she handed him an apple and took one for herself.

"What do you think?" she said, looking out at the ocean.

"I don't know," he said, quietly, so the others could not hear him. "I think things are getting worse. I don't know what all is happening, but I keep feeling the Reaper clawing at me, trying to get in my head. I just hope we're doing the right thing."

"We are."

Caleb managed a grin. "Yeah?"

"Fort McConnell was one thing," said Hawkins. "They didn't have a captain who had their back. And if we focus on an infiltration rather than a full assault, I think we've got a good chance."

"Thanks," he said. Whether or not Hawkins believed what she was saying, Caleb almost didn't care; it was good to hear some supporting words.

"What do you think of Captain Hennesey?" Caleb said, breaking the silence.

"He was not the kind of person I thought he would be from his reputation," Hawkins said. "If we can give him enough of an incentive, I think he will be there for us."

"That would be a welcome change," Caleb said, not fully convinced.

"You're worried about Aiden?"

Caleb nodded. "I dragged him into this. I dragged a lot of

people into this. I just wish I knew that I was doing the right thing."

"I'm sure the crew would like to know that as well."

"What are you saying?"

"I just mean that sometimes as a captain, you need to keep things close to your chest, but other times, you need to let them know what you're all about. Captain Kennedy started off right, but he did not end up matching the face he presented to us at the beginning. I guess you have the chance to be a better captain and learn from where he went wrong."

Caleb saw where she was going with this. "You mean the ship's articles?"

Hawkins nodded. "A mission statement is certainly a start, and even more so if you can remain true. You hold your crew to it, and we'll hold to you. Just because we've been thrown into the deep end of hell on Earth does not mean we must be devils."

"What choice do we have?" Caleb asked. "I want to hang onto hope, but the situation seems dire."

"There's always a choice to act with dignity in the face of adversity," Hawkins assured him. "You know me; I'll gladly cut down anyone who stands against me, but if we can find a choice for a respectable alternative, I would see that we face it."

"Thank you," Caleb said. "You will help me write our new articles?"

"Of course."

She subtly slid her hand over and grasped Caleb's, reassuringly. They did not vocalize their thoughts, but Caleb was almost certain he could feel a bright energy flow from her into him as she held onto his hand; while the energy from the Reaper was debilitating and unnatural, Susan's energy felt pure and healing, as if she were restoring hope in him. they stood side-by-side in silence as the ship continued to pass around the edge of the Deep.

The crew remained alert, not engaging in conversation, but putting their focus into their work. Hawkins eventually left

Caleb alone at the bow of the ship where he stood, gathering his thoughts as he looked far off at the dark sea.

The sea gradually became less threatening, and the crew relaxed. Caleb went back to the captain's cabin and requested Fullery, Hawkins, and Hanson join him.

When the four of them were inside, Caleb closed the door behind them and went around to the other side of his desk, silently considering everything that was happening and about to happen.

"I realize I may be a bit late doing this," he said, "but I believe it's important. We had articles aboard the *Vengeful Goose*. I believe many of those articles were good, and I think that if we could keep each other accountable to them, we could avoid the problems that arose there."

"Here, here," said Fullery.

"I wish to be a fair captain," Caleb continued, ignoring the interruption. "If there is something that concerns any of you, I want there to be a path for you to come to me and bring it to my attention. But we face a unique challenge ahead of us. I don't think it's a secret to anyone here that I want us to be able to stand against Benjamin Torch. I want us to keep our eyes on that task, but I also want you to feel free to address any concerns you have on the state of things.

"Mr. Fullery, you were there when we wrote up articles with Captain Kennedy. I would appreciate your hand on these. Any input you have on how we can avoid repeating the same mistakes made before would be most welcome.

Fullery nodded.

Caleb took a deep breath, then continued speaking.

"We may be outlaws here on this ship – runaway slaves, men who have escaped the gallows, and persons who have engaged in violence and theft whilst on the seas – but I do not wish that to be our legacy here and now. I believe we can aspire to be more than that.

"As someone who was raised enslaved in an unjust system, I

may have no place in civilized society anymore, but I do not wish to be the man that others have labeled me. At this point, I don't know whether it's possible for us to acquire legitimate letters of marque, allowing us to be privateers for the King – I don't even know whether that would be desirable at this point – but I believe we can behave as such. Perhaps, we could be better.

"Even if we stay on the run indefinitely," Caleb continued, "I would like to maintain dignity and integrity, and I would consider it a great favor if you held me to that."

A small chorus of affirmations echoed round the cabin, and the four of them immediately began to work together on the writing of the articles. When they were satisfied with what they had come up with, each of them put their signature at the bottom of the parchment.

They then stepped out of the cabin and called the attention of the crew. Caleb looked over the group standing in front of him and expressed his heartfelt thanks and began to go over the articles.

Much like the articles written for the crew of the *Vengeful Goose*, these new articles detailed payment for the crew and for ship provisions. Much of the crew knew or easily guessed Captain Caleb's history as an enslaved young man, so they were not surprised to hear an article forbidding the holding and selling of slaves aboard this ship.

The articles made clear that the mission of the *Troublemaker* was to fight back against the forces of Captain Torch and the dark figure they referred to as the "Reaper."

When Caleb had finished laying out the details of the articles, Kingsley spoke up.

"When the threat of the *Red Soul* is eliminated," he said, "what will become of us then?"

Caleb knew that he was being called out on the promise he had made to Santana about turning himself and his crew in.

"When the threat from Captain Torch and his undead crew is gone," Caleb said slowly, "I will make a plea to Captain Santana of the *Devil's Thunder*, requesting pardons for us."

Kingsley was skeptical. "And if he denies us?" he asked. "What repercussions will we face? Are we to surrender our fate in the hands of that hunter?"

Caleb fumbled searching for the right way to answer.

"Aiden makes a good point," said Absalom. "I think we ought to know what we have to look forward to after all this is done."

"You're right," Caleb said. "You deserve to know this. When we met with Captain Santana, I told him that I would surrender myself to him after we successfully defeat Captain Torch and his Reaper."

The men of the ship murmured amongst each other.

"And I plan to do as I said," he continued, "but I have no intention to make you all suffer for this. I will go to him alone and speak on behalf of you all. However, what you choose to do once I step down as captain of the *Troublemaker* will be up to you. I hope that you will take an honorable path, as I will strive to do.

"In the meantime, we are headed to Rogue Island to form an alliance with Captain Hennesey who will coordinate with us in a strike at Fort Levasseur, in order to retrieve a valuable prize that should turn the tide in this struggle."

Hanson thrust his fist upward, followed by a hearty cheer. The rest of the crew followed suit, shouting out in response to the enthusiasm demonstrated by Mr. Hanson.

"Now," said Caleb, "Bring us to Rogue Island."

"Aye." Hawkins consulted the charts while Martín remained at the helm. Hanson made certain the rest of the men were clear on what their duties were.

Kingsley stepped up to the quarterdeck to speak with Caleb; Kingsley could see past the brave face that Caleb was putting on for the benefit of the rest of the crew.

"You don't have to go through with surrendering yourself," he said. "I don't fancy being out here without you as captain."

"I appreciate your loyalty," Caleb said. "It was unfair of me to presume surrendering everyone to the mercy of the crown.

But I believe giving myself up would be sufficient in honoring our deal." He looked out across the ocean. "Out here, we don't have much apart from our word, and I would like to keep mine."

Kingsley's hand subtly went to something hanging around his neck underneath his shirt. Despite his attempts to be discreet, Caleb's eyes were drawn to the movement.

"What's that?"

"Oh, this," Kingsley said, unfastening the string. "It's my gris-gris." He revealed a small cloth bag, closed with a long piece of string. "Just a little something passed down from my family: a talisman to protect against bad luck or evil spirits. It's one of our top selling items at the Hex Hut. I never put much stock into that kind of magic, but I like keeping it around because it reminds me of my family. And you never know, it could come in useful. From the looks of it, we need all the luck we can get warding off evil djinn."

Kingsley opened the bag and turned out its contents. A few coins and stones emptied out into his hand, followed by several small animal bones bound together. A scrap of rolled-up parchment with some scribbled writing on it was there as well.

Noticing the attention Caleb gave to the paper, Kingsley nodded. "Some words of protection written to me by my mother's father. Let's hope it does the trick."

"You are close with your family," Caleb observed, a small tone of envy, however unintended, slipped through.

"I am," he said. "You don't have any family?"

Caleb shook his head. "I have images I have seen in my dreams of a man I believe is my father. I was separated from my family when I was too young to know them. I don't even know if they are still alive. It's probably pointless to hold onto any hope of ever seeing them again."

"I don't believe hope is ever pointless." Kingsley closed his eyes and muttered a few words too softly for Caleb to catch. He gave the piece of paper a kiss then put it and the other items back into his bag.

"I think I could make a new family out here," Caleb said wistfully. "But that's still no substitute for what I've missed."

Kingsley gave him a reassuring touch on his shoulder. "For what it is worth, you are welcome to come visit me and my family if you can avoid crossing paths with the governor."

"Thank you," Caleb said, looking out at the ocean ahead. "It may soon be a good time to ask the spirits of your ancestors for whatever guidance and protection they can offer."

They reached Rogue Island at the end of the day. Some of the crew elected to remain on the ship for the night; the rest went into town and stayed at The Twisted Hull Tavern and Inn.

In the morning, Caleb walked with Hanson, Hawkins, and Dom south along to beach towards Black Spot Point, where they hoped to find Hennesey and his ship.

As they drew close, black smoke rose from the horizon, and Caleb saw the very thing he was afraid of.

"It's Torch," Caleb said under his breath.

On the beach ahead of them, there was Hennesey's ship the *Nordlys*, fully engulfed in flame. Near the burning ship was the *Red Soul*, firing upon it. Hennesey's crew were on the distant beach, fighting a horde of skeleton men.

As they drew near, Caleb and his crew left the beach and hid in the cover of the nearby underbrush. The sound of clanging swords grew louder. Hanson peeked out from their hiding place in the underbrush and saw Captain Torch and Captain Hennesey locked in combat.

"That's him," Hanson said as he reached for his sword.

"No," Caleb cautioned. "Not like this."

Hanson disregarded Caleb's warning and stepped closer to the dueling captains.

"We have to help Captain Hennesey."

Torch locked swords with Hennesey and looked up to see Olaf Hanson approaching. Torch had no discernible expression as his face had by now completely decomposed into an exposed skull with a long red beard.

"Mr. Hanson, you have returned!" he snarled as he pushed Hennesey out of the way. Hennesey struggled back to his feet and swung his sword at Torch, who parried and countered, while speaking with Hanson. "I feared for the worst when I heard about our dear Captain Night-Heart. Poor soul." He laughed at his own choice of words.

Hennesey thrust forward and stabbed Torch, just missing his neck. Torch cried out in anger, dropped his sword, and grabbed at the one lodged in his shoulder.

"Miserable cur!" he shouted, pulling the sword out of his shoulder and pushing Hennesey away from him.

Now disarmed, Hennesey backed away, looking for an escape. Torch advanced towards him to strike a killing blow, but Hanson intercepted it.

"Well parried, Mr. Hanson," Torch spat. He raised his free hand and began to extract the life from him, causing Hanson to rapidly deteriorate. Orange flames burst forth from underneath Torch's red coat, lighting him up from the inside as he drank in the life from the Scandinavian pirate.

"Did you forget that I have power over all of you?" Torch said, looking into the lifeless eye sockets of the skeletal form standing in front of him.

Hennesey fled Torch and Hanson, who now stood side-by-side on the beach.

Still hidden behind the nearby underbrush, Caleb started to rise to his feet, but Dom and Hawkins held him down, preventing him from giving himself away.

"We cannot let that happen to you," Hawkins said.

Caleb wrestled free of their grasp, but remained down, fighting the urge to call out.

"Come with me," Torch said to Hanson. "There is much yet

to be done.

Hanson obediently walked forward beside him as they went to the water. Torch recalled his crew, and they fell in line, returning to the longboats that would take them back to the *Red Soul.*

"That's unfortunate," said Dom.

"Get to Hennesey," said Caleb.

When Caleb, Hawkins, and Dom caught up to him, Hennesey struggled for a moment until he recognized Caleb in front of him.

"You look awful," Hennesey managed to say. "What are you doing here?"

"We're getting ready for a heist," Caleb said. "We could use your help."

"You're too late," he said, wincing at the pain from his injuries. "I have no ship. The rascal just burned it down."

"I'm sorry, but can you gather your crew together? If you will join us, we are about to take something from Fort Levasseur that can help us defeat him."

"Fort Levasseur?" Hennesey repeated. "Are you mad?"

"Nearly," Hawkins said. "Come on. We'll have our doctor take a look at you."

They made their way to the beach, where they found two dozen survivors still there, left by the retreating skeleton crew. Hennesey helped rally them, and they went together back to the *Troublemaker.*

"What happened?" Fullery asked when he saw the men coming aboard. "Where's the other ship?"

"Torched," Caleb said. "We have to hurry now, because we lost Hanson. He's one of them now. He's under their control, and there's no telling what that means. It's a good bet Torch can find out all the information he has about us and our plan, so we need to get a move on now. You're my new quartermaster, Mr. Fullery."

"Aye," said Fullery. "All hands, prepare to set sail."

XXIII

FORT LEVASSEUR

The *Troublemaker* sailed southwards to Wraithbone Island. Martín remained at the helm, steering the ship with a minimal crew remaining on deck to assist him.

Dr. Gold took a look at Hennesey. When he had a chance to patch up him and the other surviving members of his crew, he sent them to see Caleb below deck. Caleb stood at a table where he had spread out a large map of Wraithbone Island and some of the nearby islands for everyone to see. A majority of his crew stood around, looking it over with him and waiting for orders.

"We're under a time constraint because we may be racing Captain Torch here," Caleb said, "but here is our current situation. The fort is on the north side of the island. We believe what we are looking for is stored in a hold that is patrolled by multiple guards. The fort regularly receives supplies, delivered by ships similar to the one that some of our men here once sailed."

"You're not wrong," said Percival, running his hand down the wall of the ship. "And the *Troublemaker* is not unlike some of the supply ships we sailed to McConnell and other forts. I can make sure we fly the proper flags and help us on the approach."

"Very good," said Caleb. "Have any of you ever been to this

island? Any information can be helpful."

One of Hennesey's men stepped forward. He had a very youthful face with flowing locks of hair and looked more like a high-class young gentleman of promising social stature than he did a seaman sailing on a rough pirate crew "Aye," he said in a soft voice. "I have been inside the fort on several occasions," he said.

"Excellent!" Caleb said. "What is your name, sailor?"

"Oddface," he said. "Stubby Oddface."

"I'm sorry," Caleb said under his breath. "How very unfortunate."

"What's that?"

"I said, how fortunate," he said in an attempt to cover his faux pas. "It's very fortunate that you are here with us."

"Oh, capital!" Oddface said with a winning smile. "I find myself fascinated by fortresses and their designs. They are quite impressive. I've been to Fort Levasseur multiple times; any excuse I could get. It's a most impressive structure. The walls are eighteen feet thick, one-hundred twenty feet high, armored with cannons. It has five levels of defenses, a network of tunnels below the surface, dungeons, and storehouses. You know, it may have a French name now, but it was actually constructed in the mid-sixteenth century by the Spanish, commissioned by King Carlos the Fifth. In fact, in those days, it was called –"

"I find all of that incredibly fascinating," Caleb lied, interrupting Oddface before he could go any further. "What can you share about this area of the fortress?" He pointed out the place on the map where he had indicated was the possible target location.

"Yes, of course," he said, looking over the very simple map. "As you said, that would be the storage hold. They hold all sorts of treasures there."

This got the attention of the other men.

"What sort of treasures?" Docks asked.

"Easy, men," Caleb cautioned, seeing the glint in some of the men's eyes. "Remember, we have one very specific purpose here."

"Aye," said Docks, "but what harm be there in lining our pockets while we're at it?"

"We mustn't weigh down ourselves with extraneous booty," Hennesey said, stepping in, "but it would be best to bring an extra bag or two to be safe."

"Can we get back to this?" Caleb insisted, his annoyance beginning to show.

"Forgive us, Captain," Hennesey said, bowing slightly, "but it is difficult to pass up such a promising score."

"I understand," said Caleb, "but we must do what we can to minimize any charges that may come up against us if we wish to enlist the help of Santana and his privateers." This was met with begrudging agreement. "On that note, I imagine there may be some resistance as soon as the book is lifted."

"Yes," Oddface agreed. He pointed to a small harbor on the map. "This southern dock is where the fort must be approached by water, but the whole south side of the fortress overlooks it with the largest arraignment of cannons. A clean escape from this point of departure would be unlikely. If you permit me, I suggest that as soon as the landing party disembarks, the ship be brought 'round the island to the rock face on the west side. It would be difficult to navigate, but there are fewer cannons on that side, and you may be able to make a more expedient getaway from there."

Caleb nodded. "Very good. I'll have the *Troublemaker* swing around as soon as our landing party disembarks. You, along with Mr. Docks and Miss Hawkins, will join me on the island under the guise of French suppliers. Mr. Docks, I understand you are an accomplished lockpicker?"

"I have some experience there," Docks said.

"Good. We will count on you to help us get behind any doors that may not be readily accessible. Mr. Kingsley," Caleb continued, "I will count on you to help us identify the book."

Kingsley stood at attention. "I'll do what I can," he said.

"And finally," Caleb said, turning to speak to Percival, "while the rest of us descend into the hold to recover the *Grimoire*, you and Dominic make your rounds on the west side and disable as many cannons there as you can, and meet us for pickup in the water below."

Percival and Dom nodded. The two of them may have worked together as merchant sailors, but they both had been prepped in methods of disabling enemy weapons.

"There's one problem we might have," Hennesey said.

Just one? Caleb thought to himself. He was already going over all sorts of problems that he had, and it was his own plan.

"If we are supposed to be a supply ship," Hennesey said, "won't they know that we aren't who we say we are when we pull up and have no supplies to deliver?"

"Ah, but we do have supplies," Caleb corrected him. "This is a new ship, fully stocked."

"So?"

Caleb gestured to the ship, waiting for him to understand.

"I still don't get it," Hennesey said. "Short of delivering your own supplies to them, how can you convince them that – oh. Oh, no."

"He gets it," Kingsley said, having already put it together on his own.

"You are going to voluntarily give these men your own stores?" Hennesey said, shocked at what he was hearing.

"Aye," said Caleb. "It will be a small price to pay for entrance into the hold of their fortress." He clasped his hands. "Shall we get to it, then?"

The crew of the *Troublemaker* spent the rest of the trip to Wraithbone Island prepping the ship, disguising it as a supply ship. Caleb went to his wardrobe and picked out an outfit that he had selected for such an occasion.

When they arrived on the east side of the island in view of the fort, the harbormaster waved them in.

They docked, and Caleb stepped out, dressed in his costume, looking as pompous and self-important has he could manage. He fixed up his face, making the wear and tear on it look like aging, presenting himself as a middle-aged, scarred sailor.

It's all about confidence, he told himself.

The harbormaster came walking up to them quickly as Fullery and Hennesey secured the ship.

"I beg your pardon!" the man said, waving to call attention to himself. He was a short, rotund man with spectacles, holding a stack of paper in one hand. "I say, I beg your pardon, sirs!"

"Yes, what is it? I am in a terrible hurry, *Monsieur,*" Caleb said smugly, in a put-on French accent. Stubby Oddface stood by his side. "We have these supplies we were bidden to deliver. Things got turned around, all messy, so disorganized – these aggressive anti-pirate measures, *non?*"

The man flipped through his papers, checking through names. "I do not see you on the schedule, Captain. What is your name?"

"This is Captain Jacques Moreau," Oddface said.

Caleb flashed a confident smile as he looked down at the short man. "And who might you be, little man?"

"Me?" He stuttered, obviously flustered about the whole situation. "I'm Sterling Smith, harbormaster. But as I said, I do not see you on the schedule."

Caleb rattled off some muttered phrases in French that he had often heard Duplantier say when in a state of annoyance. "It is just as I feared it might be. Did I not tell you, Philippe?"

He elbowed Percival, who stood next to him with a crate of gunpowder. Dom and Kingsley brought up the rear with several other crates from the ship.

"Uh, *oui!*" Percival said, but he continued to speak in his regular voice rather than put on an accent. "You said this many times, *Monsieur Capitaine.*"

"Fine, fine," Smith said, jotting down some notes. "This has happened before with the logs. They do not always tell us little people everything that is going on."

"'Us little people'?" Caleb repeated with disdain.

"Meaning myself and my colleagues, of course," Smith quickly amended. "Not you, uh, *Monsieur.*"

"*Naturellement,*" Caleb said. "I shall speak to my friend, Governor Duplantier on the Buccaneers Isle. If you please, lead the way, Smith, and we shall conclude this little diversion, and I shall get back to my own business, which I assure you is more important than anything happening here."

Susan Hawkins and Jake Docks also stepped out of the *Troublemaker.* They joined their captain, each of them carrying small crates of supplies.

"Of course it is," Smith said, writing things down on his paper. "Of course. Now, if you please, the name of your ship?" He strained to see the name written on the hull. "*Troublemaker?* That's a peculiar name for a delivery ship."

"*Mon Dieu!*" Caleb exclaimed, clasping his hand on his forehead in a display of dismay. "*Troublemaker,* indeed? It is a — what is the word? — It is a jest. A play on the words. You see, my family is a musical family. Not *Troublemaker.* It is *Treble-Maker.* They think it is funny. It is, is it not?"

Smith strained, looking at the writing. "But it is spelled 'Trouble,' *Monsieur,*" he pointed out.

"Do not challenge me, little man!" Caleb said, and he swung his hand out and slapped Smith on the face with an open palm. He nearly broke character, wincing at his own impulsive action, but he quickly recovered.

"Of course," said Smith, surrendering to Caleb's madness. "I apologize."

Kingsley and Docks stared back at Caleb with wide eyes.

"Hurry up now!" Caleb shouted back at Percival and Dom, who were lagging behind. They hurried along, carrying their crates. As they caught up, Caleb whispered to them in his regular voice. *"I am so sorry."*

From the deck of the *Troublemaker*, Hennesey and Fullery watched as Smith led Caleb, Oddface, and Kingsley up the path to the fort. Hawkins, Docks, Dom, and Percival followed closely behind. When they had finally got out of sight, Fullery addressed the remainder of the crew and had them stand by to get the ship ready to sail.

Smith led Caleb and his entourage through the gates at the entrance of the fort.

"If you will walk this way," he said, "I will alert the commodore and make your presence known."

"That is acceptable," Caleb said, dismissively, as he stepped through the gates and into the open fort courtyard.

Oddface looked at the walls of the fort and could not help but point out, "The concrete that was used in these walls is called 'coquina,' which employs a mixture of crushed shells and rocks…"

As Oddface continued speaking, Caleb glanced behind him and saw the *Troublemaker* begin to move slowly from its position.

So far, so good.

Caleb turned back to take in the sights of the fort and stopped fast as he found himself face-to-face with someone he did not expect to find here; the pale figure of Cynthia Cove stood in front of him, a coy smile on her face.

"Isn't this a surprise," she said, eyeing Caleb and his crew.

"Ah, *Monsieur Capitaine*," Smith said, noting the recognition in Caleb's face when he saw Cynthia, "I see you already know our new ambassador, Miss Cove. She arrived here this morning."

"Delighted to see you again," she said, coolly, not making any signs that she would give him away. "And Captain, is it? How quickly the world turns."

"If you will excuse us for a brief moment," Caleb said to Smith.

"I thought you were in a hurry?" Smith said. "And you'll be wanting to see the commodore?"

"There is time," he said, irritably, still feigning his French accent. "I must speak with the *mademoiselle.*"

"Suit yourself."

Smith led Caleb's crew forward into the fortress while Caleb and Cynthia stepped aside.

"What are you doing here?" Caleb asked in a sharp whisper, dropping the Frenchman persona.

"I imagine the same thing you are doing, *Monsieur*," Cynthia replied. "Reconnaissance."

"Good, good," said Caleb, looking around. "I am glad to see you made it here away from Captain Kennedy. He's not here is he?"

"I've not seen him since McConnell," Cynthia assured him. "And speaking of, I believe that the last time we saw one another, you were headed to a small spit of land in the Lost Keys. I would love to hear the particulars of your escape, but it looks like you have business to attend to. You run a supply ship now, I see?" She craned her neck to see Smith looking back at them, arms awkwardly hanging at his side.

Caleb gathered his wits and started to return to his character of the French captain. "If you wish to join us, say the word."

"I wouldn't miss it," Cynthia said with a sly smile, "*Monsieur.*"

Caleb returned to Smith, who was showing the men where to set down the crates. Smith was clearly frustrated, speaking with Kingsley as Docks was intentionally setting the items down in all the incorrect places.

Seeing that Kingsley and Docks were monopolizing the attention of Smith and his men, Percival and Dom took the opportunity to slip away unnoticed into a side corridor.

Shortly after the two had left, the commanding officer of the fort, Commodore Edwards, arrived to greet Caleb.

Edwards was a young man for such a lofty position, not much older than Caleb. He appeared to have been very pampered and had the stern face of someone who appreciated being taken seriously with no patience for any sort of "nonsense."

"What is going on here, Mr. Smith?" he asked his harbormaster without taking his eyes off Caleb. Caleb knew that look well; it was the distrustful look of someone who resented seeing an African-born man like Caleb anywhere but working in the fields. He had experienced this resentment even as a slave in the house. It had bothered him then; now, he took it in stride. As far as the commodore knew, Caleb was a successful and respected captain. As long as that did not disrupt the current mission, he would lean into this new character and embrace the commodore's discomfort.

"Munitions delivery," Smith said.

Edwards turned to face Caleb, a permanent scowl etched on his young face.

"You are late," he said. "I do not think the admiral would be happy once he hears of this disorganized mess of an operation you are running."

"The admiral?" Caleb repeated. "Yes, of course. Your father, *non?*" It was a guess, but it was a good one; judging by the redness of Edwards' face and the fact he did not deny it, Caleb seemed to have hit the mark.

"I will not be spoken to in this manner by someone of your persuasion," Edwards said. "Frenchman or otherwise. You will finish your duties. Then I will report you to whatever master you serve that you are an embarrassment to him and his company. Now, I will have your name."

"I am *Capitaine Jacques Moreau,*" Caleb said, matching Edwards' indignant tone. "And we come with greetings from the house of Governor François Duplantier of Buccaneers Isle."

"Is that so?" said the commodore. "Another incompetent Frenchman. I should have guessed." Edwards shot Oddface a glance; there was recognition in his eyes. He said nothing to him. Instead, he continued to address the captain. "Come now, what is it you have brought us this time?"

"You will see before us: guns, gunpowder, and cannonballs, Commodore," Caleb said.

"All this trouble for so little," Edwards scoffed.

"The others in your party," Smith said to Caleb, "they have already returned to your ship?"

Caleb grinned to himself; Oddface remained with them, but Hawkins had managed to take the rest of their party away into the fort while the commodore's anger was focused on him.

"And you will be returning with them now, I gather?" said Edwards.

Cynthia stepped forward and took Caleb's arm. "What hurry is there?" she said. "The captain would be wanting to see the fort. We are old friends, and he and I have some catching up to do."

"*Oui*," said Caleb. "Monsieur Oddface has told me about your setup here; I have been anxious to take in the sights for myself."

"Very well," said Edwards. "If you ask me, your journey here was entirely wasted. You tell your master the governor that if he wishes to waste my time and his with his supposed generosity, he should perhaps bring something a little more substantial."

"I will be sure to relay the message," Caleb said with a short bow.

Edwards spun theatrically on his heel and stepped briskly away.

"That was a bit of madness," Cynthia said once the commodore was safely out of hearing range.

"I know," said Caleb. "Imagine a commodore in charge of a fort called 'Levasseur' having such disdain for the French."

XXIV

THE WRAITHBONE HEIST

Kingsley kept glancing behind him, to see if they were being watched as Hawkins led him away further into the fort.

"And me without my eye patch," Hawkins said to herself as they disappeared down a dark corridor lit by torchlight. Several small windows let in minimal light as well

"Does a patch really help?" Docks asked. He had only ever worn a patch over his injured eye.

"No, it does not," Kingsley said. "It was merely a sales tactic to sell eye patches at heavily marked-up prices. It does not improve one's eyesight."

"Have you tried it?" Hawkins asked defensively.

"Nobody has!" said Kingsley.

"Keep it down," said Docks, hobbling after them, struggling to keep up due to his peg leg. "There are going to be guards down here. If they have not been alerted, we should try to sneak past them."

Though how they would get by them unnoticed in such close quarters, none of them could say. Regardless, the three of them continued walking forward into the lower levels of the fort.

They soon faced the first pair of guards blocking their way.

"Who goes there?" one guard called out upon seeing the approaching trio. He was a middle-aged man with an irritated demeanor, but he handled himself with a sense of professionalism that Kingsley suspected was for the benefit of the younger guard who stood beside him.

"I've got this," Kingsley said quietly to his companions. "I have some experience dealing with disagreeable customers." He straightened himself up and confidently stepped forward. "Good day, brothers," he said. "We have been sent by the commodore to inspect the hold below. There have been reports of disorganization and poor working conditions down here."

The two guards looked at one another, confused.

"Are you havin' a laugh?" the older one asked, holding his sword up. He approached Kingsley and brought the blade close to his neck.

Kingsley stood firm. "I am here on behalf of the Seafaring Labor Union. We look after the rights of our men on the islands. If there is a problem with the working conditions, we step in."

"Eh?" the guard said, beginning to show some genuine interest. "Go on."

"Do you feel that your situation down here is not ideal, but do you hesitate to speak out about it for fear of being reprimanded?"

The younger of the guards spoke up. "You know, I have thought that being on our feet for hours on end without a reprieve is a bit daft."

"What are you on about, Davis?" the first guard said. "It is our duty to stand guard. 'Stand' is literally the first word in our job description."

"But it is true. As the fellow says," the younger guard by the name of Davis explained, "we're down here all day, and nothin' ever happens, Mr. Jamison. It was bad enough when we were out to sea all the time, but the monotony here is even worse. They give us one small window to look outside at the sea, and that's it."

"That's exactly the sort of thing we hope to address," Kingsley said, launching into full salesman mode.

Jamison lowered his sword. "It *sounds* good," he said. He was clearly not fully convinced, but there would be no time for hearing any of his concerns, for Hawkins had grown impatient. Her hands had been making way to the throwing knife on her belt. As soon as Jamison's sword lowered, Hawkins drew the knife and flung it at him. It struck Jamison in the chest, and he went down with a strained gasp.

Kingsley cried out in alarm at the sudden show of violence.

Taking advantage of the situation, Docks used his hooked hand and pulled at Davis's coat. He threw Davis to the ground and kicked him in the head with his peg leg. Davis groaned in pain and stayed still on the floor of the corridor.

"I guess that'll do," Kingsley said, nervously rubbing at his neck.

Hawkins began searching the bodies for a key ring. As she reached into Davis's vest, he came to and grabbed hold of her wrist. She withdrew her hand and managed to snatch a small ring of keys from him, but the guard would not let go.

Hawkins shifted her body around so she stood behind Davis, twisting his arm around his back with her. The strain caused Davis to lose his grasp on the key ring, but as he let go, Hawkins stumbled and also lost her grip. The keys flew through the air, directly towards the lone window in the room. Everyone watched in disbelief as the keys landed precariously on the edge of the window.

Davis clumsily reached for the keys with his outstretched hand; his fingers knocked one of the keys, shifting the balance of the key ring. It slipped and fell out the window and into the sea below.

When Davis turned around, Hawkins was already back on him; she thrust her forearm across his neck and pinned him to the wall. Kingsley and Docks stood in silence behind her.

"Tell me there is another set of keys with your friend," she said. "Tell me where they are!"

Davis shook his head. "No more."

With a frustrated grunt, Hawkins threw Davis to the floor and kicked him. He lay there, groaning, but not moving.

"I guess we improvise," Kingsley said.

Kingsley led Hawkins and Docks down a spiraling sparsely lit corridor.

"The hold should be down this hallway," Kingsley said as they reached the bottom of the stairs. Sure enough, there was a room just in front of them filled with chests and crates, but between them and the room was a locked gate.

"When you're right, you're right," said Hawkins, looking around. "Mr. Docks, do you think you can pick that lock?"

"I can give it a try," Docks said. He opened a small pouch and brought out a few long pins and began to mess with the lock

"That's great," Hawkins said. "Is it working?"

Docks turned the pins, waiting for the satisfying *click* of the lock release. No sound came.

"No, it is not."

"Want to try my knife?" She pulled out a small throwing knife from her belt and held it up, offering it to Docks, but they both stopped what they were doing when they heard the sound of footsteps and voices coming their way, accompanying the light of a gas lantern.

"I don't suppose you could hurry it up a bit?" Kingsley pleaded.

Cynthia stepped with Caleb into the fort's courtyard. "I commend you for making your way this far," she said. "Giving them spoils from your raids was a bold move."

Caleb did not answer. Oddface remained silent as well.

"Those munitions you delivered: they *were* spoils from your raids, were they not?"

"A well-armored ship is worth nothing against Captain

Torch and his men unless we have something we can truly use against him," Caleb said.

"I see."

"What were you doing here, if I may ask?"

"I have been studying the routes of the ships, manifests, and orders given. There's more than just Captain Torch's ship out there threatening us. Empires are expanding, and they are doing so with more than just physical and ideological forces. And you're out there, making yourself a target."

"I cannot concern myself with anything more than the current threat at the moment," Caleb said. "When this is dealt with, we can face whatever comes next. And whatever that is, I hope you would face it with us. We're not alone out there. I believe we can muster a force that may have a chance against the darkness."

Cynthia studied Caleb's face. He was determined and unwavering, even more so than he had been when they first met at her home in the cemetery on Swashbuckler Island.

"It looks like I don't really have any other choice," she conceded

"Will you leave with us, then?"

"If your people manage to get what you came for, I will rejoin you."

"Can you lead us to the ramparts?" Caleb asked Oddface. "I would like to look out to the west."

"Aye, Captain," Oddface said. "Come with me."

He led Caleb and Cynthia up to the fortified walls, overlooking the western side of the fortress. As they peered out to sea, they could see the *Troublemaker* slowly circling to the side of the fortress.

"Very good," Caleb said. "Let's make our way down to meet the others."

Percival and Dom stepped confidently through the fortress but lowered their heads, avoiding eye contact with anyone they passed by. Fort Levasseur was primarily occupied by formally dressed Navy men, but there was also a small contingent of dressed-down sailors.

"This should be the place," Percival said quietly to Dom as they stepped into a doorway that led to a long hall.

"Aye," said Dom, looking about. The hall was filled with a half dozen cannons pointing out to the sea, and each cannon had a man standing nearby. "What do you reckon we do about the men? We can't very well spike these cannons with these men hanging about. We'll need a distraction to draw them away."

Percival scouted the north-facing cannons and found a coil of rope which he took and slung over his shoulder. Men stood around, looking out to sea. Dark clouds were beginning to form in the distance, and some of the men expressed concern about approaching inclement weather. In the corner was a small stack of crates filled with gunpowder. Percival fastened a piece of oil-soaked rope to one end and carefully laid the rest of it on the floor in front of him. So far, so good: the men were too occupied with one another to pay Percival any attention.

The room was lit by torchlight; Percival stepped slowly to the nearest torch and took it from its sconce. Seeing this, one of the close gunners turned and called out.

"'ey there, lad," he said. "What are ye doing with that torch?"

"Torch inspection," Percival said instinctively, his heart racing. He didn't know what that meant exactly, but it was the first thing that came to him, so he doubled down on it. "New maintenance protocols, you know? Orders from the main office."

"I wasn't notified about any torch maintenance," the gunner said. "I'll have to verify that."

"The safety conditions up here have everyone concerned," Percival continued. "After what happened at Fort McConnell last week…"

"What happened at McConnell?" the gunner asked.

"You haven't heard about the McConnell incident?" Percival asked with feigned shock. "They used outdated torches developed in the 80s and never bothered upgrading to the 1699 models that have the new safety features. If I'm being honest, it seems that these are woefully outdated. Blast it, this one seems to have a defective handling system."

He fumbled the torch and theatrically dropped it at his feet, where he had laid the end of the rope that he had set as a fuse. The rope instantly caught fire, and the fire shot quickly to the gunpowder crates.

"By thunder!" Percival cried out. "It is as I've feared!"

Percival leapt away from the crate just before it went up in flames and ignited the gunpowder, causing the crate to explode.

"Stop that man!" the gunner called out, drawing a sword.

From the western wall, Dom heard the explosion and encouraged the men at the cannons to see what assistance could be given. He was able to nearly empty the room, save for two men who remained at their guns.

As Dom was now alone with two remaining men in the room, he looked out to sea and could make out the *Troublemaker* turning the corner, coming into view.

"Oi! What's that?" Dom called out. One of the men stood to look, but as soon as he had turned his head, Dom punched him in the face and sent him to the floor.

The other gunner stood and drew his sword.

"What is the meaning of this?" he cried out, advancing on Dom. "Stand down, man!"

Dom drew his sword and defended against his attacker, who was backing him into a corner. Their swords clashed, and Dom kicked forward with both feet. The kick threw the gunner off him, but it resulted in his left arm getting cut in the process. Dom got to his feet and punched the gunner with his good arm, knocking him out. Adrenaline kicked in, and Dom kicked at the fallen man. When he calmed himself down after taking a few measured breaths, Dom tore a long piece of material and wrapped his injured arm.

"Aye, now we get to it," he said to himself, pulling out several metal spikes from his bag. He took a hammer and began driving the spikes into the vents of the cannons.

Docks held his ear to the door as he used his hook to fiddle with the lock. Hawkins and Kingsley stood behind him, attempting to keep their distance, but not wanting to stray too far.

"Is there anything we can do to help speed this up?" Hawkins asked.

"Find a key," Docks said, irritated but nearly motionless. "I need to concentrate so I can hear it when it…" He trailed off.

Click.

"That's it," he said quietly. Distorting his face in concentration, he turned his hook slightly, and the lock came free. Everyone breathed a heavy sigh of relief.

"Well done, Mr. Docks," a voice from behind them said. The three of them turned around to see Caleb standing there with Oddface and Cynthia beside him.

"Captain," said Docks with a subtle tipping of his hat.

The crew stepped forward into the room full of chests, crates, and artifacts.

"Where do we begin?" Caleb asked, looking at everything ahead of them.

"First, let's find our exit," Kingsley said. He moved forward and ran his hand along the wall. "Nothing over here," he said. "How about you?"

"There's something down here," Hawkins said. She stepped down a few steps into a mostly empty room. "There's a gap in the floor next to the wall here, but it is very small."

"There's no exit from this room other than the way we

entered," Oddface said.

"That is not encouraging at all," Kingsley said, looking down at the gap that Hawkins pointed out.

Oddface ran his hand along one of the walls and pulled out a small pocket compass from his coat. "This is the western wall," he said. "It is not the outer wall; there will be one other wall beyond this one."

"Keep on it, Mr. Oddface," Caleb said. "Mr. Docks, see if you can assist. The rest of us, let's see if we can find this book."

"Any idea what exactly we're looking for?" Hawkins asked.

"Not completely," Kingsley said, "but I imagine we will know it when we see it. First of all, look for a book."

"Right." Hawkins exhaled sharply and began turning things over, putting a few coins in her pocket as she did so.

"We're not here for the money," Caleb reminded her when he saw what she was doing.

"I know," she said. "I just thought we could use a bit to buy some replacement guns, gunpowder and cannonballs once we find this silly book."

"Very well," said Caleb, "but don't weigh yourself down too much. We have some swimming to do."

Hawkins walked into an area that was mostly empty. She rummaged through the shelves, but all the books in there stood out as being significantly insignificant.

Kingsley put his hands together and hummed slightly.

"What are you doing?" asked Caleb.

"From my studies, the spiritual energies draw upon each other. There is a connection. If I can force myself to feel it, I may be able to draw myself to the book. Now, if you please, keep silent." He spread his arms apart and walked into the room that was farthest in the back. "Do you hear that?" he asked.

There was no sound but the waves crashing outside the fort.

"No?" Hawkins said.

"I hear something. It's like a humming."

Kingsley opened his eyes. The humming that had been

growing louder inside his head stopped. Standing in front of him, inconspicuously on the back of a shelf was a sealed wooden crate. Kingsley removed the books that were blocking it and set it on the floor.

Caleb, Cynthia, and Hawkins gathered around to get a look. Kingsley took his knife and used it to pry the crate open. Inside was a large old book with a faded green cover. There were some designs on it, but they were too faded to tell what they were.

"Is that it?" Caleb asked.

"It doesn't look very magical to me," Hawkins said.

Kingsley reached in and picked up the book, turning it over in his hands. He blew the dust away, and as he did so, the designs on the cover began to give off a dull green glow. Foreign writing seemed to dissolve into a legible lettering that Kingsley could read.

"This is it," Cynthia said under her breath. "The *Golden Sea Grimoire.*"

"Golden," repeated Hawkins. "So, why is it green?"

"Two souls bound together share with one another the powers in life as well as the sting of death."

See: Ritual – Soul-binding"

– Golden Sea Grimoire

XXV

GOLDEN SEA GRIMOIRE

Kingsley opened the pages of the book sitting before him. *This was it.*

By all appearances, it was just a large, dusty book. There was some ornamentation on the spine, and the yellow pages curled slightly due to wear and tear.

"And now we come to it," Caleb said. "What do you suggest? We need to ensure it does not fall into the wrong hands. Do we burn it?"

"No," said Kingsley. "I'm not even sure it would burn if we tried."

"We pour oil on it," said Docks. "That should get it to burn."

"I don't think we should destroy it," Cynthia said. "Think of what we can accomplish with it in our possession. This is ancient knowledge culled from the minds of ancient mages of the past. It is too valuable to destroy."

"Do you see anything in there that could give us some sort of an edge?" Caleb asked. "Anything that could help us?"

Kingsley continued to pore over the contents of the tome while the others discussed its fate.

"Look here," said Kingsley, pointing to one of the pages.

253

Caleb stepped around to take a look at the page over Kingsley's shoulder, but he could not make out the writing.

"What does it say?" he asked.

Cynthia took the book from Kingsley and looked it over.

"It's a ritual," she said, reading the words carefully. "A ritual that can bind souls together."

"That's right," said Kingsley, more visibly excited.

"I don't get it," said Caleb. "What does that mean?"

Kingsley stood and paced the room, going over the situation in his head.

"Of course," he said. He began muttering to himself.

"You believe you are prepared to perform such a task?" Cynthia asked.

Kingsley nodded. "I believe so."

"What does this mean though?" Caleb asked again. "What kind of ritual are you talking about?"

Kingsley took the book from Cynthia again and ran his finger down the worn pages, skimming the information. "This passage right here. It says at the beginning of this chapter that *'Two souls bound together as one share with one another the powers in life as well as the sting of death.'* Then it refers to a soul-binding ritual."

He turned pages to find the referenced ritual.

"'One soul, bound to another: when the ritual is completed one person's existence is tied to the fate of the other.' That leads me to believe that if we can manage to link Captain Torch and the Reaper with this method, when we destroy one of them, the other is destroyed."

"That's great," said Hawkins, "but do we know either of them can even be killed in their current state?"

"Captain Torch was injured," Caleb said, "when Hennesey struck him in the shoulder. I don't believe that any of us, even in our current condition, are immortal."

"Exactly!" said Kingsley, closing the book. "I believe that his body is still mortal, even if he is elevated to a more powerful form. And consider all his other men we've destroyed. Like with the others, destroying the head will kill the body."

"There is still the matter of destroying the head," said Docks. "That won't be easy. And what was that bit about them sharing powers with one another? Will that not just make both of them even more dangerous?"

"Either way, we cannot be doing anything from here, Caleb admitted."

"What is the situation above us in the fort?" Hawkins asked. "How does our exit look?"

"The sabotage above should be causing a bit of a stir," said Caleb. "Mr. Percival and Mr. Dom should have the cannons spiked by now. We should go to the courtyard and see if we can regroup with them and make our return to the ship."

As Caleb led the others back to the courtyard, they could hear and see a commotion atop the outer wall. Commodore Edwards was shouting orders to his men who were in pursuit of a figure running along the top of the wall with a sword drawn. It was Percival.

Looking out in the sea ahead, not far from the fort's outer wall, Caleb spotted their ship, waiting to pick them up.

"Get back to the *Troublemaker*," he said to Kingsley. "Secure the book."

Kingsley nodded and scurried to the top of the wall, clutching the book in his arms.

"Stop them!" came a voice from behind. They turned to see Edwards now pointing his outstretched sword towards them.

Kingsley sealed the book back into its storage crate, jumped into the water, and began swimming out to the *Troublemaker*. Hawkins and Cynthia followed.

With a quick survey at the grounds, Caleb saw three bodies that had been felled by Dom and Percival. Caleb closed his eyes and reached out with both hands. The ground rumbled, and the three corpses stood and reached for their swords.

Their new allies struggled forward, slowed by stiffened legs and arms. Caleb fell to his knees, as though the wind had been knocked out of him from the energy he expended raising these three men.

Edwards and his guards nearly dropped their swords in surprise upon seeing the animated dead, but with measured determination, they braced themselves and prepared to fight.

"Steel yourselves, men," Edwards said. "This is the Devil's work! Strike them all back down."

The three undead attackers advanced on Edwards, drawing attention away from Dom at the door to the hall where he had finished spiking the cannons. Edwards was quick with his sword and took down two of the raised men with little effort.

Making use of the distraction, Dom fled across the top of the ramparts and dove into the sea below.

Percival, however, remained pinned into a corner by several of the fortress' guards.

"Mr. Docks, help get him out of there!" Caleb said while engaging Edwards and his men in combat.

Docks nodded and drew his sword with his good hand and went to Percival's aid. Oddface went along with him.

Two of the guards turned to face the reinforcements, leaving only one continuing to fight Percival.

Docks held his hooked limb forward, bracing himself on his peg leg, and thrust forward with his weapon. But the guard's reflexes were too quick; he slipped aside and jabbed back at Docks with his sword.

Docks caught the sword with his hook and used it to pull the guard in close.

"Looks like I've hooked me a fresh one," Docks said.

Without missing a beat, the guard pulled back his sword and shouted, "Hands off!" He twisted his sword around, slashing through Docks' good wrist.

Docks' hand, still clutching his sword, dropped to the ground in front of him. Docks cried out and brought his newly injured arm to his chest and kicked the guard, landing him on his back.

Freed from the reach of the man who took his hand, Docks scurried to the side of the fort and used his hook to bind his injury in a short sash that had been wrapped around his waist.

A longboat dispatched from the *Troublemaker* had already picked up Kingsley and Hawkins and was in the process of fishing the others from the water.

Unlucky Jake Docks braced himself for the inevitable extra pain the seawater would add to his injury and leapt into the sea.

Caleb locked swords with Edwards, but Edwards was the more accomplished swordsman; while Caleb's undead reinforcements gave him an edge, their summoning had taken a lot out of him.

"Go!" Percival called out to Caleb. He was still pinned down by two guards, and escape from them looked unlikely. "I'll tell the Devil when I see 'im to fear your retribution."

Stepping into a wide stance, Percival thrust forward and struck one of his attackers with a non-fatal injury. But his lunge opened him up to his other attacker; the second guard landed a strike with his sword into Percival's side.

Percival gasped for air. He waved his sword in a futile effort; his movements were uncoordinated, and his sword fell useless to his side.

From down the way, Caleb saw Percival fall to his knees. Their time here was up. Caleb maneuvered his fight with Edwards to the fort's wall.

"*Bonsoir*, Monsieur Edwards," he said with a flourish, and he stepped over the wall and into the water. When he resurfaced, he could see the longboat approach; just beyond it, the *Troublemaker* and its crew were hastening to prepare to set sail.

"Hullo!" Simon called out from the crow's nest. "Captain in the water to starboard!"

"Ready on the capstan," Caleb called to the ship as he climbed into the longboat.

Docks sat in the boat, clutching his injured arm and

groaning at the pain. Dom and Kingsley maneuvered the boat with the oars, bringing it quickly around to the side of the larger ship.

"Secure the longboat," Hennesey called as he stepped down from the quarterdeck. Bring them in and be ready to set sail."

The men of the *Troublemaker* made quick work bringing in the small boat with the surviving members of the shore party.

"Someone, take Mr. Docks below and tell Dr. Gold his favorite patient is back," said Caleb. "Weigh anchor and get us out of here. Let's pray the cannons were successfully rendered useless."

Paul stepped forward and ushered Docks to the hatch as the rest of the crew took to their stations, turning the capstan to bring up the anchor, setting sail, and manning the on-deck cannons.

"What's the report?" Hennesey said as the ship began to turn and leave the fort behind them. "Was the mission a success?"

"Something like that," Kingsley said, holding up the box.

Behind them, a cannon boomed.

"All hands, ready," Caleb called out. The fort's cannon missed the ship by a wide margin; it appeared to have been one of the cannons from the other side of the fort, turned in an effort to make up for the disabled cannons.

"Get us out of here. Mr. Hennesey, fire back and give us some cover."

Hennesey ordered his men to fire, and the *Troublemaker* fired back at the fort as they departed.

"Another ship off the port bow," Simon called from the crow's nest. "It's the *Red Soul.*"

In a move that stunned those who witnessed it, Cynthia Cove stepped up to Kingsley and wrestled the box that contained the *Grimoire* from him. "I'll take that," she said, knocking him down.

It took a moment for Kingsley to get his bearings, and it was a moment too late, for Cynthia was already running down the length of the ship, *Grimoire* in hand. She got to the quarterdeck and launched herself wildly into the sea.

"What was that?" Kingsley asked, dazed.

"She took the book," Caleb said, running to the quarterdeck of the ship and stopping at the railing.

"Surely, she cannot survive out there in the water," Hennesey remarked, but the *Red Soul* was already closing in on her, and several spectral figures fished her out of the water.

The *Red Soul* spun itself around to return the way it had come.

"After them!" Caleb called out. "Full sheets to the wind! Shoot them down and retrieve that book!"

But it was too late.

"In the depths of the seas, there could lie even greater magics that have yet to be studied."

– Golden Sea Grimoire

XXVI

THE EXISTENTIAL DEEP

The crew pulled the lines and brought the full wind into the *Troublemaker's* sails, but the *Red Soul* was too fast. It skirted around the islands to the east of the storms that surrounded the Deep.

Caleb stood on the quarterdeck, looking through his spyglass at the ship shrinking into the distance. Surely, he had not come all this way just to fail now. He put the spyglass down and cried out in frustration and anger at this latest betrayal.

Had it been an obvious mistake to place trust in Cynthia Cove? he wondered to himself. *And how many others left on this ship were waiting to betray him?*

"Awaiting your orders, Captain," Hennesey said.

Caleb's attention snapped back to the situation at hand. "What do we know?"

"My guess is Captain Torch is taking the ship northwards towards their refuge at Spitshine Spot," said Kingsley. "If they require anything further for this ritual of theirs, they will convene and then set out to retrieve what they need."

"That is reasonable," agreed Caleb. "And when they have everything?"

"I don't know that it matters where the ritual is performed."

Caleb nodded. "Very well. It seems that there is one option set before us. We make our way to Spitshine Spot by way of Buccaneers Isle and hope we can reach it ahead of them."

"But how can we do that?" Fullery asked. "They have a head start and a favorable wind. Their ship is the faster; it has already outrun us."

After a moment of contemplation, entertaining any thought of an alternative but finding none, Caleb spoke up.

"We cut across the Deep."

The silence that fell across the deck and the fear in the eyes of the crew was evidence enough that this was not a popular plan.

"It is the more direct way," he continued, pleading with his crew to consider his reasoning. "We know their destination. If we can beat them there, we can retake the book and be finished with this."

"But Captain," objected Hennesey, "I cannot recommend we risk this ship and crew in such treacherous waters."

"We cannot allow superstitions to guide the rudder of our destiny!" said Caleb. "The tales of the Existential Deep are built upon the fears of sailors who pass by here, and nothing more."

"You of all men should know that some superstitions might have some merit to them," said Hennesey. "You yourself have been cursed, and you're chasing a cursed ship in order to retrieve a book of magical knowledge."

"Adjust course and make way through the Deep," Caleb commanded firmly.

Susan Hawkins nodded.

"Aye, Captain," she said. She took out her compass and studied it and the sea ahead of them. "Mr. Martín, adjust course fifteen degrees west."

"Aye." Martín's voice was uneven with trepidation. Regardless, he took the helm and turned the ship into the storm.

Satisfied, Caleb stepped down from the quarterdeck and

onto the main deck of the ship, followed closely by Kingsley, whose concern was clearly growing as well. The two entered the captain's cabin, and Kingsley closed the door behind them.

"Monsters or not," Kingsley said, "sailing into this maelstrom is madness. We will not catch them this way."

"That is where you are wrong, Mr. Kingsley," Caleb said evenly. "Feel that? We are picking up speed already. The wind will launch us forward to the devils that await us!"

While Caleb seemed sincere in his plan, Kingsley knew there was something eating at him – something other than the Reaper's curse, that is.

"You don't have to give yourself up, you know," Kingsley said.

"What are you talking about?" Caleb asked, distracted. "I'm not giving myself up. We're going to defeat him."

"I'm not talking about Torch," Kingsley said. "When this is all done, you can still have a chance at a new life."

"You mean Santana," Caleb said, understanding. He opened a cabinet where there were several bottles of wine sitting there. He took one and poured a glass for himself and another for Kingsley.

"I appreciate you giving the rest of us a chance when this is over," Kingsley said, taking the glass, "but you don't have to take the fall for us. You want to take the honorable path, and that is commendable, but I think there is still the possibility to remain honorable and not suffer for simply refusing to be enslaved by another man."

"Fine sentiments, but I don't know if there is much of a choice."

"If you go back to them, how do you think Mr. Duplantier will react? Do you think life will go back to the way it was?"

Caleb shook his head. "I cannot control the actions of others. If Santana feels obligated to send me back, I can do nothing but plead my case."

"I've known you only a short while, Captain," said Kingsley, "but I get the sense that I know what kind of a man you are. You may have been enslaved by that idiot Frenchman, but a slave is not who you are; no man can be defined by what others do to them. Furthermore, you may have sailed under the black flag out of necessity, but that is also not you. I've seen you take every bit of 'fate' handed to you and redefine it into a path of your own choosing. You are no pirate. You are a leader, and you are a master of your own destiny. And I worry because I fear you might give that away after you have worked so hard to claim it for yourself. That's what I see, at least."

"Whatever I am, I'm grateful for your council and for your friendship," Caleb said, forcing half a smile in response to Kingsley's encouraging words. "All of this sounds nice, but it all may come to nothing if we cannot even navigate to Torch in the first place."

It was evident in his captain's eyes that he did not expect to make it on the other side of their mission alive and that he was resigned to his fate.

"Let's just focus on getting there for starters," Kingsley said.

"Agreed." Caleb drew in a deep, calming breath to help center himself and calm his nerves. "Thank you, Aiden. You'd make a good captain."

Kingsley chuckled softly. "I'll remember you said that. But if you leave us, my money is on Mr. Fullery taking over."

Caleb scoffed. "Ridiculous! But he may make a fine captain if he has someone like you for an officer."

He poured Kingsley and himself another drink, and they continued to drink and laugh with one another as the rain beat down heavier on the deck outside the captain's cabin.

Caleb wrapped a long strip of red material around his head and took a small tricorn hat from the desk and put it on as he reached for the cabin door.

"Let's see if we can't get our bearings," he said as the two stepped out onto the deck of the ship. Susan Hawkins provided navigational updates behind Armando Martín at the wheel. Hennesey kept the rest of the small crew busy at the rigging, battening the hatches, and bailing out water that was accumulating from the storm they were quickly approaching.

"What's the situation?" Caleb asked Hennesey at the prow of the ship.

"We're making good speed, Captain," Hennesey said, over the sound of the crashing waves, "but the water is awfully rough."

"Well done. Keep vigilant. We'll be at Buccaneers Isle in no time."

The sea opened up, and waves broke ahead of them.

The freshly patched-up Jake Docks sat high above them in the crow's nest.

"What's that up there?" Docks called out, pointing ahead. "Something in the sea, one point off the starboard bow!"

Caleb held tight to the railings at the front of the fo'c'sle and braced himself as he looked into the water ahead of them.

About a hundred yards ahead, there was a glow just beneath the surface of the waters. A giant form slowly raised itself out of the water, water crashing down as it towered above them; it was an unrecognizable red monstrosity. Giant armored legs came forth, threatening the approaching ship.

"What in the name of the sea is that?" Caleb asked.

The monstrous creature reared forward and raised two claws, each the size of one of the *Troublemaker*'s longboats, snapping in the air. Its shell was red and black, and its eyes were relatively small black orbs that peered out at them. It was like an enormous lobster, over sixty feet from mouth to tail. As the *Troublemaker* moved forward, the creature held out its massive pincers, ready to attack.

"Full speed ahead!" Caleb yelled out. "Pass by it. Put it on the larboard side. Prepare cannons and fire on my command!" The ship rocked forward, and the men loaded all the cannons.

"We are low on ammunition, captain," Fullery called out. "Enough for a full broadside, but no more to spare."

Caleb gritted his teeth. *Had the heist not only been for nothing but also made them helpless out here in the water?*

"Load what we have in the larboard side cannons, and stand by," Caleb shouted.

A giant claw reached for the ship and snapped at the longboat hanging on the larboard side. Men jumped out of its way as the claw effortlessly tore the longboat in half.

"Cut it free!" Fullery shouted to anyone nearby. "Give us more speed!"

Oddface and Absalom grabbed axes and hacked at the support ropes connected to the shattered longboat. It broke free and splashed into the sea. The ship rocked from the waves caused by the monstrosity turning in the water near them.

"Put everything into speed," Caleb ordered. Men hung onto the rigging as the ship bobbed violently through the sea. "Secure that rigging. Catch the wind. We'll be through it soon enough and we'll have a story to tell, that's for sure!"

The ship passed through, and the creature snapped at it with its claws as it went by. One blow hit the center of the main mast. The ship creaked and groaned in response. Docks dug his hooks into the sides of the small basket at the top of it all. Below him, he watched as nearly everyone in the small crew pulled on the lines and fought to catch the wind with the sheets.

A large boom swung free from the torn rigging and came flying across the deck. Fullery pushed Kingsley and Simon out of its path, taking the full force of the boom himself. He tumbled across the deck, landing violently at the door of the captain's cabin, the wind painfully knocked from his lungs.

"Mr. Odfface," Caleb called out, "Take Mr. Fullery into my cabin and have Dr. Gold see to him."

"Aye, Captain."

Oddface and Dr. Gold struggled together to drag Fullery into the cabin then hastily secured him to the captain's bunk. He had hit his head hard but had recovered his breath and was coming to, groaning from the pain. When he was satisfied that

Fullery was properly situated with the doctor, Oddface returned to the deck.

The ship sped through the storm, slipping away from the monstrosity and avoiding its other attacks. The creature reared back, and the crew could see a gaping maw full of sharp teeth opening as it came after them.

"Hard to starboard!" Caleb shouted from up on the quarterdeck, behind Martín at the helm.

Martín spun the wheel, nearly throwing the ship onto its side.

"Fire larboard side cannons!"

Four shots rang out. The monster let out a deafening screech as cannonballs struck its exposed underbelly. With a terrible bellow, it retreated back into the sea.

"If you find yourself catching fire, cease chanting immediately and contact your local physician."

– Golden Sea Grimoire

XXVII

RETURN TO BUCCANEERS ISLE

The *Troublemaker* continued to sail through the dissipating storm. Caleb watched from the quarterdeck as they left the giant monstrosity behind them.

"We're not out of this yet," said Dom, looking forward.

Caleb nodded. "Mr. Simon, make a damage report. Keep on course, Mr. Martín." He scanned the horizon behind them through his spyglass. The rain still came down, but not as violently.

"This was an experience for the books."

"I don't know what more we can take," Hawkins said, looking at the fractured mast. "And we'll need to resupply."

"We don't have time for that," Caleb said.

He stepped down from the quarterdeck and ran his hand over the fractured mast.

"We made good time," Hawkins said, "but at the cost of damage to the ship. We cannot face Torch and his men in this condition."

"It's true we cannot well fight without ammunition," Caleb conceded. "How do we fare on that front?"

"That was the last of the cannonballs," Dom said.

Simon returned from below deck, and Caleb acknowledged

267

him. "What is our situation?" he asked.

"There are some leaks below that can be boarded up," said Simon. "There is a fracture halfway up the main mast. It should be reinforced or even replaced before we go too fast. I'm sorry, Captain, but we may very well be dead in the water."

"We'll have to see what more we can push out of this ship. Can you tell us where we are, Miss Hawkins? Can we still bring it into Buccaneers Isle?"

"Yes, but it will be slow going," Hawkins said. "We should be able to arrive there tomorrow."

Caleb silently weighed his options and concluded that there truly was no option.

"Very well," he finally said. "Bring us into Port de Sang. Keep sharp. Santana may already be there waiting for us."

It was the next evening when the *Troublemaker* came to Buccaneers Isle, and the *Devil's Thunder* was already there. Docks raised the white flag of truce atop the *Troublemaker's* main mast as agreed, and they cautiously came to the dock.

"What do you think?" Caleb asked Hennesey on the quarterdeck as the ship docked.

"I think I should make myself scarce," Hennesey said.

Caleb agreed. He knew of Hennesey's reputation; he suggested that he remain in the captain's cabin until they were ready to head back out to sea.

The *Troublemaker* came to a stop at the dock, and Caleb disembarked with a few others. "John," he said to one of his men, "take Mr. Fullery into town and see if you can get him patched up in a room at the inn."

John nodded and stepped out with Fullery beside him. Fullery's bloodied head was bandaged, and his arm hung limp at his side. He struggled to stand, but he was a proud man and insisted on walking as much as he could on his own.

Dom went into town to find more able-bodied men willing to go with them to fight against Captain Torch. As Hawkins sought out the harbormaster for repairs, Caleb and Kingsley made their way to the *Devil's Thunder.* Captain Santana stood on the deck to meet them.

"Captain Caleb Keys," Santana greeted him. "You are early. I am glad to see you make it. Please, come with me."

He led the three of them into his cabin.

"It looks like you've had a rather rough time out there."

"We have repairs under way," Caleb said, "and we plan to be set in short order. We are short on time and desperately need to prevent a ritual from being performed on Torch's ship; it could summon a malevolent force from beyond our world."

"I don't know anything about malevolent forces, but I hope whatever new weapon you have to fight Captain Torch will do the job. I've fought pirates with reputations before, but tales of what he can do have grown more and more fantastical and concerning."

"We have a possible way to be rid of him. It would be using the dark magic against them, but it would involve us, particularly Mr. Kingsley here, getting onto his ship with him."

"You have experience in whatever voodoo arts that is giving him his power?" Santana asked.

"Actually," Kingsley said, hesitantly, "the magic he is using is not voodoo in the strictest sense. It's a sort of dark, ancient and forgotten practice that – "

"He does," Caleb said to Santana, cutting Kingsley off. He knew that these men would not care about such distinctions.

Kingsley reluctantly stopped explaining.

He probably wouldn't understand it anyway, he thought to himself.

"As for my men," Caleb said, shifting the subject, "when this is all over, I expect they will all be free to go?"

"If what we set out to do gets done," Santana said matter-of-factly, "your men will be free to leave. Their record, however, will not be expunged, and if they are encountered by any of the king's men or by any privateers, I cannot guarantee they will not be taken."

"I understand," said Caleb.

"And what of Captain Keys himself?" Kingsley pressed.

"He will come with me for questioning when this is concluded," said Santana. "Depending on his actions, I will plead his case, and a decision will be made whether he can be given a commission."

Kingsley shot Caleb a glance; Caleb no doubt knew this would be an unlikely result, particularly with his history with the governor of Buccaneers Isle, but they agreed to the arrangement.

Santana laid out the next course of action and sailing plans for Torch's refuge at the nearby Spitshine Spot. The last of the supplies were brought aboard, and he ordered his men prepare to set sail.

Repairs on the *Troublemaker* were ongoing, under the watchful eyes of Hennesey and Hawkins. Caleb and Kingsley returned to the port town's square to make final purchases and preparations ahead of their departure.

The streets might have been empty, but the Happy Souls Tavern remained lively. As Caleb approached it, he could hear music and many men conversing loudly inside. Dom exited the tavern and took Caleb aside.

"Mr. Fullery is being looked after," he said, "and I managed to sign two dozen men for the voyage."

"Two dozen?" Caleb repeated, impressed. "Do they know what they are up against?"

"Aye," Dom assured him. "Torch is making life on the sea treacherous for everyone, and it seems these men are ready to fight back against it all. I think they're hopeful for impressive plunder when the *Red Soul* is ultimately taken. The booty from that kind of a ship is tempting for anyone, I suppose."

"I hope they won't be disappointed, then," said Caleb. "I'm

under the impression Torch's goals are less tangible than silver and gold."

"You know that, and I know that," said Dom, "but I see no reason to be so upfront about it all." He patted Caleb hard on the shoulder. "It might give rise to some unnecessary concern."

Caleb gave in. "I see."

Dom left Caleb alone in the street and made his way back to the docks, where the *Devil's Thunder* had just cast off.

Caleb watched the ship begin to leave.

It was nearly time.

A lone figure slowly stepped out into the sunlight in the middle of the port town's square, between him and the docks. Caleb squinted his eyes and stepped forward to get a better look.

"Caleb!" The voice was unmistakable. "Or should I call you Captain Keys?"

"Stephen Kennedy," said Caleb. "What are you doing here?"

"We have unfinished business," he said. "I have been hearing some interesting rumors around Captain Santana. Apparently, he was here to meet a young pirate captain to set sail together against some sort of 'demon pirate.' And with you being here, I gather that your foolhardy mission was a success?"

"If you mean that we were able to successfully take the *Grimoire* from Fort Levasseur, then yes," Caleb said.

"And where is it?"

Caleb hesitated. Kennedy divined the meaning of this and grinned wickedly.

"I see."

Caleb cautiously drew his sword and prepared to engage his former captain in combat.

Kennedy drew his sword as well.

"We had a little misunderstanding," Kennedy said. "You wanted the get the *Grimoire*, as did I, but you did not trust my methods. You were, as always, impatient and insubordinate. That is what got you marooned, Caleb. Believe me, we were going to go to the fort, but there is an order in which things must be done.

I can't expect you to understand strategy."

"Was it not you who recklessly attacked Fort McConnell and got your ship sunk? And was it not you who, in the quest for a little bit of gold, broke the articles we signed together?"

"Again, with those ridiculous articles!" Kennedy shouted, striking a nearby street display with his sword. "Captain Torch knows that the world is not fair, and he's going to do something about it. It cannot easily be fixed, so he's going to burn down the old world, the world that made outlaws out of you and me, and he's going to be able to rebuild it."

"Not if I have anything to say about it."

Caleb advanced upon Kennedy with his sword, but the experienced captain was more than a match for him. With a furious yell, Kennedy drove Caleb back towards the island interior, away from the town center.

"You feel the fire burning within you," he growled. "That is why you pushed your ship and your men to the breaking point. They will not be coming to help you now."

He kicked Caleb in the stomach, knocking him onto his back on the dirt pathway leading out of town.

"So much death surrounds you, young one. Will you kill me now?"

"If you don't stop."

Caleb returned to his feet and began to slowly circle Kennedy with his sword outstretched.

"We can build a better life," Caleb cautioned, "But we cannot do it if we welcome Torch's master into this world. He will tear us all apart. He will consume everything in its path if he is set free here. But if you are so willing to meet him…"

Caleb struck decisively at Kennedy with his sword. Kennedy parried, but Caleb swung twice more, knocking the sword out of his hand. Caleb struck again, plunging his sword into Kennedy's chest. He pushed through to the hilt and looked hard into his fallen foe's eyes.

"…Tell him I'm coming for him next."

Kennedy gasped and fell onto the dirt pathway.

Caleb stood over Kennedy's body and looked down, breathing heavily. As Kennedy's life left him, Caleb felt a great pulse of energy shoot from the fallen body into him. He could feel a tingling all over him, like he had been stung by a hundred eels. His hands and face burned.

He sank to his knees. Flames beneath his skin erupted. He covered his face as all he could see was fire. He sat there, reeling from the pain. Even then, his thoughts went to his ship.

What of his crew? he wondered. *Had they heard any of that?* He stumbled into the woods, cutting through them back towards the edge of the town, crawling on his hands and knees.

Fire engulfed his hands, and as he put them in the water, they hissed, and the water steamed. The pain shifted into a numb sensation, like when you have been sitting on your foot for too long, but this feeling was all over his body. He pulled his hands out and looked at them; the flesh and muscle tissue had all burned away, and all that was left was a bony skeleton. He looked into his reflection in the water, afraid of what he may see.

It was as he had feared. The flames went out, and his flesh appeared to have burned away. Staring back at him, though through fiery eyes, was a fully-exposed skull.

XXVIII

SKULDUGGERY

Caleb looked up towards the dock. Men were finalizing repairs on the *Troublemaker*. He hastily removed his hat and took the long red cloth from his head and wrapped it over the lower part of his face, hiding his features. He then put the hat back on his head and stepped back into the open, approaching the docks, where he ran into Kingsley.

"Aiden," he said in a hoarse whisper.

"Captain?" Kingsley said, nearly dropping the small barrel of apples he was carrying. "Is that you? What are you doing? Why is your face covered?"

"There's no time. We have to get the ship moving. Have Mr. Hennesey take charge in my stead. I will keep to my cabin until we near our destination."

"Aye, Captain."

Kingsley threw the barrel of apples back over his shoulder.

Caleb finished masking the lower portion of his face with a long strip of material, leaving only a narrow space for his eyes to peek through. The shade cast by his hat concealed the rest of him.

They hurried to the ship, stepping swiftly even as they

boarded. A brief quizzical look flashed on Dom's face as he greeted them, but he dismissed his concerns to give his report.

"The new men are ready," he said. "Essential repairs are complete, and we are prepared to set sail."

"Well done, Dom," Caleb said. "Weigh anchor and get us moving."

"Aye Captain." Dom turned to address the men. "Weigh anchor, set sails, and secure tacks and longboats!"

Caleb stepped up to the quarterdeck and faced the crew, keeping his face in the dark.

"We're short on time," he said. "Those of you who do not yet know me, I am Captain Caleb Keys. Welcome aboard the *Troublemaker*. We sail to Spitshine Spot where we will encounter and confront Captain Benjamin Torch of the *Red Soul*, with the aid of the *Devil's Thunder*. It will be a difficult voyage, but the rewards will be great. Be prepared to stand and fight, for the enemy is ruthless. I trust we can be as well."

There was a shout of agreement from the crew.

"Mr. Docks!" He called up to where Docks was perched. "Fly the king's colors."

"Aye!" Docks called back as he searched for the English flag.

"There is much I have yet to prepare for," Caleb continued, speaking to his crew, "so I will be in my cabin. I leave you now in the very capable hands of my bosun, Reginald Hennesey. He will take charge as I go over our strategies."

The crew murmured amongst themselves at this. Hennesey was well known, particularly as a rival to Benjamin Torch, but also as the captain who had laid siege of Bogtown on Swashbuckler Island five years ago.

"Susan," Caleb said, turning to speak to Hawkins, "set the course to Spitshine Spot.

Hawkins produced her compass and consulted it. She looked back at the trajectory they were taking from the island and compared it to the markings on a small map she carried around with her.

"North-northeast," she said to Martín at the helm. She secured the eye patch over her good eye, shielding it from the rising sun.

Caleb opened the door to his cabin, where Reginald Hennesey stood, waiting for the go-ahead to return to duty.

"Did I hear correctly?" he asked. "Why would you relinquish your command at this pivotal hour?"

Rather than answering directly, Caleb first removed his hat, then unwrapped the material covering his face, revealing the skinless bone underneath.

Instinctively, Hennesey's hand went to his cutlass.

"You have earned my trust and respect," Caleb said. "I need to work a few things out for myself. I hope the crew can be made to understand by the time we arrive at Spitshine Spot. Nevertheless, it's important we get there in the first place, and I leave that task to you."

Hennesey relaxed his hand and moved it away from his sword.

"I see."

"I hope that you will also share our articles with the crew and keep them as well as me on task. I don't know what power Torch might have over me. If there is a doubt where my loyalties lie, do what needs to be done."

Caleb paused, then added, "But please try talking me down first."

"Of course," Hennesey said with a short bow. He turned on his heels and stepped out to the deck without another word.

Caleb remained in his cabin, and from there he could hear the ship's articles being recited to the men. Then there was the busied movement as Hennesey bellowed instructions to the crew. For the greater part of the voyage, Caleb sat in his chair behind a large table where maps and other papers were littered about.

A map of Swashbuckler Island showed Spitshine Spot on the northwest side. He knew that the details of the map might not be exact, because most common cartographers would steer clear of the small island due to its reputation.

Caleb recalled the day he had jumped ship and left the others on the *Red Soul,* just as they had approached Torch's stronghold. His thoughts went to Mr. Knave, the poor soul whom Torch had first reduced to a state of living death. He had seemed a mindless husk, but now Caleb wondered if that was actually the case. And if Knave was truly a mindless form bent to Torch's will and of there could have been a path back for him, Caleb wondered if that was to be the end for everyone under the Reaper's thrall.

If they reached Torch, and the Reaper was let into this world, would anyone under his influence be able to resist his commands?

His thoughts went to his friend Hanson, who had been his first true ally in this whole messy ordeal. He hoped against hope that he would not have to face him in combat.

His mind swimming with all the possibilities ahead of him, Caleb looked at his degloved hand; it was nearly entirely bone. It occurred to him that he was likely already more than halfway on his way to death.

Maybe death was the only way out for any of them.

Caleb closed his eyes, focused his mind on the steady rocking of the ship and on the sound of the waves outside, and began to draw upon the energy around him. He let the troubles ahead slip away as he steadily exhaled. Since the fight with Kennedy, everything was wreathed in flame. But now, darkness began to envelop him as he looked inward, thinking now on those who had remained loyal and true to him.

He thought of Aiden Kingsley and his friendship. Then his thoughts strayed to Susan Hawkins and her loyalty and kindness – her comforting hand in troubled times. He envisioned her taking his hand in hers and just being there for him.

The cabin was now completely silent. There was no rocking. There were no waves. As he breathed, his breath was loud and clean in the darkness. He looked up, and everything around him came into sharp focus. The movement of the ship and the sounds around him returned.

He stood and went to his dressing mirror, dropping his hat and the strips of linen he had used to hide his face.

He regarded himself in the mirror, and his old self had returned and stood before him, his skin back to its natural, healthy brown. He saw scars that he had not noticed before; it was like they were working to cover his condition, as if his body was fighting back the Reaper's curse.

Gradually, Caleb once again became aware of the rocking of the ship and the sound of the men outside and the crashing of waves. The commotion seemed to grow as the sound of Hennesey's voice barked orders that were muffled by the walls of the captain's cabin. *Maybe—*

The blast of cannon fire interrupted Caleb's thoughts. Were they already to their destination? Surely not.

Putting on a worn hat and re-wrapping his hand, he stepped out of his cabin and ascended the stairs to the quarterdeck.

Hennesey was there, looking through a spyglass at a brigantine bearing down upon them. As he lowered the spyglass, he gave his captain a double-take.

"Captain," he said, straightening up. "You're looking well."

"Yes," said Caleb, brushing the matter aside. "A good bit of meditation works wonders. What's the situation?"

"Just our luck," Hennesey said, handing Caleb the spyglass. "It's the French. What the blazes are they up to?"

"They've begun patrolling these waters." Caleb recalled the conversations he had overheard between Mr. Lansky and Governor Duplantier the day he had made his escape. "They're likely here trying to disrupt the shipping routes in the area. I guess everything's still not well between them and the English."

"And as our luck would have it, Santana has us flying the English flag," said Oddface.

"I'd wager that they'd be on us even if we weren't," Caleb said, taking his turn with the spyglass. He handed it back to Hennesey when he was through. "Any sign of Santana?"

Hennesey shook his head. "We're on our own here."

"Let's see if we can't disable her."

"Aye, Captain."

Caleb held up a halting hand as another idea came to him. "On second thought," he said, "belay that. Hoist up the white flag of truce. Be ready to defend the ship as necessary, but I'd like an audience with her captain. Let's see what words might accomplish."

"Aye." Hennesey leaned over the rail to look at the men on the main deck. "Absalom, sound the bell. Dom, call the men to quarters. Docks, fly the flag of truce!"

Absalom nodded and began ringing the ship's bell. As Dom shouted orders and organized everyone to their stations, men ran about, loading cannons and readying their muskets and boarding hooks.

Caleb held up his hand, encouraging his men to hold off the attack.

"Steady, men," he said. "Be ready but make no unprovoked movements."

The ships approached each other; a voice came from the other ship.

"Prepare to be boarded," the heavily-accented French voice commanded over a speaking horn, "by *Capitaine* Louis Matisse and the men of *La Charrue.*"

"Stand down," Caleb said to his crew.

Hawkins spoke quietly in Caleb's ear. "Do you really mean not to fight?"

"There are ways to battle besides the sword,"

"Exactly," said Hawkins, "which is why the cannons are standing by."

But Caleb gave no such order. Hooks came flying across the *Troublemaker's* railings, and when the ships were settled, a plank was secured, bridging the two ships. A dozen men boarded, led by a fancily dressed captain, the man who had ordered their surrender. He had a long black mustache and a neatly trimmed goatee. There was a notable contrast between his highborn looks and manner and the rough men of the *Troublemaker*, and his attitude showed he was acutely aware of this distinction.

"I am *Capitaine* Louis Matisse," he said. "Am I addressing the *capitaine* of this…" He paused as he looked around at the crude repairs done following the passage through the Deep. "…this vessel?"

"You are," Caleb said with a courteous bow. "I am Captain Caleb Keys. We have recently come through the storms of the Existential Deep, and I'm afraid it has left our ship rather battered."

"I see," said the French captain, showing no sign of being impressed. "And what is your business in these waters? You fly the flag of truce, but it does not escape me that you were flying English colors before we came upon you."

"That's true." Caleb gestured to the cabin. "If you will join me in my cabin, we can talk over the situation."

"We can speak here," he said curtly, nearly stepping on Caleb's words.

"Very well," said Caleb, eyeing his men and hoping they would be able to keep from making a spectacle of themselves, "I am just wondering if you are familiar with the 'honorable' François Duplantier, governor of Buccaneers Isle?"

"*Tu prononces le nom du traître lâche!*" Matisse spat on the deck of the ship. "*Oui*, I am familiar with him. What of it?"

"You know of the deals he has made with the English to hunt pirates near his island?"

"Such matters are not my concern."

"Of course," said Caleb, now speaking in a lower voice, "but privateers targeting French strongholds in these waters on the payroll of the Royal Navy, I would guess that would be your concern. I'm in pursuit of an English privateer ship, the *Devil's Thunder*. We fly the Union Jack to avoid drawing unwanted attention."

"Renault," Matisse said, addressing one of his men standing next to him, "*Connaissez-vous Le Devil's Thunder?*'

The man nodded. *"Oui, Capitaine,"* he said. He made a statement to the captain in French that Caleb could not quite make out, but he heard the name "Santana" mentioned and guessed that the report was accurate.

"As I said," Caleb continued, maintaining his calm straight-laced demeanor, "our current voyage has us on the trail of Captain Rafael Santana. We have reason to believe he will be crossing north of Ramrod Island by tomorrow."

"Is that so? It is a good story," the captain said, "but it could be a clever ruse as well. We have no reason to put our trust in you. You could very well be sailing for him and leading us into a trap."

Caleb's heart sank. The deceptions he had been forming were catching up with him. There seemed to be no solid way to convince these men the truth that he was, in fact, sailing against Governor Duplantier. And now he was in danger of facing yet another adversary.

He put his hand into his hip pouch and idly felt around. His fingers stopped on a piece of parchment, and his countenance lifted.

"You'll not find friends of Duplantier here," Caleb assured him. "Governor Duplantier enslaved me from a young age; I only recently managed to procure my freedom."

He pulled out the parchment from his hip pouch and threw it to Matisse, who caught it and began to look it over. It was the small handbill with Caleb's picture drawn on it, accompanied by the reward offer.

"I am Captain Caleb Keys," he explained, "formerly of Buccaneers Isle. Governor Duplantier took my life from me; I took it back, and he resents me for it. And now, I sail against him and his allies. You can clearly see here the resentment he has for me."

Matisse studied the picture of Caleb in his hands. "It is a fair likeness," he said. "And this looks authentic enough. So, you are a runaway?" He looked over the rest of Caleb's unsavory looking crew around him. "And what about the rest of you?"

"I'm a sailor chasing my own destiny," Caleb said, "seeking fortune and freedom where we can find it. Our allegiance is not to any nation, but we do have those out there who hunt us. My crew follow me for their own reasons."

"And this *Devil's Thunder*," Matisse said, "where might she be?"

Caleb took back the handbill and returned it to his pouch.

"I am glad you asked."

"When the paths to the beyond are opened, the seas will run black, the skies will turn red, and the sun and moom will pale."

– Golden Sea Grimoire

XXIX

A TEAR IN THE SKY

Captain Matisse returned to *La Charrue* and broke away to the southeast side of Swashbuckler Island while the *Troublemaker* moved north along the west coast of the island.

"Keep us close to the land," Hawkins said to Martín at the helm. "Bring us towards the Bogtown port on the northern peninsula. Captain Torch and his ship should be waiting for us at their stronghold at Spitshine Spot to the northwest. Keep a weather eye out for Santana."

Caleb stood ahead at the fo'c'sle, looking ahead across the bow, having just finished his evening meal, though it did not seem to satisfy. He held a tankard of watered-down grog in one hand, though it rarely touched his lips. The sun set behind them, casting its rays on the trees of the approaching beach. Ahead of them, dark clouds began to fill the sky, indicating the formation of a storm.

After a long moment of silent observation, Caleb stepped back to address Kingsley.

"What do you think we can expect?" he asked.

"It is hard to say. I don't know what all is needed for the soul-binding ritual. Hopefully everything will be available to us.

283

Usually for something like this, we would need an item from both parties: an article of clothing, blood, bone, that sort of thing. Ms. Cynthia is the one to watch out for right now. If she can be stopped before she finishes her ritual that opens the gateway, we can all go home early. If not…" He trailed off.

"It'll be up to you," Caleb said, finishing the thought that Kingsley did not wish to say aloud.

"Yes," Kingsley said, feeling the pressure build on him. Caleb put a reassuring hand on his shoulder.

"I have faith in you, and when we get out of this, you'll return to your shop a hero."

"I don't know that 'hero' is in the books for me, but maybe I can be fine with going back into obscurity, if that's possible."

"You can use some inspiration from your travels for some new merchandise," Caleb suggested, prompting a weak smile from Kingsley. "Regardless, I imagine you'll be free to go wherever you would like to after all this."

This talk reminded Caleb that when all of this was over, he himself would still be on the run, no matter the outcome.

Hennesey maintained a respectful distance during the conversation, but as the ship moved closer to the island and closer to the dark clouds ahead of them, he broke his silence.

"Captain," he said, "a storm seems to be forming ahead."

"Indeed, it is," said Caleb. "What do you think, Mr. Kingsley? Could it have to do with the ritual?"

"It is a possibility, of course. The chaotic energy in the area could be agitating its environment. Or it could just be this unpredictable weather. If you don't like it, just wait a few moments, am I right?"

He nudged Caleb in the ribs.

"Only in the Caribbean," Caleb remarked.

Whatever the reason for the dark skies, Hennesey knew that the crew would need to be attentive to it.

"What are your orders?"

"Yes, of course," Caleb said, clearing his throat as he realized he was just now coming to the same conclusion. "Mr. Docks," he called out to the crow's nest, "What do you see in the storm? Is a ship there?"

Docks scanned the storm with a long spyglass. "Aye!" he called down. "That be the *Red Soul* for certain." He shifted his gaze to the west. "Another ship approaching from the southwest, Captain. It's the *Devil's Thunder*, coming in fast, flying the King's colors."

"Well done, men." Caleb fixed his tricorn hat on his head and raised his voice so the crew could hear. "Hoist the Union Jack. Strike the top-gallant sails. Run into the wind and ready the cannons. Mr. Hennesey, as we board the *Red Soul*, the *Troublemaker* is under your command. Coordinate your attack with Captain Santana as we deal with Torch and his men.

"Miss Hawkins, assemble a boarding party and join me as we take the *Red Soul*. Our first primary target is Cynthia Cove. Stop her from completing the ritual and retrieve the book she will be using. Be mindful of Captain Torch's cursed men: they are hearty, and their numbers will increase with each man they bring down, so for the rest of our sake, don't let them cut you down. Go for the head. If you dismember them, throw their parts into the sea, lest they continue to cause trouble."

He took a moment to look over his crew, an impressive assortment of men cobbled together from merchant ships, slaver galleys, privateer ships, as well as former thieves and murderers – bad men and good men, all working together under his command. Caleb felt a brief swelling of pride that was new to him. He held onto that for a satisfying moment, then tucked it within himself and focused his energy.

"Armando," he said, "move us in."

"Aye, Captain," Armando Martín called back as he adjusted course, turning the ship into the storm.

As the *Troublemaker* approached the *Red Soul*, it was clear she was the center of the atmospheric disturbance. The area directly surrounding the ship was calm, acting as the eye of a storm.

"On my word, give them a volley of cannon fire as we board her," Caleb said to Hennesey, "then circle around us and protect the ship." He lowered his voice. "Beware of any trickery from Santana. Do not let him use the situation to move against us."

"Aye, Captain," said Hennesey. "I will not surrender the *Troublemaker.*"

Caleb clapped Hennesey on the shoulder. "Thank you, Captain."

Rain fell hard over the *Troublemaker* as it pressed forward. The *Devil's Thunder* closed in, keeping on the *Troublemaker*'s stern. Hawkins stood by Caleb, with a boarding hook in hand and a cutlass ready at her side.

"On your order, Captain," she said.

Looking through his spyglass, Caleb could see Cynthia Cove, sitting in the center of the deck of the *Red Soul,* her face downcast, focused on the *Grimoire* laid open on the floor in front of her.

"It may not be too late," Caleb said. "Hennesey, signal Santana to join us on the *Red Soul.*"

"Aye."

He retrieved a speaking trumpet and went to the back of the quarterdeck to address their approaching allies. The anticipation of the impending mêlée blocked everything else out of Caleb's mind; he could barely hear any of the words shouted out to the other ship. It was time for his swordsmanship to be put to the test, and doubt was gnawing at him that he was in any way prepared for this encounter.

Nevertheless, it was here.

"Fire!"

On Caleb's order, the *Troublemaker* let loose a deafening blast as the starboard cannons all fired, mostly aimed at crewmen and the main mast. Shouts could be heard as men on the *Red Soul* were hit and thrown into the sea.

A volley of cannon fire came from the other side of the *Red*

Soul as the *Devil's Thunder* had begun firing. Minimal damage was done; it was as if the ship had been strengthened in some way. Part of some curse? Or maybe it was just good, sturdy crafts-manship. The *Red Soul* was a legendarily tough ship, even before its captain had become the Reaper's right-hand man.

Shots rang out as the *Red Soul* fired back, even as a half dozen hooks were released from the crew on the *Troublemaker.*

Caleb dodged splinters as a cannonball crashed into the railing next to him. He gave the order to board, and a dozen men began climbing lines to the other ship.

The storm continued to swirl around the three ships, though the *Red Soul* remained relatively untouched. Wind blew water and debris as men from both the *Troublemaker* and the *Devil's Thunder* boarded, met with a crew of cursed pirates, all of whom were now fully skeletal in appearance.

Standing over all of them on the raised quarterdeck of the *Red Soul* was their captain, Benjamin Torch himself, identified by his towering stance, his unmistakable red wool jacket, and his wide-brimmed black hat. His orange-red beard was now fully wreathed in flames, his face an expressionless skull with small orange lights like dim candles behind the eye sockets.

He certainly recognized Caleb, for he began marching towards him in a jerking motion as soon as he set foot on the deck. Caleb drew his cutlass to face off against his former captain.

Caleb recognized Atsadi, the tall quartermaster who had first given him work when he sailed with Santana. Expertly wielding a sword that seemed nearly twice the weight of any of the other swords carried on the ship, Atsadi powerfully and methodically plowed through the ship's skeletal crew.

When Atsadi reached Cynthia in the center of the ship's deck next to the main mast, he looked down at her and raised his hefty sword, preparing for the heavy death-dealing blow. She read aloud from the *Grimoire,* her voice growing louder. Atsadi and two other men from the *Devil's Thunder* began to lower their swords, as if compelled by Cynthia's chanting. As they stepped forward, Cynthia lifted her head up and faced them.

Their eyes locked. Cynthia's pupils had either rolled backwards or had just vanished; she looked back at them with empty milky-white eyes and stopped speaking.

Cynthia's assailants began to cry out in terror and pain as they fell to their knees. When their knees hit the deck of the ship, Atsadi and the other two men crumpled like burned rolls of paper and blew away with the wind.

"Hold back!" Hawkins called out, sliding to a stop when she saw what had happened in front of her. Skeleton men with their swords raised moved on Hawkins; she fought back, leaving Cynthia to recite the rest of her summoning rites.

The two captains – Benjamin Torch and Caleb Keys – circled around the deck, facing off against one another. Caleb swung away furiously to keep up with Torch's more practiced hand. Flames surrounded Torch's face. He was himself not burning; rather, flames seemed to fix onto him like a hellish aura. As he spoke, his voice was gravelly, distorted by the curse.

"Come to offer your soul up on the pyre?" he growled. "There is room enough for yours and your crew's."

Another skeletal husk stepped up beside his captain, the skull atop his shoulders expressing no emotion.

Caleb recognized the tattered coat it wore, though.

"Hanson."

"Aye," Torch confirmed, "I can take you at any time the way I took Mr. Hanson." He made two powerful thrusts with his sword. Caleb hit back, deflecting the blows, but expending a great amount of energy in doing so.

"Then why don't you?" Caleb shot back, instinctively.

Torch halted his attack, as if he were now planning to do just that.

Oops.

Caleb took a step back, now fearfully awaiting the inevitable. Torch raised his hand.

Another hand clasped Caleb's shoulder firmly from behind.

Caleb turned with a start; it was Aiden Kingsley. With his other hand, Kingsley clutched his small gris-gris bag and chanted something in a strange tongue. He finished by speaking a blessing in English.

"I humbly call upon the loa Baron Semedi. I beseech you to not prepare a grave for Caleb Keys. May the spirits of my ancestors guard his soul, and may it not be torn away from him."

He opened his eyes just in time to dodge a strike from Torch. Kingsley exclaimed in alarm and backed away.

Torch returned his focus back to Caleb, who stood with his sword in front of him in a defense posture. Caleb braced himself as Torch attempted to remotely draw his soul away from him.

It felt to Caleb as if a strong wind was blowing from him to Captain Torch as the semblance of life seemed to pass away. His skin burned as his outer body became engulfed in flame. Charred ashes blew off him revealing exposed bone. Caleb's head was bowed as he braced himself for the traumatic loss of self-control; any moment now, he knew that his will could be turned over to Torch.

But that moment never came.

"Come here, Caleb," Torch commanded with a forceful tone.

Caleb slowly raised his countenance; flames burned under his collar, and as his face lifted, all that remained was a flaming skull, matching Captain Torch's look. He raised his cutlass in a threatening posture.

"Come here, Benjamin," he said.

Torch cried out in frustration and swung his sword at Caleb, pushing him towards the side of the ship. Caleb leapt onto the railing and cut one of the lines. Taking hold of the rope, he swung himself back to the circling *Troublemaker* with Torch hot in pursuit.

The mêlée continued on the *Troublemaker* as both crews fought against one another on both ships.

Captain Santana had just boarded the *Red Soul* from *The Devil's Thunder*, which also continued to circle the ship in tandem with the *Troublemaker*. He and Hawkins stepped side-by-side, approaching the chanting Cynthia Cove, but they were stopped by Kingsley.

"Do not go near her," Kingsley warned. "She has given herself a protection against anyone who looks upon her too closely."

"She has to be stopped," said Hawkins, raising her voice over the commotion around them.

"Aye," said Santana, "but how do we stop someone we cannot look upon?" He drew his sword to fend off Torch's approaching crew as Cynthia sat there over the opened *Grimoire*.

Hawkins' hand went up to her face, feeling the patch that covered her darkened glass eye.

"I've got this," she said, switching the eye patch over to her good eye.

"What in the blazes is she doing?" Santana asked while beating back a particularly angry cutlass-wielding skeleton.

"Will this work if I cannot look directly at her?" she asked Kingsley, hoping for some sort of confirmation.

But Kingsley could not say. He shrugged and drew his own cutlass to defend himself as the fighting around them grew only more intense.

"I don't know," he said. He was drawn away as another group of angry cursed pirates moved in on them.

Hawkins, now blinded by her own doing, thought back to the training she had been putting herself through. She smelled the foulness of the air, the salty sea water splashing around them, and the sulfur from the burning hoard of skeleton crewmen. She heard the shouting around her, the clashing of swords, and the creaking of the ship. She felt the vibrations of the planks beneath her, the heat from the fire...

...and the bony fist of a cursed skeleton pirate punching her in the face.

Hawkins instinctively threw her sword in front of her and blocked the thrust of another pirate's cutlass. She parried two more blows then thrust her sword into the middle of her attacker's torso. She felt the crunching of its exposed bones as her sword was embedded in him. With a concerted effort and a shout, she swung her sword to the side, flinging the attached skeleton crewman over the side of the ship and into the sea.

Hawkins stumbled forward towards where she recalled the main mast was, bumping shoulders with crewmen from all three ships on her way there. When she finally arrived, she could hear the chanting of Cynthia grow louder; Cynthia repeated the same phrase, her voice growing more and more strained, possibly as a result of her defenses having no effect on Hawkins.

As Hawkins swung her sword where she imagined Cynthia to be, it was intercepted by another sword. With her free hand, Hawkins drew her swordbreaker from her belt and held it up. She pressed a switch on the hilt and two smaller blades separated from the main blade at an angle. The attacker's sword came down and got caught between two of the blades. With a quick twist of her left hand, Hawkins snapped the sword from its hilt and kicked the stunned pirate out of her way.

The fist of another pirate landed on the side of Hawkins' face. She spat out some blood along with a bloody molar and blindly cut the fiend down.

Cynthia spoke her invocation louder as she raised her hands, and the wind blew her black hair around her pallid face. She repeated the final phrase three times, which gave away her position to Hawkins who stood blindly in front of her.

Hawkins, listening to the raised voice, thrust her sword into Cynthia's chest.

While groping weakly at the sword stuck in her, Cynthia tried to gasp for air. She fell backwards onto the deck of the *Red Soul* and silently lay there in the midst of the commotion around her.

There was a rumbling around them all as the whole ship shook. Shockwaves sent out from the *Red Soul*, impacting the other two ships. Hawkins shifted her eye patch back to her glass eye and looked up at the sky.

A bright light like lightning flashed in the dark sky, but unlike a regular bolt of lightning, it did not disappear. With a crack of thunder, the light widened like a doorway in the sky just in front of the bow of the ship. Standing in the center of the bright doorway was the shadow of a figure wearing a tattered cloak and holding a large sickle in one hand.

Kingsley ran to where Hawkins was standing over the fallen body of Cynthia Cove. He picked up the large book and clutched it to his chest as he regarded the Reaper in front of them.

"We're too late."

"Be sure to stretch 10 to 15 minutes before and after performing a dark ritual."

– *Golden Sea Grimoire*

XXX

THE HAND

The cloaked figure in the sky floated down towards the bow of the *Red Soul*. All who were gathered around stopped what they were doing in order to watch; those on Captain Torch's side awaited some sort of reward for their allegiance, while the crews loyal to Caleb and Santana stood with their swords and flintlock pistols ready, anticipating the next attack to come.

But the Reaper did not attack. Instead, he floated through the air as if it were water, slowly sinking towards the *Troublemaker*, where Torch and Caleb stood. He stopped just ahead of the two captains.

"Benjamin Torch," he said with a low voice that seemed to resonate across the ship, "Thou hast prepared the way for mine return. The lives thou hast taken hath fueled me, and I hath slit the bonds that held me in purgatory. Now, as mine conquest of the land of the living cometh to pass, I welcome thee as mine right hand."

Coming down the steps from the quarterdeck, Captain Santana positioned himself by the main mast of the *Devil's Thunder* and fired a shot from his flintlock pistol. The shot went through the tattered cloak of the Reaper, leaving him unfazed as he stayed hovering between the two ships. Santana strapped his pistol back onto his belt and took out a throwing knife and flung it with precision directly at the center mass of the Reaper.

The Reaper's eyes flashed with fire, and the knife passed through his chest as if he were made of smoke. He spun and caught the blade with his long, outstretched fingers. The knife tore a small piece of the Reaper's tattered cloak but did no damage to the Reaper himself. In one fluid motion, he whipped around and launched the knife back to its origin. It lodged deep into Santana's shoulder, knocking him off his feet.

Santana struggled as he fell back onto the deck with the wind knocked out of him, clutching the knife stuck in his shoulder.

"Come with me," the Reaper said to Torch, "and we shalt fashion the world anew to our desire. Mine power shalt be made known. And the treasures of the world shall be thine."

Torch held his sword aloft as the flames circling his skull intensified.

Reacting to the gesture, Caleb held out his sword as flames danced around his own exposed skull.

"Surrender your ship, boy," Torch growled. "You must lay down your arms and rejoin my crew before it is too late for you. Let us waste no more time here."

"Why's that?" Caleb countered. "You have somewhere you need to be?"

Admittedly, it sounded better in his head. The comeback did little to dissuade the other captain.

"Even if you could defeat me," Torch said, locking swords with Caleb, "it would do you no good. The Reaper has come, and he is ready to lay waste to this world."

Caleb stumbled backwards, away from the stronger captain, keeping his sword up and ready to defend himself.

Across the way, on the deck of the *Red Soul*, Reginald Hennesey dispatched several of Torch's men and threw them over the railings into the sea just in front of Hawkins and Kingsley, gaining their attention.

"You have the book," Hennesey said. "Fall back to the safety of the *Devil's Thunder* and do what you need to do there."

They all knew that none of the three ships could reasonably be considered "safe," but for the moment, Santana's ship had the fewest hostiles on board.

"Aye," Kingsley said, securing his hold on the *Grimoire*. He began to climb the *Red Soul*'s rigging up towards the main mast with Hawkins close behind, fending off attackers with her cutlass.

When the way was clear enough, Hawkins pulled out a rope with a grappling hook and swung it across the gap between the two rocking ships.

"You first," she said, handing Kingsley the rope.

Tucking the book under one arm, Kingsley took the rope and braced himself as he swung over to the allied ship.

When he was safely across, Kingsley threw the rope back. Hawkins reached for it as it came near, but she was interrupted by a large skeletal figure who came up behind her, swinging its sword.

"Go on," Hawkins said over her shoulder to Hennesey.

Hennesey nodded, took the rope, and followed Kingsley onto the other ship.

Hawkins found herself pushed towards the center of the ship, next to where Cynthia Cove had fallen, but she noticed the floor there was now empty. She had only a moment to consider this as she knocked down her attacker when she suddenly found herself face to face with the lifeless form of Cynthia; she stood there, her eyes glazed over and vacant. Her face was still as pale as it had been in life. She held the cutlass of one of her fallen comrades.

"You again?" Hawkins said, annoyed that she had to face off

against Cynthia once more.

Without speaking a word, Cynthia sprang into action, swinging with an unexpected strength at Hawkins, who defended herself with her own sword.

On the fo'c'sle of the *Devil's Thunder*, Aiden Kingsley looked upwards toward the foremast. An empty nest near the fore top-gallant sail appeared to have a decent vantage point. Once again, tucking the *Grimoire* under his arm, Kingsley closed his eyes, gave his gris-gris bag a kiss, muttered a quick prayer, and began to climb the ship's rigging.

From the relative safety of the nest, Kingsley could see a clear view of the other two ships as well as the hovering figure of the Reaper floating ominously above them.

Kingsley situated himself and laid the book open in front of him. He thumbed through the pages until he reached an entry labeled "Ritual: Soul-binding."

"Two souls bound together as one share with one another the powers in life as well as the sting of death," he read aloud. "Perfect." He skimmed through the ritual, familiarizing himself with the components and incantations. Most of the required components seemed simple enough, including the sorts of things he kept on him in his bag strapped on himself. Of course, there were personal items that would be needed from both parties.

Looking down at the ships from his high vantage point, Kingsley scanned the battlefield. It still appeared chaotic even from up here, but he could at least make out more clearly what was happening and who was who.

As he looked down, he saw Hennesey make his way over to the *Devil's Thunder*, underneath him. He was attending to Captain Santana, hastily bandaging up his shoulder with a blood-stained wrapping.

As Hennesey helped him to his feet, Santana raised a flintlock pistol and fired at one of Torch's approaching men.

Hennesey stepped aside to avoid being caught up in the crossfire. He looked down at the knife he had removed from Santana's shoulder and noticed the bit of material that was stuck to it. He recalled what Kingsley had said earlier concerning necessary components to the binding ritual.

"Aiden Kingsley!" his booming voice called out. "Ahoy, there!"

Kingsley waved back from his perch.

"Ahoy, Cap'n Hennesey, what news do you have?"

Hennesey held up the knife. It took a brief moment for Kingsley to understand the significance. He reached into his bag and pulled out a small spyglass to help him get a better look at it. Through the magnification, he noticed the cloth stuck to it, and he realized that it was from the shroud of the Reaper.

"That will do!" he said, putting away his spyglass. "I'll come down to retrieve it. Just give me a minute."

Hennesey put the material away into his jacket and pulled out his flintlock pistol to help deter any of Torch's men as they attempted to board the ship. Standing back-to-back with one another, Santana and Hennesey fired, knocking approaching skeleton pirates from the rigging and into the sea, where they quickly broke apart on the crashing waves.

"I don't suppose this will count for anything?" Hennesey called over his shoulder, knowing Santana had been hunting him for years.

"Let's get out of this first," Santana said between breaths. "There may be a letter of marque awaiting you."

Hennesey laughed heartily and fired away at the approaching cursed men.

Kingsley reached the base of the foremast next to Hennesey, who was busy reloading his flintlock. He put it away and retrieved the knife with the scrap of cloth from the Reaper still stuck on it.

"I don't know what good it is," Hennesey said, handing

it over, "but I heard you may be needing something from both parties for the ritual."

"It's a start," said Kingsley, removing the cloth and putting it into his bag. He handed the knife back.

"What else might you require?"

"Something from Captain Torch, certainly. Preferably, something with blood, a bit of skin, or even bone, if possible. Other than that, I should have everything else, no small thanks to Miss Cove."

"Aye, that's a tall order, for certain. Why not choose someone else to be bound to him? Someone who might be easier to take down?"

"There is already a great bond that exists between the two, and that is critical. This is beyond anything I have attempted. It must be based on two individuals with an existing connection, and I can think of no person the Reaper might have a closer connection to at the moment. The energy that has already passed between the two gives me something certain to start with."

"I'll see what can be done," Hennesey assured him. "Now, get yourself back up into your loft, and we'll fetch you what you need."

On the *Troublemaker*, Caleb kept his distance from Torch as the fighting continued. It seemed that even as Torch's skeleton crew were defeated, their numbers did not dwindle, for they continued to resurrect the fallen men from Caleb and Santana's crews to fight for them.

Hennesey boarded the *Troublemaker* to help fight the growing numbers.

"We need something from Torch for the ritual," Hennesey told Caleb. "A piece of him, as it were."

"He's too strong." It was a difficult thing for Caleb to admit, but he knew that reckless pride would only hurt them now. "I can't get close to him."

Hennesey nodded. It was up to him now. He had long waited for the chance to confront Benjamin Torch face to face, and now was the opportunity to test his strength. He fought through the chaos and approached Captain Torch, who greeted him with a showy flourish of his fiery sword.

"Reginald," the flaming Torch greeted him, "I am pleased to finally test my skill against you in combat."

Although Torch was the one who was cursed and he had the advantage of having the powers of given to him by the Reaper, he was still a rather trim man and seemed small in comparison to the stocky beast of Hennesey towering over him.

Hennesey was both a stronger and more experienced swordsman than Caleb and was able to press his advantage on Torch, but Torch's mastery of fighting on rough seas evened the odds a bit.

With Torch occupied, Caleb shifted his focus to the protection of his crew. Back at the helm, Martín hung loyally onto the ship's wheel while being protected by Dom, who fought off three of Torch's skeleton men. Caleb saw this and ran to their aid.

"Captain, I'm not sure how much more of this we can take," Dom said, furiously swinging his sword at the three men.

As he approached the scuffle, Caleb recognized that one of the men had been Mr. Hanson, still under the mindless thrall of Captain Torch. If there was a way that he could reach him…

He focused, and the fires in Caleb's eyes dimmed. He remembered the energy he felt as Torch had attempted to take his will from him and how he resisted; he latched onto that feeling.

"Olaf Hanson," he spoke softly. Caleb reached out his hand and a wave of energy passed from him into Hanson, agitating the flames around him.

The skeleton that used to be Hanson turned his head to face Caleb. It was difficult to discern the expression, but from the hesitancy of his hand on his sword, and from the movement of his head as he looked around for some sort of external guidance, he seemed to be fighting for some sort of direction.

"Olaf Hanson," Caleb repeated louder, "come back to yourself." Another wave of fiery energy shot from Caleb, this time knocking Hanson backwards onto the deck.

Hanson rose to his feet with his sword lowered. His two fellow cursed comrades turned their swords in unison towards him.

Their attention diverted, Dom swung his sword and lobbed off both skulls from their bodies. Caleb and Dom threw the two skulls overboard into the ocean, followed by the bodies.

"Caleb?" Hanson finally managed to say as he stood up straight in front of the captain.

"Well, blow me down," said Dom.

Caleb took Hanson's hand. "We have little time. Will you help us?"

"Aye," said Hanson. "I'll carve a piece of the old captain for you."

Together, the two cursed men moved towards the bow of the ship, where Hennesey and Torch continued dueling; Hanson kept up the ruse that he was still under the thrall of Captain Torch.

Hennesey was looking more battered and bloodied, his coat tattered and burned from Torch's attacks, but his determination had not waned. As he went for a more powerful swing, however, Torch slipped out of the way, causing Hennesey to stumble. With his backhand, Torch knocked Hennesey off his feet and threw down Hennesey's sword.

Hennesey awaited the killing blow, but it did not come. Torch's sword was intercepted by Hanson, who stepped in and blocked the blow with his own sword.

"Cursed fool," Torch said, furious at being robbed of the deathblow. "Have ye lost your vision?"

Hanson swung wildly with little form as he advanced upon

his former captain around the ship's fo'c'sle.

Caleb helped Hennesey to his feet. His hands were both bloody from the combat; it was likely pure adrenaline that had allowed him to continue fighting as long as he had.

Torch raised his sword against the barrage of blows coming from Hanson. He executed five or six chopping motions, all stopped by Torch's sword, then shifted his weight and swung for Torch's unprotected left hand, slicing it off at the wrist.

The hand fell to the deck, and Torch let out an inhuman cry, equal parts rage and pain as fire and smoke emitted from the place where the hand had been cut. Torch pulled back with his other hand and thrust his sword into Hanson's chest. Hanson tried to move, but the position of the sword wedged in him made it impossible. Torch released his hold on the sword and grabbed Hanson by the throat. Hanson shuddered involuntarily until he became so overwhelmed by a surge of the captain's fiery energy that he finally collapsed into a pile of charred bones at Torch's feet.

Torch kicked the bones and reached down to retrieve his sword from Olaf Hanson's remains.

"To avoid muscle cramps, do not go into the water until at least an hour after being cursed."

– Golden Sea Grimoire

XXXI

FACE OF THE REAPER

From the nest atop the *Devil's Thunder*, Kingsley had laid out items gathered from Cynthia Cove's ritual as well as a few of his own items that he always kept close by. In the center of it all was the *Golden Sea Grimoire*, weighted down with several rocks resting on the open pages.

He had gathered nearly everything required and set all the components in front of him, needing only something from Captain Torch himself to begin.

From his vantage point, he could see commotion happening near the bow of the *Troublemaker*, but what exactly was happening he could not say.

The Reaper himself continued to hover above the *Red Soul*, taking no action; its role at the moment seemed to be just an observer, looking on with a cold indifference.

"All the better," Kingsley said to himself.

His eyes scanned across the *Red Soul*, where he could see the resurrected form of Cynthia Cove still fighting against Susan Hawkins.

Cynthia was not nearly as skilled with the sword as Hawkins, but she did have the advantage of being undead. She would get

302

struck in a normally vital place and continue to fight. The only way it seemed Hawkins could defeat her would be to remove her head and then throw her into the sea.

So that is what she did.

Hawkins had already defeated her once, and this time, she did not have to be blind to fight.

Kingsley found himself preoccupied watching Hawkins dispatch Cynthia, so that he nearly dropped everything when he heard a voice from below calling his name.

"Aiden Kingsley! Ahoy, there!"

"Hullo?" Kingsley peered over the edge of his nest and was pleased to see Stubby Oddface standing at the base of the foremast.

"Need some assistance with the ritual?" Oddface shouted up to Kingsley. "Allow me to come up, and I'll give you a hand!"

"I just need the final component," Kingsley called back. "Something from Mr. Torch."

Oddface revealed from behind his back the severed hand of Benjamin Torch.

Kingsley's face lit up. "Yes, bring that up, quickly now."

Oddface climbed up the rigging to Kingsley.

"The sooner we can be done with this, the better," Oddface said. "It's madness down there."

Kingsley took the skeleton hand of Captain Torch and placed it in front of him. He pulled out the piece of material from the Reaper and held it against the hand. He poured some black sand from a vial in front of him, creating several circles on the floor and began to recite the incantation from the book.

The clouds above darkened as the rain intensified. The Reaper's attention turned to the two young men in the crow's nest of the *Devil's Thunder.* As he floated towards them, his hood blew away, revealing his deathly countenance underneath. It was a gaunt, pale face that looked neither young nor old. His eyes were black and reflected the lightning that flashed around the ship. He stopped just in front of the crow's nest.

Kingsley continued to recite the words from the book which he held in both hands, fighting against the circling wind.

The Reaper reached out and grabbed at Kingsley and the *Grimoire* he held in his hands.

"You're too late," Kingsley spat at the Reaper while struggling to keep the book in his grasp.

Oddface took a dagger from his belt and stabbed at the Reaper, knowing in his heart that it was a futile gesture.

The spectral being seemed uninjured by the knife, but he was certainly not pleased. With a hellish shriek, he tore the *Grimoire* from Kingsley's hands. Kingsley stumbled back in the crow's nest. He and Oddface scrambled to their feet to look down at the ship below them. Kingsley swore as he saw the book disappear into the ocean below.

The Reaper turned his attention to the battle happening on the *Troublemaker*. Kingsley and Oddface looked at one another and silently decided that they, too, should return to their ship where their captain might need whatever help they could give them.

As they descended the foremast of the *Devil's Thunder*, Kingsley and Oddface could see the *Red Soul* close by, connected by a knotted mess of rope ladders and grappling hooks. They crossed the ropes and found themselves back on the *Red Soul*, where Susan Hawkins greeted them.

"The binding is done," Kingsley told her. "We need to get back to Captain Caleb and see if we can't finish this."

"Right." Hawkins put away her sword. "Come with me. This squall does not seem to be calming down, but we might be able to swing ourselves back there as she comes 'round."

Torch still stood at the front of the *Troublemaker*, his hurt arm tucked into his cloak. In his right hand, he wielded his sword against both Caleb and Hennesey, who struggled with his injuries but stood strong.

The Reaper flew down in the midst of them, throwing Caleb towards the middle of the ship and knocking Hennesey down once again onto the deck, grunting from the pain.

Caleb rose to his feet, fighting the increasing pitch and yaw of the ship from the storm. He fell backwards, grabbing onto the railing for support as he walked the steps up to the quarterdeck.

Martín was there, loyally manning the helm against the might of the coming storm. When he saw Caleb, he cried out in surprise, still not used to seeing his captain in this form.

"Is this what was supposed to happen, Captain?"

Caleb looked around, first at the Reaper at the bow of the ship, then up towards the other ships. A boarding hook flew towards him from the direction of the *Red Soul*. As it landed, Caleb and Dom secured it on the railing and waved over their comrades.

Hawkins led the party back to the *Troublemaker*, with Kingsley and Oddface close behind her. When they were safely on board, Dom produced a hatchet and cut the ropes connecting the ships.

"Tell me some good news," Caleb said, turning his countenance to Kingsley, who nodded in confirmation.

"I think we are looking at two linked entities," he said.

The ritual had been completed. The Reaper himself was now joining in the battle.

"Aye," Caleb said. "All according to plan."

He said this, but he knew his skills were no match against the captain of the *Red Soul*. And now the Reaper was circling close by, threatening anyone who came near Torch. Even Hennesey was backing away from the protective Reaper.

"Hang on!" Martín cried out as he braced himself on the wheel.

The waves raised the back of the ship up then back down again in a dramatic motion, causing everyone to nearly lose their footing. Caleb took hold of the railing and rode it out, but a thought came into his head.

"Give me your sword."

Martín gave him a quizzical look, but not wanting to argue with the captain, he took a long knife from his scabbard and handed it over.

Feel the waves as it rocks the boat down, he thought, remembering the words of the man who had sold him this ship, claiming that the wood used gave the deck an extra bounce to it. *Feel as it goes down...*

The back of the ship rocked down again. Caleb stepped forward and planted his feet firmly in the center of the quarterdeck behind his helmsman and bent his knees, holding his sword in one hand and Martín's long knife in the other. The back of the ship rose sharply on the next wave.

Feel the waves bring it back up, and...

Jump.

The back of the ship reached its highest height, and Caleb stretched his legs out and let the ship spring him into the air. Rain poured down around him, waves crashed, lighting flashed, and Caleb found himself launched higher than he had accounted for, just barely missing the masts and tearing through the sheets with a coordinated swing of both of his swords. He shot through as if he were fired from a cannon and found himself closing the distance to Benjamin Torch, who turned to face him in surprise.

Caleb's sword landed in the center of Torch's torso and went clear through to the hilt; the force of the impact pinned him to the ship's bowsprit behind him. For good measure, with the knife Martín had just given him, Caleb removed Torch's skull with a heavy blow.

His skull flew off and rolled across the deck.

Above them, the Reaper let out a mournful wail. Then, in a surprisingly understated finish, he collapsed to the deck, reaching out with an outstretched arm. His flesh and bones turned to white ash and washed away with the seawater on the wooden floorboards.

The localized tempest that had gathered around the three ships calmed, and the clouds parted, revealing the full moon and the starry night.

Martín peered across the length of the ship, both hands gripping tightly onto the ship's wheel as the waves rocking the ship calmed down.

"*Hijole*," he exclaimed under his breath. "*¡Qué viaje!*"

He chuckled, wiped his brow, and turned to address Dom, standing over the bodies of defeated foes nearby.

"Is that it?"

Dom held up a covered lantern, its golden glow aiding the moonlight now shining down upon the *Troublemaker*. They looked out and saw the men of Torch's cursed crew, many now standing as their old selves and others falling to the deck, succumbing to the wounds they had received in the battle.

At the bow of the ship, standing tall, was Caleb. The fiery aura around him had been extinguished. As he raised his head and removed his hat, he revealed his face: it was back to his old, flesh-covered self again.

"Make safe the ship," he said to his crew. "Take any surviving crew of the *Red Soul* to the brig and prepare to set sail."

"Aye, Captain," said Dom, stepping down from the quarter-deck to help enforce the orders.

XXXII

RETURN TO THE SEA

As preparations for setting sail were hastily made, the *Devil's Thunder* came about, and Captain Santana stood at the railing closest to the *Troublemaker.*

"Captain Caleb Keys," he called out with the aid of a speaking trumpet, "the victory is yours! Come aboard, and we will speak of granting you clemency."

"Cut ties from the other ship," Caleb said to his crew, paying no heed to Santana's request. He made a quick visual scan and determined that none of his crew remained on either the *Red Soul* or the *Devil's Thunder.*

"Haul the mainsail out and brace the bowline leeward. Set course west past the Lost Keys."

Kingsley's spirits were lifted seeing Caleb fight for himself rather than putting himself at Santana's mercy.

Hawkins was ready to carry out the orders, but she had a concerned look about her.

"At our current position," she said, "it is likely the *Devil's Thunder* will overtake us easily."

"Noted," Caleb said, preoccupied with executing his own plan. "Mr. Docks," he called up to Unlucky Jake, still situated in the crow's nest atop the main mast, "strike the Union Jack and fly the French colors."

"Aye, aye!" he called back down. He opened up the flag box with his hooks and produced the appropriate flag.

"Heave to and prepare to be boarded," came the voice of Santana's first mate Johansen from across the way. "There's still a chance for you to come peaceably."

But Caleb paid no heed to his calls.

"I hope you know what you're doing," Kingsley said. This was an unexpected move for Caleb, and the ramifications of this choice was anyone's guess.

"Ship approaching two points off the starboard bow!" Docks called from his perch. "It's *La Charrue.*"

A smile forced itself onto Caleb's face. "*Bienvenue à la fête, Capitaine Matisse,*" he said quietly.

"Keep the sheets tight," he called to the crew with a newfound air of confidence about him. "Now, steady the bowline and get the tack aboard. Let go and haul."

The sails unfurled, and the *Troublemaker* picked up speed in the water as it sailed quickly away from the *Devil's Thunder,* which attempted to pursue, but was quickly cut off by the approaching French ship.

The boom of cannons rang out as Matisse had his eyes set on his English prize, giving the *Troublemaker* a chance to flee.

"Come about!" Santana called out to his men.

The *Devil's Thunder* turned itself quickly around the far side of the *Red Soul,* which remained dead in the water, most of her crew having been lost in the sea.

Standing proud on the quarterdeck of the *Troublemaker,* Caleb watched the other ships shrink away in the distance. He turned to look over his cheering crew and reveled in the victory they had been a part of and the escape that they had just managed. He closed his eyes and basked in the sun, delighting in the feeling of the wind on his uncursed face.

As they continued to sail westward past the keys, Caleb

thought back to the time he had been marooned there with Susan Hawkins; it seemed a lifetime ago. Even more remote in his memory was his old life on Buccaneers Isle and the life he had spent in the service of a horrible man – a life that, because of the law of the land, was never his own.

Buccaneers Isle was close, and they would arrive by dawn. It was where he had spent his formative years, but it was not his home. He returned to his cabin to think of his life choices and of the crew around him who had remained faithful and committed to him.

There was a knock at his door.

"Yes," he said. "Come."

The door opened and Aiden Kingsley stepped in.

"Aiden." Caleb rose to his feet and embraced his friend. "Please, come in. Have a seat."

Kingsley took a seat on a cushioned bench near the window beside the captain's desk. A look of concern in his eyes did not go unnoticed.

"Something troubles you," he said as he produced a bottle of celebratory wine from a cabinet. He fetched some glasses and poured drinks for him and his friend.

"I wanted to thank you," Kingsley began as he accepted the wine from Caleb. "You put your faith in us to do what I never really knew could be done. But in doing so, I am afraid that I may have pushed you away from an opportunity."

"What's that?" Caleb said, not quite grasping what he was getting at.

"Captain Santana," Kingsley said. "What if he was intent on offering you letters of marque? You could have gone legitimate and been a privateer in the King's navy, and I'm afraid I steered you away from that."

Caleb paced a bit as he thought that over.

"That's a possibility. It could have been a true offer, or it could have been a ruse. It's impossible to know at this point. I have no regrets in my decision. In the end, my actions were my own, and what's done is done; focusing my concern on things that happened in the past or in a future that will not be is fruitless, unless we can find a way for it to inform our decisions.

"Years ago, I could not have dreamed that I would find myself a captain and be making such choices. Now, being here with the opportunity to make decisions, good or bad, is a freedom and responsibility that I gladly accept. Whatever consequences come, they come from something that I had power over."

Something still nagged at Kingsley, and it was evident by his hesitation.

"Is there something else?" Caleb asked.

"It's the *Grimoire*," he said. "It's lost again."

"Ah." Caleb nodded. "That is a shame, for sure, but I think we are just fine without it. It has served its purpose. Besides, what would we have done with it? You could not neglect your shop! The Hex Hut is a Caribbean landmark, and I'm not sure your niece Corine is quite up to the task of managing it herself yet."

"No, not likely," Kingsley laughed.

There was another knock at the cabin door; Susan Hawkins let herself in.

"Captain," she said, "we will be coming up to the southern side of Buccaneers Isle soon."

"Very good." He poured a glass of wine for her as well and handed it over.

"If I may say so," she continued, "I think you may have found your calling out here. I thought you performed amicably, and the men followed you well."

Caleb fought against the proud grin forming on the side of his mouth but ultimately gave in to it.

"Is that so?"

"She's not wrong," Kingsley said, raising his drink for a toast.

"Thank you," Caleb said. The three raised their glasses. "To the *Troublemaker* and her crew."

"And to her captain," Hawkins added.

They all drained their glasses.

Caleb looked out the window and into the distance. "We'll be coming to the hut presently, Aiden. Is there anything else you need from us before we drop you off?"

"I have what I need," he said. "If there's anything I forgot, I'll just get it next time I sail with you."

He and Hawkins joined Caleb at the window.

"My sister makes an awfully good breakfast Would you care to meet the rest of the family while we're here?" He motioned to Hawkins as well. "You are both invited, of course."

Caleb shot Susan a glance.

"I can think of nothing better."

Flags of the Cursed Seas

Caleb Keys - *Troublemaker*

Blunderbuss Bailey - *Vengeful Goose*

Benjamin Torch - *Red Soul*

Stephen Kennedy - *Vengeful Goose*

Reginald Hennesey - *Nordlys*

Night-Heart the Bloodletter - *Death-Blade*

Rafael Santana - *Devil's Thunder*

Follow Matt Nielsen on social media:

TikTok.com/@nielsenstories

Instagram.com/nielsenstories

Facebook.com/nielsenstories

YouTube.com/@mattnielsenstories

About the Author

Matt Nielsen lives in Dahlonega, Georgia, where he owns and operates a small video production company. His interest in storytelling started early in life, and he has always been involved in some form of telling stories since his undergrad years at Berry College in Rome, Georgia.

When he's not writing or working on his video production business, he enjoys creating cosplays for conventions and playing sea shanties on his concertina.